THE DEVIL'S
RED NICKEL

By Robert Greer

The Devil's Red Nickel
The Devil's Hatband

ROBERT GREER

THE DEVIL'S RED NICKEL

THE MYSTERIOUS PRESS

Published by Warner Books

A Time Warner Company

Mysterious Press books are published by Warner Books, Inc.,
1271 Avenue of the Americas, New York, NY 10020.

 A Time Warner Company

The Mysterious Press name and logo are registered trademarks of Warner
Books, Inc.

Printed in the United States of America

First printing: March 1997

10 9 8 7 6 5 4 3 2 1

Library of Congress Cataloging-in-Publication Data

Greer, Robert
    The devil's red nickel / Robert Greer.
        p.   cm.
    ISBN 0-89296-652-1
    I. Title
PS3557.R3997D49   1997   96-42031
813'.54—dc20   CIP

Dedicated to the memory of my father, Robert O. Greer, Sr., and for my mother, Mary, and my brothers, Darryl and Dwight.

Acknowledgments

I am grateful for the support, dedication, and resiliency of my editor, Sara Ann Freed, my agent, Nat Sobel, my publicist, Susan Richman, my secretary, Kathleen Hoernig, and the promotional efforts of Wayne Kral.

Special thanks to a Rocky Mountain and West Coast crew of friends who helped me keep this train on schedule and never let the music leave my head: Everil Bell, Laura Griffith, and Lee Young in Los Angeles; Stephanie and George Sigue in San Francisco; and Tom Vandermee, Connie Oehring, Ike Moore, and Stephen White in Denver.

And as always, thanks to my wonderful wife, Phyllis, for her unwavering encouragement.

Author's Note

The characters, events, and places that are depicted in *The Devil's Red Nickel* are spawned from the author's imagination. Certain Denver, Chicago, and Western locales are used fictitiously, and any resemblance between the novel's fictional inhabitants and actual persons living or dead is purely coincidental.

The time lines for the major Denver Public Works projects that are described in *The Devil's Red Nickel* have been fictionalized so as to appear coincident. Finally, as far as I can determine from Colorado history, there is not now nor has there ever been a town called Montcliff, Colorado.

"I don't think anybody steals anything;
all of us borrow."

—*B. B. King*

THE DEVIL'S RED NICKEL

One

June seventeenth turned out to be a six-biscuit day, and Vernon Lowe hated six-biscuit days. *Biscuit* was the name Denver General Hospital pathology residents reserved for bodies awaiting autopsy, and for twenty years Vernon, a five-foot-seven, bug-eyed, flashy-dressing slip of a black man and DGH chief morgue attendant, had been in charge of prepping and eviscerating the dead. Six bodies meant he had more than a full day's work staring him in the face.

Ten years earlier, on a similar bone-dry, hazy, early summer day, a pasty-faced resident named Aaron Leibowitz had burst into the morgue and announced, "Hey, Vernon, they're bringing down another biscuit to pop in the oven." After that the name just stuck. It had never made sense to Vernon that a refrigerated cooler for storing bodies should jokingly be called an oven, or that a dead human being should be referred to as a biscuit, but then Vernon had never had much insight into the gallows humor of pathology residents, and he never would.

Vernon worked part-time at DGH. The rest of the time he was a mortician at Hubble's Mortuary in Five Points, where for two decades he had painstakingly prepared Denver's black folks to be laid to rest. Vernon was the kind of man who took dying seriously, so for him death could never be a joke. Making light of what he always referred to simply as *passing on* was as close as anyone could come to achieving blasphemy.

Vernon was clearing his sinuses with a loud snort just as a fifth-year pathology resident marched into the morgue. She was two steps ahead of an orderly who was pushing a stainless-steel gurney—the noncollapsible, old-fashioned kind that always announced its occupant was on a one-way trip. Vernon could see the outline of a body beneath the two layers of sheets looped around the gurney's side rails. The sheets were tucked neatly beneath the safety railing—hospital safety protocol at work, even in death. Two meaty size-fourteen feet protruded beyond the sheets, silently announcing that sometime that day Vernon was going to have to wrestle with the sandbag weight of a very large man. The sheets ballooned up at midgurney, where a medical chart rested precariously on an elevated abdominal hump. A large head bulged up beneath the sheets at the gurney's other end.

"Park him over by the cooler," Vernon said to the orderly, sounding very much like a traffic cop.

The casual, un-Vernon-like remark made the resident smile. She was wearing a faded shamrock-green scrub suit, a necklace with an oversized silver cross, and clogs. Her hair was pulled back in a tight, efficient-looking bun, and her scrubs were at least a size too small, accentuating the fact that she was curavaceous and very well endowed. Vernon tried not to stare. He was a modest man—a Five Points community leader and a deacon in the Mount Carmel Baptist Church. All his life he had avoided alcohol, loud music, and things of the flesh. He had always wanted to tell the resident that she wore her clothes too tight, but it would be ungentlemanly, and besides, she was in the final year of her residency and would soon be gone.

Vernon had never understood why any woman would choose to specialize in pathology. Now, women baby doctors, that made sense. But a woman slogging through a distended, foul-smelling, decaying body racked with cancer or AIDS, up to her elbows in pus and blood, sifting through ravaged limbs, feces, and mangled brains, had always struck Vernon as odd. In addition to being modest and churchgoing, Vernon was an old-fashioned, center-of-the-family, salt-of-the-earth, lean-on-my-shoulder, chauvinistic kind of guy. In Vernon's world, men and women just naturally tended to settle in their rightful places, and as he saw it, a morgue was never intended to be a woman's natural place.

"Got a fresh biscuit for you, Vernon," said the resident. Her clogs tapped a staccato cadence across the cold gray institutional tile toward the morgue's bank of stainless-steel coolers. A yellowing certificate from the Joint Commission on Hospital Accreditation taped to the wall beside the coolers announced: "Refrigeration units must be available at the rate of six per four hundred hospital beds, routinely serviced, and maintained at a constant 37 degrees C."

"Word's out we're pretty full up," said the resident,

swinging open one of the cooler doors and eyeing the soles of two pale, lifeless feet.

"Try the middle row, to your left," Vernon said, without looking up from the bone saw he was cleaning.

She opened one of the middle-row doors and the hum of the massive refrigeration units kicked up an octave, a sure sign of an empty berth. "Roll him on over here, we've got a vacancy," said the resident, looking back at the orderly. The orderly, who hadn't budged since wheeling in the body, did as he was told.

Vernon laid the saw down on one of three gleaming stainless-steel autopsy tables and walked across the room as if to help, knowing full well that he wouldn't. Shoving bodies into coolers wasn't part of his job. Vernon's work didn't start until he pulled the body back out for the postmortem. The rules of union collective bargaining took precedence over everything, even in death. When the orderly pulled back the sheet and started to guide the body in, Vernon glanced down for a quick look. The body was that of a six-foot-five, two-hundred-forty-pound black man who looked to be in his late sixties. His hair was wiry, salt-and-pepper gray, and closely cropped. He had a Mona Lisa smile on his face, and only his right eye was shut. Vernon reached over and lowered the other lid while he calculated the day's overtime in his head. The resident cleared her throat to remind Vernon of her presence. "Probable MI," she announced, using the medical jargon for a heart attack.

"Gotta metastatic breast cancer case and a gram negative sepsis ahead of him," Vernon said.

"I'm sure he won't mind waiting his turn," said the resident, forcing a smile.

Vernon grimaced. "Guess not."

The orderly pushed the body into the cooler until there was a cold-sounding thump. Then he folded up the sheets, placed them neatly back on top of the gurney, and pushed the gurney ahead of him out the door.

"You got a permission?" asked Vernon, staring coldly at the resident.

"No need. He's a coroner's case."

Vernon looked surprised, knowing that coroner's cases didn't require permission from the next of kin and that more than half of all coroner's cases ended up on the bad side of the law. Even worse, they always pushed him way past his normal four o'clock quitting time. "Thought you said he had an MI."

"I did," said the resident. "But I didn't say what punched his ticket."

Vernon did something he did only once or twice a year. He rolled the body back out and bent over for a quick reassessment of the dead man. The man's skin was smooth, amazingly so for someone in his sixties, and except for a couple of white patches the size of large Band-Aids on his right bicep, there wasn't a single thing to distinguish Denver General Hospital's latest biscuit from the last hundred bodies Vernon had prepped for a post.

While Vernon was doing his reexamination, the resident walked over to retrieve the medical chart that the orderly had left on the autopsy table nearest the door. The chart was slim, no more than three or four pages thick, not the kind of voluminous medical record typically associated with a person with long-standing cardiac disease. She flipped through the pages quickly before announcing, "He came in drunk with a chief complaint of chest pains and a history of a bad heart, all right, but all the preliminary tests for a coronary were negative. He was just in for overnight observation. He's a medical examiner's case because a nurse's aid found him sprawled across the bathroom floor this morning. You know the routine, Vernon, all unexplained inpatient deaths get at least a peek from the ME." She put the chart down.

"Then we better let the coroner do his job," said Vernon, refusing to use the resident's shorthand. "Who's up?" he added, hoping it would be a pathologist who wouldn't take three hours to autopsy a man who had had a run-of-the-mill MI.

"Dr. Woodley," said the resident.

Vernon grinned, knowing that Woodley would have a quick answer to what had killed the man that would be uncomplicated, accurate, and rawboned straight. His chance of punching out on time was suddenly starting to look close to even money.

The resident picked the chart back up from the autopsy table for a second look. As she did, a business card dropped from one of its pockets and fluttered to the floor. She retrieved the card, and a puzzled look crossed her face. "Looks like our biscuit here might have had a problem with the law," she said, examining the card closely before handing it to Vernon.

Vernon gave the card the once-over:

CJ Floyd
Bail Bonding Twenty-Four Hours a Day
112 Delaware Street
Denver, Colorado 80218
303-555-4406

A note written on the back read: "Floyd can help. Call him ASAP." Beneath the note someone had signed, "C."

Vernon handed the card back to the resident and looked down at the dead man. Years of prepping bodies made him stare a little longer than usual at the man's enormous size and the white patches on his right arm. He began to wonder whether Denver General Hospital's latest biscuit had met his maker courtesy of something more sinister than a standard heart attack. He wouldn't know the answer until the autopsy was done, but he did know that he was already scheduled to meet his friend CJ Floyd that evening at six.

TWO

The fat bastard's dead, all right. I watched them roll his greasy black ass down to the morgue a couple of hours ago." The man speaking was standing in Sunken Gardens Park across from Denver General Hospital talking into a cellular telephone and watching a foul-plagued pickup basketball game unfold on a crumbling asphalt court about ten yards away.

"You sound cellular," said the voice on the other end of the line.

"Yeah, I'm outside the hospital in a park. I wanted to get to you before I headed over to Coors Field to catch the Rockies and the Braves."

"You're a dumb shit, Johnny. Sometimes I think you've got scrambled eggs for brains. Anybody can listen in on a goddamn cordless. Don't you ever read the fucking papers?"

"Everything's cool. I'll make it short."

"Before you ramble on, did you find out if that son of a bitch had the tapes?"

"Couldn't," said the man in the park. "Fucker croaked before I got a chance."

The man on the other end of the line sighed. "We're gonna buy some trouble out of this, Johnny. I can feel it in my bones."

"Over some coon dog's death? Not a chance." Johnny Telano slipped the phone away from his ear momentarily and watched a pint-sized black kid with a head full of cornrows steal the ball from a two-hundred-pound man-child twice his size, dribble the length of the court, and jam the ball home.

"You listening to me, Johnny?" asked the other man.

"Sure."

"What the hell's that ringing noise in the background?"

"Nothing, just some kids dribbling a basketball."

"You're a freakin' lunatic, Johnny. A freakin' brain-dead, hophead sports nut with a gun. Before you go betting your pension on a park full of jungle bunnies in baggy pants, and maybe end up shooting one of 'em's balls 'off when the wrong team wins, why don't you do what I sent you up there for in the first place and follow up on our boy Doo-Wop. Then, if you can tear yourself away from the big-city sports scene, get your ass on I-25 and back down here." He slammed the receiver down.

Unfazed, Johnny Telano watched the ebb and flow of the game for another ten minutes before deciding there was no need for a wager. For one thing, the two teams were too evenly matched, but more importantly, there was no one to lay a bet with. He started to tuck the cell phone away in the left inside pocket of his sport coat but remembered that the pocket was already weighted down with his .45 Colt Commander. So he left the park swinging the phone by its antenna, glancing back over his shoulder at a game that was now knotted at forty-all.

Three

On his final break of the day, Vernon Lowe called CJ Floyd at his office on Bail Bondsman's Row to remind him to be at Denver's Five Points community Juneteenth Steering Committee meeting at six o'clock sharp.

"And this time don't be draggin' your behind in late," Vernon reminded CJ, following up his admonition with a worn-out sigh.

"You sound beat," said CJ.

"One of those six-biscuit days," Vernon responded, checking his watch.

CJ could relate to Vernon's weariness. He had just returned from a fifteen-hundred-mile trip the night before, and his mind and body were still crying foul.

"One of my biscuits was carrying your business card," said Vernon, "and I think maybe he was having trouble with the law. I'll fill you in tonight."

Before CJ could respond, he was listening to a dial tone. He knew that impatience was par for the course whenever Vernon was staring overtime in the face, so he remained slumped, red-eyed, and bone weary in the worn but comfortable leather chair behind his desk and ignored being left hanging on the line. When he finally bent down to rub the charley horse lingering in his thigh, the offending knot seemed to enlarge.

In addition to being a bail bondsman, CJ was a collector of Western Americana, and he had just returned from a six-day, full-tilt, cross-country hunt for antique license plates. His license-plate odyssey had taken him zagging across North and South Dakota, through what now seemed like every remaining blade of short-grass prairie in the West. He wasn't looking forward to suffering through a Juneteenth celebration committee meeting. He'd been on the committee for six months, and during that time he had never been to a meeting where more than half of the members showed. But he knew that that evening committee members would be out in full force so they could finalize plans for the two-day celebration.

Denver's Five Points Juneteenth Festival commemorates June 19, 1865, the day that slaves in Texas belatedly learned that they had been freed by Abraham Lincoln's Emancipation Proclamation two and a half years earlier. The Confederate government of Texas had concealed the news from the state's slave population in a historical shell game as slick and as simple as street-corner three-card monte. They had simply kept their mouths shut about the new law of the land. But they couldn't keep quiet forever, and in the years that followed, blacks in Texas and nearby states, including Colorado, came to celebrate June 19, known colloquially as Juneteenth, as a day of black liberation.

The two-day celebration, Denver's thirtieth, had mushroomed from a simple two-block parade into a street fair extravaganza with over a hundred artisans and street vendors hawking everything from Poppa Loomis Kinnard's famous barbecued chicken, ribs, and smoked hot links to Nation of Islam's *Mohammad Speaks.*

CJ had been a reluctant Juneteenth committee member. His two-year term had been suggested by Mavis Sundee, the feminine soft spot in CJ's otherwise hard-boiled reclusive life, and pushed through by her father, Willis, longtime Five Points businessman and a Juneteenth committee member himself. Willis owned Mae's Louisiana Kitchen, CJ's favorite eatery and hangout, but Mavis ran the place. It had taken Mavis and Willis weeks of arm twisting and old-fashioned hard sell to convince the Juneteenth committee's executive board to appoint CJ. Most of the committee members thought a quick-tempered bail bondsman and no-holds-barred bounty hunter didn't fit the image they wanted. Realizing that his bittersweet relationship with Mavis would suffer if he didn't attempt to keep his promise to lock the door on his temper and try to become more active in the community where he had spent most of his life, CJ had attended every committee meeting since his appointment.

Unfortunately, his trip to the Dakotas hadn't left CJ in much of a Juneteenth mood. The dry, dusty trek in a gas-guzzling, rough-riding, three-quarter-ton pickup accompanied by two gamy ex-rodeo cowboy friends, Morgan Williams and Dittier Atkins, had been cramped and exhausting. Morgan and Dittier had tried to eat their way across the Great Plains at CJ's expense, and the lingering dried-sweat smell of the two former pro rodeo cowboys, who now eked out a living collecting cans on Denver's streets, had left CJ wondering whether they really smelled that bad or if he was coming down with a sinus infection. But more than anything, it had been the truck that made the trip a pain in the ass from the start.

Three weeks earlier, the octane-thirsty pickup had been offered to CJ as partial collateral against a bond that he had posted for Doucette Roundtree, a friend he had known since grade school. Doucette had decided to use his IBM PC, an aging web offset printing press loaned by a local Denver fence, and paper stolen from a Boise Cascade warehouse in Washington State to go into the counterfeiting business. When his twenties couldn't pass muster on the street, Doucette found himself facing local, state, and federal counterfeiting charges. When Doucette's mother, a former girlfriend of the drunken uncle who had raised CJ, came begging for help, CJ grudgingly took Doucette's truck as collateral against the $12,000 it took to get the legal ball rolling and Doucette out of jail. The rest of the bond had been collateralized by Doucette's mother's Five Points home.

Things went smoothly until a week later, when Doucette disappeared, leaving behind an apartment that was empty except for thirty-six cartons of Old Spice aftershave and an equal number of cases of Comet and Tide. It turned out that in addition to his counterfeiting, Doucette had also been fencing stolen toiletries and janitorial supplies. At Doucette's hearing, the judge gave CJ twenty-four hours to locate his friend. When CJ couldn't and Doucette failed his court appearance the next day, the judge issued a bench warrant for his arrest, declared the two-part bond in forfeiture, and instructed CJ to immediately ante up $12,000 and fees to the court. Doucette's mother began the process of losing her house, and CJ ended up $12,300 poorer and the owner of an aging fire-engine-red Dodge muscle truck.

CJ eased the chair away from his desk, rubbed the knot in his thigh again, and drummed his fingers on the desktop. He hoped that Vernon's information about the dead man who had been carrying his business card would translate into work, since his antique-license-plate odyssey, including food, lodging, gas, and $700 in truck repairs, had left him $900 overdrawn at the bank. The trip hadn't been a total loss. CJ had stumbled across two mint-condition 1919 Sioux Falls municipal license plates and a couple of hundred-year-old chewing tobacco tins, but those purchases had delivered the final death blow to his bank account.

Now, suffering in soreness in the silence of his office, CJ finally had to admit that recently he may have been living just a little too large. His high-cotton lifestyle had started when he tracked down two men who had killed a judge's daughter and his bail-bonding profile shot through the roof. The surge in business had lasted from Thanksgiving until the first of the year, most of it coming from giddy white people who had seen his name in the paper or his face on TV. But by Valentine's Day he was back to being just another black bail bondsman doing business with Five Points bottom feeders and small-time hoods. Doucette Roundtree's bond had been his biggest in months. When Doucette skipped his bond, CJ knew he should have tightened his belt. Now he was thinking about what his dead uncle who had taught him about the bail-bonding business used to say: *Fast money and high times is what keeps colored folks poor.*

He finally swiveled around in his chair to face the opposite wall and the rogues' gallery of more than eighty photographs of the bond skippers he had brought to justice. He scanned the rows of photographs slowly, searching for a spot for Doucette Roundtree's pitiful face. After picking one out, he ran a few hard numbers in his head. If he wholesaled Doucette's truck for ten grand even, he'd still be two thousand dollars short of the $12,000 he had originally anted up, but at least he'd be able to meet his monthly expenses and keep his secretary, Julie Madrid, on the payroll. In a few months, maybe things would even out.

CJ reached into his vest pocket, pulled out a cheroot, and lit up. The pungent cigar smoke drifted toward the room's open bay window. He smoked the cigar halfway down before placing it on the lip of a black lacquered ashtray inlaid with golden dragons that he had brought back as a souvenir from his two navy tours in Vietnam. Finally he got up from his chair, walked over to his rogues' gallery, and pinned a two-by-three-inch sixth-grade yearbook photo of Doucette Roundtree in place. He reached back for his cheroot, secure in the knowledge that sometimes friendships just naturally burn themselves out.

Four

CJ pulled his bad-luck truck into the Five Points Community Center's pothole-filled parking lot ten minutes early for his committee meeting. Half a dozen cars were already scattered across the lot. CJ recognized most of them as belonging to Juneteenth Steering Committee members. Dodging potholes and broken glass, he headed for a corner space where he knew he could angle the truck into a spot that wouldn't leave its bed sticking out like a rooster's tail ready to be clipped by some neighborhood drunk. He had decided to take his financial lumps and sell the truck the next day.

The moment he turned off the engine, Vernon Lowe pulled up next to him in his rusted-out ten-year-old Honda Civic. The egg-yolk-yellow Civic was known around Five Points as the dead canary because Vernon had purchased it from the widow of a man who had asphyxiated himself in the car shortly after learning that his wife was having affairs with his two best friends. Vernon hopped out of the Honda, resplendent in an iridescent powder-blue linen suit, a red silk shirt, white silk tie, and shoes shined to a mirror gloss.

"Today was a killer diller—one body after another all day long. And, like I told you on the phone, one of 'em's sure enough linked up to you." He paused and dusted off the arm of his coat. "I barely had time to get buttered up."

Vernon's body language told CJ that before they discussed any business, he had better comment on Vernon's suit. "One thing about you, Vernon, you know how to style."

Vernon beamed. "Picked this baby up on sale at Bernardo's. One of a kind. They wouldn't be able to fit no big horse like you, though, CJ, not in threads like this."

Bernardo's specialized in clothing for the trim man, and CJ didn't fit the clothier's mold. Even so, at six-foot-two and 220 pounds, he was fifteen pounds lighter than he had been in years, courtesy of a rigidly enforced Mavis Sundee diet. "Guess I'll have to stick with Neiman Marcus," CJ said as he and Vernon headed stride for stride toward the community center's front door.

Halfway to the entrance, Vernon gazed back over his shoulder. "Ain't that Doucette Roundtree's truck you're driving?"

"It was," said CJ.

Vernon looked surprised. "I knew sooner or later that little toad was going to end up bumping his behind. I heard they caught him passing funny money. But I didn't realize you was his bank. I figured he stuck some white boy."

"Guess he went a little color-blind," said CJ, glancing back at the truck and gritting his teeth.

They were met at the door by four other Juneteenth committee members. After a series of handshakes and some small talk about when the drought might break, three of the people peeled off together and headed down the long hallway toward the center's gymnasium for the meeting. The remaining man, Winston Dunn, one of Denver's assistant city attorneys, ignored CJ, hooked his arm in Vernon's, and started easing him toward a small anteroom to the left of the entrance. Before they disappeared into the room, Vernon turned back to CJ. "Got that business card I told you about here somewhere," he said, fishing in his pockets.

"It can wait," said Dunn, slamming the anteroom door shut before CJ could respond—and loving it. Dunn had been a vocal opponent of CJ's membership on the Juneteenth Steering Committee from the day CJ's name had been proposed. He had a deep-seated disdain for bail bondsmen in general, and CJ in particular.

Dunn had appeared in Denver fifteen years earlier, coming from Detroit with nothing but a half-empty beat-up Samsonite suitcase and a freshly minted Marquette University law degree. He and CJ had had a run-in within a week, immediately after Dunn told one of CJ's DUI regulars that he needed a lawyer handling his case, not some trash-rooting bondsman. When CJ found out, it had taken his best friend, Rosie Weaks, twenty minutes to convince him not to go over to Dunn's office and stomp in his face. In the decade and a half since that day, when it came to Dunn, CJ's temper was always seething below the surface.

Dunn was the same age as CJ, forty-five, with a formal education that had come late in life. The word on the street was that Dunn had been a street thug who in his twenties had to choose between the classroom and ending up dead. Dunn chose the former, and once he left Detroit for Denver, he was smart enough to weave his way into the kind of political circles that eventually helped him land an assistant attorney's job.

Encounters with Dunn nearly always ended up giving CJ a sour stomach. CJ thought about kicking in the door that Dunn had just slammed in his face, if for no other reason than to let Dunn know it was rude. But before he had a chance to act, two people brushed past him, defusing his temper and jostling him back into reality. When CJ realized that he was blocking the flow of traffic, he cursed Dunn under his breath, then turned and headed for the gymnasium.

Willis Sundee caught up with CJ about halfway to the gym. "Vacation's over, time to roll up your sleeves, CJ. Juneteenth's here for real," said Willis.

CJ put Winston Dunn behind him and smiled. "I'm ready," he said as he and Willis continued down the hall. A few minutes later Vernon and Dunn reappeared in the foyer, grinning from ear to ear and looking like million-dollar Lotto winners.

The rec center's ventilation system had been a low-bid item. The gymnasium reeked of sweaty Air Jordans and Reeboks, fried food, and chlorine from the swimming pool next door. The instant CJ and Willis entered the gym, Willis began working the crowd, offering pleasantries to committee members and making certain to shake every hand in the room. Juneteenth committee busi-

ness wasn't the only issue on his agenda for the evening.
For months he had been on a one-man mission to put an
end to Denver's proposed transportation darling, an elevated monorail rapid transit system. The rapid transit system was a dog bone that had been tossed to the public by
Denver's newly elected black mayor, who had been swept
into office on the wings of his political savvy and campaign slogans like "Ride the Rockies: Gateway to the
West." The mayor was a new-age Rainbow Coalition pop-
ulist, and Willis knew he had no interest in catering to the
needs of a neighborhood like Five Points, regardless of the
fact that Five Points was the heart and soul of the black
community. The cold, hard facts were that Five Points just
had too few votes for the mayor to consider its needs a
top priority. A high-profile, politically correct issue like
rapid transit was something the mayor's constituents in
larger districts with high voter turnouts could sink their
teeth into. The inaugural leg of the new monorail system
was planned to run squarely down the middle of Welton
Street, effectively splitting the Five Points business district
in half with concrete and steel. Willis knew that when the
monorail system was complete, white commuters would
use the system to whisk them from their outlying homes
to work every day, and they would have no intention of
stopping on the way to rub shoulders with a bunch of
dark faces or to polish off a meal of fried catfish and
greens while they lingered. A construction period of two
years was being projected. Willis, who owned three businesses on both sides of Welton Street, including his community landmark, Mae's Louisiana Kitchen, was smart
enough to realize that although two years of construction
might not bury his businesses, they would destroy several

fledgling black-owned businesses that were just beginning to grow. Three of the ten people on the Juneteenth committee were also on the mayor's monorail task force, and Willis was busy working his way around the room with much more than simply Juneteenth festivities on his mind.

"Got to look real close at this monorail business, Otis," Willis said, loudly enough for everyone within earshot to hear. The remark was directed at Otis Ketchum, a Smally Junior High School teacher and a member of the mayor's task force. Ketchum responded with a weak grin. The mayor expected his committee members to follow the party line, but he hadn't counted on Willis Sundee's powers of persuasion, or the fact that Willis had a lifetime's worth of bass fishing with Otis Ketchum working on his behalf. Otis had always been the kind of man who liked to butter both sides of his toast, and Willis expected that sooner or later he'd persuade Otis to take a long, hard look at his side of the monorail bread.

"I'll have a fact sheet for you to take a look at in a couple of days," he said to Ketchum. "Then maybe you'll think twice before moving ahead on monorail."

CJ had made his own handshaking rounds, and he ended up back with Willis. "Pretty tough on Hiz Honor's pet project, aren't you, Willis?"

"As tough as Hades on a block of ice." Willis turned to Otis with one last comment. "The real story on monorail is gonna make you weep."

Otis was spared from responding when the booming voice of a tall, full-bodied woman, who was standing at the head of a long aluminum banquet table beneath one of the gym baskets, demanded that everyone take their seats.

Vernon Lowe and Winston Dunn were the last two people to enter the gymnasium. When they reached CJ and Willis near the midcourt stripe, Willis stopped Vernon, grabbed his hand, and started pumping his arm. "The mayor's selling political rope-a-dope, Vernon. Don't let him sucker you in on monorail."

Vernon gave Willis the kind of look that said *I'll talk to you about it later*, but Dunn wasn't as generous. He shot Willis a hateful back-alley stare and said, "Fuck off. You're a day late and a dollar short, Sundee," he added. "Vernon has the people's interest at heart. Go push your propaganda someplace else."

It wasn't until then that CJ connected all the dots and realized that Vernon must also have been appointed to the mayor's task force on monorail. Vernon remained silent, looking as if he had run a red light.

Willis sensed Vernon's predicament and flashed him a look of reassurance before turning to Dunn. "Slavery's over, counselor, or haven't you heard about Juneteenth?"

Dunn didn't have a comeback. Instead he looked at Vernon. "Let's grab a seat." They both headed toward the woman with the booming voice.

Willis and CJ chose seats at opposite ends of the banquet table just as Retha Clark's deep baritone voice resounded again, calling the meeting to order.

Three hours later, the final details of Denver's thirtieth annual Juneteenth celebration, including exactly how many Smally Junior High School student pooper-scoopers would trail the parade's twenty-three horses and exact seating arrangements for the passengers who would ride in CJ's 1957 convertible Chevy Bel Air, had been nailed down. The meeting broke up in a rush. After an evening of nonstop talk, arm twisting, budget massage, bitter coffee, and two-day-old Dunkin' Donuts, most of the committee members couldn't be blamed for making a beeline for the door. Winston Dunn tried to hustle Vernon out with him, but when Vernon said he needed to talk to CJ, Dunn slithered out the door by himself.

Only CJ, Willis, Vernon, and Retha Clark remained. Retha, a six-foot, one-hundred-eighty-pound former Roller Derby queen, refused CJ's and Vernon's offers to help pack away the banquet table and chairs. She had been captain of the San Francisco Bay Area Bombers, years ahead of her time as the only black lead jammer on the women's circuit. When she said no, she meant it, and Vernon and CJ knew better than to ask twice.

The sound of Retha stacking chairs echoed throughout the gym as Willis, Vernon, and CJ walked over to the gym's 1940s-vintage foot-pedal-style water cooler, just to the left of center court. Vernon took a sip of water and swallowed hard. It was obvious to both CJ and Willis that he was thinking about the monorail discussion earlier. Vernon straightened up and looked Willis in the eye. "I ain't no puppet for nobody, Willis Sundee. And that includes you and the mayor."

"I know that," said Willis. "What I said earlier was meant for Dunn."

Vernon wasn't entirely satisfied with Willis's answer, but he didn't like to argue. "I'll hear you out on this monorail thing, Willis, but don't you never forget I'm my own man."

"All I'm asking you to do is to keep an open mind."

Vernon nodded, but Willis sensed that he was going to have one hell of a sales job on his hands and some prideful feathers to smooth before it was over. He decided that he had waved his anti-monorail flag enough for one evening. "It's getting past bedtime for old folks like me. Think I'll head up the street and help Mavis close up Mae's before I go home and dream about being twenty-one again."

"Later," said Vernon, still steamed.

"Tell Mavis I'll see her tomorrow," said CJ. "And remind her this Saturday we've got Rockies tickets."

"Sure thing, Romeo," said Willis. He reached the gym door just as Retha dimmed the westside bleacher lights.

Vernon and CJ stood in the subdued light for a moment without saying anything, and except for the intermittent sound of folding chairs banging to rest against the gymnasium wall and the noise of Retha Clark's size-twelve Reeboks screeching across the parquet floor, the gym was silent.

Vernon finally said, "Autopsied a real big, dignified-lookin' brother by the name of Polk today, and I'm sure he must have been looking to sign up with you to do some business." Vernon pulled the business card that had been in LeRoy Polk's medical chart out of his coat pocket. "You know I ain't supposed to take nothing out of people's charts." He handed the card to CJ. "But I figured you might want to knot up any loose ends."

"Thanks," said CJ, looking the card over before shrugging. "Beats me. Haven't talked to anybody named Polk about a bond."

"Maybe it's a bounty-hunting job," said Vernon,

lowering his voice to a whisper because he considered bounty hunting a sin.

CJ examined the card again. "Don't think so. The writing on the back's real pretty, though." He handed the card back to Vernon.

The words had barely left CJ's mouth when the unmistakable sound of high-heeled shoes clicked toward them across the hardwood floor. In the dim light CJ didn't recognize the face of the woman approaching him, but he couldn't help but notice her rehearsed, seductive walk. It was a walk so enticing that at first CJ barely noticed the man at her side. By the time they had closed to within fifteen feet, CJ had already sized them up as if they were fodder for his rogues' gallery. The man, who looked to be in his early forties, was stylishly dressed in a three-piece seersucker suit. He was black, but very light-skinned, and straight-haired enough to fool anyone but another black person into thinking he was white. He was wearing expensive European framed glasses that were too large for his slender oval face. When he realized that both CJ and Vernon were staring at him, he diverted his eyes to the floor. *The flunky*, thought CJ.

The woman was younger, thirty tops, and dressed more casually in a loose-fitting yellow silk blouse and tailored linen sacks, but there was no mistaking that her clothes screamed *real money*. When she stopped within handshaking distance of CJ, he strained to find a single wrinkle in her exotically beautiful cocoa-brown face. *The boss*, thought CJ.

She seemed to purposely keep the water fountain between them, and she didn't offer her hand. "You're a hard man to run down, Mr. Floyd." The slight hint of a

Southern accent cushioned her soft, warm voice. The self-preservation computer in CJ's head was still turned on. Since he had never laid eyes on her before, he wondered how she knew not only who he was but how to locate him at ten-thirty at night. "I haven't been hiding," CJ said, more defensively than he would have liked.

The expression on the woman's face said *I'm not here to banter,* but the look disappeared the instant she said, "I need your help." Even so, the remark sounded more like a command than a request. When she looked at Vernon as if she expected him to disappear, the man with her bent down and casually took a drink from the water fountain as if he had been a Five Points Community Center gym rat for years.

"I usually make it a habit of finding out the names of people who say they need my help before I offer it," said CJ.

"Sorry; I'm Clothilde Polk, and this is my brother Tyrone."

CJ glanced at Vernon as if to say, *The chickens are coming home to roost.*

Tyrone straightened up and shook CJ's hand. Clothilde did the same, but it seemed to CJ that she offered her hand reluctantly.

"I'll get straight to the point, Mr. Floyd. I've had your name for a while; a mutual friend, Charlene Gentry, gave it to me. I should have acted sooner. Originally I wanted you to act as a bodyguard for my father. Now, unfortunately, I need you to look into his death." The words *wanted* and *need* rolled off her tongue more softly than the others, as if they were meant for CJ's ears alone.

CJ, who liked to sort out every player in the game,

nodded toward Vernon before responding. "This is Vernon Lowe." Vernon smiled without saying hello.

"Vernon, how about letting me have another look at that business card of yours," said CJ.

While Vernon fished the business card back out of his pocket, CJ could see Clothilde trying to figure out the CJ-Vernon connection. CJ decided during the pause that if he and Clothilde Polk were ever to do any business at all, he needed to set a few ground rules. "Just for the record, Ms. Polk, I'm not a bodyguard. I'm too old and way too slow. And since I'm not a PI, a pathologist, or a cop, I normally don't investigate murders."

Clothilde answered as if she had expected CJ's response. "I know the things you do, Mr. Floyd. I know you aren't adverse to—shall we say—hunting people down and lashing them to the hood of your Jeep. I also know that you bail despicable people out of jail and that you've even shot people before. I think I can make you the kind of offer that'll convince you to track down whoever killed my dad."

CJ didn't know where Clothilde could have gotten her inside dope, except from Charlene, who was the sister-in-law of his best friend, Rosie Weaks. Regardless of the source, Clothilde Polk knew enough about him to make him nervous. And to top it off, she wasn't the least bit shy about throwing it in his face. Vernon finally handed CJ the business card he had asked for.

"I'm guessing you wrote the note on the back," said CJ, handing the card to Clothilde.

"I did," said Clothilde, glaring at CJ and then at Vernon as if they were Watergate coconspirators. She was about to ask how Vernon had gotten the business card when he spoke up.

"I assisted on the autopsy on your father," Vernon said politely.

Clothilde finally made the connection between Vernon, her father, and CJ. Before she could ask Vernon what the autopsy had shown, Tyrone beat her to it. "What killed him?" asked Tyrone, sounding more like a cop than a grieving son.

"Don't know," said Vernon. "That's the coroner's job."

"I'll know by tomorrow morning," said Clothilde. "The coroner promised." The look of determination on her face told CJ that by the next morning Clothilde Polk would have some kind of answer about what had killed her father or the Denver General Hospital medical bureaucracy would pay a heavy price.

"My dad was murdered," said Clothilde, reaching into a small clutch she was carrying. She handed CJ her own business card. "I want to know why and by whom. I have an idea, but to prove it I'm going to need help from someone who's used to operating on Denver's streets." She stared directly into CJ's eyes.

CJ was used to clients thinking that his work was one step above that of a street thug, so he wasn't surprised by Clothilde's remark. What surprised him was the order in which Clothilde wanted to have the issues surrounding her father's death addressed: why, then by whom. He glanced at her business card which read, "Polk's Stax of Wax—Chicago, Denver, and Beyond." The high-profile lower downtown central Platte Valley address and phone prefix made CJ wonder why he had never seen or heard of Clothilde Polk or her brother Tyrone before, and that made him question again where Clothilde had gotten all her information on him. "Tyrone needs to know what happened too," said Clothilde. "Why don't we all meet at our place tomorrow morning. I'll have more information for you by then, and I'm certain you'll assist us once I have the opportunity to spell things out."

CJ had never liked being in situations where he felt lectured, and normally he would have told someone like Clothilde Polk to take a hike, but two things stopped him. He was determined to find out how a total stranger seemed to have half of his life's story tucked away in her head, and he wanted to see Clothilde Polk in the light of day.

"Ten o'clock at the address on the card," was all Clothilde said before doing an about-face, nodding for her brother to follow, and walking seductively back across the hardwood court and out the doors of the gymnasium.

Retha Clark had finished stacking chairs, and she had caught the last of CJ's and Clothilde's conversation from just a few feet away. "Kind of sizzles, don't she, boys?"

"If you like your potatoes hot," said CJ.

Retha let out a booming laugh that seemed to be the cue that started Vernon and CJ walking slowly toward the exit. "Think somebody really killed her old man?" Vernon asked once they were outside.

"You opened the man up; what do you think?" asked CJ, surveying the empty parking lot. There wasn't a sign of Clothilde or Tyrone.

"I'd say he just had a bad ticker. We get 'em every day."

CJ was about to pursue Vernon's assessment when a mammoth silver-and-blue tow truck, the kind usually reserved for towing buses and semi-trailers, pulled into the parking lot. Midway across the lot, the driver stopped, shifted the wrecker into reverse, and, with his high beams aimed directly at Vernon and CJ, backed up and squared the business end of the wrecker off with the bumper of CJ's truck.

CJ stood mesmerized until the driver swung his sumo-sized body out of the cab and flipped a lever just above the wrecker's rear wheel well, and he heard the hydraulic hum of a towing rig engage.

"Son of a bitch." CJ streaked for the tow truck, leaving Vernon in his wake. He slid to a stop behind the wrecker and jumped into the space between his truck's rear bumper and the towing rig that was now resting on the asphalt drive. "What the hell's going on?"

"This your truck?" asked the driver, who was chewing on a Popsicle stick.

CJ thought he knew every tow truck driver in the city, but he had never seen this one before. New acquaintances seemed to be the order of the evening. "Damn straight," he said, holding his ground between the two trucks.

"Got an order to impound your chariot, Hercules." The driver pulled a crumpled piece of paper from his back pocket and handed it to CJ. The grease-stained document was a judge's order to impound a 1988 three-quarter-ton Dodge pickup truck, VIN 664429384, as material evidence in the City and County of Denver's case against one Doucette Roundtree.

"The title you're holdin' on this baby's counterfeit, my man, light as a three-dollar bill. Your vehicle actually belongs to First National Bank," said the tow truck driver, slapping the pickup's side rail.

CJ swallowed hard. He suddenly wished he had nailed the grade school photo of Doucette Roundtree to his rogues' gallery wall with a spike between the eyes instead of a piece of Scotch tape.

"Just be glad you didn't take no money from him too. I hear he stuck his mama with funny money worth twenty grand."

"The man ain't Christian," said Vernon, who had walked up just as CJ got the news about the title. He stood shaking his head in disbelief through the rest of the tow truck driver's declarations. CJ sucked in and out on his right cheek several times, a childhood habit that surfaced when he was angry, before he regained his composure and stepped out from between the two trucks.

"Wise choice," said the driver. "Always makes things a lot easier."

CJ watched silently as the man hooked his towing bar up to the truck, double-checked all the chains and linkages, and hoisted the rear wheels off the ground. The hoist abruptly stopped humming when the truck's rear wheels reached their zenith. The pickup's recoil made CJ realize that he was as close as he had ever been to what his uncle used to like to call "sure 'nuff down home broke." His uncle had suffered through sixty-eight years of ups and downs, but even on his alcoholic roller-coaster ride through life, he had never come close to being flat-

out broke. Probably because, unlike CJ, he had never collected expensive antiques, owned two vehicles, held Broncos and Nuggets season tickets, or even once in his life
come close to having fifteen seconds, much less fifteen
minutes, of fame. CJ knew that his recent stab at high living had pushed him to the brink of insolvency, and he
felt embarrassed.

The tow truck driver didn't say another word to
Vernon or CJ. He double-checked his hitches and the
lock set on his hydraulics. Then he swung back up into
the cab, turned over the truck's guttural diesel engine, and
fastened his seat belt.

CJ considered starting out after Doucette Roundtree
right then. It was a thought that surfaced between trying
to figure out how he was going to keep his office open
and where the next week's meals were going to come
from. He knew he could always slap a mortgage on the
aging Victorian building on Bondsman's Row that was
both his home and office. But he suspected that if he did,
the vision of his uncle, who had worked a lifetime to pay
the old painted lady off, would burn more brightly in his
subconscious as a sign of failure than the neon signs outside his office that flashed BAIL BONDS ANYTIME: DAY
AND NIGHT. Suddenly he felt the kind of low-gut queasi-
ness settling in the pit of his stomach that used to haunt
him when his navy swift boat was on sunset patrol during
Vietnam.

The wrecker driver gunned his engine and engaged
the flashing red light atop the truck's cab. CJ watched the
light spin for a while, wondering whether the driver was
going to turn on the truck's flashing lights to announce
his stupidity too. It wasn't until the truck lurched forward

that CJ decided what he had to do. He turned to Vernon. "You know, Vernon, my work's a lot like yours. You don't always get to handpick your jobs." He pulled Clothilde Polk's business card out of his pocket and stared at it.

The arc of a smile formed on Vernon's face as they watched the wrecker dodge potholes and disappear into the night with CJ's truck trailing behind.

Five

The next morning just before sunrise, CJ woke up coughing and sweating like some iron-pumping jock in a Gatorade commercial. Whenever Denver's temperature broke 85 degrees and the relative humidity dipped below 15 percent, CJ's second-floor apartment above his office turned into a convection oven. The building's twelve-foot-high Victorian ceilings weren't enough to overcome the fact that turn-of-the-century construction included a ventilation system from hell.

CJ fumbled with the alarm clock on the nightstand next to his bed in between raspy coughs. When he saw that it was five forty-five, he set the clock face down. The previous summer he had promised himself that he was going to upgrade the building's ancient ventilation system, but a year had passed, and when the conditions were just right CJ still woke up sounding like a mustard-gassed World War I vet.

He stumbled out of bed, flipped on a light, and cursed the overhead ceiling fan that hadn't worked in twenty years. Bleary-eyed, he headed straight for the bathroom sink, where he turned on the cold faucet and gulped a handful of water. His coughing stopped, but the events of the previous night surfaced just at the edge of his subconscious. After splashing a couple of handfuls of water on his face, he decided to brew a pot of coffee and get ready for another desiccation-jar kind of day.

He walked back to the bedroom, slipped on a pair of faded University of Colorado athletic department jogging shorts that he had won as part of an Orange Bowl bet with his friend Dr. Henry Bales, a University of Colorado medical school pathologist, and ran a comb through his hair. He walked down the narrow hallway to the kitchen. Six months earlier he had switched from on-sale brew to flavored decaffeinated coffee as part of a Mavis Sundee—instituted healthy lifestyles diet. She made certain that he always had four or five flavors to choose from, but the only flavor CJ could stomach was the hazelnut. As he reached for the coffee tin and pulled out his ten-year-old Mr. Coffee, his thoughts turned to the leggy Ms. Clothilde Polk. She was still on his mind when the rich aroma of Colombian hazelnut began to fill the air.

Twenty minutes later CJ remained at his kitchen table, picking at the crumbs of what had been an overly generous slice of carrot cake. The business card with Clothilde's note to her father was lying in the center of the table along with his car keys, where he had tossed them the night before. The card and the note had been festering in the back of his mind like a week-old splinter. He couldn't stop asking himself why Clothilde had picked him out to help, and he kept wondering why LeRoy Polk hadn't called him ASAP, like the note on the back of the card said. Maybe he simply hadn't had time to call before someone punched his ticket. Then again, maybe Clothilde's whole *my father's been murdered* story was just a piece of Wizard-of-Oz dreamland fiction. CJ calculated the odds of Clothilde charming a provisional diagnosis of murder out of a crusty old pathology warhorse like Charlie Woodley. He was betting she couldn't. When it came to murder, pathologists usually confided in cops, not next of kin. What he needed was the straight poop on whether LeRoy Polk had been murdered before it filtered its way to Clothilde or the police.

CJ glanced down at the CU logo on his jogging shorts and broke into the smile of a man who has just drawn an inside straight. He almost said Dr. Henry Bales's name out loud. CJ knew that Henry could call up what pathologists referred to as a provisional anatomic diagnosis from the state's pathology laboratory consortium computer network before Clothilde's long, lovely legs made their first sensuous out-of-bed stretch of the day, and long before Denver's finest clocked in for the day watch. CJ finished his coffee and tried to imagine what to expect at his ten o'clock appointment with Clothilde at Stax of Wax.

Clothilde's business address was in Denver's lower downtown district, known as LoDo, and it seemed vaguely familiar, but it wasn't the address of a building he could visualize, perhaps because every time he tried to place the address, Clothilde Polk's face and seductive walk kept filling his head.

When CJ pulled his '57 Bel Air convertible up in front of 2959 Inca in the Prospect Heights section of the city northwest of Coors Field, future home of Polk's Stax of Wax, he knew that LeRoy Polk must have been either a gullible fool or a man truly ahead of his time. The address that he hadn't been able to place earlier now had him shaking his head and muttering, "I'll be damned." When Clothilde opened a side door to let him into the boarded-up Quonset-hut-style behemoth that had been one of Denver's first Safeway supermarkets, CJ felt as though he had just stumbled thirty years back into his youth. He was still trying to imagine what LeRoy Polk could possibly have wanted with the dilapidated old building when Clothilde grabbed his hand and pulled him inside. She was wearing lightweight lime-green running shorts that floated loosely around her upper thighs, a gray Moorehouse College athletic top, cut to the midriff, and glow-in-the-dark running shoes that matched the color of her shorts. Her hair was pulled back in a ponytail, and beads of perspiration dotted her forehead just beneath a handwoven Navajo headband.

"Just finished a jog," she said, pulling a washcloth from her fanny pack and toweling off her face. "What do you think of the place?"

CJ looked around the dingy, mildewing edifice to supermarket nostalgia and remembered it as teeming with people and stocked with enough junk food, hot-rod magazines, and soft-drink varieties to forever capture the fantasy of a twelve-year-old Five Points kid.

The building had outgrown its usefulness long ago and
had been left behind in lower downtown to decay and share
the Platte River Valley with winos, derelicts, and rotting
railroad cars until the revitalization of LoDo had begun
several years earlier. The construction of Denver's new
baseball stadium, Coors Field, coupled with the move
of Elitch's, Denver's venerable old amusement park, to
the central valley had miraculously transformed LoDo
into a mecca of restaurants, high-priced lots, sports
bars, and art galleries. CJ didn't like the gentrified, fake-
neighborhood, sandblasted-brick sameness of the new
LoDo. It was all too pat. For him, real neighborhoods had
homes and schools, insurance agencies and barbershops,
hardware stores and groceries, not just art galleries,
restaurants, and bars. But at least the revitalization had produced the new baseball stadium, and CJ
was happy about that.

The old Safeway building sat just far enough away
from the center of quick-buck speculation and looked
so run-down that it had escaped rehabilitation, even in
the mad rush to revitalize. Maybe LeRoy Polk was a
man with a greater vision than most, CJ thought to
himself.

"It's got possibilities," said CJ, choosing his words
carefully, still surveying the space.

Clothilde laughed. "You're a hell of a diplomat, CJ.
The place is a dump. But give me twelve more weeks
and it'll be the R&B mecca of the West. My daddy had
been planning to revive the Polk's Stax of Wax record
label for years, but there was always something or somebody stopping him. Now the job's up to me." She bit
her lower lip nervously as she tried to hold back tears.

When she realized that CJ wasn't fully comprehending the scope of her plans, she added, "We Polks are in the music business. Have been all our lives. From talent searches to platinum records—rock and roll to rhythm and blues. Don't tell me you've never heard of Daddy Doo-Wop Polk?"

The name Daddy Doo-Wop Polk stopped CJ's assessment of the space cold. "Doo-Wop Polk was your old man?"

"Nobody but."

"Damn," was the only word CJ could muster. He would never have linked Clothilde to the king of Chicago soul.

LeRoy Polk, or Daddy Doo-Wop, as he preferred to be called, had started his career in 1953, fresh home from the Korean War as a $3-an-hour DJ spinning records for an obscure black-owned radio station in the steel town of Gary, Indiana. After two years as a steel-city journeyman platter jock at WWCA, he got the break of a lifetime when Willie Hopkins, a light-skinned black man from Chicago who owned six northern Illinois and Indiana Coca-Cola distributorships and more often than not passed for white, tuned him in on a trip to Gary. When he heard LeRoy's unique part-country-boy, part-city-slicker DJ banter and listened to him play the songs that he predicted would be hits, Hopkins knew it was time to diversify from soda pop to soul. With the help of a few politicians and a little underworld Chicago muscle, Hopkins bought WPTN, a 50,000-watt South Side ratio station that could be heard all the way south to Nashville, east to Philadelphia, and on a crystal-clear day as far west as Denver. The first person he hired at WPTN was LeRoy Polk.

Polk changed his name to Daddy Doo-Wop, drove the thirty miles around the tip of Lake Michigan from Gary to the Windy City, and set up shop at WPTN dispensing his own special brand of rapid-fire, rat-a-tat soul chatter and rhythm and blues. At the time, seven hundred thousand of Chicago's three million residents were black, and they didn't give a rat's ass about Sinatra or Como. They were starved for music they could call their own, and within a year LeRoy Polk had developed a constituency that would eventually propel him into the Rhythm and Blues Hall of Fame.

CJ first caught Daddy D's act in the late 1960s, during his reclusive lone-wolf early teenage years. By then WPTN had boosted its wattage to 80,000, and Daddy D, who was near the end of his disc-jockey career, had branched out to pressing records for five different record labels, talent scouting, promoting black singing groups, and pushing his own label, Stax of Wax. But at least one day a week, when the airwaves were uncluttered and the weather gods were smiling, CJ could still tune in Daddy D on his Motorola transistor from a thousand miles away and receive his weekly dose of Chicago soul.

CJ looked at Clothilde and thought about the times he had pedaled his balloon-tired JC Higgins bicycle from Five Points to the Inca Street Safeway to buy a sixteen-ounce grape NeHi and a twenty-four-ounce bag of Fritos to snack on while he listened to her father spin his intoxicating web of chatter and Chitown R&B. He had the urge to tell Clothilde that her father had been a lightning rod for him: a black man who talked to the world. A fast-talking record wizard who played what felt good to him and called his own shots. LeRoy Polk had brought CJ something he could relate to, but it wasn't until years later that CJ realized what that something was—independence. CJ suppressed his urge to open up to Clothilde, instead saying only, "I caught your father's act once or twice."

"You and half the black folks in America," Clothilde said with a sly smile.

She said it as if black folks owed LeRoy Polk something more than he had gotten from them during his life.

"What are your plans for this place?" said CJ, back to surveying the building again.

"I'm going to turn it into an R&B music palace," said Clothilde proudly. "A combination Tower Records superstore, record plant, and rhythm and blues museum. The museum is going to be the jewel, twenty thousand square feet designed to look like the old R&B Regal Theater on Chicago's South Side." She pointed toward the back of the building, outlining the space in a hand sweep. "It's even being designed to mimic the Regal, right down to the Spanish baroque look and dark Moorish mahogany. Every R&B *Billboard* chart recording from 1942 to the present will be available. I've got photos, letters, stylesheets, records, studio equipment, costumes, sales data, and stories from some of the greatest legends in rhythm and blues to fill the place. Any way you look at it, it's a win-win."

Clothilde's plans sounded fantastic, but the poorly lit front half of the building where he and Clothilde were standing still had six rows of avocado-colored checkout counters standing at the ready. Instead of music, CJ expected to hear cash registers start ringing any minute. A few yards beyond the checkout counters were dozens of tightly bunched empty supermarket shelves lined up Indian file, row after dusty row. The building beyond the shelves had been gutted. Electrical wiring jetted from the ceiling, and rolls of pink insulation were stacked in pyramids against the back wall. Several pallets of drywall were distributed across the floor, and it wasn't until CJ squinted into the semidarkness that he realized he and Clothilde weren't alone. A man and woman were standing by one of the drywall pallets talking. The man looked like Clothilde's brother Tyrone, but from forty feet away CJ couldn't be certain. CJ's lingering stare made Clothilde say, "It's just Tyrone and Vanetta Ebson, my father's accountant, checking up on the construction. They like to keep our contractor on time and honest."

"Looks like your plans are serious."

"Serious enough to have gotten my daddy killed." Clothilde adjusted her headband and grabbed a bleached-out sweatshirt from one of the nearby countertops. In one fluid motion she slipped the sweatshirt over her head without so much as moving a hair out of place. As she matter-of-factly tucked the sweatshirt under, she said, "Got a stereo system at home?"

The question seemed strange, but CJ nodded.

"Components or built in?"

"Components. Turntable, receiver, speakers, and an amplifier that would shake this building if I tweaked it right. Even got an old reel-to-reel."

"I'm on to you now," said Clothilde. "Old-fashioned. I like that. Most people trashed their components years ago. Any man with a turntable has to have a stash of forty-fives."

"Got enough in my basement to fill half a dozen shopping carts and change." CJ was beginning to wonder where Clothilde was headed on her trip down memory lane.

"Better hang on to them," said Clothilde, gesturing toward the renovation. "Because with or without my dad, I'm bringing the Polk's Stax of Wax label and old-time vinyl records back from the dead. My daddy was two months away from pressing records again, and it got him killed. I want the killer to pay, and I don't have time to wait on white folks' slow-as-molasses plea-bargain law. That's why I need you, CJ." She swallowed hard, but it couldn't stop the flow of tears. CJ had the urge to wrap his arm around her. While he tried to decide whether to play with fire, Clothilde regained her composure, blotting tears on the sleeve of her sweatshirt.

Somehow CJ couldn't picture Clothilde Polk as helpless. He felt as though she were weaving him in. The tears and her declaration had him wondering why anyone would want to kill an out-to-pasture rhythm and blues disc jockey just for wanting to manufacture some old-style vinyl 45s and rekindle a few brief minutes of fame.

CJ's skepticism must have shown because Clothilde blotted her eyes again and looked straight through him. "There's a hell of a lot more to this than you think. The sale of forty-fives jumped eighty percent from five hundred thousand to nine hundred thousand last year.

Percentagewise, that leap tops the growth of cassettes and videos combined. Not only was Daddy going to press records again, and make money at it, he was going to distribute, market, and sell vinyl like it was 1955. He wanted the Stax of Wax label to be king again." She paused, looking like an actress who had suddenly forgotten her lines, before adding, "Lots of people didn't want my father mucking around in the past."

"You make it sound like some kind of hit."

"You're tuning in," Clothilde said with a wry smile. "I wasn't even born when Daddy was riding the crest of fame, but there're people left over from that era, including an ex-wife, who didn't want to see him treading back across old stones and muddying up their waters. I can give you names, but first I need to know if you're going to help."

"Assuming your father was murdered, and we aren't even certain of that, what's wrong with letting the police handle it?"

Clothilde looked at CJ as if he had just tripped a blind person in the street. "Are you black, or just playing the part? I don't trust white folks in bellboys' uniforms, much less white cops. You obviously don't know a lot about the Stax of Wax label or our problems with the law."

CJ was a second away from telling Clothilde where she could shove her job, in language he knew she'd understand, but he reminded himself of two things: she was a woman, and he was a step away from being broke. He chalked Clothilde's insult up to the impatience of a grieving daughter and decided he wouldn't ask her the other question that had been on his mind all morning:

why she hadn't just hired one of Denver's high-powered PIs. He made a mental note of Clothilde's remark before giving her the kind of earnest *I'll even the score sooner or later* kind of look he reserved for clients he didn't trust. "This could go places you might not want it to go. Turn up some things you didn't expect."

Clothilde clamped her hands to her hips. "I've been through worse. I'll have Dr. Woodley's provisional report on what killed Daddy by this afternoon. It'll say he was murdered. You can count on that."

CJ was about to ask Clothilde how she could be so sure about what a preliminary autopsy report would say, but he remembered his financial situation and decided not to look a gift horse in the mouth. "I'll buy in," he said reluctantly.

"Fantastic," said Clothilde, sounding like a realtor who had just closed a million-dollar deal. "What's your hourly rate?"

CJ smiled. Clothilde's question told him that despite her bluster, she was a novice in the world she was about to step into. The magnitude of the construction project that Doo-Wop Polk had left behind also told him that Clothilde was well off. "I charge by the day. Three hundred dollars plus expenses. Two weeks in advance." He could always judge a potential client's ability to pay by watching the reaction to his fee. If the client blinked, coughed, hemmed, or hawed, he always demanded every penny of his fee up front.

Clothilde's response was strange. She adjusted her headband and said, "I'll be right back." Then she headed toward the new construction, leaving CJ wondering what in the hell made Clothilde Polk tick. She came back with Tyrone and a tall, slender, impeccably dressed black woman in tortoiseshell glasses in tow. The first things CJ noticed about the brown-skinned woman in addition to her painfully ugly glasses were the over-sized false eyelashes that fluttered beneath the glass rims and her thin, shapeless build. Her hair, which had seen years of straightening, was swept up in a big wave hairstyle in front, giving her the look of a country-western singer. Her glasses rested well below the bridge of a broad, oversized nose that overwhelmed her slim but pleasant face. CJ guessed she was probably in her early forties, although her glasses made her look older.

Clothilde smiled apologetically, as if she were try-ing to make up for challenging CJ's blackness earlier. "This is Vanetta Ebson. She handles the financial side of Stax of Wax." Clothilde's arm was hooked inside Vanetta's, best-friends style. "I'm hiring Mr. Floyd for a month. He is going to find out who killed Daddy."

Vanetta took her arm out of Clothilde's and looked CJ up and down. The look said, *We can do better.* "Is he a private investigator?"

"No. CJ's a bail bondsman, and finding people's his specialty." Clothilde's reassurance only made Vanetta push her glasses up on her nose and give CJ the once-over again. CJ was sure she was about to shake her head in one final burst of disgust. Instead she said, "I'll have a check for you before you leave."

It was obvious to CJ that Vanetta was used to tak-ing orders from one Polk or another, and whether or not she agreed with Clothilde's decision to hire him, she didn't seem like the type who was about to start refus-ing Polk's requests now.

Tyrone, who hadn't uttered a word during the entire exchange, finally spoke up. "We're behind schedule, Clothilde." His voice rang with more authority than the previous night.

"Then push them to make it up."

There was a tension between the two that CJ hadn't fully appreciated the previous evening.

"I'll do my job. Just make sure you do yours," said Tyrone.

Clothilde didn't respond. Instead she turned to Vanetta. "Go cut CJ a check." Vanetta moved off hesitantly. Clothilde then flashed Tyrone an icy stare that sent him following Vanetta back to the construction area like a scalded dog. When Clothilde was sure they were both out of earshot, she turned her attention back to CJ. "Vanetta's not used to taking orders from me. She was keeping the books for a nursery before Daddy hired her. Sometimes I think she's sniffed too many flowers. And you know, Tyrone's not my real brother. He's my half-brother from Daddy's first marriage. Just thought you'd like to know."

"Every bit of information helps."

While they waited on Vanetta, Clothilde gave CJ the world's greatest sales pitch for old-style vinyl records, including her theory that they possessed the kind of vibrant warm analog sounds that could never be captured on the icy compact disc. When she finished, CJ knew one thing for certain—Clothilde Polk knew the record-making and distribution business from A to Z.

Clothilde ended her mini-lecture just as Vanetta Ebson returned, carrying a large leather-bound business checkbook. She tore out a check that had been drafted for $4,200 and handed it to Clothilde, who signed it and gave it to CJ. The bold black letters at the top of the check spelling out "Polk's Stax of Wax" dwarfed Clothilde's signature. As Clothilde handed the check to CJ, Vanetta shot him a look that said, *Now, Mr. Hired Gun, go earn your money.* She tucked the checkbook under her arm and walked away.

CJ slipped the check into his pocket, hoping that the job would turn out to be the kind his uncle always liked to call easy money. Like he always did when he started a job, he calculated his chances of success on a scale of one to ten, ten being a certain success. In his mind, this job was an eight. "I'll need a list of people who could have benefited from your father's death."

"It could get pretty long, depending on how far back you want me to go."

"How about back to when he started out as a DJ?"

Clothilde thought for a moment. "Five people for sure, maybe six. I can have you their names, addresses, and their reasons for wanting to kill my father and maybe even their favorite colors, if you want them, by this evening."

"That many people wanted him dead?" said CJ, so surprised by the size of the enemies list that he almost missed the fact that Clothilde had obviously been keeping score.

"Yes, but only two would be at the top of my list." Clothilde looked away from CJ toward the stacks of drywall, insulation, and hanging wires. "Tyrone's mother would be number one—followed by Tyrone himself. I want you to investigate them first." The instant she finished speaking, several sheets of drywall thundered to the floor. CJ couldn't see Tyrone or Vanetta through the haze of dust that was rising in the air, and for a brief instant he wondered if the drywall hadn't been toppled by some mysterious combination of supermarket and R&B ghosts left over from his youth.

Six

CJ slipped on a scratchy-sounding, ten-year-old Muddy Waters tape as he nosed the Bel Air down Blake Street past Coors Field and out of LoDo. Clothilde had promised to call him with the names and background information on the other people she suspected might have killed her father, even though she kept insisting that Tyrone or his mother, Mabel, was the culprit.

The stadium entrance marquee announced that the Colorado Rockies and the San Diego Padres would do big-league battle TODAY. CJ patted the check in his shirt pocket and told himself that for the time being he couldn't trust anyone associated with Polk's Stax of Wax entirely, and that included Clothilde.

CJ had seen only one game all season, a late-May extra-innings nail-biter that he, Henry Bales, and Rosie Weaks had agonized through until the Rockies' pitching had failed in the eleventh inning and they lost 7 to 5.

The outing had been memorable, not so much for the Rockies' late-game ineptitude as for the game's seventh-inning stretch, when for a fleeting couple of minutes there had been thunder and lightning in the foothills and Rosie had sworn that he felt a few brief spits of rain. But even in a drought the grass at Coors Field, with its elaborate half-a-million-dollar watering and drainage system, had been as green as springtime in the Emerald Isle.

The rest of Denver was dying of thirst. Drought restrictions allowed for lawn watering only once a week, and the city had unleashed a bevy of water restriction enforcement officers, known unaffectionately as the toilet bowl police, on Denver's residents. The TBP cruised around town on ATVs making certain that every Mile High City resident either complied or paid a hefty fine. Whether you owned a home, a high-rise office building, or a taco stand, if you had grass you were classified by the water cops as either a circle, a diamond, or a square, and once a week, according to your geometric ID, you had four hours to water like hell. The problem with the TBP system was that any living thing that could do without water for an entire week belonged not in Denver but in the desert.

During the first week of June, CJ had given up on trying to maintain the patch of lawn around his building. The flower garden that his secretary, Julie, had painstakingly nurtured for years had turned into a mound of rock-hard clay and he had decided to resod the lawn and replant the flower bed when the drought broke, so he was letting Cicero Vickers, the bail bondsman in the building next door, who was a circle, water on his diamond day, toilet bowl police be damned.

Muddy Waters had just started a gravelly refrain bemoaning the fact that the repo man had stolen his wife and his car when CJ eased down the 20th Street on-ramp and into the I-25 noonday rush of traffic. He couldn't explain exactly why, after Vietnam, he had come to prefer the guttural, gut-wrenching sounds of the blues to the melodic, poetic music from Motown's stable of balladeers. Deep down he suspected that it had a lot to do with the damage war had done to his youthful soul. Two tours as a navy ravine swift boat gunner's mate patrolling the twisted branches of the Mekong River hadn't made him any more of a loner than he was the day he left the States, but they helped end a brief childhood-sweetheart marriage to a woman who needed more than the morose, untrusting, twenty-year-old jungle rat who came home. After Vietnam, the blues and CJ just seemed to be more of a musical fit.

CJ eased off the interstate and headed across town for the University of Colorado Health Sciences Center as Muddy Waters began to grumble about someone taking his place at home in the middle of the night. A blues man's world never changes, thought CJ.

As he breezed down Sixth Avenue, he wondered if he should have called Dr. Henry Bales before dropping by unannounced. But since it seemed that he was now going to have to stay a step ahead of Clothilde as well as the cops, he decided he needed Henry's input on just how Doo-Wop Polk had died before the information was passed on to Clothilde or some homicide cop. Henry was a creature of habit, and CJ expected to find him eating lunch in his research laboratory, devouring his daily ham-and-swiss-cheese Dagwood, heavy on the tomato and mayo, with a Coke and a bag of potato chips near at hand. CJ and Bales had served together in Vietnam when Henry, fresh out of Navy Corpsmen School and as green as Bermuda algae, had been assigned by Uncle Sam as a medic aboard the *Cape Star*, CJ's patrol boat. When Henry returned home, he had pursued medicine instead of going back to his father's five-thousand-acre Durango cattle ranch. Now he was a surgical pathologist at CU's medical school, where he had access to the provisional anatomic diagnosis on Clothilde Polk's father, and CJ knew that in the space of a couple of minutes he could find out whether the old R&B DJ had been murdered.

To CJ, the forty-million-dollar research building that housed Henry's gene-splicing recombinant DNA virology laboratory seemed almost as spooky and filled with ghosts as Clothilde Polk's old Safeway building. There wasn't a soul stirring out front of the mammoth edifice to modern-day science when he pulled into the parking lot. He wondered if everyone on the medical center campus locked themselves in their laboratories over the noon hour like Henry and chowed down on the same meal they had been eating for the past twenty years.

On his way up to Henry's eighth-floor lab, CJ was serenaded by the kind of easy-listening elevator music that made him realize why he loved the blues. The slow ride also gave him time to reflect on a question he needed to get answered the next time he saw Clothilde Polk. Why was she feuding with her half-brother Tyrone?

The elevator door opened as CJ reminded himself that he also needed to find out exactly where Vanetta Ebson's loyalties stood now that LeRoy Polk was dead. He knew from experience that when it came to murder,

the next best thing to having an eyewitness is having an
inside source. Besides, Vanetta had struck him as the kind
of employee who knew exactly where all the family skele-
tons were buried.

The entire southwestern wall of Henry Bales's lab
had four-foot-high windows with a soaring falcon's view
of the Rocky Mountain Front Range. Even without its
usual year-round snowcap, due to the drought, 14,264-
foot Mt. Evans sparkled in the distance. CJ took in the
view as he walked the length of the thirty-foot-long laboratory and headed for Henry's cramped office at the far
end. Henry was finishing off a bag of wavy Lay's potato
chips when CJ walked in. Stacks of papers, medical journals, and DNA gels littered every foot of usable space.

"Those things'll kill you, Henry, or hasn't your doctor told you about saturated fat?" asked CJ.

A broad, been-through-hell-together kind of grin
that is seen only on the faces of men and women who
have observed humankind at its worst crossed Henry's
face. He pushed the bag of chips aside and stood up. He
was a couple of inches shorter than CJ, not nearly as
muscular, and looked like some Hollywood casting director's version of a brooding, sensitive, grade-B Western
half-breed. Henry might have said so himself since he
was equal parts French Canadian and Oklahoma Chero-
kee. During Vietnam he and CJ had even called themselves Blood and Breed, daring their shipmates to use the
terms.

"I'm not worried," said Henry, knotting his fist and
lightly tapping it against CJ's outstretched palm. "I'm
working on a cure for high cholesterol." He popped a

handful of chips into his mouth. "And I'm testing it out on myself."

"Call me when your heart explodes," said CJ.

They broke into the in-synch laughter of longtime friends.

"Shove those papers over there out of the way and rest your behind, Mr. Bounty Hunter," said Henry, sliding a stool CJ's way. "Then tell me whose badass you're after this afternoon."

CJ nudged a two-foot-high stack of computer printouts on the floor to one side with his foot and eased onto the stool. "No badasses today, Henry. Believe it or not, an exploding heart's what brings me over to the Halls of Ivy."

"You and Mavis short-circuit again?"

"No. And just for the record, Don Juan, I'm not on wife number three."

Henry smiled. "Some of us Wild West types just don't like being pinned down."

"You quoting *Rolling Stone* or the *New England Journal*?"

Before Henry could respond, a slender woman in a heavily starched lab coat poked her head through the open doorway. "That androgen receptor gene long gel you wanted is done, Dr. Bales." She flashed an innocent, first-job-in-the-real-world kind of smile before she disappeared.

Henry caught the *not again* look in CJ's eyes. "She's my new postdoc," he said defensively. "And she doesn't give a damn about polyunsaturated fat." He finished the last of his potato chips and toweled off his greasy fingers with microscope lens paper. "Whose heart exploded?" he asked, tossing the paper into a wastebasket.

"An old-time R&B DJ named LeRoy Polk."

"Not Daddy Doo-Wop. Shit, he's the man who hooked me on R&B. Hell, I couldn't have been more than thirteen. What's your tie to an old platter jock like him?"

"Your medical brethren at DGH say he had a heart attack. His daughter claims he was murdered. I was hoping you'd pull up his PAD and help me close the loop."

Henry frowned, but CJ knew the frown was staged. "Damn, CJ. Every time I turn around you're asking for help on a murder case. Maybe it's time I applied to be a bondsman. This one doesn't involve chasing after another set of lunatics with a killer virus, does it?"

"I doubt it. But just in case, at least this time you've got your own vaccine." CJ picked up Henry's empty potato-chip bag and waved it in the air.

Henry shook his head, rolled a chair over to a workstation in the corner, and turned on his computer. He motioned for CJ to pull over his stool. After a series of high-pitched beeps, Henry tapped a couple of keys and the computer screen lit up with a listing of every hospital along the Front Range. He scrolled down to Denver General Hospital, entered two more commands, and the next thing CJ saw as he looked over Henry's shoulder was a bold heading that read CONFIDENTIAL INFORMATION—ACCESS LIMITED. Beneath the heading were the words FRONT RANGE PATHOLOGY CONSORTIUM RECORDS.

"What day did he die?" asked Henry, looking up from the screen.

"The seventeenth."

Henry accessed the date, and the heading PROVI-

SIONAL ANATOMIC DIAGNOSES filled the screen. Henry
scrolled his way down the list of PADs to LeRoy Polk's
name. "Old Vernon Lowe must have had one hell of a
busy day," said Henry, freezing LeRoy Polk's PAD on the
screen. "Half of the names I scrolled by were DGH
cases."

Henry tapped a key, and instantly the six principal
pathologic findings from LeRoy Polk's autopsy appeared
below his name.

"He had a heart attack, all right," said Henry. "But
that asterisk next to his primary diagnosis, the one at the
top that says myocardial infarction, tells me there's something more."

Henry tapped the keyboard once again, and the
words PRELIMINARY TOXICOLOGY appeared, followed by a
paragraph of medicalese that CJ couldn't decipher even
after three quick reads. But the fact that Henry Bales
whistled loudly and shook his head was all CJ needed to
tell him that LeRoy Polk had been murdered.

"Unless old Doo-Wop was smoking twenty packs a
day, he was murdered, all right," said Henry. "He had
enough nicotine in his blood to stroke out a horse. Says
here Charlie Woodley was the attending pathologist.
Let's see if he issued a preliminary to the cops." Henry
called up Dr. Woodley's preliminary summary. It was
brief and to the point:

At autopsy, two Nicoderm smoking cessation transdermal patches were
evident on the right forearm 5 cm. below the condylar level of the
humerus. When the body was rotated for ventral surface examination
of lividity, two additional Nicoderm patches were identified on both
upper thighs at the mid level of the quadriceps. A final patch was

found adhering to the undersurface of the scrotum. Plasma levels of nicotine were 210 mg./ml. at the time of death, ten times the recommended daily dosage in a patient with a known history of cardiac arrhythmia and angina. The nicotine was most certainly a contributing factor and likely caused the patient's death, although a blood alcohol level of .18% was also noted.

CJ reread the summary for the fourth time, frowning at the comment about the strange placement of the patch on the genitalia. "How much medical knowledge would you need to pull off a doping deal like that?" he finally said, looking up at Henry.

"A good little bit. More than what you could pick up from just reading the package insert. The real difficult thing about pulling it off would be getting the opportunity to deliver the drug to the patient in the first place. You'd almost have to have the run of the hospital, like a doctor or nurse, or be family to get that close. And you'd have to deliver it when the patient was out of it. But since his blood alcohol level was so high, I'd say Mr. Polk was stewed enough for someone to slip him the patches without his knowing it."

Opportunity was something CJ hadn't fully considered until that very moment, but as soon as he did, Tyrone and Clothilde Polk's names came to mind.

"How much of this information would Woodley have told Polk's daughter?" asked CJ.

"Cause of death would be just about it for now. He wouldn't go much beyond confirming a heart attack. I doubt that he'd say it was nicotine-induced."

"Good. For the moment I need to stay a few steps ahead of the pack, especially since right now I don't know which wolves are friendly and which ones might want to take a bite out of my ass."

"Anything else, *mein herr?*" asked Henry, turning off the computer with a salute.

"No. But take my advice and lay off the chips," said CJ, retrieving the empty potato-chip bag from Henry's desk and crumpling it up into a tight ball just as Henry's postdoc walked back in. He was sure that now that the noon hour had passed, she was chafing at the bit to move medical science into the next millennium.

CJ checked his watch. "You coming to Juneteenth?"

"Don't think so," said Henry. "Got too many experiments going."

"You work too hard, Henry." CJ walked past Henry's postdoc, who looked poised to rid the world of pestilence and disease. As he headed past her and out the door, CJ knew that Denver's Juneteenth celebration was the furthest thing from her mind.

When CJ got back to his office, his secretary, Julie, was busily watering the dozen plants that filled her cramped little office. Since the drought had robbed her of any opportunity to tend her backyard flower garden, she had moved the garden inside. Geraniums, ficuses, begonias, black-eyed Susans, and succulents ringed her desk and lined the office walls. Julie was attending to a bushy, healthy-looking, two-foot-tall ficus in front of her desk when CJ slipped up behind her, clapped his hands together, and boomed, "Toilet bowl police." Julie didn't so much as flinch. She had been CJ's secretary too long to bite, and she knew every one of his half-dozen tired old pranks as well as she knew how to breathe.

"You've got a bunch of messages," she said, straightening up and adding, "Does this ficus look healthy to you?"

"As healthy as a tree in the forest," said CJ, giving the plant the briefest of looks.

Julie shook her head in disgust. "You're worthless." She walked around her desk and retrieved several message slips. "Clothilde Polk called four times. I tossed her first three messages; they were just callbacks. The last time she called she sounded like she was ready to pop a synapse. I wrote down the message verbatim." She handed CJ a slip that read, "It's about my father. Call me ASAP."

Something about the message struck a chord with CJ. It took him a few seconds before he realized it was the fact that Clothilde liked to use the acronym ASAP. He was still concentrating on the idiosyncracy when Julie handed him his other messages. He flipped through them until he came to one from Mavis that said to call her immediately. Choosing between whether to call Mavis or Clothilde wasn't really a choice. He left Julie fighting her personal war against Denver's drought, walked into his office, and dialed Mavis's number at Mae's Kitchen. She answered on the first ring. There was a tension in her voice that made the muscles in CJ's face tighten.

"A couple of city health department inspectors were here a few hours ago. They cited us for eight health-code violations. It's got something to do with Daddy's opposition to monorail," Mavis said angrily. "I told him he's too old to be screwing around with today's brand of political cutthroats. He's from another time, CJ. You've got to talk some sense into his thick skull before he runs into the mayor and his entourage tomorrow at Juneteenth and they decide to make an example of him. The next time the mayor's flunkies might just close us down."

It took CJ a few minutes to calm Mavis down. She began to sound normal only when he said he'd try to convince Willis to back off on his opposition to monorail when they met for dinner that evening at Te Carte's Mexican Grill. Mavis hung up with the plea, "Help me cool his jets."

A couple of minutes later, CJ called Clothilde.

"Dr. Woodley's calling my father's death a murder," were the first words out of her mouth after CJ identified himself. He was still thinking about Mavis and didn't feel like sparring with Clothilde over the phone, so he asked her to have a list of everyone who might have wanted to see her father dead, and at least one good reason why, ready for him and he'd be by to get it within the hour. When she said she was tied up on business until seven PM, CJ told her he was going to be tied up for the evening also and to meet him at seven-thirty the next morning at Rosie Weaks's garage, the staging area for the beginning of the Juneteenth parade. As he cradled the phone, he wondered how Clothilde had been able to get Woodley to give her a PAD so fast and why someone who had been screaming bloody murder to speak to him two hours earlier was now so willing to wait until the next day for a meeting. Clothilde Polk was a black woman with money who was turning out to be volatile, manipulative, and unpredictable. Traits that his uncle always said should worry the dog shit out of any poor black man.

*   *   *

Dinner that evening with Mavis and Willis turned out to be a war of wills. Willis had his mind made up about monorail, and he made it clear to Mavis and CJ that no amount of health-code violation blackmail or threats from the mayor would make him change it. When the evening ended, CJ had a headache from playing referee and gas from too many deep-fried tacoritos. Mavis left Te Carte's exasperated and more than a little scared.

When CJ got home a little past nine, he called Clothilde Polk to see if he could settle their business about a list of possible suspects that evening and skip her interfering with his plans for Juneteenth. All he got for his efforts was a curt voice-mail message that said, "Polk; leave your message at the tone." Thirty minutes later CJ was tossing and turning his way through six hours of restless sleep and dreaming that he was wandering the Mojave Desert, stalked by two beautiful women with their pigheaded fathers in tow. Unfortunately, Denver's thirtieth annual Juneteenth festivities turned out to be a whole lot worse than CJ's dreams.

Seven

For two decades Roosevelt Weaks's 1950s-style full-service gas station, known to everyone in Five Points as Rosie's Garage, had served as the staging area for the Juneteenth parade. Rosie and his wife, Etta Lee, had transformed the once-ramshackle Welton Street eyesore into a thriving Five Points business and a city landmark. When it came to servicing cars, Rosie's could provide you with everything from a gas cap to a new engine, and at the full-service pump islands, high school and college-aged attendants in gray pin-striped uniforms still washed your windows, checked the air in all four tires, and checked your oil each time you stopped for gas.

Juneteenth was one of the few times during the year that Rosie, a six-foot-four, ruddy-complected black man with an enormous head, no neck, and huge shoulders that made it appear as though he were always wearing football pads, ever complained. He didn't mind that the annual celebration put a cramp in business for a couple of days, or that the festivities gave Etta Lee a chance to ignore him and socialize with her girlfriends for the better part of a week. But he did hate the fact that too many Juneteenth revelers preferred his restrooms to the city's portable johnny-on-the-spots, and he despised cleaning up after the yearly visit from the Budweiser Clydesdales or pooper-scooping for the Black Rodeo Cowboys' Association's temperamental quarterhorses.

Clothilde Polk was standing next to one of Rosie's antique 1940s globe-style Conoco gas pumps. She was dressed in a figure-flattering linen slacks suit, and Darryl Gentry, Rosie's eighteen-year-old nephew, was filling her Lexus with gas. Darryl had met Clothilde a week earlier at his house, when his mother, Charlene, had introduced Clothilde to him during his lunch break and informed him in her high-pitched soprano voice that Clothilde and her father were going to put Denver on the world's musical map. Darryl had been in a rush, and he hadn't paid much attention to the lady sharing the living room sofa with his mother. "Pleased to meet you and sounds great" had been his only words as he rushed into the kitchen to make himself a sandwich. Now it was all he could do to keep from staring wide-eyed at Clothilde, who looked every bit the part of an *Ebony* fashion-fair model about to take the runway.

"Your mother and I go back a long way. We were in nursing school together in Chicago," Clothilde said as Darryl finished topping off the tank. Darryl searched for something witty to say, but all that came out was, "She says you're building a R&B museum."

"We're doing more than that." Clothilde adjusted her

stance so that one hip was cocked ever so slightly higher than the other.

Darryl swallowed hard, wondering what else the greatest-looking woman he had ever seen was planning, and wishing he were a few years older. "It's great that you two got a chance to hook back up," he said, moving to clean the car's back windows. It surprised him when Clothilde followed him around the car, and it floored him when she asked, "Do you know CJ Floyd? Your mother says he's pretty good at what he does."

Darryl had once gotten himself involved in one of CJ's bounty-hunting cases, and it had cost him a night in jail. The episode had nearly scared his hyperexcitable mother to death. "There's no one better," he said, now cleaning the driver's side of the windshield, thinking back on the episode with relish.

"That's good to know," said Clothilde, glancing at her watch. CJ was now fifteen minutes late.

Darryl finished cleaning the car's windshield and moved to check the air in the tires, saving the tire closest to Clothilde for last. When she handed him a fifty-dollar bill while he was capping the valve stem, Darryl bolted up as if he had been blessed by a priest and hurried off toward the garage for change.

As Darryl entered the garage, a dozen East High School band members who until then had been milling around the garage's Welton Street entrance scattered like bowling pins as a tractor-trailer carrying six Budweiser Clydesdales pulled into the drive. The driver stopped and set his air brakes with a loud hiss. Two other men swung down from the cab and proceeded stonefaced to the rear of the huge horse trailer. A couple of minutes later, the first horse out of the trailer christened Rosie's driveway with the inaugural road apple of the day.

Within half an hour parade marshals had queued up two other high school marching bands and the half-dozen convertibles reserved for dignitaries. Twenty members of the Colorado Black Rodeo Cowboys' Association had staked out their places in line, and representatives from several downtown banks that had only recently realized that black people could be loanworthy stood champing at the bit to get the Juneteenth show on the road.

Clothilde was standing near the end of the line, fuming. She was about to go inside the garage to call CJ and tell him that she was going to stop payment on his check when his Bel Air pulled up into Rosie's south-side driveway and stopped at one of the diesel pumps. Mavis and Willis Sundee were in the Bel Air with CJ, and not one of them looked the least bit happy. Mavis was seated behind CJ. Her jet-black curly hair was tossed and windblown, and her customary girl-next-door smile had been replaced by an irritated *why me* kind of frown. CJ and Willis were in the front seat, and Willis was staring blankly into the queued-up crowd.

CJ got out of the car first. When he folded his seat forward to let Mavis out, Willis reached over the back of his own seat and started gathering together a half-dozen signs he had placed on the backseat. Once he had them squared up and their wooden standards aligned, he got out, reached into the rear seat, and gathered up the protest signs from inside the car. Each alabaster-white sign carried the same bold blue message punctuated with a red exclamation mark: MONORAIL—A BLAST FROM THE PAST, FIVE POINTS DON'T NEED CITY HALL PORK BARREL!

While Willis wrestled with the signs, Clothilde made a beeline for the Bel Air. Before CJ could brace himself for her fury, she lit into him. "I've been waiting here listening to the off-key warmup screeches of pimple-faced musicians and inhaling the sickening odor of beer-commercial horses for over an hour. If you expect to work for me, we need to get something straight right now, CJ. When we set up a meeting, I expect you to be on time."

CJ was so surprised by her outburst that all he could muster was, "Sorry." He could tell from the expression on Clothilde's face that she was in no mood to throttle back, but with CJ Floyd, one *sorry* was all you got.

Mavis was heading for the driver's side of the Bel Air to find out who the hot-tempered woman pushing CJ's buttons was when a parade marshal rushed up and interrupted. "You need to pull your ride in line, CJ. You're holding up the works. Swing in around behind Ben Hickman's Buick."

Tired of orders, CJ shot back, "I'm not driving. This year Rosie's doing the honors."

"Well, find him and get his ass in gear," said the marshal, rushing off to put out another fire.

CJ turned around to find Mavis and Clothilde smiling at one another awkwardly. "Same zoo every year." He shook his head disgustedly before making introductions.

"Clothilde Polk, this is Mavis Sundee. Mavis is the one responsible for me being in the middle of this mess."

"But I didn't make him late," said Mavis, extending her hand to Clothilde. "That honor goes to my father." She turned to look for Willis, who had gathered up his signs and was now halfway to the garage entrance.

"Clothilde's a client," said CJ, emphasizing the word *client*.

"I see," said Mavis. The way she said it let CJ know that although she was currently more interested in her father's movements than in Clothilde's, his relationship to the fire-breather who had extracted a *sorry* from him was going to have to be explained.

"We can deal with CJ's problem with being on time later," said Clothilde. "Right now, I just want to get away from this foul-smelling place."

CJ looked at Mavis and shrugged. "Can you handle Willis and his gang of six alone?"

"I'll try," said Mavis. She wanted to add *Can you handle Ms. Polk on your own?* but didn't.

Willis had linked up with two of his six fellow monorail protesters, Morgan Williams and Dittier Atkins. Dittier was struggling to control the one-hundred-fifty-pound California red river pig he had won in a New Year's Eve raffle. As usual, the pig was tugging at its leash, front hooves off the ground, trying to break free.

"Hold your horses, Geronimo," admonished Morgan. "The parade ain't started yet. Dittier, give Geronimo some cheese or he's gonna have a fuckin' fit."

Dittier, who was mute, pulled a chunk of cheddar out of his pocket and dropped it on the driveway. Geronimo scarfed the cheese up as if it were a truffle.

"You and Dittier ready for your signs?" asked Willis, amazed at how quickly Geronimo had devoured the donut-sized hunk of cheese.

"Damn straight," said Morgan.

"Remember to make sure people can see your signs

from both sides of the street." Willis demonstrated, turning his sign from side to side.

"How can they miss with Geronimo out front dancing the jig?" said Morgan.

Dittier grinned and leaned forward with his sign. As he did, the leash in his other hand went slack and Geronimo, feeling a sudden surge of freedom, let out a squeal that sounded like an automobile horn blaring in a tunnel. He shot forward like a bullet, and it took all of Dittier's strength to hold him back. When the pig was finally back under control, Willis, Morgan, and Dittier started over to the procession line with Geronimo out front, nosing at every crack in the concrete, knifing his way through the bystanders, grunting, snorting, and sounding like a dying man's death rattle. Mavis followed behind the foursome, regretting that she hadn't asked CJ for help.

CJ and Clothilde threaded their way through a maze of cars, horses, and high school bands into Rosie's Garage. Inside, the office area was remarkably neat. Two stacks of oil cans were arranged pyramid fashion almost to the ceiling, and several stacks of Michelin tires dominated the room. A U-shaped counter with an antique cash register stood off to one side, crowding a door that opened to the garage's three service bays. For people who had never set foot in Rosie's Garage, the 1950s charm could be intriguing and a nostalgic period piece. But Rosie's differed from other gas station garages in at least one other respect. On weekends, the mammoth storage room behind the service bays doubled as a local gambling casino known as "the den." The den was a place where CJ knew he could talk to Clothilde in private and afterward be back out in the thick of the Juneteenth celebration within minutes.

Rosie, whom his closest friends called Red, was stationed behind the cash register, looking more like a bouncer at a topless bar than Mr. Goodwrench. His eyes widened when he saw CJ walk in with Clothilde. CJ shook his head as if to say *It's not what you think, Red,* before saying, "They're waiting outside for you to chauffeur the Bel Air."

"It'll have to wait a minute till Darryl finishes the car up on the rack." His words were directed to CJ, but he was staring directly at Clothilde. CJ decided it was time to end Rosie's suspense. "The woolly mammoth guarding the cash register is Rosie Weaks."

Rosie grinned.

"Clothilde Polk." Clothilde extended her hand.

"Clothilde's a client," said CJ. The words came out defensively.

Clothilde smiled back at Rosie briefly before turning to CJ. "Is there somewhere private where we can go over the list I put together?"

"That's why we're here," said CJ.

The message that Clothilde wanted privacy came through to Rosie loud and clear. Without asking, he handed CJ the key to the den. "Lock up behind yourself and give the key back to Darryl."

CJ and Clothilde walked through the garage's service bays just as Darryl hammered a stubborn greasy fitting on a '72 Olds. The metal-on-metal sound startled Clothilde, and she flinched. *She's human after all,* thought CJ. After several more bangs Darryl dropped the hammer, and a few seconds later they heard the thump of a grease gun.

The den was much cooler than the garage, and without the benefit of its patrons or poker tables and roulette wheels, which were rolled in only on demand, the room had an empty, forlorn look. Rosie rented his gambling paraphernalia as needed. The rest of the time he kept the storage room looking like an unused basement. A card table, an out-of-commission riding mower, several folding chairs, and a huge tarp-covered bar were the only things occupying the room.

CJ unfolded a couple of chairs and slipped them up to the card table. "Awfully large storage room for a gas station," said Clothilde.

"Rosie thinks big."

If Clothilde suspected that the room was meant for more than storing thirty-weight oil, she didn't say so. What Rosie Weaks did with his garage was his own business. She adjusted herself on the rickety chair before digging into her pocket and pulling out a folded piece of legal-sized paper. She slapped it down on the table. "Here's the list of people you wanted. And it starts with Tyrone and his mother, Mabel."

"Let's see what you got." CJ unfolded the paper. He ran his fingers down a list of names printed in bold capital letters. Clothilde had taken the time to write a brief summary beneath each name. As he read down the list of names a second time, he remembered one of his uncle's favorite sayings: *Momma birds do a lot of wing-flappin' to hide what's in the nest.* CJ decided against asking Clothilde about Tyrone or his mother and went straight to Roland Jefferson, the third name on the list. "What about Jefferson?"

Clothilde was irritated that CJ skipped to Jefferson first. Her answer was terse. "During the late fifties and early sixties he was Daddy's business partner, and to hear him tell it, he once owned fifty percent of Stax of Wax."

"And you're saying he didn't?"

"Only Daddy knew for sure, and he can't answer."

"Is Jefferson black?" asked CJ.

The question caught Clothilde off guard and she hesitated before answering. "As a bowling ball."

Her hesitation made CJ wonder whether she had inside dope on Jefferson that she wasn't sharing. He was about to go on to the next name when Clothilde surprised him. "Roland's wife, Willette, is white. Before they got married she was a backup singer for a group out of Gary, Indiana, called the Corsairs. Daddy put her under contract to Stax of Wax, and from what I've heard he wanted to do more, but with Roland on the scene, Daddy ended up in second place."

CJ was surprised at Clothilde's candor. He chalked it up to what he suspected was just show-business talk: tell everything you know to hide the hurting feelings inside. The name Lawrence Hampoli was next. Clothilde had printed just one word, "wiseguy," next to his name. "Pretty short rap sheet on Hampoli," said CJ.

"*Wiseguy* says it all, if you know what I mean," said Clothilde.

"Mob?"

"He lives here in Colorado, down in Pueblo, I think. According to Daddy, he never worked a day in his life; his best friends fly in and out of Las Vegas and New Jersey a lot and cruise around in long, black cars."

CJ smiled at Clothilde's description. She could have been describing a funeral director, but he got the point. He thought for a moment, trying to connect the name Hampoli to Colorado's nucleus of organized crime, but all he drew was a blank.

The name Juney-boy Stokes was next, but there wasn't a summary after his name. "Stokes a wiseguy too?" asked CJ.

"No. But one thing for certain, if he had ever laid eyes on Daddy, he would have killed him on sight."

"Why?"

"He thought Daddy destroyed his life."

"How?"

"Beats me. Daddy never said."

CJ made note of the fact that Clothilde seemed to need to skip past Juney-boy's name. He wondered if she was lying or just afraid. He scrutinized the list of names again and began thinking about a strategy for tracking down a couple of sixties R&B has-beens, a purported mobster, and a man with a schoolyard nickname who would have killed LeRoy Polk on sight. After pondering his options, he drummed his fingers on the table and looked up at Clothilde. "Tyrone's right here and Hampoli lives in Pueblo. They'll be easy enough to find. What about Roland Jefferson and his wife and Tyrone's mother, Mabel, and this brother, Stokes?"

"You're pretty quick at figuring out how to limit your legwork, CJ. As far as I know, Roland and Willette still live in Chicago. Mabel lives right here in Denver. Has for years."

"Does she still use the name Polk?"

"No. Dropped it after the divorce. She uses her maiden name, Pitts."

CJ swallowed hard, hoping that somehow he had heard Clothilde wrong. He had known Mabel Pitts for years. He had run errands for her as a child, mowed her lawn as a teenager, and during his years as a bail bondsman he had helped her evict more ne'er-do-well tenants from the four apartment buildings she owned than he cared to count. Why hadn't he known about Tyrone? Now that Mabel was close to seventy and crippled with arthritis, CJ made certain that every fall Morgan Williams and Dittier Atkins, the two homeless ex-rodeo cowboys who helped him on cases from time to time, trimmed her trees and raked up the leaves in her yard. CJ's feelings for Mabel were plastered all over his face.

"You know that witch?"

"Yes."

"She took Daddy for a ride. Tyrone's probably not even his. She's a gold-digging shrew, and Tyrone's a clone."

CJ could see that as far as Clothilde was concerned, Tyrone and Mabel might as well march into the District Three police station that instant and admit they had killed LeRoy Polk. CJ didn't relish having to investigate Mabel, but now that he knew she was Tyrone's mother, he tried to recall if he had ever seen Tyrone before the other night. "Has Tyrone ever lived in Denver?"

"No. He lived with Daddy after the divorce. That's why you probably never saw him."

Satisfied with Clothilde's answer, CJ went back to thinking about having to confront Mabel.

"Where are you going to start?" said Clothilde, breaking his train of thought.

"Right here in Denver with Mabel and Tyrone. Then I'll check out your wiseguy, Mr. Hampoli. If nothing pans out here in Colorado, I'll give your two aging rock and rollers in Chicago, Roland Jefferson and his wife, a look. Maybe I'll find Juney-boy Stokes back there hiding under a rock."

"You won't need to go to Chicago," said Clothilde. "It was either Daddy's love life or his ties to the underworld that did him in, and both of those connections are right here in Colorado."

CJ would have normally put a pushy know-it-all like Clothilde in her place, but the $4,200 check she had given him earlier made him think twice. He swallowed his pride and ran the list of suspects back through his head. "Wasn't Willette Jefferson a love connection too?"

Clothilde frowned. "I wasn't there. All I know is that Daddy always claimed she had a better voice and more stage presence than Diana Ross."

CJ rubbed his chin, reached into his shirt pocket, and pulled out a cheroot. He was about to light up when Clothilde said, "I wish you wouldn't."

CJ shoved the cheroot back into his pocket and sucked in on his cheeks to check his disgust at having to acquiesce to Clothilde Polk once again. "Where'd you hook up with Charlene Gentry?"

"Back in nursing school in Chicago. Charlene finished, but I washed out. Two years of changing bedpans was all I could take."

CJ didn't know much about nursing, but he suspected that Clothilde had enough medical knowledge to have killed LeRoy Polk, so he mentally added Clothilde's name to the suspect list.

He now knew several things for certain. It wouldn't have been a big deal for someone to fly in from Chicago to send LeRoy Polk to an early R&B grave, especially if the old doo-wop king really had offended an organized crime figure. But it would have been just as easy for a Colorado connection like Lawrence Hampoli or even Mabel

Pitts to have killed him one evening on their way home from the 7-Eleven. CJ realized that, like it or not, he was going to have to do some serious digging. He had a question for Clothilde about why Daddy Doo-Wop had decided to set up shop in Denver, but he was tired of playing twenty questions and decided to save it for later. "Let's head back outside to catch the parade," said CJ, reaching for a cheroot.

Clothilde rolled her eyes and dusted off the arm of her jacket as CJ lit up. "Hope the barnyard smell's gone."

As she brushed past CJ toward the door, he caught the faint hint of jasmine in her perfume, and he found himself hoping that Clothilde had forgotten everything she had ever learned about medicine.

The Juneteenth parade was in full swing when CJ and Clothilde stepped back out onto Welton Street and into a crowd of people lining the sidewalks for blocks. The hickory smell of Poppa Loomis's Georgia smokehouse barbecue permeated the dry morning air as the Montebello High School band marched by, strutting to a fast-paced 160-beats-per-minute cadence.

"I want you to wrap this thing with my father up in a couple of weeks," said Clothilde.

"Thought you said you'd need me for a month," said CJ.

"The two additional weeks are just for insurance. From what Charlene says, you won't need the extra time. Either way, you come out ahead."

Clothilde's generosity made CJ wonder if he was being set up. But with his finances in the shape they were, he wasn't about to argue. "Let's head for higher ground. There'll be less people up near Mae's Kitchen."

"Good. My car's parked that way anyway," said Clothilde, feeling a bit claustrophobic. She took the point and seemed to relish running interference as they wove their way through the crowded sidewalk toward Mae's. Each time CJ nearly caught up with her, someone cut him off. After a block and a half CJ caught sight of Dittier Atkins standing in front of Mae's Kitchen waving a monorail protest sign above his head with one hand while Geronimo's leash tugged at the other. A Lincoln convertible filled with Winston Dunn, the councilwoman for District Seven, and someone CJ didn't recognize cruised past Dittier. Even from a distance, CJ thought he saw a hint of a scowl on Dunn's face.

Clothilde stopped two doors down from Mae's, in front of Prillerman's Trophy and Badge, waiting for CJ to catch up. When he did, she said, "I've got to head down to LoDo to check with Tyrone on the construction. How long before you can give me something concrete?"

"Give me a week." CJ knew that by the time the official autopsy findings on LeRoy Polk worked through the Denver General Hospital bureaucracy and the cops finally sank their teeth into the case, he'd have a head start.

Dittier caught sight of CJ and began waving his protest sign frantically as he worked his way toward CJ and Clothilde. CJ responded with a raised arm and clenched fist. Dittier and Geronimo were about fifteen yards away when the front of Mae's Kitchen exploded in a mass of flying glass, splintered wood, brickbats, and hundred-year-old tin ceiling tiles that sliced through the air like boomerangs.

Instinctively, as if he were back in the jungles of Vietnam, CJ hit the ground, pulling Clothilde with him. Almost in unison, the crowd let out a low, piercing howl, but the loudest and most distinctive noise that CJ heard as he rolled on top of Clothilde and felt the crush of bodies falling on top of him was a guttural, endless squeal coming from Geronimo.

Eight

Roland Jefferson was walking down Cottage Grove Avenue along the western boundary of what in the early 1950s had been Chicago's rhythm and blues mecca, headed for Wing Gipson's Original House of Chicago Soul and dreaming about the past. Gipson's was where Roland had spent most of the mornings in his life for the past twenty-five years, talking music and shooting the breeze with friends. The puffy, irregular circles under his eyes and the crazy-quilt pattern of missing hair that had resulted from years of battling a hereditary form of eczema, alopecia, and diabetes made him look much older than sixty-eight.

He was dreaming about sporting a wavy, processed marcel, wearing $250 Stacey Adams shoes, and having a closet full of $500 sharkskin suits. But most of all he was thinking about LeRoy Polk and the late 1940s, when he and LeRoy had started in the music business as red nickel runners by hooking up with a couple of mob-connected white boys they knew from Calumet City, Indiana.

Organized crime controlled the lucrative jukebox industry as R&B was spreading its wings and moving north from its Southern roots into cities like Chicago and Detroit. The mob began by establishing regional control of the R&B side of the record industry. Once it had control, it determined what songs went into the jukeboxes, using runners like Roland and LeRoy. In order to maximize gains as it moved into the large Midwestern industrial markets, the mob initiated the notorious red nickel practice of double-dipping from the jukes. Any establishment that took a mob-controlled jukebox, from swanky cabarets to chitlin-circuit dives, had to show a certain amount of coin play per jukebox unit or make up the difference at the end of the month, when Roland and LeRoy or other runners like them showed up to make sure that the owners were in compliance. Owners were forced to purchase a certain number of indelibly red-striped coins to be used whenever they gave change for the jukebox. The red coins were then collected from the jukes and exchanged at a mob-favored discount with the owner, effectively giving organized crime a double cut of the action. LeRoy had always said they were collecting the "devil's red nickels."

Roland and LeRoy had started out as runners in Gary, Indiana, collecting jukebox proceeds and distributing their red nickels in black-run establishments. LeRoy eventually transformed himself from a bagman to what the world came to know as Doo-Wop Polk. Roland remembered being swept along in LeRoy's wake until they eventually sat at the head of their own record company, Stax of Wax. He remembered their midnight recording sessions with the Diamonds, the Satires, Sam Rushdon and the Dreams, and Barry Tremain. He even remembered how Alan Freed, the king of the 1950s payola scandals, had coined the term *doo-wop* after the mannered, harmonizing sounds that he recognized as coming straight out of the black church, and how LeRoy Polk had appropriated the name for himself.

As he stopped for a light at 47th Street he thought about meeting Willette when she was singing at a club in Gary, about how smooth and mellow her alto voice had sounded, and how throughout thirty minutes of gut-wrenching choreography onstage, Willette never seemed to perspire. He couldn't help but think about all the wrong turns he had taken in his life, from letting LeRoy Polk tell him that friends never need a contract to forcing Willette to give up her singing career. When LeRoy decided to make records on his own, Roland should have backed away from the venture instead of pumping money in and jumping headfirst into a record company that ten years later turned out to be nothing more than a name on a piece of paper with no assets.

The light changed, and Roland stepped off the curb and headed for an unimpressive, abandoned-looking, one-story gray brick building halfway up the block. In the middle of the intersection it hit him anew that above everything else, he never should have introduced LeRoy Polk to Willette, a naive white country girl from Louisville who was no match for LeRoy's charm. Although Willette had stayed married to him for almost thirty-five years, Roland knew that LeRoy was the man she had truly loved. Their intermittent, long-term affair had never bothered him as much as the fact that LeRoy had money to offer Willette and he didn't. Over the years he and Willette had stuck to their Southern Baptist roots, lying in the bed that they had made for themselves, unwilling and unable to change the course of events.

When Roland had heard through the Chicago rhythm and blues grapevine that LeRoy was in Denver with a potful of money, resurrecting Stax of Wax, it was all he could do to keep from choking to death on the backflow of anger. After a week of sleepless nights and mornings filled with roller-coaster stomach gyrations that made him woozy, he had decided to make a trip to Denver. He wasn't the least bit sorry he had.

Roland reached the deserted-looking building and tightened his grip on the strap of his duffel as he walked through the badly warped door. A sign above the entrance read WING GIPSON'S: THE ORIGINAL HOUSE OF CHICAGO SOUL. Inside, a woman in go-go boots and snug-hugging black pants greeted him. "Where you been, honey? Missed you and Wing the last couple of days." She entwined her arm in Roland's and snuggled up to him like an alley cat looking for scraps. "You heard about LeRoy Polk? He's dead."

Roland didn't answer. He stood perfectly still, drinking in the atmosphere of the room. The sounds of the Drifters' hit "There Goes My Baby" mushroomed up from somewhere in the deep recesses of the building. Roland listened to the music, staring off into space for almost a minute. Then he slipped the duffel off his arm, unzipped it, and pulled out a reel-to-reel tape. "Tell Wing to get out here. I got something I picked up in

Denver he needs to hear." The woman nodded okay and hurried off in the direction of the music to get Wing Gipson. When the song ended, Roland remembered what the woman had said about LeRoy Polk. He smiled and muttered to himself, "Ain't that a shame."

Nine

CJ could feel the ambulance gaining speed, its high-pitched sirens screeching as the driver dodged horses, concession booths, rollerbladers, city dignitaries, and a platoon of policemen and reporters with TV cameras at the ready who had gathered in front of Mae's in the twenty minutes since the restaurant had exploded. CJ and Clothilde were among a group of a dozen people with non-life-threatening injuries who had been triaged by EMTs in the front office of Prillerman's Trophy and Badge, two doors down from what was left of Mae's, before they were placed in an ambulance. Willis Sundee hadn't been as lucky. He had entered Mae's a few seconds before the building had disintegrated into flying debris and had suffered a fractured collarbone and burns over 10 percent of his body. Willis and a man who had run half a block down Welton Street with his hair and clothes on fire had been in the first two ambulances to leave the scene. Mavis's trek up Welton Street had been obstructed by the mass of parade onlookers, which had probably saved her from being seriously injured or killed. She had lagged behind Dittier and Morgan as they leapfrogged from one side of Welton Street to the other, waving their protest signs. She was forty yards away from the blast when it occurred. CJ had last seen Mavis shivering uncontrollably in obvious shock as she followed Dittier Atkins into the back of the third ambulance to leave the scene.

It was that image that haunted CJ as the ambulance he was riding in turned onto Broadway and headed for Denver General Hospital. He was holding a blood-soaked gauze pad up to a three-inch gash in his forehead, staring across the aisle into the eyes of the calm, efficient EMT who was kneeling between him and Clothilde. "Now, go backwards from one hundred," she said firmly to Clothilde.

"Ninety-nine, ninety-eight, ninety-seven, ninety-six."

"What city are you in?" asked the EMT.

"Denver," said Clothilde.

"Where are you right now?"

"In the back of a goddamned ambulance."

The paramedic looked around at CJ. "Guess we can forget about a concussion."

CJ smiled and thought, *Join the club; you've just met Clothilde Polk.*

The ambulance hit a pothole that sent Clothilde slamming against the padded wall. "How fast is this Batmobile going?" asked Clothilde.

"Fifty, fifty-five," said the paramedic.

"We're not dying. Get the lunatic driving this buggy to slow it down."

The paramedic pounded on the bulkhead three times

with her fist, and as the ambulance slowed she turned her attention to CJ. "You need a new dressing," she said, examining his forehead. In one fluid motion, she pulled a roll of gauze, some tape, and a pair of scissors from a kit on the floor and began redressing CJ's wound. The gentleness of her touch surprised CJ.

"Your friend's feisty." She nodded at Clothilde. "Hope she's always like that. Wouldn't want to think it's shock." She placed the gauze and tape back in her kit and snapped the scissors onto a black velcro strap above her breast pocket. Her movements reminded CJ of a sleepy-eyed, gregarious Pillsbury Doughboy of a medic he had served with in Vietnam. The medic had treated most of the *Cape Star*'s crew members, from lancing gum boils to digging shrapnel out of the executive officer's rear. Doughboy, as he was known, had two weeks left on his tour when the *Cape Star* headed out on a routine rescue mission looking for a downed helicopter pilot. For some unknown reason, that day he decided not to follow his usual routine of reading romance novels belowdecks and ended up catching a sniper's bullet in the jugular vein. He flopped around on the deck like an oversized flounder for the minute and a half it took him to bleed to death. CJ had never been big on psychology, but he realized that something more than a minor head gash had him connecting events that were twenty-five years and two worlds apart.

When CJ realized that he was staring directly into the paramedic's eyes, he nodded toward Clothilde, trying to explain away her behavior. "She's had a pretty rough few days."

The EMT, who had been traveling the Mile High

City's streets for years, didn't take Clothilde's outburst personally. She went back to arranging things in her kit. CJ looked across the aisle and took his first long, hard look at Clothilde since she had come crashing down on him during the explosion. Her hair was matted and her eyes were glazed, her expensive outfit ripped at the shoulders and thighs. The heel of one shoe was missing, and she looked defeated. When CJ smiled at her, it took her half a minute to respond.

"Don't think for a minute that some little explosion is going to sidetrack our business." Her response was disconnected and out of synch.

CJ didn't know if she expected his reassurance that he wasn't going to turn tail and run or whether she really was drifting off into shock.

The EMT looked up at Clothilde, reached over and checked her pupils and pulse, got a quick blood-pressure reading, then nodded to CJ that Clothilde was okay before going back to closing up her kit. By the time she finished, CJ's thoughts had drifted from Clothilde to whether the explosion at Mae's had been accidental and whether Mavis was all right. He remembered someone looking back at him, giving him the thumbs-up sign, but couldn't recall if it had been Mavis or Willis. He rubbed his throbbing temples, trying to bring things into focus.

For the next few minutes, a kaleidoscope of disjointed events kept running through his head, always beginning with the mayor standing on a giant podium giving a speech in support of monorail and ending up with a Hollywood special-effects explosion. In between, dozens of dwarf-sized city health inspectors dressed like Pillsbury Doughboys were screaming insults at Mavis and Willis

Sundee as they danced in Mae's newly renovated kitchen. The ambulance veered sharply to avoid a pickup and sent CJ arcing forward into the EMT.

"You okay?" she said, recovering, noticing the glaze in CJ's eyes.

"Yeah, just running a bad movie through my head."

"Put this on your forehead." She handed CJ an ice-cold towel from a chest that had the word *Igloo* peeling from its side.

CJ pressed the towel against his forehead and his back against the wall. He had just started to feel the soothing effects of the compress when Clothilde announced, "You have four weeks to find out who killed my dad. That's all, four weeks."

CJ couldn't determine if Clothilde was repeating herself or whether a new movie had started to thread its way through his brain. It didn't matter. He didn't feel like talking. The rest of the fifteen-block ride to Denver General was completed in silence.

Half a dozen people met the ambulance at Denver General's ER entrance. The EMT who had been attending CJ and Clothilde waved a group of trauma doctors and technicians off as she stepped out of the back of the ambulance. "Got two here. Both with assorted bumps and bruises. One with a head laceration. Vitals are okay. But this woman's a little shook," she said, looking at Clothilde, "and he's still woozy. They can navigate on their own." Two nurses stayed with CJ and Clothilde while the rest of the crew moved down the circular driveway to await the next ambulance.

The flurry of activity at the entrance was just what Johnny Telano needed to camouflage his movements. He was dressed in an expensively tailored European suit, and a pilfered DGH ID card hung from his lapel. In the excitement, he moved in and out of the cluster of hospital workers with ease. Every now and then he smiled at a nurse with an exaggerated grin that showed off $10,000 worth of porcelain crowns. He made sure CJ and Clothilde had disappeared into the emergency room before he turned to one of the EMTs and asked in an authoritative voice, "What went down? That's the fourth one of our buggies I've seen pull up here in the past twenty minutes." He nodded toward the ambulance that had just delivered CJ and Clothilde.

"Some kind of explosion over at Juneteenth," said the nurse.

"I'll be damned; nobody killed, was there?"

"Don't know," said the nurse, trying her best to place the man asking the questions.

Sensing her apprehension, he turned and started moving away. "There's some sick people out there nowadays. Makes you wanna puke."

The nurse nodded in agreement before heading for a newly arriving ambulance. When she looked back, Johnny Telano had disappeared through the entrance to the emergency room. With his hand in his right pocket and feeling safe again, he was busy running a mixture of loose change and dum-dum bullets through his fingers.

The emergency room patient waiting area had recently been renovated, transformed from a cold gray 1960s-era sterile box with a classroom arrangement of folding metal chairs to a room with vaulted ceilings, textured alabaster walls, and ergonomic furniture upholstered in warm pastels. The only thing that remained from the earlier incarnation was the musty institutional smell of dried sweat and deep-fried food.

CJ and Clothilde were ushered through the waiting room into a small alcove set up for trauma triage. Dittier Atkins and Morgan Williams were on their way out as Clothilde and CJ entered.

"I'm telling you, he headed west toward I-25," said Morgan, spitting his words at Dittier, who was stomping his feet and shaking his head back and forth in disagreement. Several people in the waiting room stared intently at Morgan as if expecting him to do or say something that would calm Dittier down.

When Morgan spotted CJ, he shot him a look of exasperation. "I've been trying to calm Dittier down for half an hour." Then, noticing the bandage on CJ's forehead and the glazed look in his eyes, he added, "You okay?"

Before CJ could answer, Dittier ran up to him, eyes darting in every direction, and shoved Geronimo's broken leash into his hand.

"Damn pig ran off," said Morgan, taking the leash from Dittier. "Don't think he likes explosions. Dittier's about to pee his pants. You ain't seen Geronimo, have you?"

"No." A trickle of blood worked its way down CJ's forehead onto his right eye, and he realized that he was still bleeding.

"Damn," said Morgan. He was about to add *fucking crazy hamhock* when Clothilde tugged on his sleeve and said, "Your pig took off toward that gas station where the parade started."

"Are you sure?" asked CJ, wondering if Clothilde was as disoriented as he. Her stare told CJ she didn't like being second-guessed. "I saw him streaking away before the bodies started falling. Like I said, he headed toward that gas station."

Dittier ran over and grasped Clothilde's hands in his, a silent *thank you* forming on his lips. Before she could say anything, Dittier had let go and was dragging Morgan toward the door. CJ followed, hoping that maybe they could tell him what had happened to Mavis and Willis. He also wanted their take on the explosion. It was only then that he noticed the backs of both ex-rodeo cowboys' forearms were heavily bandaged. Before Morgan was fully through the door, CJ stopped him. "Notice anything out of the ordinary before the explosion?"

"We ain't senile yet," said Morgan, glancing at Dittier. "Me and Dittier had a front-row seat. But if I don't let Dittier start after Geronimo this instant, he's gonna have a conniption."

"Then you better get going. But after you locate Geronimo, how about stopping by the office? We'll compare notes, and you can tell me if you noticed any strange faces on that protest march of yours."

Dittier was still tugging at Morgan's arm.

"No need to stop by your office for that. You know me and Dittier. We don't forget a face. I seen plenty I recognized—and a few I didn't. One white guy in particular—with real long arms and a toothy grin. He didn't pay me or Dittier no attention. He was too busy looking past us down Welton Street—behind us, more in your direction. Besides him, I don't remember nobody else looking out of place. But I'll think on it. Dittier will too."

Dittier gave Morgan's arm one last tug, and the spark-plug-sized ex-rodeo bullrider was through the doorway and out of the emergency room before he could say any more.

CJ was feeling less woozy than he had earlier. He patted the bloody gauze on his forehead and watched Morgan and Dittier disappear. When he turned back to look for Clothilde, an ER doctor was hovering over her like a mother hen.

"You're going to be fine, Ms. Polk," said the doctor. "Just fine." The smile of reassurance on his face disappeared when he looked up and saw the bloody bandage on CJ's forehead. "Let me take a look at that dressing. Looks like you've still got a bleeder." He removed the blood-soaked bandage and examined the wound carefully. "It'll be easy enough to close, but you're going to have a nasty little scar."

"Guess I'll have to learn to live with it," said CJ.

"Step around to the table on the other side of this partition. The one with the contraption sitting on it that looks like a big heat lamp. The resident over there will have you patched up before you can say stitch." The doctor smiled, looking at CJ for a response to his attempt at humor, but CJ was busy trying to shake the lingering cobwebs from his head. He headed for the minor-surgery table without responding.

While CJ took thirteen stitches to his forehead, Clothilde sat mute and motionless in a chair against the opposite wall. The week's events had taken their toll. Her father had been murdered, the construction on their Stax of Wax superstore was six weeks behind schedule, $100,000 worth of furnishings and inventory were scheduled for delivery in a week, and to top it off, she had just missed being blown to kingdom come.

Clothilde was close to the point of succumbing to mental and physical exhaustion when Vanetta Ebson charged into the waiting room looking like a lost dog in search of its master. She saw Clothilde and gave a little scream of relief before running over to her, pulling her out of the chair, and wrapping her in a bear hug. "I've been on ER patrol for over an hour. This is my third stop. If you hadn't been here I think I would have lost it." She smoothed Clothilde's hair back out of her face just as CJ walked up, and acknowledged his presence with a darting glance. "News about the explosion's on every channel. They're saying it was a bombing. I nearly died when I looked up at the screen and saw you being loaded into an ambulance. You're lucky to be alive." The words came out in a furious rush.

With one arm still wrapped around Clothilde, Vanetta straightened up to her full five-eight height and eyed CJ as if he were a thug who had just been in a street fight. "I figured you for a street scrounger, but I didn't expect you to take Clothilde along with you on your daily chores."

"We were in the wrong place at the wrong time," said CJ defensively, realizing that no explanation was going to endear him to Vanetta.

Vanetta looked disgusted. "Most people I know conduct business in their offices, not at street fairs packed full of dopeheads and drunks. You do have an office, don't you, Mr. Floyd?"

CJ had learned long ago not to argue with someone who sees herself as another person's savior. Vanetta was playing the big-sister act to the hilt, and he knew better than to bite on one of her insults. "No chance the explo-

sion resulted from a gas main break or a propane leak?"
asked CJ, trying to get some answers about what had happened and at the same time deflect Vanetta's wrath.

"*Bombing,*" said Vanetta, raising her eyebrows, rolling
her eyes, and spelling the word out in midair.

CJ checked the urge to tell Vanetta, *You've made your
point, sister; let's move on.* His first guess was that the bomb
had been intended for Willis, to silence his opposition to
monorail, but he wanted to gauge Clothilde's reaction to a
second possibility. Clothilde seemed to have regained her
composure in the face of Vanetta's overbearing presence.
"Anybody on that enemies list you gave me have a reason
to go after you with a bomb?"

"I wouldn't know why, unless it was someone who
didn't want me to open the new Stax of Wax and R&B
museum," said Clothilde in a half whisper.

CJ looked at Vanetta for a response.

Vanetta shrugged her shoulders. "Maybe someone
was after you, Mr. Bird Dog, or perhaps someone wanted
to send the people who own that restaurant that blew
halfway to Kansas a message. What makes you think
somebody had it in for Clothilde?"

"Just covering all the bases," said CJ, fighting the
urge to remind Vanetta that Clothilde was the one paying
him. But before he had a chance to say what might have
cost him a job, Clothilde patted herself down as if she
were checking to make certain that she was still all in one
piece and, with the fire of suspicion in her eyes, she
looked at Vanetta and asked, "Where's Tyrone?"

"Haven't seen him all day," said Vanetta. She glanced
at CJ. "Maybe Tyrone's the one you should be asking

questions, Mr. Floyd. And while you're at it, don't leave out his mother, Mabel."

"It's a place to start." CJ had finally come to terms with the fact that no matter how hard he tried to dodge the issue, sooner or later he was going to have to question Mabel Pitts.

Vanetta hooked her arm in Clothilde's the same way she had the day she and CJ had met. Vanetta looked every bit the part of a towering big sister. "Come on, girl, let me take you home where you can soak your body and clear your head." She looked at CJ as if he were the newly hired yard man. "Meter's running, Mr. Floyd. How about some results?" She tightened her grip on Clothilde's arm and walked her toward the doorway.

At the doorway, Clothilde looked back at CJ. The secure look of a child who has just found its baby blanket spread across her face. "Start with Mabel and Tyrone. I thought I told you that once," she reiterated before disappearing.

CJ already had an agenda, one that first included finding out whether Mavis and Willis Sundee were all right. Forty-two hundred dollars or not, Clothilde Polk's problems were just going to have to wait their turn.

Ten

CJ left DGH with a pulsating headache and the vision in his right eye dancing between semi-blindness and a fuzzy blur as he tried to regroup and find out what had happened to Mavis and Willis. The only thing he knew after fifteen minutes of tangling with the patient information bureaucracy was that they hadn't been admitted to DGH. Carless and still groggy, he hailed a cab, deciding to head back to Five Points and see if anyone there knew where Mavis and Willis had been taken.

When he got to Five Points, CJ found that a four-square-block area around the explosion had been cordoned off by the police. He headed for Rosie Weaks's garage, whose driveway sat just beyond the southern edge of the police perimeter.

Welton Street had been transformed into a media staging area, crowded with a maze of TV reporters, *Den-*

ver *Post* and *Rocky Mountain News* writers, and dozens of people milling around talking about the explosion.

Inside Rosie's a bombastic talking-head TV news reporter blared nonstop from the fourteen-inch black-and-white TV in Rosie's waiting room, jabbering, vulturelike, that his station had been the first to bring viewers on-the-scene reports of what he was now dramatically calling the "Bombing at Juneteenth."

"Flip it to another channel," CJ said, giving the overzealous reporter the finger and then high-fiving Rosie. "SOB sounds like he's fucking happy about what happened."

When Rosie flipped the channel, another reporter was lamenting the fact that the police had roped off the area and they were offering no comment on the cause of the explosion, as if he should have been informed immediately. Before CJ could ask Rosie to change the channel again, the reporter said, "Miraculously no one was killed, and all the victims are being taken to Denver General Hospital, University Hospital, or Rose Medical Center."

CJ commandeered Rosie's front-office phone, found the University Hospital patient information number in the phone book, and called University Hospital first. He got the same runaround he had gotten at DGH. Exasperated, he finally had the sense to call Dr. Henry Bales for help and waited for information on Mavis and Willis. Henry got back to him ten minutes later. "Willis has been admitted, but I couldn't get any particulars on his status." CJ held his breath, staring at a miller moth trapped inside one of Rosie's grease-stained light fixtures, waiting for Henry to give him news about Mavis.

"Mavis is fine. You'll need to check with patient information services for more news. That's all I could get."

"Thanks," said CJ, exhaling in relief. He immediately redialed the University Hospital patient information service, where this time he got through to a nasal-sounding PR type who told him in a robotic monotone that Willis Sundee was listed in fair condition in Room 521 and that Mavis Sundee had been treated and released. After five more minutes of persistent dialing, CJ got through to Willis's room and spoke to Willis's son, Carl. "How's Willis?"

Carl Sundee immediately recognized CJ's voice. "He's hanging tough."

"And Mavis?"

"She's okay physically, but she's operating in a fog. The doctor gave her a prescription for a sedative. And I took her home and made her go to bed. I told her not to come back down here until this evening to check on Dad."

"You okay?" asked CJ.

"Yeah."

"Good. I'll get there when I can. I'm going to check on Mavis."

"She's asleep by now."

"I'll wake her up." CJ slammed down the phone and rushed past Rosie, who was engrossed in what someone being interviewed down the street was saying on TV. "Gotta go check on Mavis," said CJ, rushing out the front door.

He almost ran over a Channel 4 camera crew as he gunned the Bel Air across the drive and down Welton Street. The question of whether the bombing had been a

retaliation for Willis Sundee's opposition to monorail, a
botched attempt to kill Clothilde Polk, or a message for
him to stop looking into LeRoy Polk's murder nagged at
him all the way to Mavis's.

If someone had intended to send Willis a message
to back off on his opposition to monorail, the message
had been delivered in one hell of a big package, and political swamp rats like the mayor and Winston Dunn
were too smart for that. The construction trades, who
stood to lose millions of dollars and didn't mind getting
their hands a little bloody, were a different matter. But
knowing the mayor's penchant for keeping all his people
in line, it was unlikely that he'd let a few union hotheads
get in the way of his taking credit for the fourth largest
public works project in Denver's history.

The possibility that someone had wanted to kill
Clothilde Polk made more sense, especially if Clothilde
hadn't told him the whole story about her father's ties to
organized crime. But a bombing at an event already
teeming with reporters seemed out of character for Colorado's underworld types, who preferred maintaining a
low profile. There was a final possibility. The bombing
had been a message for him to back off from looking
into what had happened to LeRoy Polk. He stopped at a
red light, lit up a cheroot, and thought back to something a navy SEAL frogman had told him one night in
Vietnam as the *Cape Star* ferried six SEAL commandos
down a Mekong Delta estuary for a midnight river drop
on their mission to blow up a Viet Cong fueling port.
The commandos were black-faced, decked out in knit
caps, wetsuits, and flippers. When a newly arrived *Cape
Star* boatswain's mate began cracking up at the SEALs'

James Bond attire and calling them toad frogs, one of the frogmen gritted his teeth and said, "Sometimes it takes a toad frog to deliver Prince Charming's message, sonny." He then jammed his fist into the boatswain's mate's stomach so hard that the mate threw up. If someone was sending CJ a message to stay away from Daddy Doo-Wop's death, it had been received loud and clear.

CJ turned onto Clarkson Street with the frogman's message still fresh in his head. A block away from Mavis's house, he started toying with the bandage above his eye as he tried unsuccessfully to blink the eye into focus. When he pulled the Bel Air into Mavis's driveway, her house seemed to jump out at him in 3D. He took a series of deep breaths before smoking his cheroot down to a nub and waited until he saw only one house in front of him.

Mavis lived in one of the half-dozen mission-revival-style homes that lined the west side of California Street, the buffer-zone boundary between Five Points and the neighborhood of Curtis Park. Most of the houses in Curtis Park were small restored Queen Annes and Victorians, and for almost ten years a steady stream of yuppies had been moving in, causing the value of everything in the neighborhood to nearly double. Ornate replicas of turn-of-the-century-style gaslight streetlamps had recently been installed along California to achieve what the mayor and city council were calling a return to Curtis Park's "turn-of-the-century grace." But Mavis, who knew Denver's architectural and neighborhood histories as well as any college history professor, had told CJ one evening, while they were on a twilight stroll admiring the newly installed lights, that there had never been gas-lamp lighting in Five Points or Curtis Park. Both neighborhoods at the turn of the century had been a maze of feedlots and horse corrals. Mavis had laughed as they had turned toward home, saying, "Mayor Wiley's more malleable than white folks' history."

CJ now stood beneath the dormer that protected the side entrance to Mavis's house, enjoying one last drag on his cheroot. He rapped the horseshoe-sized, wrought-iron door knocker close to a dozen times before Mavis pulled back the door. Her eyes were bloodshot and puffy from a combination of sleep and tears, and she looked smaller and less self-assured than the take-charge Mavis that CJ had always known. Her jet-black curly hair was brushed back, windblown straight, and her normally warm, rich cocoa-color skin was the muted color of clay. Without saying a word she looked at CJ's bandaged forehead and swollen eye, shook her head as if to say *not you too*, hugged him, and closed the door. They walked in silence holding hands down a brightly lit, Spanish-tiled hallway to what Mavis called her reading room. It was a cozy, cluttered room filled with inviting overstuffed California-mission-style furniture. The walls were peppered with family photos, including pictures of Mavis as a Denver Owl Club debutante and Boston University debate team captain. There was a photo of brother Carl and her father and Rosie Weaks standing out in front of Mae's, grinning at CJ the day he came back from Vietnam. And on an end table along with a lamp covered with etchings of black rodeo cowboys, there was a photograph of CJ and Mavis hugging sweetheart-style in the Bel Air. The photograph had always been her favorite.

Before CJ could ask her if she was okay, Mavis turned to him in the middle of the room and in a hushed tone said, "They tried to kill him, CJ." The words came as if she had been holding them in, saving them for someone who cared. CJ draped his arm over her shoulder and walked her to an easy chair in the corner. Mavis dropped into the chair like a rock, looking up at CJ helplessly.

CJ brushed her hair back a couple of times, a gesture meant to soothe him as much as Mavis. "You okay?"

"I'm fine."

"Are you sure Willis was the target?" CJ stroked her hair back again.

"Yes." Mavis forced back a flood of tears. "They want Daddy out of their hair. Mayor Wiley and his imagine-a-perfect-city goons. He's too smart to have dirtied his hands, but you can bet Winston Dunn is in this up to his fat jack-o'-lantern pumpkin-shaped head."

As much as CJ disliked Dunn, it was hard for him to believe that Dunn would stoop to bombing Mae's in order to get the monorail issue to go the mayor's way. There were too many other effective ways to skin that cat, like greasing the right palms or outmaneuvering Willis when it came to playing to the voting public. There was always the outside chance that Dunn played even dirtier than CJ thought. For years there had been rumors that Dunn had connections to the Detroit mob and that he had even done a stretch of time before moving west to Denver. But a bombing seemed out of character. CJ sat down on the arm of the chair, reached over for Mavis's hand, and cradled it in his. "I know you think the mayor's people had something to do with this, but you could be wrong."

Mavis's eyes glazed over, and she sat back in the chair. "First a city health inspector drops in and threatens to close us down, then Daddy organizes a monorail protest, and the next thing you know the business it took him half a lifetime to build is blown to kingdom come. Am I missing something here, CJ?" She clenched her teeth to keep from crying.

"It's possible the bomb was meant for someone else." CJ lowered his eyes to the floor.

It was a telltale look Mavis knew all too well. She had helped navigate CJ through mountaintop highs and rock-bottom lows, and she knew that when he wouldn't look her in the eye, it was usually because he was holding something back. She was way ahead of him. "That Polk woman you were with this morning. She had something to do with the explosion. It's plastered all over your face."

CJ adjusted his weight on the arm of the chair, trying to fathom why he was such an easy read.

"You and Ms. Polk got any other secrets I should know about? I wouldn't want to be the odd woman out."

"No. And don't be so hard on her. She just lost her father."

CJ's answer and the similarity between her own situation and Clothilde's struck a chord with Mavis. She squeezed CJ's hand softly. "I could use a shot of Jack Daniel's about now. But I've got a migraine, and my blood pressure's probably out of orbit, so how about sharing a fruit smoothie with me instead?"

"If you add a shot of something that's ninety-proof to mine."

CJ and Mavis hadn't shared anything completely in years, preferring instead to play a cat-and-mouse game of on-again, off-again romance. CJ assumed the part of the brash loner raised by an alcoholic, threatened by anyone who tried to get close enough to him to care. Mavis had settled into the role of the cherished firstborn, perfect in every way except the fact that she hadn't been a son. CJ had been so busy wearing his coat of lone-wolf armor and Mavis had become so involved in running her father's businesses and trying hard to please that until CJ was nearly killed trying to chase down the killer of the daughter of a federal judge the previous year, their relationship had never been allowed to follow its natural course. It had only been in the past few months that the two of them had been able to fight through the self-imposed barriers that had separated them and begin acting like people who cared deeply about one another.

Mavis reluctantly pulled her hand out of CJ's and headed for the kitchen. "Are bananas and vanilla ice cream okay?"

"Sounds good to me," said CJ, finally getting his injured eye to focus.

Mavis returned with two banana smoothies topped off with mountainous dollops of whipped cream. Her eyes were still bloodshot, and her color hadn't returned to normal, but the earlier look of helplessness was gone. She placed the smoothies on the coffee table in front of the sofa, patted one of the cushions, and motioned for CJ to join her. "Yours is the one on the left."

CJ scooped off a spoonful of the thick, creamy

concoction and thought about all the years that he and
Mavis had let slip by. "Hits the spot."

Mavis let CJ enjoy a couple more heaping spoon-
fuls. "I'm scared, CJ. I need you to tell Daddy to forget
about this monorail business."

"I'll do what I can, but you know how stubborn he
can be."

"I'm counting on you. God knows he won't listen
to me or Carl."

CJ slowly twirled the spoon around in his
smoothie, deep in thought. Besides his uncle, the two
people most responsible for saving him from a thug's life
on the streets during his mercurial teens had been Willis
Sundee and Mabel Pitts. Now Mavis was asking him to
start barking orders to one of them, and Clothilde Polk
wanted him to hang a murder rap on the other. He
spooned off another mound of smoothie and sat back,
thinking about how to approach the problem.

Mavis could see the wheels already turning in CJ's
head. "Don't even think about running interference for
him, CJ." She patted the patch above his eye. "I don't
want both of you ending up morgue fodder for Vernon
Lowe."

"That makes two of us. Besides, that hospital Lysol
smell ties my stomach up in knots."

CJ's weak attempt at reassurance hadn't worked.
Mavis knew his propensity for attracting trouble, and
she understood his hardheaded get-the-job-done-at-all-
cost stubbornness as well as her father's. But her emo-
tions were drained and she didn't care to argue. All she
could say was, "Don't do anything foolish. And don't
share any smoothies with Clothilde Polk."

CJ was about to offer a rebuttal when Mavis leaned over and gave him a soft, lingering kiss. He was surprised at how deliciously warm her lips were for someone who had been eating a near-frozen smoothie. He pulled her close to him, deciding that a rebuttal was clearly out of the question.

Eleven

The fare served at Richie's Grub Steak Diner was as far removed from a fruit smoothie as pork and beans from crème brûlée. Richie's had been a north Denver landmark for fifty years. The forty-five-ton prefabricated club-car-style diner came to Denver after World War II from New Jersey, secured to two flatbed railroad cars, with its new owner, Toastmaster Richie Dupree, riding in a Pullman sleeper at the rear. Dupree, who was part French, part Italian, and 100 percent Jersey con, had earned the nickname Toastmaster by virtue of the fact that he had once been an MC at Minski's Burlesque Theater in New York. Richie found the term MC insulting, and until the day he died he always referred to himself as the Toastmaster.

The diner's trademark, a forty-foot-high neon cowboy complete with a white hat, silver spurs, purple kerchief, and a red kitchen apron, stood in front of the diner's entrance beckoning passersby to drop in for a

hearty meal. A full-sized palomino horse feeding at a
trough stood atop the diner's roof, Richie's theatrical exclamation mark to the cholesterol-laden delights inside.

Richie Dupree had been dead for twenty years, done
in by a combination of high blood pressure, his two daily
packs of Lucky Strikes, and too many years of his own
gravy and grease. His son, Richie, Jr., had run the diner
without so much as a single menu change since his death.
The breakfast special remained Philly steak and eggs,
ranch fries, and Texas toast, and patrons still bellied up to
the diner's counter by the hundreds all day long to order
Denver's largest grilled jumbo frank and "Jersey shore hot-
to-trot" chili for $2.25.

Three kinds of people frequented Richie's: north
Denver locals who considered the place a historical landmark and knew a feedbag bargain when they saw one;
tourists who had read the weekly north Denver *Tribune's*
popular restaurant insert, "Neighborhood Dining on a
Dime"; and descendants of the dozen or so East Coast
underworld figures who had followed Toastmaster Richie
Dupree from New Jersey to the Rocky Mountains in
1947 to help him organize and fine-tune what until then
had been the Wild Western stepchild of the organization.

In the years that followed Richie Dupree's death, in-
fighting between competing factions within the Western
intermountain crime families eventually resulted in two
equally powerful branches of Colorado organized crime,
one in Denver and a second ninety miles to the south in
Pueblo. Unlike the East, where turf battles could erupt
simply because of proximity, Colorado had thousands of
square miles of blue sky and wide-open spaces to facilitate
peaceful coexistence.

Johnny Telano, the man who had been on the cellular phone in the park just after LeRoy Polk's body had been rolled down to the morgue for autopsy, was a member of what longtime Colorado residents called the Pueblo mob. He was also Richie, Jr.'s third cousin. Whenever Johnny was in Denver he made a point of dropping by the diner to shoot the breeze, polish off a meatloaf special, and settle up on a few overdue bets. The day of the explosion at Mae's, Johnny was busy collecting his winnings from half a dozen diner employees and an equal number of friends of friends who had been naive enough to believe that the Cincinnati Reds could win two out of three against the Colorado Rockies in a recent Rockies home stand. Johnny and Richie, Jr., were seated in a booth reserved for family.

Richie, Jr., watched Johnny Telano finish the last of his mashed potatoes and gravy, surprised as always at how fastidious Johnny was when it came to eating. "You were just here day before yesterday, Johnny. Keep running up and down I-25 like that and they gonna reserve you one of them lanes like they do for buses. What's the attraction? You got a new Denver honey you poking?"

"Nah, I'm working."

Richie Dupree's eyes widened. There were rules for doing business that the Denver and Pueblo members of the organization followed, including not stepping on the other person's toes and rigidly observing their unique missions. The niche in Denver included bookmaking, prostitution, political graft, and drugs, whereas the centerpiece of the southern Colorado operation in Pueblo, a city that had once housed the largest steel mills in the West, included controlling organized labor, transportation, and the distribution of goods.

"Don't piss your pants, Richie," said Johnny. "I ain't squeezing your grapes. I'm bird-dogging a sweet little piece of dark meat for Hamp—name of Clothilde Polk."

Lawrence Hampoli, who preferred to be called Hamp, had been Johnny Telano's boss for fifteen years, ever since Hampoli had moved to Pueblo from Chicago. Before crossover music became the rage in the seventies, Hampoli had spent twenty-five years with his hand deep in the Chitown soul music till, taking his cut of the rhythm and blues money pie from the slew of black artists he recorded, managed, distributed, and controlled. Once crossover music became a part of the national music-industry psyche, the same singing groups became free agents, signing on with huge conglomerates like Atlantic and MCA, and Hampoli's world turned to dust. He moved to Colorado with a nest egg built from years of helping to orchestrate the mob-controlled Chitown soul music sound and set up shop in Pueblo, where his expertise in marketing and distribution of goods was received eagerly.

"Hamp still partial to colored girls?" asked Richie, leering. "Or did he get over that when his wife threatened to cut off his nuts?"

Johnny Telano's one admirable quality was loyalty. Besides giving a three-thousand-dollar annual donation to a halfway house for glue-sniffing addicts because he had once been a resident there himself, and buying his last five jet-black Camaros from the same car dealership in Pueblo because they sent him flowers on his birthday, he never allowed anyone to express disrespect for Hampoli. He grabbed Richie's right ear and twisted it. "This one ain't for pokin'. In fact, worst comes to worst, she's a lady I just might have to cap," he said tersely before letting go.

Richie's eyes teared up as he rubbed the circulation back into his ear. He looked around to see if anyone had been watching. "Don't pay to demean a man in a legitimate place of business." Despite his underworld ties, Richie liked to think of himself as a stand-up family-values kind of businessman, and although he was one of the largest distributors of poached game and non-government-inspected meat in the West, he didn't appreciate Johnny's intimidation or his matter-of-fact mention that he might have to kill someone, especially with customers around. Before Richie could protest further, a man wearing tight-fitting polyester pants and sporting a 1950s-style crewcut walked up to the booth, coughed once to let Johnny know he was there, and immediately handed Johnny three crisp one-hundred-dollar bills.

Johnny broke into an ear-to-ear grin, enjoying the fact that the man had felt the need to announce his presence. He liked having a sense of power without having to inflict any pain. "Shit, Rusty. I figured you for being smarter than to bet on a baseball team owned by a woman who everybody knows French kisses her dog. Cincy ain't nothing but a bunch of Ohio riverboat losers."

The man grinned boldly and rocked back on the heels of his lizard-skin boots. Before he had a chance to rock forward again, Johnny reached out, grabbed a handful of polyester and testicles, and squeezed. The man grunted and dropped to his knees.

"Johnny, Johnny, lighten up," said Richie, his eyes nervously darting around in every direction.

The man in polyester was coughing and twitching as

if he were in the throes of a seizure. Johnny held firm for the better part of a minute before letting go. "Try the stock market the next time you wanna gamble." Johnny looked at the man in disgust. "Now, how about the other two hundred?" Still on his knees, the man reached in his pocket, pulled out two one-hundred-dollar bills, and puked.

"That's unhygienic," said Johnny, reaching down to pick up the bills. "Richie, get one of your people over here to clean this up." He pointed at the pool of vomit.

Richie had had enough. "No more business dealings in here today, Johnny. Save your crazy shit for the streets."

The man in polyester was back on his feet, shuffling away from the table, glad to be walking. He knew that some other time Johnny might not have been in such a forgiving mood about being shortchanged. Johnny considered late and partial payers deadbeats, and he had been known to break their thumbs or even shoot off their toes. Crushing a mere testicle was child's play.

Johnny pocketed the bills. Then, grinning, he looked at Richie and said, "I love it when a plan comes together."

A waitress wearing form-fitting leotards and the Grub Steak's standard-issue gingham apron walked up and started clearing the table. "Got any apple pie left?" asked Johnny with a wink.

"Sure do." She beamed as if she had made the pie herself.

"Bring me a slice." Johnny glanced over at Richie, who was still beside himself. "And bring one for Richie too—ice cream on the side."

She looked at Richie. Knowing that he didn't eat pie because it gave him heartburn, she expected him to say no to the order. But he nodded for her to do as she was told, and she hurriedly walked away.

Johnny eased back against the booth's blue tuck-and-roll vinyl, then looked up at the ceiling as if he were checking for leaks. "Ever heard of LeRoy Polk?"

Richie didn't want to answer. He wanted Johnny out of his restaurant and on the way to Pueblo, but he realized Johnny probably knew that he had heard of Polk, and if Johnny was fishing for any possible way Richie and LeRoy might be connected, he didn't want to piss him off. He decided to play it straight. "Of course. My old man gave me an introduction to Polk back in Chicago during the fifties, when I was a kid. Polk and the old man did a lot of business back then. What's your interest?"

Johnny slapped Richie on the shoulder. "You got a good memory, Richie. Real good. That piece of dark meat I'm trailing is Polk's daughter. Sorry to say old LeRoy's gone on to meet the maker."

Richie, always nervous about his place being bugged, looked around quickly to make sure no one was listening. "Lower your voice." In a near whisper he added, "What's Polk's connection to Hamp?"

Johnny picked up a glass saltshaker and began rolling it back and forth in his right hand. The sound of glass clicking across Johnny's three rings irritated the hell out of Richie, but he kept it to himself.

"Seems like back in Chicago, Polk was the kind of guy who needed a retirement plan. During the fifties Hamp heard him spinning records on a colored radio station, and he offered him the part-time job gettin' some local Chitown R&B singers he hung out with to sign on with Hamp's record label. Polk wasn't supposed to be nothin' more but a gofer, your local ghetto shill, but it turned out he was a damn good con. Hamp says Polk spent damn near three years gettin' everybody in the organization to trust him. The same three years he was buildin' his rep as Chicago's hottest colored DJ. The coon eventually got so hot that Hamp let him do studio tapings on his own. Hell of a mistake," said Johnny, clicking the saltshaker back and forth. "Turns out that while Polk was playing your perfect Uncle Tom for Hamp, he was settin' aside some real valuable things for himself. Like several reels of never-released master tapes Hamp never knew he recorded."

Their waitress returned with two giant slices of apple pie, each flanked by a tennis-ball-sized scoop of vanilla ice cream. As soon as she set Johnny's dessert down, he picked up a spoon and nudged the ice cream away from the pie, making certain that the two didn't touch.

"Polk's dead now; what difference does it make?" asked Richie, staring at his dessert and hoping he wouldn't offend Johnny by not digging in.

"You know, Richie, sometimes I'm thinkin' you spent too many years up here in Denver making meatloaf. In Pueblo we don't like over-the-hill turncoat zigs like LeRoy Polk yanking our chain. The son of a bitch stole a bunch of recordings that belonged to Hamp. He had no right. Hamp says he should've known better than to let a sly country dog like Polk freelance. Shit, he should have known the nigger was gonna steal. Son of a bitch's lucky he's dead." Johnny took a spoonful of ice cream, rolled it around slowly in his mouth, wine-tasting fashion, and swallowed. After a few seconds he looked at Richie disapprovingly. "Still too cheap to carry the good stuff, huh,

Richie? I hate the way this cheap shit leaves that cardboard aftertaste." He took a bite of apple pie, chewing it slowly before swallowing and smiling. "Pie's good, though. Gotta admit that."

Richie cracked a half-smile. Getting a compliment out of Johnny Telano was never easy. "Think his daughter has Hamp's master tapes?"

"Probably," said Johnny, taking another bite of pie. "Like I said, the fucker wasn't stupid. Hell, he was plannin' to set up a one-man coon booth pressing and distributing the stolen recordings from right here in Denver. Son of a bitch probably would've got away with it, at least for a while, but he made the mistake of testing the market. He pressed a few forty-fives, short runs, Hamp thinks, no more than three or four hundred, from the stolen tapes to see how they would sell, and they ended up in the hands of some of our people in Chicago. Hamp says he knew what he was doin'. There's supposedly enough dumbshit collectors out there looking for never-released oldies by legendary R&B names from the past that Polk could've started churning the market. Hamp says that with the masters now rerecorded on his own label, the old fart could've cleared half a million a year even with having to pay something to the artists. Not a bad retirement program."

Richie whistled so loudly he surprised himself. "I didn't know old records were worth that kind of money."

"Normally they ain't. But LeRoy socked away tapes of some pretty big names. Who would've thought that some fifties platter jockey would've had enough guts to not only steal from us but steal the kind of music that was gonna increase in value over the years?"

"Sounds to me like Polk has you by the nuts," said Richie, thinking about what Johnny had done to the man in the polyester pants. "You're forty years down the road from his stealing. You don't have anything to prove that what he took belongs to you, and he's dead. Even if he wasn't, how do you expect to get Hamp's tapes back?"

"Friendly persuasion," said Johnny with a wink. "The kind that sugar-titted daughter of his'll understand." He took another bite of pie before placing his fork down with Emily Post grace.

It wasn't often that Richie reminded himself that he wasn't just another Denver small businessman. Whenever he forgot, it seemed like Johnny Telano was the one to jog his memory. Richie knew what Johnny meant by persuasion, and a cold twinge worked its way down his spine. "Suppose she doesn't cooperate."

Johnny smiled without answering and finished the last of his pie. Then he sat up perfectly straight and wrapped arms that were much too lengthy for his short, stocky body around the back edge of the booth. "Ever heard of a colored bail bondsman named Calvin Floyd?"

"No. I try to stay clear of needing those kinds of services," said Richie, singing his solid-citizen song.

Johnny adjusted himself in the booth. His pelvis moved, but his arms stayed put. "Looks like Floyd's running interference for Polk's daughter. She called him four times the other day."

Richie looked at Johnny disappointedly and shook his head. "You tapping people's phones again, Johnny? I thought they broke you of that habit." He knew that a few years earlier a phone-tapping charge had cost Johnny two years behind bars.

Johnny grinned, unwrapped his arms from around the tuck-and-roll, and finished off the last of his ice cream. During the entire conversation, not once had he allowed the pie and ice cream to come in contact. "I'm smarter now. I've learned to subcontract." He wiped off his hands with a napkin. "I'll tell you one thing, though: shine or not, Polk's daughter's a ten. Ass, tits, and butter-smooth brown tropical-island skin. I followed her and that Floyd guy to that Mau-Mau festival goin' on in Five Points today. Shit, just watching her walk down the street made my pecker jump. A couple of minutes more and I would've had to tie the hog down. But just then some soul-food greasy spoon blows sky high." Johnny smiled, and his arms shot straight up in the air.

Richie nearly bolted out of his seat. "Goddamn, Johnny, don't tell me you're the one that took out that restaurant. Shit. It's been on the news all day." Richie's head was bobbing back and forth in disbelief. "You're gonna draw heat, Johnny, and I don't like that."

Johnny Telano had never cared about his cousin's likes or dislikes, and he didn't answer Richie's question. He was too busy watching the rear end of the waitress taking the order from a couple in the booth across the aisle.

"You know the rules," said Richie, trying to get Johnny's attention. "Denver's north, Pueblo's south." He drew an imaginary line across the top of the table with his finger.

Johnny turned his attention from the waitress, looking back at Richie as if he weren't there. He knew about rules. Rules that had forced him to live in the cellar of a fat, abusive aunt who never bathed, and eat nothing but dog scraps and cold noodles and gravy every day for the first twelve years of his life. Rules that made kids look at his muscular physique, long, spindly arms, dark, oily skin, and thick black mop of hair and call him gorilla. He knew about rules, all right, but in all of his thirty-six years no one had ever been able to convince Johnny Telano that rules applied to him. He glanced down at his empty pie plate, then back at Richie. "How about tellin' that waitress across the aisle to dish me up another slice of pie?"

Before Richie could say anything, the waitress turned around and found herself staring directly into Johnny Telano's dark, sunken eyes. She didn't notice that he had tucked his long, hairy arms out of view beneath the lip of the table, or that his barrel-chested physique actually did resemble a gorilla's.

Twelve

CJ left Mavis's reluctantly only after she threatened to have his Bel Air towed, never speak to him again, and cut off his love life if he asked her one more time if she was okay. Before leaving he made two phone calls: one to Willis Sundee, who was well enough to still be lambasting the mayor's monorail plan, and the second to Charlene Gentry, Rosie Weaks's sister-in-law. He asked Charlene to stay put because he wanted to stop by and talk to her about an old friend, Clothilde Polk. Charlene, who had just pulled an oncology unit double shift at Saint Joseph's Hospital, wasn't too happy with CJ's request, but since she had been the one who had given Clothilde CJ's name, she felt obligated to talk to him. "Be here in thirty minutes or I'm not answering the door," was her exact response.

There had never been any deep-seated dislike between Charlene and CJ, just a life-long, gritty, salt-in-the-wound, sibling-rivalry kind of animosity. Most people in Five Points figured the two should have had a closer connection, especially since her brother-in-law, Rosie Weaks, and CJ had been best friends all their lives and Charlene and CJ had known one another for years.

There had been dozens of reasons for their friction, but for the past five years the heart of their bickering had been Charlene's only child, Darryl. As hard as she tried, Charlene was no match for a fatherless teenager with a junker car, an uncle who owned a garage, and CJ's classic Bel Air. She didn't mind Darryl's attachment to Rosie, but she hated playing second fiddle to a roughneck bail bondsman and part-time bounty hunter, whom she couldn't see as a role model for her child.

Ebony-skinned and with the short, solid build of an Olympic gymnast, Charlene was a woman with a cast-iron will. Her husband, a Denver firefighter, had been killed in an insurance-fraud arson fire sixteen years ago, and since his death Charlene had lavished all of her grief-stricken love on Darryl.

Charlene and Darryl lived in a small, lovingly restored Five Points Queen Anne house at the intersection of Washington and Tremont. They had lived in Five Points for Darryl's entire life, but Charlene had grown up in Chicago.

Darryl was heading out the front door when CJ arrived close to six o'clock.

"CJ, how's it hangin'?"

CJ smiled, knowing that Charlene would have been beside herself if she had heard Darryl's greeting. She spent too many of her waking hours making sure that Darryl didn't become addicted to the language of the streets.

"It's your world, Darryl."

Darryl broke into the kind of respectful smile a teenager on the threshold of manhood offers up to someone he admires. "I'm heading to the garage to help Uncle Rosie and Sweet Roy rewire Colin Phillips's old deuce and a quarter." He stared at the bandage above CJ's eye. "What's with your head?"

"A souvenir from the explosion at Mae's."

"Heard about that. Missed it, though. I was up in Idaho Springs, playin' ball." Darryl was a shortstop on a summer prep-league team; he had major-league potential, and Charlene hated it. "Take care of that head."

"Sure thing, young blood, and tell Rosie I said not to burn your throwing arm out on doin' car repairs."

"Will do." Darryl brushed past CJ in a rush and ran down the steps. He took a long, loving look at the Bel Air before he headed up the street.

In Darryl, CJ recognized the same gasoline-alley enthusiasm that he had had for cars when he was eighteen.

"Charlene, you there?" said CJ, stepping into the house.

"In the kitchen—come on in."

Charlene was seated in the sunny breakfast nook that she and Darryl had painstakingly remodeled the previous summer, pouring herself a cup of decaf. The evening light streamed through the slightly off-kilter sliding glass doors behind her and over the built-in hourglass-shaped table where she sat. CJ had once asked her why the table had such an unusual pinched-in-the-middle shape. Charlene had responded by saying that the table had been designed to accommodate only two. "Pull up a chair, super blood, take a load off your feet, and while you're at it tell me about that bandage over your eye."

CJ ignored Charlene's *super blood* reference and slipped into the restored antique straightbacked Vickers chair at the opposite end of the table. "Juneteenth," he said.

"I see." Charlene knew CJ's line of work earned him lots of cuts and bruises, so she didn't pursue the issue. "Coffee?" She pushed a Denver Broncos mug CJ's way.

"Half a cup." CJ added a splash of cream and thought about adding sugar, but remembering the smoothie he had had earlier and his chronic weight problems, he decided not to. "Thanks for sending me Clothilde Polk. I needed the gig."

"You're welcome. Figured you could use a job, especially if what they're saying about Doucette Roundtree stiffing you on a bond is true."

The mention of Doucette's name gave CJ a bitter taste in his mouth. Normally he would have had a comeback for Charlene, but after nearly getting his head blown off and then trying to find out what had happened to Willis and Mavis for most of the rest of the day, he didn't have the energy to play their usual game. "Clothilde says she went to nursing school with you in Chicago."

"She did, at least for a few semesters. What happened? Did she stiff you on your fee?"

"Nah, just doing some checking. How long's she been here in Denver?"

"Four, five months. But she didn't ask me about hooking up with you until last week." A puzzled look spread across Charlene's face. "Why all the questions?"

CJ hesitated and took a sip of coffee.

"No cat-and-mouse today, CJ. I just pulled a double shift because of the bombing. I'm too tired."

CJ looked at his watch and realized that he'd been running on adrenaline for nearly ten hours. "Fair enough. Clothilde hired me to look into her father's murder."

"That sweet old man? No way."

"Afraid so. He died from a nicotine overdose. Somebody slapped a bunch of those time-release Nicoderm patches on him and stopped his heart. Did you know he had a bad ticker?"

"Yeah." Charlene sounded genuinely sad. "Clothilde told me about it when we were in nursing school. It bothered her something terrible that she couldn't do anything about it. The fact that he smoked two packs a day and drank like a fish didn't help."

"Clothilde wouldn't have had any reason to kill him, would she?"

Charlene looked at CJ as if he had just started screaming obscenities in church. "You been smoking danks?" Danks, cigarettes dipped in formaldehyde, had recently become the preferred method of getting stoned for Denver gang members.

"No." CJ took a long sip of coffee and leaned forward uncomfortably in his chair. "Did you know Clothilde has a half-brother and that LeRoy Polk was once married to Mabel Pitts?"

"You need to spend more time hanging out with the girls, CJ. If you did, you'd know that's yesterday's news. And as close as you are to Mabel, I figured you'd already know all about her and LeRoy Polk."

CJ couldn't admit to Charlene that Mabel had never discussed LeRoy Polk or Tyrone. It would be admitting that he wasn't as close to Mabel as he had thought. "Would either Tyrone or Mabel have had any reason to kill the old man?" CJ surprised himself at how effortlessly the question had surfaced.

Charlene frowned. "I don't know about Tyrone. I've only met him once. As for Mabel, I can't believe you'd ask me a question like that!"

CJ peered into his coffee, wanting to retract his words.

Charlene decided to offer CJ some relief from his guilt and give him a few facts about Doo-Wop Polk. "Did you know LeRoy had ties to the Chicago mob?"

"Clothilde told me about that. Even named names, starting with some wiseguy from Pueblo named Hampoli. But it sounded like ancient history to me."

"Don't bet on it. When I was in nursing school I spent a few hours in nightclubs on Chicago's South Side, where the folks were serious about rhythm and blues."

"You didn't!" CJ feigned shock.

"It wasn't against the law. Now, let me finish what I was saying. I knew a piano player before I was married to Freddie, God rest his soul, who said that Doo-Wop Polk had been one of the few black men in America who had been in on the original payola scams. You know, those pay-for-play deals they had back in the fifties where DJs were paid under the table for giving certain songs air time and making them hits."

CJ gave Charlene a *don't lecture me* kind of look.

"Don't get defensive, CJ; hear me out. That same piano player told me that LeRoy had enough dirt on Chicago's mob-controlled recording industry to write his own ticket to either heaven or hell. He said that by keeping his mouth shut, LeRoy was making certain he wouldn't have to take a quick trip to either one."

"Did you ever discuss what you knew about her father with Clothilde?"

"No. Why would I?"

"No girl talk?" asked CJ, smiling.

"Good girls don't talk about things like that."

CJ swirled the last of his coffee around in his cup and finished it off. "You didn't have any other LeRoy Polk contacts back in Chicago, did you?"

"Just the piano player, and he was an old man back then. I don't even remember his name."

Suspecting that sooner or later Chicago was going to end up in his travel plans, CJ watched the sunlight behind Charlene knife its way over her shoulder and onto the narrow midsection of the table. The beam of light seemed to emphasize their separation. "One last thing, Charlene." He moved to get up from the table. "What percentage of the patients you see are on Nicoderm patches?"

"Not a lot. Mainly those on smoking intervention protocols for upper-airway disease."

"Any reason to ever stick one of those patches onto someone's scrotum?"

This time Charlene looked at CJ as if he had just shot someone in church. "I'd say you've got a sickie on your hands, CJ."

"No shit," said CJ, turning to go, thinking about how fast he could get home and crash. He was almost to the front door when he heard Charlene repeat, "Real effing sick."

Thirteen

First thing the next morning CJ checked in with his secretary, Julie Madrid, and then headed for a meeting with Mabel Pitts. He had called Mabel the night before, after swinging by University Hospital to check on Willis, and filled her in on his connection to her ex-husband, LeRoy Polk. It had been close to eleven when he called, but he knew Mabel would be up because she had a habit of telling anyone who would listen that the only people who died from arthritis like hers were the ones who spent a lifetime making love to a bed. In all the years that CJ had known Mabel, he had never known her to sleep more than four hours a night. He told her he needed her to tie up some loose ends about LeRoy, knowing that if anyone would level with him about LeRoy Polk, it would be Mabel.

The day had started sunny, but a bank of clouds had rolled over the Front Range and into Denver by the time

CJ left his home for Mabel's. On the short trip from Bail Bondsman's Row to Five Points he kept glancing skyward in hopes that the clouds would bring the Mile High City some rain. He caught a red light at Broadway and Colfax, dug into his glove compartment and found a John Lee Hooker tape, and plopped it in the tape deck. As the old bluesman began to sing, CJ mulled over the list of people who may have wanted to kill LeRoy Polk. He didn't like having to include Mabel, but Tyrone was another matter. He was an insipid Milquetoast with a half-sister who kept him under her thumb and a big payday on the horizon if his father's record barn and R&B museum really took off. He could have had a motive.

CJ had Julie checking out Lawrence Hampoli's ties to LeRoy Polk as well as Hampoli's role in Pueblo's organized crime. Julie could be as effective as a tabloid reporter when it came to finding people's dirty laundry. She had two years' worth of night-school credits toward a law degree, a gift of gab, and a nitpicking need to always get things straight that guaranteed she'd find the dirt. Since the other people on CJ's list of suspects, Roland Jefferson, Willette Jefferson, and Juney-boy Stokes, all supposedly lived in Chicago, he decided to scrutinize them later.

He nosed the Bel Air onto the 2400 block of California Street and headed for Mabel's duplex in the middle of the block. Mabel had lived in the same Five Points duplex for thirty years. She had never told CJ why she moved to Denver from Chicago and he had never asked, but now he suspected that her journey west probably had some connection to LeRoy Polk.

Mabel's duplex was across the street from Rufus G. Tibbits Memorial Park. CJ parked the Bel Air directly in

front of the park's entrance. The park was listed in the
Colorado Registry of Historic Places, as the three-by-
three-foot granite marker out front announced. A grue-
some historical event had earned the park its name.
Tibbits, the first black man to work for the old Denver
Power and Light Company, was murdered by his supervi-
sor, Jim Gribaldi, the night of August 10, 1925, on the
site where the park now stood. An argument between Tibbits and Gribaldi over a big-boned mulatto woman was
said to have been the spark that lit Gribaldi's murderous
rage. In an attempt to cover his tracks, Gribaldi set Tibbits's body on fire and ran. He was later captured, tried
for murder, and sentenced to ten to fifteen years in prison
for second-degree murder. He served six years of the sentence before being released.

After his release from prison, Gribaldi couldn't hold
a steady job, ultimately becoming a vagrant begging on the
Denver streets. One night while camping in a Depression-
era hobo jungle on the edge of Five Points, Gribaldi suffered a stroke, fell into his own campfire, and died. The
hobo jungle eventually became an unnamed Five Points
park. For years the residents of Five Points tried to have
the park named in honor of Tibbits, but no one suc-
ceeded until after Martin Luther King, Jr.'s assassination
in 1968, when Bible Back Brown, a Five Points folk hero
who had toted Bibles on his back from door to door in
the neighborhood for forty years, and Willis Sundee
teamed up with the Colorado Historical Society and suc-
ceeded in getting the park named for Tibbits. For many
years after its naming the park had served as a welcome
neighborhood retreat, but recently it had turned into a
haven for gangs. CJ and his friend Billy DeLong, a wiry

cowboy and recovering alcoholic who helped CJ with cases, had made more than a few dollars rounding up gangbanging bond skippers in Rufus G. Tibbits Park.

CJ was thinking about going down to Pueblo to confront Lawrence Hampoli as he bounded up the steps to Mabel's duplex and rang the doorbell. He stood on the front step for a couple of minutes watching two ten-year-olds on dirt bikes take turns charging up and then back down a hill just to the right of the park entrance. The boys weren't wearing helmets, and their heads had been shaved cueball clean. CJ wondered what kind of parent would allow a ten-year-old to shave his head until he thought back to the size of his mid-sixties Afro. One boy stalled three-quarters of the way up the hill and fell face first into the dirt. The other boy laughed.

"Don't be laughing at me," screamed the boy who had fallen. "I'll stomp your fucking ass."

The other boy lit into him like a rocket. They flailed at one another and screamed obscenities as they wobbled end over end down the hill. CJ shook his head, wondering whether in a couple of years they would be going after one another with guns.

Mabel Pitts answered the door with her intricately carved Jamaican walking stick looped over her arm and a geranium-filled flower pot in her hand. She was a stoop-shouldered woman whose every motion was calculated to avoid arthritic pain. Her shriveled body looked every bit of its sixty-six years, but her eyes were sun-up bright, and her smile was broad and infectious. She was the kind of deeply religious lady who felt guilty for a month if she missed a single Sunday of church. To remind her of her commitment to her faith she kept inspirational gospel music playing from the time she got up in the morning until she crawled into bed each night. The Mighty Clouds of Joy, her favorite gospel group, were belting out their 1977 rendition of "There's Love in the World" when CJ stepped inside. With her walking stick swinging from her arm and her flowerpot gripped tightly in gnarled arthritic fingers, she reached up and hugged CJ, then stepped back, eyeing the bandage on his forehead sympathetically. Mabel's embrace was as close as CJ had ever come to a mother's hug.

"Battle scar from my Juneteenth wars," said CJ, noting Mabel's scrutiny. "Yesterday I was seeing three of everything."

"Oh, the bombing. I heard the blast. Terrible, terrible thing," she said, fighting back the urge to mother, and shaking her head, surprised at how, at forty-five, CJ still seemed to take his encounters with death so lightly. "You just missed Morgan and Dittier." She stepped back and placed her flowerpot on the deacon's bench that overwhelmed the entry hall. "Dittier's all tied up in knots over losing that Red River hog of his in that explosion. If he could talk, I'd be afraid to hear what might come out of his mouth."

"Geronimo means a lot to him."

"I expect so. But he needs to get a hold of himself. He's a grown man—an ex-rodeo champ to boot. He can go out and buy another pig." When Mabel noticed that the look on CJ's face didn't quite mirror her assessment, she eased off a bit. "If he needs that pig so bad, maybe you should help him and Morgan find it."

"I'll do what I can. But runaways ain't my stock in trade."

"You tracked down that zonked-out judge's daughter and those environmental kooks who were trying to kill off the cattle industry last year," said Mabel, sounding as proud as any parent.

"She wasn't a runaway, and besides, when I found her she was dead."

Mabel adjusted her weight onto her walking stick. "I expect you're right. Guess you're better at digging up doo-doo on dead disc jockeys." A mock frown spread across her face. "Might as well get this mess with LeRoy over with," she added, turning to go inside.

They walked down a narrow hallway past the living and dining rooms and into a brightly lit modern kitchen. No matter when CJ came to visit Mabel, whether it had been to mow the lawn and rake leaves as a child or to bring her up to date on how he had dealt with one of her unsavory tenants, they had always done business in the kitchen.

Mabel was from a small town in Louisiana that claimed to be the birthplace of America's hottest hot sauce, and she could easily have been a first-rate chef. Every cooking utensil a gourmet could desire, from expensive Swedish cutlery to graduated fourteen-, twelve-, ten-, and eight-inch-diameter cast-iron skillets, filled the nooks and crannies of the room. Oversized restaurant-style double ovens and a custom-built minirotisserie covered an entire wall. CJ's mouth started to water as soon as they walked into the room. When he caught sight of a five-gallon pot of gumbo simmering on the stove and inhaled the aroma of baking crackling bread, his stomach started growling.

"Take a load off your feet and sit a spell," Mabel said with a smile.

CJ pulled one of Mabel's antique poolroom stools from the corner, slid it up to the built-in center island with its tile-rimmed cooktop, and sat down. It was all he could do to keep from bending over the pot of gumbo and inhaling.

Mabel sat down across the cooktop from him on an identical stool. She leaned both elbows on the cooking island and breathed in the rising steam from the gumbo. She couldn't resist asking CJ about his head injury again. "How bad did you hurt your noggin?"

"Not bad; in fact it's pretty minor compared to what happened to Willis Sundee." CJ patted the bandage above his eye as if he expected the knot below it to be gone.

"How's he doing?"

"A broken collarbone, some burns, and a mild concussion, but he's gonna be all right."

"Tell Mavis if she needs any help, give me a call. That's if you can keep your hands off the girl," Mabel advised with a snicker. She loved to hassle CJ about keeping his romance with Mavis close to a state secret. "And when you see Willis, tell him word on the street is that he better lighten up on city hall. I was in the Safeway this morning, and the buzz up and down the aisles was that us Five Points folks better get to lovin' that monorail if we don't wanna end up like Willis."

"That place is worse than a barbershop after a Broncos loss. I'd take anything I heard there with a grain of salt."

"I would if I didn't know Winston Dunn. That treacherous little leech probably wired Mae's and blew it himself." Mabel looked at CJ, expecting him to give her his take on who was behind the bombing at Juneteenth.

Normally he would have, but he had been so worried about Mavis and Willis that he hadn't had time to look into the bombing. In addition, he didn't want Mabel, who wasn't past spreading a little gossip herself, to unwittingly start putting out warning signals to the bombers that he was going to be a source of smoke on their tail. CJ decided that for the moment he'd stick with what he'd come to see Mavis about, Daddy Doo-Wop Polk. "Let's get back to Dunn later. Right now I need to know about LeRoy Polk."

Mabel shrugged her shoulders fine-by-me style, sat back in her chair, and shook her head. "I expect LeRoy died the same way he lived. Chasing after his dreams." A look of genuine sorrow crossed her face. "LeRoy never wanted to believe his time had come and gone. He lived in a fantasy world. Take that record barn and R&B museum he and that stuck-up daughter of his are building north of LoDo. It's gonna turn out to be nothing but an ice palace in the sun. Nobody's going back to buying forty-fives. I told him that the day he told me about the deal. I said, 'LeRoy, you can't go back.' But he winked at me, saying he had an inside straight. I never talked to him about what that was. Next thing I know, he's dead."

CJ ignored Mabel's assessment of LeRoy's business acumen. He was more interested in the fact that she and LeRoy had been close enough to have discussed his plans before he died. CJ took a pack of cheroots from his vest pocket and tapped one out. "How'd you hook up with LeRoy?" he said, lighting up.

"You might not believe it, CJ Floyd, but I wasn't always an arthritic heap. I did my share of tail-feather shaking back in Chicago when I was young." She wiggled around on the stool for emphasis.

CJ couldn't help but smile. In his eyes, Mabel had always been a proper churchgoing lady and a rock-solid Five Points citizen. He had a hard time picturing her as anything else. But the twinkle in Mabel's eyes told him that deep down beneath her arthritic church-lady shell, she was a woman who had been a four-star diamond when she was young.

"Is that how you met LeRoy, shakin' a tail feather?" asked CJ, imitating Mabel's wiggle.

She laughed at CJ's stiff rendition. "Sort of. Actually I met him a few years earlier over in Gary, Indiana. A friend of mine introduced me to him in a little back-alley blues hole called the Ricochet Lounge. LeRoy had just signed a couple of local singing groups to the record label he was starting, Stax of Wax, for a thousand bucks apiece. He had the record contracts in his pocket, pulling them out and waving them around every chance he got, and he was buying rounds of drinks for everyone in the place. He bought me a couple of drinks, laid a line ten yards long on me, and offered me a job as his secretary on the spot. The job sounded better than what I had been doing, emptying bedpans at Cook County Hospital from four to twelve, so I took it. We started out in a cramped little crackerbox on Forty-second and Cottage Grove. Four months later we were married. Five months after that I had Tyrone." She scanned CJ's face for signs of disapproval and added, "I was young."

"How long did you stay married?"

"Five years. Until LeRoy's eye started roving so much

I couldn't take it anymore, and until the kind of people who made my skin crawl started coming by our house all hours of the day and night. Evil, lowlife, trashy scum." She emphasized every syllable.

"Any names I might recognize?" asked CJ.

"It's been over thirty years, CJ. Half of the names I never knew, and I'm glad I didn't. But I knew they were part of the Chicago mob, and I knew they had their fingers in the Chitown rhythm and blues pie." Mabel paused and frowned as if what she had to say next was going to be a dirty word. "There was one man in particular I remember. If you saw him on the street back then, you'd have sworn he was a banker." She looked apprehensive. "I always suspected he killed people. Probably still does. His name was Larry Hampoli."

It surprised CJ that Mabel seemed unaware that Hampoli now lived practically on her doorstep, just ninety miles south in Pueblo. He had a strange, uneasy feeling that Mabel was holding something back from him. "I know about Hampoli. Julie's checking out his pedigree right now." He leaned forward and put his elbows firmly on the countertop before asking his next question, as if he needed additional support before asking it. "LeRoy's roving eye ever make you want to get even?"

"Of course not. Not then and not now. LeRoy couldn't help it. The Lord gave him too many hormones, so he spent most of his life marking his territory and sniffing up rears like a frustrated dog. One thing for sure, his sniffing wasn't limited to the opposite sex."

Mabel's statement caught CJ so off guard that his right elbow slipped out from under him.

"Bet that sweet-talking shrew of a daughter didn't tell

you that. Old LeRoy was a wine before his time. Bisexual as the day is long. Ms. Sweet-Pea Clothilde ain't never been able to come to grips with it. I could, though. I left his behind. I wanted to take Tyrone but . . ."

"Did Tyrone know?"

"Beats me. We've only been back on speaking terms the past couple of years. I tried to put the past behind me, pretend it didn't exist, including Tyrone. That's why in all these years, I never mentioned Tyrone to you. LeRoy kept Tyrone under wraps away from me most of the time he was growing up. But knowing LeRoy, the only side of himself he'd ever have let Tyrone see would have been Mr. Macho Man." Mabel eased forward on her stool to check the simmering gumbo. She lifted the lid, and the tantalizing spicy smell mushroomed through the room. "Welcome to come back this evening for dinner," she said, stirring the pot.

"Think I will," said CJ, salivating.

"But you have to promise me, no more questions about LeRoy Polk."

"Then let's get the rest of them out of the way right now."

"Might as well," said Mabel, continuing to stir the gumbo.

"Did you know LeRoy's second wife, Clothilde's mother?"

"No. But I heard she was a real knockout, and I know she's dead. Tyrone told me she had a stroke. Knowing LeRoy, he probably drove her to it."

CJ sat back and rubbed his hand across a patch of cheek stubble his razor had missed. In Clothilde Polk's glowing synopsis of her father, she had omitted the tidbit about his being bisexual, and she had never mentioned her mother. He wondered what other important details she had left out. "Why the war between you and Clothilde?"

"Because she steals. She stole all her daddy's affection from Tyrone when he needed his rightful share. She stole Tyrone's self-worth, or maybe you haven't seen the way she leads him around on a chain like one of Cinderella's ugly stepsisters; and although I can't prove it, she was probably stealing cold, hard cash from LeRoy till the day he died."

"Not a ringing endorsement of my client."

"She's a hateful little shrew, CJ. Don't let that beauty-contest smile and sexy body of hers fool you. She's full of black-widow venom. I'd watch out for her bite if I was you."

"I can take care of myself. Can Tyrone?"

Mabel beamed the knowing smile of a mother. "Tyrone's tougher than he looks. Clothilde may think he's just another puppet, but she's wrong. You know, she had no intention of including Tyrone in that new record company extravaganza of theirs. Even claimed that it was her idea, not LeRoy's, to resurrect Stax of Wax. She tried to convince LeRoy to leave Tyrone out in the cold. But Tyrone raised holy hell. The fact that he's in on the ground floor should answer your question."

Mabel seemed to be a lot wiser about LeRoy's plans for Stax of Wax and his R&B museum than she should have been. CJ chalked it up to the fact that Tyrone was feeding her inside dope, but the scope of her knowledge bothered him. "What made Clothilde finally agree to let Tyrone in?"

"LeRoy laid down the law. Told her blood was

thicker than water. But believe you me, sooner or later Clothilde'll find a way to try and X Tyrone out."

"Think she's capable of murder?"

"Thought I already made that clear. She's a black widow."

CJ hesitated before stumbling over his next question. "Clothilde says, ah, maybe you killed LeRoy."

Mabel stabbed her spoon into the gumbo, then grabbed her dangling walking stick from the countertop and began waving it Zorro fashion in the air. "If I didn't have arthritis so bad, I'd beat that little hussy to a pulp."

CJ hadn't seen Mabel so animated in years. He decided to give her time to cool down before asking any more questions.

Mabel thumped her walking stick on the floor as her head swiveled from side to side in disbelief. When she sat back down she was shaking. When he felt that the demons had safely passed, CJ finally spoke up. "Clothilde claims that some of LeRoy's old-time music cronies may have been after him. Know anything about Roland Jefferson or Juney-boy Stokes?"

"That witch sure makes a lot of claims," said Mabel, hanging her walking stick back over the counter's edge. "Roland and Juney-boy. Now, those are real names from the crypt." She paused and sampled the gumbo. "Should be dynamite by night. Back when I knew him, Roland was just a pretty-boy spook who loved the idea of having a white woman hanging on his arm. He didn't have an ounce of common sense, and he never seemed to realize that chasing after white girls was even dumber in 1955 than it is today."

"Clothilde says Jefferson claims to own fifty percent of Stax of Wax."

Mabel burst out laughing. "And I own the Sears Tower. Roland never had brains enough to come in out of the rain, and the only thing he ever owned in his life was a '57 Chevy like yours. Now, that white wife of his, Willette, she was sharp as a tack. If anybody had a piece of Stax of Wax besides LeRoy, it would've been Willette."

"Why not you?"

"Because LeRoy's lawyer made sure I didn't. Just like he made sure I didn't get custody of Tyrone. After all, I was dealing with Daddy Doo-Wop, and even back then he had enough money to hire the kind of people he needed to look after his interests. Like I said before, I was young. I left the LeRoy Polk merry-go-round the same way I came in, with a couple of hundred dollars in my pocket, a half-empty suitcase, and a bus ticket back to Gary. It was an amicable enough split, not like when Juney-boy Stokes and LeRoy parted ways."

"Nasty?" asked CJ.

"As a pigsty. So nasty, in fact, I thought they might brain one another. Juney-boy claimed LeRoy stole his songs."

"Did he?"

"Probably."

CJ was surprised at Mabel's matter-of-fact response, and it showed.

"Don't look so surprised, CJ. Everybody in the music business steals. It's a way of life."

"Clothilde says Juney-boy would have killed LeRoy on sight."

"That's overstating it. But he hated LeRoy enough to

try and burn down the Stax of Wax offices. Cost him two years in Joliet and a marriage he never should have been in."

CJ adjusted his weight on the stool and sighed. "What a menagerie."

"No worse than today's pack of entertainment wolves," said Mabel.

"Guess not."

The aroma from the simmering gumbo had CJ on the verge of asking for a bowl right then, but before he could, Mabel put the top on the pot and turned off the burner. "Should be something special tonight," she said before looking at CJ pensively and asking, "How did LeRoy die?"

"Somebody slipped him enough nicotine to kill a horse."

Mabel frowned, and a battery of wrinkles spread across her forehead. "Think he knew what hit him?"

"No." CJ recognized Mabel's question for what it was: the inquiry of someone who had once cared deeply about LeRoy Polk.

Mabel blushed. "Don't twist anything around in your head, CJ. Me and LeRoy Polk finished our business long ago. I just don't like the idea that somebody cut him short."

"You don't think Tyrone could be involved?"

Mabel cringed. "Don't even think about it. I'd follow up on Roland Jefferson, Hampoli, and Little Miss Sweetness, Clothilde. Those three are birds of a feather. Money makes 'em tick. If anything got LeRoy killed, you can be certain money's somewhere in the mix."

CJ nodded his head knowingly and stood up from his stool. "What time's the feast?"

Mabel shuffled over to a cupboard next to the microwave and pulled out a packet of gumbo filé. "Six'll be just fine. And before you get to thinking you're somebody special, you should know Tyrone's coming too. Just remember, no discussing LeRoy Polk."

CJ smiled, admiring Mabel's persistence. There'd be no talk about Doo-Wop Polk, but at least he'd have the chance to talk to Tyrone without Clothilde dancing around in the wings. He watched as Mabel dumped the packet of filé into the gumbo. "I'll start fasting now," he said, patting his stomach.

"Bring some wine. My joints are screaming too loud for me to run out shopping this afternoon. Tyrone likes wine."

"Done," said CJ, turning to go.

Mabel followed him out of the kitchen and down the hallway in a slow, arthritic waddle. She was relying on her walking stick much more than when CJ had come in. At the front door, Mabel offered a warning. "Watch yourself, CJ. I can't speak for all the folks you're trackin', but I wouldn't take Hampoli lightly."

CJ turned and gave her a quick peck on the cheek before bounding down the front steps two at a time.

Mabel stood on the porch leaning on her walking stick until she saw CJ ease off in the Bel Air. She felt guilty about not telling CJ the whole truth about Juneyboy Stokes. Perhaps it was her female vanity. It didn't matter. She knew that sooner or later CJ would find out for himself.

She didn't see Johnny Telano's metallic, inky-black

Camaro parked half a block down the street from the Bel Air, and she wouldn't have recognized it anyway. Johnny was seated behind the wheel reading the baseball box scores when CJ drove past him. When CJ turned off California Street and onto 23rd, Johnny neatly folded the *Rocky Mountain News* into quarters and placed it on the passenger seat.

The two kids who had been roughhousing in the park earlier walked past the Camaro just as Johnny got out.

"Nice ride," said one of them, eyeing the car.

Johnny didn't respond. He punched the lock button on his key-ring remote and the Camaro's locks clicked shut as he crossed the street and headed past Mabel's, patting the eavesdropping device he had in one pocket and his Colt Commander in the other.

Fourteen

Winston Dunn was nervously pacing the asphalt driveway in front of garage number three at the Turkey Creek Canyon ministorage, reflecting on forty-eight hours of rotten luck. To add insult to his misfortune, one of the lanes of U.S. 285 up the canyon had been closed for paving, and he had had to follow a conga line of semitrailers spewing diesel fumes and black smoke the fifteen miles from Denver into the foothills of the Rockies. The ministorage facility was in Clear Creek County, a stone's throw across the Jefferson County line, and Denver's mayor, Arcell Wiley, had been leasing garage number three for fifteen years, ever since his first term as a Denver city councilman. He had first leased the space after a reporter had asked him in an interview, shortly after he took his city council seat, whether as Denver's first black councilman from a predominantly white district he had ever considered how history would judge him. Within a week of the interview, Wiley, who dreamed of one day becoming as big a historical figure as Martin Luther King, Jr., started stockpiling the garage with Arcell Wiley memorabilia that included everything from all-American red-white-and-blue campaign buttons to a full-sized wooden replica of an Angus cow with the words BEEF INDUSTRY FOR WILEY stamped across its hindquarters.

Thirty-mile-per-hour wind gusts had Winston Dunn ducking in and out of the protection of the garage's covered apron, cursing his luck, trying to come up with the names of political adversaries who might have hated the mayor or his monorail plan for Five Points enough to bomb Mae's Louisiana Kitchen and direct suspicion at the mayor. Since the bombing, the *Rocky Mountain News* and the *Denver Post* had run nearly identical front-page headlines, JUNETEENTH BOMBING MAY SCUTTLE MONORAIL, along with editorials suggesting that Mae's and Willis Sundee may have been specifically targeted by the mayor and calling for a full-scale investigation of the project.

Over his usual breakfast of black coffee and two sugar donuts, the mayor had read the headlines and editorials, called Dunn, and issued him an ultimatum. "Have your ass up at Turkey Creek Canyon by two o'clock sharp with some answers." Scuttlebutt among the mayor's inner circle was that when he asked for a face-to-face at the Turkey Creek Canyon location, you were about to be fired.

Dunn was huddled out of the swirling wind, staring at a U.S. Forest Service fire-danger marker that was rotating back and forth and thinking about how to save his rear, when the mayor's Lincoln town car rounded the corner and headed down the asphalt toward him. Dunn swal-

lowed hard, noting that the arrow on the Forest Service
marker was registering in the extreme-fire-danger red
zone. When the car slowed to a stop in front of the
garage, the swirling wind momentarily ebbed.

Mayor Wiley, a stocky, dark-skinned, balding man
with muttonchop sideburns and a middle linebacker's
physique gone to seed, stepped from the backseat. He was
wearing a cheap tan wash-and-wear summer suit that
looked out of place on a man decked out in $500 Italian
loafers, a solid gold Rolex, and a custom-weave hundred-
dollar European silk tie. The mayor made it a habit to
wear the same grassroots campaign suit whenever he
wanted to wring the vinegar out of a wayward aide.

"Windy today," he said, clutching his suit jacket as a
gust hit him head-on.

"Hear it's always windy up here," said Dunn boldly,
letting the mayor know that he was aware of the stories
about Turkey Creek Canyon.

The mayor didn't seem impressed. He pulled a set of
keys from his pocket and motioned for his driver to pull
off the asphalt and into a small clump of trees. "Let's get
in out of the wind." He had the door to the garage open
and had stepped inside before Dunn could respond.

Dunn had only heard gossip about what was stored
in the garage, tales that it was chock-full to the rafters
with the nuts and bolts of the mayor's political life. Now
that he was seeing it for himself, he could hardly believe
his eyes. The thirty-by-thirty-foot room was cordoned off
into eight separate bays with movie-theater red velvet
rope. Six of the bays were jam-packed with campaign literature, signs, furniture, storage boxes, word-processing
equipment, file cabinets, liquor, and even a stack of red-

white-and-blue banners that read TAKE A TURN WITH
WILEY, from the mayor's early city council years. A bay
near the back of the garage, reserved for more recent
items, contained several life-sized cardboard blowup photos of Mayor Wiley shaking hands with the vice president. One bay was empty.

"Let's step over toward the back," said the mayor,
pointing to the empty bay and beckoning for Dunn to
follow. "And grab a chair on the way."

Dunn walked past half a dozen chairs before finally
grabbing an old dusty straightbacked rocker tucked between boxes of WIN WITH WILEY buttons. He noticed
that the mayor didn't take a chair. When they got to the
empty bay, he realized why.

"Put it in the middle over there," said Wiley, pointing to the center of the bay, "and have a seat."

Dunn did as he was told. The stress of the situation
suddenly had him thinking back to his days as a teenage
hoodlum in Detroit, and he wondered how he had evolved
into an ass-kissing flunky for some washed-up athlete
turned big-city mayor.

The mayor began circling him like a prizefighter circling an opponent. After a couple of round trips he
stopped directly in front of Dunn, leaned down, hands on
his knees, and said, "We're not in a cockfight, Winston.
We don't have to peck out the other guy's eyes."

Dunn looked up at the mayor, trying to look innocent.

"Don't play numbnuts with me, Winston. I know
you sicced city health inspectors on Willis Sundee, and I
know about some of the other shit you've got up your
sleeve. You're playing stupid. We don't need to operate on

that level of stupidity for monorail to succeed. I'm just hoping you didn't lose the whole goddamn blood supply to your brain yesterday and decide to try and take out Willis Sundee."

Dunn was about to respond, but the mayor cut him off. "Whether you did or didn't is immaterial now. What's important for you to understand is where we go from here. I don't like loose cannons in my operation, and I won't tolerate being second-guessed. Got it?"

Dunn cleared his throat, looked down at the floor, and focused on a crack in the concrete running between his feet. He thought about where he had come from and where he was now. He thought about cold orphanage showers and kids making fun of him because he had no parents. He remembered searching for his mother after his rough years on the streets and finding out she was an addict. He never did find his father. His moment of reflection lingered, haunting him, until the mayor repeated, "Got it?"

Dunn looked up slowly. "I can handle the agenda."

"Good, because this morning I had my own chief of police ask me a whole series of embarrassing questions about the bombing. Questions I didn't have answers for. Questions that could make my whole political future turn sour. I told him you and I were scheduled for this little talk and assured him that by this evening you'd be able to give him the kind of information he needs to have his people start looking under the right kind of rocks for a bomber."

The mayor's message was loud and clear. *Get the spotlight off him.* "We can start by having the police turn up the heat on our local Five Points gangbangers," said Dunn.

"Willis Sundee's been trying to push them out of Five Points for years. Maybe they decided it was time to settle the score." Dunn smiled at how quickly at least one solution to the mayor's problem had come to him.

"And then there's always CJ Floyd. He was Johnny-on-the-spot when the restaurant went up. I've been wondering why ever since yesterday. Could be he was the target."

"Or the triggerman," said the mayor.

Dunn smiled again. The mayor's solution sounded even better. "I'll find something on Floyd that's meaty enough for the police to dig their teeth into."

"Do that. And while you're at it, think about trying to serve the chief up a few other bones to chew on. We're done here." He gestured for Dunn to get up from his chair. "Let's head back down the hill."

A sense of relief flooded through Dunn as they walked back out into the late afternoon sun. Wind gusts kept kicking up fiercely, sending swirling dust devils across the parched prairie grass. The arrow on the fire-danger marker never stopped rotating back and forth.

When the mayor's driver caught sight of the mayor, he moved the town car around to meet him. As Wiley lowered his bulky frame into the front seat, he looked back at Dunn with a determined win-at-all-costs intensity. "I've traveled a long way on my journey, Winston, and I'm expecting it to be an even longer trip. Remember that." He swung his legs into the car. "And by the way, I've asked Sergeant Fuller to help you with your assignment."

The car pulled away, leaving Winston Dunn walking into a forty-mile-an-hour headwind as he started toward his own car. Puzzled and intimidated because the mayor now had a homicide detective nursemaiding him, he wondered what he could turn up on CJ Floyd that would make him the focus of a bombing investigation.

Fifteen

It had taken CJ's secretary, Julie Madrid, half a lifetime, including six years of a gut-wrenching marriage to an abusive, Ritalin-popping husband, to realize that she didn't have to take guff from anyone. So the smug, holier-than-thou reincarnation of Jabba the Hutt, calling himself a water restriction officer, seated on the porch railing outside CJ's office, nodding his head disapprovingly and writing a hundred-dollar citation for unlawful distribution of city water, had her blood boiling.

"What's your beef?" said Julie, who had just returned from the library. "Today's a diamond watering day—we're a diamond." She pointed to the odd-numbered address above the front door.

"Technically you're correct, madam," said Jabba. A pendulous loop of skin swung bulldog-style at the margin of his lower jaw as he talked. "But the law clearly states that lessors, lessees, tenants, and property owners may make use of their water only for themselves, their lessors, lessees, or tenants. You may not divert, subrogate, or otherwise barter your unit's water rights to others." He nodded toward a leaky garden hose running from CJ's building to the yard of Cicero Vickers, the bail bondsman who operated out of the three-story Victorian office building next door. "The statute's quite clear. It stems from a hundred-year-old Colorado ranching and irrigation law."

"You see any cows grazing out there?" Julie pointed toward the brown patch of dead grass that had once been a vibrant green front lawn. "We let the guy next door use our water because our lawn's dead and his isn't. We're just being neighborly."

"Precisely why I'm citing you, Ms. Madrid," said Jabba, saliva pooling at the corners of his mouth. "The water delivered to this residence is for your use and your use alone."

Julie rolled her eyes and mulled over whether to argue statutes with the bureaucratic maniac, let him continue writing the citation, or push him over the railing. She had just spent all morning at the stifling downtown Denver Public Library, where the space-age air-conditioning system had been on the blink, scanning microfilm, digging through slow-as-molasses computer databases, reviewing dusty old newspapers that still had her sneezing, and sifting through cartons of documents from Colorado's now-defunct Organized Crime Strike Force for information on Lawrence Hampoli. She now knew not only the color of wool-blend socks that Hampoli preferred but the name of the southern California hair-weave firm that supplied his toupee and half a dozen reasons for a recent split with his wife. The Benadryl she had taken to stop her fits of sneezing had made her lightheaded and irritable, and she had little tolerance left for the toilet bowl police, but she decided against shoving Jabba over the railing.

The man finished writing the citation and handed it to Julie.

"You a real cop?" she said, looking at the slip of paper, knowing that he wasn't.

"No." Jabba jammed the citation book in his back pocket.

"Then you better go find one, because here's what I think of your fine." Julie ripped the paper into several pieces, tossing them over the railing into a gust of wind.

Jabba looked at Julie as if she had suddenly gone mad, then leaped up from the porch banister and ran after the fluttering fragments just as CJ pulled the Bel Air up in front of the building, returning from his meeting with Mabel.

Normally CJ would have pulled into the garage behind the house, but since he was only planning a pit stop to have Julie bring him up to speed on what she had found out about Hampoli, he decided to park in front. He knew that something was wrong the instant he spotted the orange-sherbet-colored ATV parked out front.

Jabba, who CJ later learned was Ernest T. Teller, came barreling down the porch steps, propelling his nearly three hundred pounds in the direction of the fluttering scraps.

He and CJ met midway up the flagstone walkway. "I'll prepare another," Teller screamed back at Julie, "and another after that if necessary, Ms. Madrid. I don't take my job lightly."

CJ stared at the panting water restriction officer, who was pawing for paper scraps. Then, slowly, his eyes followed the length of the garden hose to the neighboring yard. He shook his head as he watched water gurgling from the hose. Realizing that Julie's low tolerance for bureaucracy had probably gotten the best of her, he went down on one knee to assist Teller. "Let me help."

Teller was caught off guard. He nearly said *thanks*, but instead he stared at CJ and the street-warrior bandage above his eye with disapproval, forced a *Don't interfere here* kind of look, and continued pocketing the scraps.

"Is there a problem?"

"The lady on the porch has the problem." Teller nodded in Julie's direction, grabbing the last fragment of paper.

"Then I've got one too," said CJ as they stood up in unison. "She's my secretary."

"And the building. Does it belong to you?" Teller scrutinized CJ, half smiling, realizing that the last laugh might still be his.

"It's mine, lock, stock, and barrel."

Julie had taken a seat in one of the wicker chairs on the porch. Her head was partially obstructed by the porch railing, and Teller couldn't see her face. She seemed much smaller to him than she had a few minutes before. "Then I'll give you the citation," he said, breaking into an all-out grin. "You're watering improperly and out of sequence." He pulled his citation book out of his back pocket, scribbled out a new ticket in less than thirty seconds, jammed the book back in his pocket, and handed CJ the new paperwork. The fine had increased to $200, and Teller had checked a box next to the words "obstruction of officer."

He looked back up toward Julie. "Your secretary needs a course on rules and regulations, Mr. . . . ?"

"Floyd," said CJ.

"She's just cost you an extra hundred dollars, Mr. Floyd." He licked the corners of his mouth. "From now on, I'll be watching you. Now, how about turning your water off." He tugged at his belt, adjusting his trousers, cast a final ice-dagger stare toward Julie, and walked away. When Julie heard his ATV fire up and pull off, she stood up, leaned over the railing, and gave Ernest Teller the loudest raspberry CJ had heard in years.

"Sorry I missed your performance," said CJ, stepping onto the porch. The eighty-year-old cedar planking creaked with age. Red, yellow, and green neon tubes shaped to spell out OPEN 24 HOURS and BAIL BONDS ANY-TIME hung from the ornate porch fascia and hummed continuously above his head. CJ rolled the ticket up diploma-style. "Must have been some show." He slapped the ticket into his palm. "And all I got was a bill."

"He caught me off guard," said Julie, scrutinizing CJ to make certain that the Juneteenth injuries she had seen only briefly earlier that morning were really minor. Satisfied that they were, she added, "And besides, he doesn't know what he's talking about. Denver can't enforce century-old irrigation laws that were intended for open cattle range. We can fight it, CJ. It'll be a piece of cake."

CJ eyed the ticket, knowing that if he gave Julie the okay to contest the citation she'd unleash a personal war on the TBP that would teach them to steer clear of a determined Puerto Rican woman with two years of law school under her belt. But at the moment he needed Julie focused on helping him find out who killed LeRoy Polk.

"Let's save that battle for another day." He slipped the ticket into his pocket. "Right now I'd rather hear about what you dug up on our friend Lawrence Hampoli."

A look of disappointment spread across Julie's face. She looked at their gurgling garden hose and thought about the now-barren vegetable patch and flower garden behind CJ's building that she had nurtured for years. "Better pull the plug on our pipeline to Cicero," she said, heading inside to get her notes on Hampoli. "We wouldn't want any more fines today."

CJ nodded in agreement as the screen door slammed shut behind Julie. He stepped off the porch, turned off the faucet beside the steps, and rolled the leaky hose back up on its rusted wheel.

Julie came back outside with a legal pad full of notes and a frown on her face. "I missed a call from Mabel while I was out here sparring with that toilet bowl cop. It was on the answering machine. Your dinner tonight's been changed to seven o'clock."

"Good; that gives me time to figure out how I'm gonna get Tyrone Polk to tell me about his father's sexual preferences before we have to sit down to dinner with Mabel."

Julie's eyes ballooned. "Is this case going to turn freaky?" She remembered a bond skipper whom CJ had had to chase down in the White River National Forest near Aspen. The man turned out to be the leader of a cult of eagle worshipers who killed the endangered birds, ground their beaks to make an aphrodisiac, and snorted the gummy residue, claiming that the powder cured impotence and made their arousals last for hours. CJ had kept a jar of the stuff sitting on his desk for months afterward, and every time Julie looked at the jar she wondered whether he had ever had the nerve to try any.

CJ's eyes narrowed as he caught on to what Julie was thinking. "I don't think we have any eagle killers here. I'm just trying to cover all the bases."

"Glad to hear that." Julie sat down and flipped the first page of her legal pad over. "I hate playing library mole. The dust kicks my allergies up." She looked at her notes. "Before I started sneezing my brains out, I was able to put half a tablet of notes together on your friend Mr. Hampoli. You want the good news or the bad news first?"

"Good. I've had enough bad news for one day." CJ patted the pocket with the ticket.

Julie fought back the urge to recommend fighting the ticket again. "The good news is that two months ago Hampoli left his wife, and since no one likes being dumped, she's been putting his business in the street ever since. The Pueblo papers have been eating it up. News stories, editorials, even a feature piece in the Sunday supplement about his longtime ties to organized crime."

"Has she been talkative enough to let us know why Hampoli might have wanted to kill LeRoy Polk?"

"No. But she also sicced the Colorado Bureau of Investigation on him, and he's been bobbing and weaving, trying to stay out of their way and screaming like a scalded dog for months." Julie flipped to the third page of her notes and ran her finger down the page. "His lawyers have been running interference, trying to skirt charges of receiving stolen goods, interfering with union organizers, and violating interstate commerce laws. So far he's managed to stay out of jail."

CJ leaned back against the porch railing deep in

thought, digesting the good news, anticipating the bad. "Those charges are love taps for a guy like Hampoli. His lawyers'll end up swatting them away like flies. Now, Mrs. Hampoli—sounds like she's pissed enough to keep up the heat. Maybe she and I need to talk."

"Makes sense. She's been dropping tidbits about Hampoli's activities like somebody on Ex-Lax. She just might know something about LeRoy Polk."

"Anything else on the good side of the ledger?"

Julie paged through her notes. "Hampoli has a link to the Pueblo social set. He's past president of the Pueblo Rose Society. He must be feeling the need to reinvent himself because one of those Sunday-supplement fluff pieces in the *Pueblo Chieftian* said that he's planning to re-marry and return to a former business interest, record sales and distribution. Sounds like a LeRoy Polk connection to me."

CJ leaned his entire weight into the railing, testing to see if Ernest Teller's three-hundred-pound load had caused permanent damage. "What's the bad news?" He moved to the wicker chair across from Julie, assured that the railing was still safe.

"Hampoli plays for keeps. According to reams of just-released Colorado Organized Crime Strike Force documents, he has a business associate named Johnny Telano who makes people disappear."

"Tough group," said CJ. "Anything else?"

Julie ignored CJ's nonchalant response. "Just one more thing of interest." Her eyebrows shot straight up, a sure sign that what she was about to say was important. "Telano's a shipmate of yours. He spent two years in the navy before he started working for Hampoli, and guess what his specialty was." Before CJ could answer, Julie said, "Demolitions. Seems he's an expert at blowing things up."

Julie's pronouncement caught CJ off guard. Suddenly the image of Mavis Sundee shivering uncontrollably in shock and the entire front wall of Mae's Louisiana Kitchen hurtling toward him reemerged in his head. The vision of the exploding restaurant faded quickly, but the helplessness he had seen on Mavis's face lingered. A foggy, trancelike look of revenge filled CJ's eyes.

Julie knew the look, and she knew how vulnerable CJ could be when he acted on impulse. She knew she needed to get him to focus on something other than revenge. "It's amazing what kind of stuff surfaces when you dump your wife," said Julie, hoping that CJ wasn't about to lose sight of the fact he was tracking a murderer. "Maybe Hampoli and his wife should kiss and make up. Bet it would cut down on his appearances in the Pueblo papers. Maybe that's what we should do too, kiss and make up with the TBP."

Julie's TBP reference broke CJ's trance. He added the tidbit about Johnny Telano's demolition expertise to his growing list of connections between the Juneteenth bombing and LeRoy Polk and rubbed the sore knot above his eye. Then he pulled the ticket out of his pocket and handed it to Julie. "Pay this. We'll have to figure out another way to get Cicero his water." As they moved to go inside, CJ added, "You know, Julie, the way you dig up dirt on people, sometimes I think you should be working for *60 Minutes*."

Julie smiled at the backhanded compliment. After seven years of working with CJ she knew the remark was as close as he could come to telling her she had done a good job.

CJ spent the next five minutes in his office on the phone with Mavis, who told him Willis had developed a bronchial infection and she was headed out the door to University Hospital. Her soft, sad voice echoed on the other end of the line as if it were coming from inside a tunnel.

"I'll try to come by this evening after I leave Mabel's," said CJ.

"Has another one of Mabel's worthless tenants refused to cough up the rent?"

CJ hesitated for a moment before answering. "No. Mabel fixed gumbo."

"Enjoy," said Mavis. "I've got to run; see you later."

CJ recradled the receiver, controlling the urge to get up right then and head for Pueblo after Johnny Telano. Calming down, he shoved a pile of failure-to-appear warrants, normally his bread and butter, to one side of his desk. Then he called an old navy friend who was now a Denver bomb-squad sergeant to see if he could get any new information on the Juneteenth bombing.

"Shit, the brass have a lid on this Juneteenth thing tighter than Dick's hatband," said the gravelly-voiced sergeant after he and CJ exchanged a few pleasantries. "The only thing I can tell you for sure is that the bomb was crude and it was triggered by a remote. It's a wonder the damn thing worked." There was a pause while CJ listened to the sergeant dress down some subordinate. When he returned to the line, his desire to be informative had waned. "Remember, CJ, you didn't get a damn thing from me. See you at a Rockies game." He slammed down the receiver.

CJ sat back in his chair and lit up a cheroot. A remote trigger meant the bomber had probably been at the scene, watching to see if their Tinkertoy had worked. Even with the new knowledge that Hampoli's man Johnny Telano had been a navy demolitions expert, something about the bombing still didn't fit. He laid his cheroot in the black-lacquered 42nd River Patrol Group's tenth reunion souvenir ashtray on his desk and was watching the smoke rise toward the ventilation grate in the ceiling when Julie walked in to announce that she was going to take a late lunch. "When you get back, run a check on that guy Telano for me. Find out if he was a navy SEAL." CJ picked up his cheroot and took a long drag.

"Done," said Julie, looking at the pile of skip warrants and unreturned phone calls on CJ's desk. As he headed out the door, she wondered when things were going to return to normal.

CJ checked his watch. He had almost a full afternoon to work on the LeRoy Polk case before his dinner date with Tyrone and Mabel. That gave him time to drop in on someone he knew who had tenuous ties to Denver's old-time organized crime. He finished his cheroot, watching as Julie's fire-engine-red Honda Civic eased backward past the bay window of his office and down the driveway. Then, shaking his head, he shoved the pile of papers he had moved earlier back to the middle of his desk, stood up, and walked out.

CJ's one solid connection to what remained from the glory days of people like Toastmaster Richie Dupree was a seventy-three-year-old curmudgeon named Mario Satoni who ran a secondhand furniture store in north Denver and smoked the foulest-smelling cheap cigars CJ had ever run up against. Satoni lived in a drab brown bungalow in the middle of an industrial park where, over the years, he had managed to stash a cellarful of boxes of vintage, mint-condition license plates that made a collector like CJ drool. Among the hundreds of other things Satoni hoarded that CJ collected were movie posters, occupied-Japan ceramics, and a serious cache of Depression glass.

The first time they met, Satoni had sold CJ a 1913 Deer Trail Colorado municipal license plate that CJ had been searching for for years. CJ had paid him $500, though they both knew it was worth twice that. As Satoni wrapped the plate in newspaper for CJ, he had explained the reason for the bargain price. "I'm old, and I don't want my merchandise going to my asshole disbarred lawyer nephew who tells people I'm a gangster and spends his afternoons counting the days till I croak." Since their initial meeting CJ had purchased six license plates from Satoni in his effort to complete his collection of first of state issues from every state in the United States and finish off his Colorado municipality collection.

CJ's passion for collecting American memorabilia wasn't limited to license plates. He had one of the finest collection of cat's-eye marbles in the West. When people asked him why he collected things, he always told them it was for the same reason he bounty hunted: the thrill of the chase. But deep down CJ knew he surrounded himself with his handpicked treasures in order to fill the void of never having been treasured himself.

The drive from his office to Satoni's house in north

Denver's warehouse district took CJ fifteen minutes. He hadn't called ahead because he knew that Satoni, who ran his life like an old-time railroad schedule, locked the doors of his furniture store each day promptly at four-thirty and returned home by five. It was five forty-five when CJ nosed the Bel Air to a stop behind Satoni's classic '53 Buick Roadmaster. On the drive over he had been thinking about how to ask Satoni what he knew about Larry Hampoli without becoming the object of a string of the kind of obscenities Satoni usually reserved for his nephew.

Satoni was one of only a handful of Denver's remaining "papa bears," native Coloradans who in the late forties had helped people like Toastmaster Richie Dupree settle into Colorado and set up their organized crime infrastructure by introducing them to the right people and telling them who might play their kind of ball and who wouldn't. The papa bears had always been careful to stay clear of any frank underworld involvement themselves.

A layer of thin cirrus clouds filtered the sun as CJ headed for Satoni's back entrance. "I don't like people looking at who or what I've got comin' and goin'; always use the back," Satoni had told him after their first transaction. Satoni was hosing down his grass when CJ closed the rickety backyard gate behind him. He was wearing faded yellow Bermuda shorts, and his ghostly white, spindly legs announced that the shorts were an uncommon part of his garb. An antique cowbell attached to the gate alerted Satoni. It took him nearly a minute to find his sunglasses, put them on, and bring CJ into focus. "Calvin," he said, smiling. He never called CJ by his initials. Too new-world, he had told CJ once. "Come on in. I thought you might be the TBP." He started unscrewing the nozzle off the hose. "I gotta start keepin' that gate locked. You know, I water an hour every day," he said with a snicker.

"It shows." CJ was amazed at the lushness of Satoni's lawn.

Satoni shuffled over to the water faucet, turned it down, and left the hose trickling in the middle of the grass. "Hell, they won't see a trickle, and if they do I'm just a shriveled-up old man who forgets what day he can water—fuck 'em." He rubbed his hands on his shorts, then walked over and shook hands with CJ. "What brings you up my way?" He expected CJ to ask him if he had any new license plates, and knowing that he had two newly ac-quired gems that CJ would fawn over for hours, he was ready to dicker.

"I'm here on different business than usual, Mario." CJ tried unsuccessfully to sound as nonthreatening as pos-sible.

Satoni was as perceptive as an animal being stalked. His eyes narrowed, and the hint of a frown creased his forehead. "Hope it's not about the kind of business my asshole nephew swears I'm in."

"Afraid so," said CJ. "Need to know a little about Lawrence Hampoli."

Satoni clamped a thumb and two fingers over his lips. "Damn, Calvin, are you for real?" Satoni dropped his hand.

"As this bandage over my eye." CJ patted the ban-dage.

Satoni focused on the bandage for the first time and thought for a moment before clamping his thumb and fin-gers back in place. He liked CJ and considered him a man of dignity. In all their dealings, CJ had never once treated him as if he were a rancid old prune, the way other people did, including his family. CJ had always paid in cash, and they had the same taste in classic cars from the fifties. But this time CJ was pressing him to the edge.

He dropped the hand again reluctantly. "I'll be brief. That way I ain't givin' and I ain't takin'. Above all, I ain't stepping on any loyalties." He paused, looked CJ straight in the eye, and said, "Stay the fuck out of Hampoli's way. He'll cut off your nuts."

"That bad."

"Or worse."

"He got any backup?" asked CJ, expecting Satoni to name Johnny Telano.

"A hot-wired, gorilla-looking lunatic, name of Johnny Telano, with a chest like an ape and arms as long as an orangutan, sweeps up for him."

"Anything else?"

Satoni frowned at the request. "Nothin' I can talk to you about."

CJ tucked the information in the self-preservation compartment in his head. Knowing not to push Satoni any further, he said, "Got any license plates for me to look at?"

Satoni smiled. "Now you're askin' the right kind of question. Let's go inside and have a look. This could be your lucky day."

CJ followed Satoni toward the door that led to the basement of his house as his thoughts turned to how he was going to approach Hampoli and Johnny Telano without being castrated. He held the screen door open while Satoni fumbled with a wad of keys the size of a tennis ball. On the way down to the cellar, CJ decided that Hampoli and Telano posed enough of a threat that he needed someone to cover his own unprotected rear. As soon as he left Satoni's he planned to call his friend Billy DeLong up in Baggs, Wyoming, and tell him to bring his rough-cut cowboy butt down to Denver. It looked like he was going to need some help.

Sixteen

CJ stopped at a phone booth in front of Leckman's Ball Bearing Warehouse half a block down the street from Mario Satoni's and called Billy DeLong. He had just paid Satoni $450 for the most perfect Minneapolis, Minnesota, municipal license plate he had ever seen. The alabaster-white porcelain on gunmetal-gray iron, license plate number 36, was now wrapped in newspaper and bubble wrap, and he carried it tucked under his arm like a child unable to part with his security blanket. When he dialed Billy's number in Baggs and got an answering machine, he nearly choked. Billy wasn't the kind of man who would spring for such space-age communications hardware. A reclusive, one-eyed, hard-as-nails Wyoming cowboy living in a teetering line shack on the side of a mountain hardly needed an answering machine. But CJ left a message for Billy to get his butt to Denver as quickly as he could, signing off with, "It's time to cover my ass again."

Still smiling at Billy's unexplained excursion into the world of telecommunications, he fumbled around in his pocket until he found a quarter and called Clothilde Polk to tell her he was having dinner with Mabel and Tyrone. Since Clothilde was certain that either Tyrone or Mabel had killed her father, CJ wanted to find out if she had uncovered any additional information that might point a finger at either of them. He also wanted to know if Clothilde had had a visit from the cops, in order to gauge how far he needed to stay out of their wake. Vanetta Ebson answered the phone. The unmistakable sounds of building construction in the background muted her voice, but not enough to tone down a perfunctory, distrusting "Oh" when CJ announced who he was. "I'll get her," Vanetta said protectively when CJ asked to speak to Clothilde.

Clothilde came to the phone, sounding out of breath. "Yes," she said curtly, as though she were trying to give some pesky salesman the brush-off.

"How are you doing? Are the cobwebs gone since the bombing?"

"Everything's fine. What do you need?"

CJ didn't need a third cold response. He decided to get to his reason for calling. "I've got a meeting with Tyrone and Mabel this evening to flesh a few things out. Anything new on your end that might help me out?"

"No, just do your job. One of them will admit they killed Daddy in the end."

It was the same song Clothilde had been singing all along, except that now she sounded almost blasé, as if her father's murder had taken place twenty years ago and the killers were already serving time. CJ wanted to tell Clothilde she was still wrong about Mabel, but recalling his uncle's old axiom, *Don't duke it out with your clients,* he swallowed the urge and decided that for the moment he'd be a good soldier. "Have the cops been around to talk to you yet?"

"Twice. They move faster than I thought. I suggest you do the same or I'll have to ask for my money back. No use paying privately when their service is free."

CJ came as close to biting his lip as he had in years. The day before, Clothilde had been vengeful, blubbering over her father's death, begging for his help. Now she was ready to cuddle up to the criminal justice system. Her pronouncements not only caught him off guard, they made him nervous.

"Do what you have to." CJ felt the weight of the $450 license plate tugging at his arm as he wondered what he'd do if he had to return any of Clothilde's money.

Sounding slightly less threatening but just as dogmatic, Clothilde responded, "I've got a business to run; I gave you a timetable from the start. Get with it. I expect results," and then hung up.

CJ stood dumbfounded, clutching the receiver in his hand, thinking that either Clothilde had been watching too many old movies where the killer comes out of the woodwork screaming *I did it! I did it!* or she was now up to her sassy neck in the business of trying to keep her father's Stax of Wax boondoggle afloat, and his murder had become a second-tier problem. CJ wasn't sure which answer applied, but he found it ironic that the prospect of going broke might have suddenly changed Clothilde's point of

view about what was important. CJ hung up the receiver
and then fished in the coin return for his quarter. As he
walked back to the Bel Air coinless, he kept thinking
about Clothilde's abrupt about-face, wondering if she was
holding back something important or maybe even setting
him up.

CJ headed for Clyde Simkins's Five Points cut-rate
package store to buy wine for dinner at Mabel's thinking
that there could be another reason for Clothilde's sudden
flip-flop; a reason that included the possibility that she
might somehow have been involved in her father's murder,
and she now needed someone like CJ between her and
Hampoli. The idea left its own grainy, low-budget film
imprint on CJ's consciousness.

The only reason a bottom-feeding ne'er-do-well like
Clyde Simkins had a food service and retail liquor license
was that his brother Zek, a building contractor and Dem-
ocratic precinct whip, had been delivering the Five Points
ethnic vote to Mayor Wiley for years. Clyde called the
hole-in-the-wall liquor store and pizza joint, where he
served the stringiest cardboard-tasting pizza in the state,
Simkins's Double Crust Pizza & Beer. He managed to stay
in business serving up his tasteless, rubbery concoctions
only because 90 percent of the beer, wine, and liquor he
sold was stolen.

CJ pulled into one of the half-dozen parking spaces
lining the south side of the chartreuse cinder block building that Clyde and Zek had built fifteen years earlier with
materials Zek had pilfered from city construction jobs.
He turned the engine off and looked up Welton Street as
he listened to the end of a Z. Z. Hill tape, humming
along briefly as Z.Z. lamented in his raspy trademark

bluesy baritone that his wife was leavin' 'cause he was "nursin' the needs of too many other women on the side."

Welton Street was deserted except for an orphaned white late-model Ford parked up the street in front of Mae's. In the wake of the Juneteenth bombing, the normal late afternoon Five Points bustle and street-corner chatter had given way to a fear and sadness that had CJ worried. The restaurant that had been not only a neighborhood gathering place but a home away from home for him all his life was now a bombed-out shell, and even though he knew that Willis and Mavis were insured and Mae's would be rebuilt, he wondered if things would ever be the same.

Mae's had never been much to look at, no more than a long, narrow box along the lines of a New Orleans shotgun house. It was the first place CJ had ever paid any attention to Mavis. When he was thirteen, on an early fall day, his uncle had sent him pedaling his JC Higgins from the office to Mae's to pick up two catfish-and-collard dinners and a sweet-potato pie.

Mavis, who had seen him ride up and whose head barely cleared the countertop, rang him out at the cash register and asked him how he planned to balance his dinners and a sweet-potato pie while pedaling home. Somehow he managed, but it was another thirty years before he and Mavis were able to balance their own relationship.

He had been at Mae's for sad affairs after funerals and at celebrations following weddings, and his uncle had thrown a welcome-home dinner there when CJ came back from his second Vietnam tour. There was no way CJ could imagine Five Points without Mae's.

The Z. Z. Hill tape came to an end. A van pulled up beside CJ, and two teenagers, one in dreadlocks and the other with a woolly eagle's nest of hair, got out and headed for the front door of the Double Crust. CJ followed them to the corner of the building, where he stopped to look again up an empty Welton Street toward Mae's. The restaurant and the two buildings on either side of it, the Rossonian Club and Benny Prillerman's Trophy and Badge, were still cordoned off. Two white men in dark suits were surveying the damage. They could easily have been mistaken for insurance men or lawyers, but when one of them reached through the open window of the Ford parked out front and pulled out a spiral notebook, exposing his shoulder holster, CJ knew they were cops. As he watched the man leaf through the notebook and jot something down, CJ wondered just how intensely the police were planning to investigate the Juneteenth bombing. He expected that whether the probe turned out to be superficial or deep, sooner or later his name would pop up in some policeman's notebook.

He headed into the Double Crust, trying to remember whether Mabel preferred cabernet or merlot. He and the two teenagers were the only customers. CJ watched the teenagers move slowly up and down the liquor aisles. Their darting eyes made him follow their movements. The fact that their hands never left their pants pockets made him nervous. Clyde Simkins was standing at the checkout counter, viewing the teens through three strategically placed convex shoplifter mirrors and a video camera. Clyde glanced intermittently at the video and then at the illegal sawed-off twelve-gauge he kept beneath the cash register. Still uncertain of Mabel's wine preference, CJ selected a bottle of cabernet and a bottle of merlot and headed for the checkout.

Clyde was still eyeing the video monitor when he walked up. He shot a quick glance at the bandage on CJ's forehead. "What you celebratin', CJ? Mavis finally giving you the time of day?" His eyes barely left the camera.

"Mabel's gumbo," said CJ, glancing back at the two teenagers, who had now disappeared behind a Mogen David display.

"Fuckers better not get frisky." Clyde shot another quick glance toward his twelve-gauge. "Thirty bucks even." He slid a paper bag out from the middle of a six-inch-high stack beside him and tapped the rest of the bags back into place.

Knowing that Clyde's regular customers always got their prices rounded to the lowest dollar and that Clyde never added tax, CJ figured he was a couple of bucks ahead for the night. He handed Clyde two twenties and looked toward the back again. The two teenagers still hadn't come out from behind the display.

"Funny thing you should drop by this evening," said Clyde, sliding a ten back across the counter and sounding as if he had just remembered something important. "Couple of cops were in here earlier askin' about you. Wanted to know if I saw you on Welton anytime close to when Mae's blew. Told 'em the only thing I saw was folks haulin' ass. Thought you'd like to know."

"Any boys in blue I'd know?" asked CJ, trying to determine if the inquiry had come from downtown or the precinct.

"Never seen 'em before. But I'm guessin' these boys was from pretty high up. No uniforms or such; you know the kind I mean—button-down collars, shiny wingtips."

"Did they ask you anything else?"

Clyde cocked his head to one side and was stroking his chin in contemplation when he glanced at the video monitor and saw one of the teenagers fumbling for something in his back pocket. He swung his shotgun up from behind the counter so fast that the barrel almost caught CJ in the chin. CJ jumped away from the counter, back arched, as if he were trying to avoid a roundhouse upper-cut.

"Get your asses out where I can see 'em," boomed Clyde, aiming the sawed-off barrel squarely at the Mogen David display. "Now, or I'll turn you into fuckin' potted meat."

The two boys emerged from behind the cardboard display, grinning sheepishly. "You got fifteen seconds to have your skinny Rastafarian asses out of here."

The two boys looked at one another. The one with the bird's nest of hair stood his ground, staring defiantly at Clyde. When the safety on the shotgun clicked off, both boys were through the door in a matter of seconds. Clyde kept his shotgun up at the ready, aimed at the front door, for a good thirty seconds before lowering the weapon to the countertop. He looked at CJ and shook his head. "Too many baby cockroaches infectin' our society today. It's a damn shame." Then, as if the incident had never happened, he added, "The cops did ask me where they could find Dittier Atkins and Morgan Williams. I told 'em Dittier and Morgan was street bums; their guess was as good as mine. That was it. They didn't say no more. Just up and left." He slid the shotgun off the countertop and put it away.

"Thanks for the info." CJ swept his two bottles of wine off the counter.

"Need a sack?" Clyde eyed the bag he had teased out earlier.

"No," said CJ, swinging a bottle in each hand and heading for the door.

"Later." Clyde was now back to eyeing the video camera even though there wasn't another soul in the store.

Some habits are hard to break, thought CJ as he walked out the door into the twilight.

Seventeen

On the drive over to Mabel's from the Double Crust, CJ kept thinking, *What the hell's thirty bucks? Mabel's family.* A layer of broken clouds filtered the fading sunlight into beams that ricocheted off the Bel Air's hood, and the evening heat radiated off the asphalt like southern swamp gas. CJ was halfway down California Street when he caught sight of the flashing blue and orange lights on top of a police cruiser parked in front of Mabel's. At first the cruiser didn't strike him as unusual, since the police were a common sight around Tibbits Park. But when he spotted a cop coming out of Mabel's front door, a knot formed in the back of his throat. He eased the Bel Air up behind the police cruiser. Forgetting about the wine on the front seat, he jumped out of the car and headed for the house. When he reached the front steps, he realized that Tyrone was standing on the porch talking to a black cop for whom CJ had as much use as an infected toenail, Sam Glenn.

Tyrone looked as if he had just had the wind knocked out of him and couldn't catch his breath. He gulped a mouthful of air, and he and Glenn simultaneously looked down the steps at CJ.

"Come on up and join the party," said Glenn, motioning like a traffic cop. "Heard you'd be coming. Nice patch," he added, eyeing the bandage on CJ's forehead.

CJ took the steps two at a time, ending up on the cramped porch sandwiched between a fidgeting Tyrone and the tall, lanky Glenn. An overpowering smokehouse smell emanated from Glenn's uniform, telling CJ that Glenn had eaten at Poppa Loomis Kinnard's Bar-B-Q sometime that day.

"She's dead," said Tyrone, staring right through CJ, without noticing CJ's bandage.

CJ clenched his teeth until his jaws popped. For him, Mabel Pitts had been more than just some colorful Five Points gospel-loving old woman. She had seen him through the roughest of times, especially during his teens. Mabel had been the closest thing to a mother he had ever known. She had encouraged him to come to grips with the kinds of nurturing failures that too often untrack a man for life. It was Mabel who had convinced him that his uncle, lush though he was, had raised him the best he knew how and that above all, the old man was family. Mabel had always been there to add a sense of stability to his life. A week earlier as they were having a meal at Mae's, he remembered her being in one of her advice-giving moods. "You're forty-five now, Calvin; better close the loop on your relationship with Mavis. If you don't water it, it's gonna die or get planted in somebody else's pot," she had told him. CJ cleared his throat and swallowed, releasing the tension on his jaws. "What happened?" He stared at Sam Glenn, his eyes pleading for an answer.

Glenn was about to say *None of your business,* and he would have if Tyrone hadn't been standing next to him. Glenn and CJ shared grievances that went back to their high school gym-rat days. In deference to Tyrone, Glenn buffered his animosity. "Somebody cut her bad. Somebody with one hell of an aim." Pausing before delivering his punch line, he looked CJ up and down and added, "This your first trip out here tonight?"

Ten years earlier CJ would have shoved Glenn backward down the steps, but he had gotten better at restraining his temper. He also knew that District Three cops always traveled in pairs, and he didn't want to give whoever was probably inside the house a reason to come out shooting. "You're a fuckin' credit to your race, Sam. Yeah, this is my first time by tonight. Got any more dumb-ass questions?"

"Don't fluff your feathers with me, CJ. I can make this easy, or Sergeant Fuller inside can make it hard." The hint of a smile formed at the corners of Glenn's mouth.

CJ rolled his eyes in disgust. Fuller, a six-foot-four, two-hundred-fifty-pound water buffalo of a white man, was an old-school, streetwise cop who could be a lot meaner than he had to be if you pushed him. CJ knew that whenever a politically well-connected detective sergeant like Fuller hitched a ride with a lowly precinct cop like Glenn, it was because he had orders from higher up. The smile on Glenn's face broadened.

"Can I go inside?"

"No. You can cool your heels right here till Fuller comes out."

Feeling helpless, CJ turned to Tyrone. "What time did you get here?"

Tyrone swallowed hard, fighting back the tears. "A little past six-thirty. The house was open. I walked right past her at first." He paused and inhaled deeply. "There was so much blood."

Before Tyrone could say anything else, Sergeant Fuller ducked his beefy head beneath the doorjamb. When he saw CJ his eyes lit up and the dark, baggy circles beneath his eyes began jiggling. "Well, I'll be. I leave the precinct in search of Denver's most famous bail bondsman of color on a purely different matter, and lo and behold I stumble across him at the scene of a murder. Ain't that a kick."

Squeezed between Fuller's bulk, Tyrone's shaking, and Sam Glenn's barbecue odor, CJ felt claustrophobic. The look of surprise on his face forced Fuller into a full, toothy grin. "Guess I should explain myself. Since Five Points isn't my normal turf, Officer Glenn here's been helping me interview people who might have had a connection to the bombing at Juneteenth. Believe it or not, you were pretty close to being next on my list. The way I hear it, you and Tyrone's sister were right at center court when Mae's blew."

"Thought you were here to deal with a murder," said CJ, ignoring Fuller's preamble.

"I'm here doing my job, Floyd. We got dispatched here as the closest car to a crime scene. That's my reason. What the hell's yours?"

CJ glanced over at Tyrone before answering. "We were invited to dinner."

"What time?"

"Seven."

Fuller checked his watch. "You always show up half an hour late for your dinner dates?"

"I stopped off to buy some wine."

"Where?"

"Clyde Simkins's."

"Guess you were shopping for bargains."

When CJ didn't respond, Tyrone answered instead. Tiny bubbles of spittle had accumulated at both corners of his mouth. "My mother's been murdered, and you're here playing twenty questions with us as if we had something to do with it. How about finding out what really happened?"

Fuller had no real reason to believe that CJ or Tyrone had been involved in Mabel's murder, but he had half a dozen reasons to grill CJ about the bombing at Mae's. "Why don't you take Mr. Polk's statement," he said, turning to Glenn. "Floyd, follow me inside. We'll have a little chat while I'm waiting on the boys from the coroner's office." He ducked back under the doorjamb, nodding for CJ to follow. "And don't touch a goddamn thing."

Once they were in the hallway, CJ heard noises coming from the living room, and he suspected that a police criminalist must have already shown up. He knew Fuller would never have allowed him to set foot inside the house unless the investigator in the living room had given him clearance. He also knew police procedure well enough to realize that he and Tyrone were being interviewed separately in order to see if their statements meshed. He still hadn't figured out why a homicide cop like Fuller would be out nosing around about the June-teenth bombing when no one had been killed. Then he remembered that for years when Mayor Wiley was a councilman, Wiley, Fuller, and Winston Dunn had played Police Athletic League basketball together. Fuller was a skilled detective who knew every precinct in the city like the back of his hand. He had probably been sent out on a little side job to beat the bushes for bombing suspects and take the heat off the mayor.

"I'll get back to the business here in a minute. First I want to know why you ended up thirty feet from that explosion at Juneteenth," said Fuller.

"Why so many questions about a bombing with no fatalities? Thought you were a homicide cop. Somebody got you dancing for your supper?"

Fuller jammed his forearm across CJ's neck, forcing him back against the wall, leveraging his weight into CJ's windpipe until he could barely breathe. "Cut the finger-pointing crap, Floyd. I know you're working for Clothilde Polk. Her daddy's case is in a folder some-where in my pile of slush, and we've already talked to her twice. If you think I'm as dumb as the lowlifes you dick around with every day, think again. I know all about LeRoy Polk, and I know he was friendly with the kind of people that wouldn't think twice about doing a facelift on your girlfriend's restaurant, especially if they figured it would send you and that daughter of his a message to back off. If there's any finger-pointing to be done, I'm the one who'll do it, got that?" He removed his elbow, leaving CJ gulping for air.

Fuller dusted off his sleeve while CJ caught his breath, but he stayed right in CJ's face. "I've got two people dead, and both of them jigsaw right up to you and Ms. Polk. To top it off, the victim here is Polk's ex-wife. There's a bad smell coming from you and that Polk woman, Floyd. A real bad smell. I'll find out how the two of you are tied to that bombing and the murders soon enough." He smiled, finally stepping away.

CJ was breathing almost normally, thankful that he had quit carrying a weapon full-time. A petite black woman in uniform stepped into the hallway from the living room. She was carrying an oversized black valise in one hand and a clear plastic bag in the other. CJ couldn't make out the bag's contents. "Done in the living room," she said, directing her response to Fuller but staring at CJ. Content that Fuller had things under control, she shrugged matter-of-factly and moved on. "The coroner can wrap up in there," she called back, disappearing into the kitchen.

"How about letting me take a look in the living room?" asked CJ. "I'd like to pay my respects."

"Read about it in the papers, Floyd. This is as far as you go." Fuller had finally pushed the wrong button. CJ started toward the living room.

He took three steps before Fuller hooked him with his right arm and slammed him into the wall. "Don't push me, Floyd. I haven't forgotten about that sugar-plum-fairy job you pulled on me last year, withholding information about that Mathison girl and her band of environmental kooks. Count that as the last time you dance around me. This time we're all traveling in the same boat. Now, how about giving me a nice military-style about-face and heading back outside. When I'm done here I'll be back out so we can chat some more."

CJ's jaw muscles had turned to rock-hard knots, and his stomach was gurgling in an adrenaline rush of frustration. Knowing that Fuller had no official reason to detain him, he looked past him toward the living room and thought about the odds of making it to the end of the hallway before Fuller had him for dessert. Instead of acting out his frustration, he thought about all the times when he was a teenager that Mabel Pitts had told him, *You're a colored boy, CJ, mind your manners in the face of the man.* Deciding that he and Fuller could settle up later, he shot Fuller the kind of look that said *Kiss my ass*, pivoted, and started back toward the door. The muscles in his face were twitching and the same foggy, lost-soul look that had haunted him for the first six months after he returned stateside from Vietnam was plastered on his face. A strange mixture of memories, ranging from the noise of machine-gun fire peppering the hull of the *Cape Star* to the sound of Mabel Pitts's soothing, worldly voice, played themselves over in his head. Once he was outside on the porch he stared as if hypnotized toward the entrance to Tibbits Park until Tyrone touched him cautiously on the shoulder and broke the spell.

"You okay?"

CJ looked up California Street toward a slowly approaching medical examiner's station wagon. "Yeah, I'm fine."

"Feel like I'm on trial." Tyrone nodded toward Sam Glenn, who was standing at the curb awaiting the station wagon. "That cop down there asked me every question in the world but whether or not I had two nuts."

"Don't take it personal. Glenn's just a chauffeur for the big bull inside. Start to worry when Fuller wants a piece of your hide."

The station wagon parked directly in front of the house and a rangy-looking man got out on the passenger side, opened the back doors, and pulled out a collapsible stretcher, grunting as the legs snapped down into place.

"Let's get off this porch," said CJ. They walked down the steps onto the sidewalk and toward the street, veering into the front yard to let the stretcher by. The two men carried the stretcher up the stairs and disappeared inside the house.

Tyrone dug a handkerchief out of his pants pocket and blew his nose. CJ swallowed repeatedly, fighting back tears. They watched as Sam Glenn prepared to deal with a cluster of nosy onlookers who had moved out of the park and were easing their way toward the house.

When they brought Mabel's body out, CJ forced himself to look the other way and lit up a cheroot. The lanky man from the coroner's office stopped and said something to Tyrone, and the next thing CJ heard was the rear panel doors of the station wagon slamming shut. When he looked back around, the station wagon was pulling away.

"How about a drink?" said CJ, staring into nowhere, crushing out his partially smoked cheroot on the sidewalk.

"Sounds good," said Tyrone.

Sam Glenn was busy moving the onlookers off the lawn back toward the street.

"Hey, Glenn," said CJ as he and Tyrone started toward the Bel Air.

Glenn looked back without answering.

"Tell Fuller that if he needs me he can try my office, and if I'm not there he can check for my whereabouts in the newspaper. He'll understand."

Glenn hadn't been instructed to detain CJ, so he assumed CJ was being his usual smart-ass self. He continued moving the crowd off the lawn without responding.

"Did Sergeant Fuller want you to stick around?" asked Tyrone.

"Yeah, and people in hell want ice water," said CJ as they got into the Bel Air.

Eighteen

Clothilde hated visiting the drafty old Safeway building at night. Her late-night excursions always conjured up disturbing images of being trapped in an abandoned airport hangar in some grainy 1940s film noir. The temporary lighting wire looping from the high, arching rafters cast a net of menacing shadows across the floor, and she felt as though she were transgressing in an Egyptian tomb. She eased her way between two stacks of lumber, motioning for Vanetta, who disliked being there as much as Clothilde did, to follow.

"After dark this place gives me the creeps," said Vanetta, catching her skirt on the edge of a jutting four-by-six. "Shit." She reached down to check whether her skirt was torn. Satisfied that it was intact, she followed Clothilde over to a large plywood table that was covered with blueprints. Some had been flattened out; others were still scrolled. "What makes you think they're ripping you off?"

"I'm not sure. Just a funny feeling I have," said Clothilde. "That and the fact that I don't trust Tyrone." She flipped through several pages of blueprints. "Greek to me. Blueprints were my father's area." She dusted off her hands, stepped back from the table, and surveyed the immediate area, stopping at a six-foot-high stack of drywall. "You're tall, Vanetta; count out how many sheets of drywall are in that stack over there."

Vanetta walked over to the pallet of drywall and began counting.

Clothilde pulled a crumpled invoice and a calculator out of her pocket and placed them on the table, trying her best to ignore the gridwork of shadows undulating across the tabletop. She studied the figures on the invoice for a while before she started adding up the numbers. She was halfway down the list of itemized materials when Vanetta called out, "Eighty-eight."

"Look at the edges and see if they're stamped half-inch or five-eighths."

"Half." Vanetta dusted off her hands and walked back to Clothilde.

"I knew it," said Clothilde, tapping her index finger on the invoice half a dozen times. "This invoice is for a hundred sheets of three-quarter-inch drywall. They're not only shorting us but delivering that flimsy half-inch shit. Goddamn it, I told my father not to bring Tyrone in on this deal. I knew there had to be a reason that Tyrone's been kissing that construction superintendent's butt." She refolded the invoice, slipped it into her pocket, and looked at Vanetta. "Have you paid for all the drywall yet?"

"Paid for it yesterday," said Vanetta with a shrug.

Clothilde's forehead arched into an unbecoming frown. "Damn!" The word echoed off the walls.

Clothilde gave herself a minute to cool down. "I know how to deal with Tyrone. I'll fix his little prep-school wagon."

Vanetta's eyes widened. "What about Floyd? Maybe you should tell him."

"I don't trust that street rat. Besides, I can handle Tyrone on my own."

"Then why'd you hire him?"

"To take the bullets," said Clothilde.

"Don't be so sure he'll do everything you say."

Clothilde smiled widely. "He will. I checked him out from the start. He needs the money. Besides, if things get funky, I'll charm him. My bet is he needs his testosterone tanked up just like every other man." She winked and ran her hands down her hips seductively.

"Does he know about your father's tapes?"

Clothilde shot Vanetta a look that told her she had just overstepped her bounds. "He knows what he needs to know. That I'm finishing my dead daddy's dream and that my half-brother and his mother probably killed him."

"Trust me, Clothilde; Floyd's the kind that'll dig deeper than that. He'll find out about the tapes."

"So? Even if I'm wrong about Tyrone and Mabel— and I'm not—sooner or later he'll stumble across who killed Daddy, and that's all I care about. If he doesn't, the cops will. It's always better to have two gofers humping for you than one. If CJ runs headfirst into Hampoli, so be it. He's the kind of lowlife trash Floyd's used to dealing with. Seems to me like the odds are even."

Vanetta shrugged. "I just don't want one of those ghosts from your father's past or that Mabel Pitts woman providing the two of us with cement overcoats."

Clothilde laughed. It was the insecure, thready laugh of someone who wanted to be convinced of what she was about to say. "That's not Mabel's style. Besides, the mob doesn't do that anymore, Vanetta. Nowadays everybody negotiates. And I'm betting that when push comes to shove, Hampoli and I'll be able to work out a deal before he finds out that Mabel Pitts has a duplicate set of tapes. Besides, my nest egg's locked away. Hampoli won't do anything stupid as long as I'm holding the golden eggs."

Vanetta ignored Clothilde's boastful arrogance. *A hard head makes a soft behind,* she thought, her eyes darting around the room. "Let's get out of here; this place is giving me the willies."

"Think about what it's going to look like in a month," said Clothilde, sensing Vanetta's agitation.

"Then's then—now's now—let's go."

Clothilde looked at her lanky, bespectacled companion and smiled. "It'll be okay," she said, suddenly feeling sorry for Vanetta. Her father had hired Vanetta away from a mundane bookkeeping job with the promise that when Stax of Wax and his rhythm and blues museum were finished she would be in charge of an accounting staff of seven. She wanted to move up in the accounting world, and Clothilde knew that Vanetta hadn't hired on to become a bodyguard or a sleuth. Vanetta was full of idiosyncracies. She was a squeamish vegetarian because, as she saw it, "Chickens, cows, and fish either peck at, eat, or swim around in their own feces," and she couldn't tolerate consuming anything that did that. Loud noises frightened her, and, surprisingly for someone working for an old R&B kingpin like LeRoy Polk, she didn't much like music, especially R&B. She kept Mace at her Curtis Park apartment and in her car and purse, and she had attended the Denver downtown YWCA's self-defense school twice in one month. Clothilde wasn't the least bit surprised that a rawboned, rough-around-the-edges woman like Vanetta was overly suspicious of everyone and perpetually scared.

As they made their way out of the building, a new web of construction shadows followed them across the floor. The shadows seemed to be gaining on them until Clothilde flipped off the lights near the entrance and they disappeared.

Nineteen

CJ wasn't sure what psychological demons had driven him to plop in his funkiest-sounding Z. Z. Hill tape and take off up the hairpin curves of the Lookout Mountain road in the Bel Air at eleven at night. But he knew he had been drawn there by a force that was pushing him to pause and reflect.

His view of Denver from the Lookout Mountain scenic marker pull-off was spectacular. Millions of kilowatts of electricity illuminated a Front Range Rocky Mountain basin that 120 years earlier had been nothing more than a backwater trading outpost at the confluence of the South Platte River and Cherry Creek. Except for Denver's brown cloud haze and the ever-expanding parade of lights into the plains, the view hadn't changed that much since CJ was in his teens. On a clear day you could still see fifty miles south to Castle Rock and make out the outline of Pikes Peak in the distance.

After leaving Mabel's, he and Tyrone had gone to the Empire Lounge on East Colfax, CJ's favorite Mexican greasy spoon, hoping to take the edge off their grief. They had ended up wolfing down four soft-shell tacos apiece, sharing a quart of Johnnie Walker, and talking about Mabel.

During the first fifteen minutes that he and Tyrone shared their cramped booth in the drab, smoky neighborhood lounge, they just stared around the room, nursing their drinks without saying more than ten words to one another. Tyrone finally opened up when CJ asked him what had made him come to Denver. "My father's grandiose scheme to rebuild Stax of Wax was the first enticer," Tyrone had said. "I was always a sucker for his hype. Right after that Mabel sent me a Christmas card with a photograph of her sitting on a horse with snow up to its withers. She looked like a snow carnival queen, and for the first time in my life I began to wonder what she was like. Up until then she had just been the woman who left me behind and lived out West. My father never said much about her except that she was as tenacious as a tick, and that I should stay clear of her at all costs. I needed to find out about her for myself."

They sat in silence for another five minutes before Tyrone said, "I only knew her briefly, but it was like she had been there all my life." He clammed up while they each polished off a couple more tacos, feeding their sorrow. Then he surprised CJ by blurting out, "I have a feeling she knew why my father was killed."

For the better part of the next half hour, CJ tried to get Tyrone to explain himself, but Tyrone only got drunker, repeating intermittently, "I think she knew. I

think she knew." When Tyrone finally stared sullenly off
into space for a solid ten minutes, CJ decided that the
dark side of Tyrone Polk's subconscious and too much
Johnnie Walker had taken over for the night, and he wasn't
going to get another word out of him if they sat there
until dawn.

CJ was still sparring with his own personal anguish
when he dropped Tyrone off at his Washington Park
apartment. Realizing how unsteady Tyrone was, he walked
him to the door. The midnight chill had them both shivering. As CJ helped him into the house, Tyrone said, "I'm
gonna try and bury her day after tomorrow." When CJ
turned to head back for the Bel Air, he knew he was
headed for Lookout Mountain.

The lights from downtown Denver blended so uni-
formly that CJ was having trouble finding a landmark that
would help him identify Five Points. After searching for
several minutes he gave up, leaned back against the Bel
Air's warm hood, and shook his arms to ward off the
mountain chill. Then, resting his palms against the Bel
Air's ten coats of collector's-edition lacquer, he thought
about the times Mabel had warned him during his unset-
tled late teens, "Don't drive drunk or like a fool in them
mountains." He fumbled around in the pocket of his vest,
pulled out his last cheroot, and smoked the sweet-smelling
cigar in silence while he watched the lights from the queen
city of the plains flicker below.

He stubbed out his cheroot knowing that now he
had to find not only LeRoy Polk's killer but Mabel's as
well. When Tyrone was coherent he'd talk to him again
about his suspicions, but he suspected that Tyrone's
pronouncements about Mabel knowing who had killed

LeRoy Polk had been precipitated by Johnnie Walker. Tired and impaired himself, CJ tried to organize a game plan in his head. First he'd go see Dr. Henry Bales and try to get the lowdown on just how Mabel had been killed. Then he'd meet with Clothilde. After that he'd head for Pueblo and pay a visit to Lawrence Hampoli. Now that Mabel had been murdered, he was certain that Clothilde needed to tell him the rest of her story. She had lured him in with crocodile tears and cash up front, but in his business half-truths could end up costing you your payday and your life.

CJ eased his 220-pound frame off the Bel Air's hood and felt a twinge of arthritic pain in his hip. He smiled and thought about Mabel Pitts's perseverance as he limped back to the car. When he turned the engine over and flicked on the headlights, a white-tailed deer darted out from the underbrush, freezing in the headlights just long enough for CJ to catch a glimpse of the startled fawn at her side. They took off down the steep embankment in front of the car, vanishing as quickly as they had appeared.

CJ drove back down the Lookout Mountain road cautiously, Mabel's warnings ringing in his ears. Forty-five minutes later he pulled into his driveway behind a battered Dodge pickup truck with Wyoming license plates. The Bel Air's headlights flooded the cab as the back of a man's head popped up in the truck's window.

"Billy," said CJ so loudly that he surprised himself. He turned off the Bel Air's engine, leaving the high-beam lights on. The truck's rusted door creaked open, and a sleepy-looking Billy DeLong stepped onto the running board. He was a little man with thick, curly black hair, a squared-off mustache that stopped right at the corners of his mouth, and cinnamon-colored skin. CJ broke into a graduation-day smile. Billy DeLong was family, and what he needed more than anything right then was family.

"Get those high beams off me. I can't see a damned thing." Billy reached back to the cab and pulled out an army duffel bag, a battered old Boy Scout canteen, and a set of binoculars.

"Come help me with this stuff," he grumbled, sounding like an army boot-camp sergeant. "Firepower's in the back." He nodded toward the truck bed.

CJ walked over to the pickup bed and looked inside. He and Billy had worked on cases and bounty hunted together before, so he knew what he'd find: a Winchester magnum, a Remington twelve-gauge riot gun, and the old wooden milk crate Billy used to steady his aim. CJ tossed the crate by the garage door and hung the two gun cases over his shoulder. He was already thinking ahead. If things worked out with Clothilde in the morning, by ten he and Billy would be on their way to Pueblo. He walked back to the Bel Air, reached inside, and turned off the lights, leaving Billy standing in the dark. He could feel the gun case straps digging into his shoulder. Looking up into the starless night, he had the eerie feeling that he was nineteen again and aboard the *Cape Star*, searching for the enemy, starting out on night patrol. As he headed for the building's back stairway, he turned back to Billy and said, "Mabel's dead."

Twenty

Damn, CJ, I'm a gene splicer, not Quincy." It was six-thirty A.M. and Dr. Henry Bales was seated to one side of the desk in his research laboratory office with his right hand deep in a sixty-four-ounce bag of Lay's potato chips and an open can of Coke in the other hand, eyeing the thirteen subcutaneous stitches above CJ's eye and thinking, *Nice work.* CJ had trashed his cumbersome bandage the previous night, telling Billy then and Henry just a few minutes ago that the bandage made him feel like a three-eyed pirate. A banana and a bottle of Centrex multiple vitamins sat in the middle of the leather blotter on Henry's desk.

"Funny," said CJ, "I could have sworn the sign on your office door said 'Henry Bales, M.D., Ph.D., World-Renowned Pathology Professor.'"

Henry dug out a handful of chips and started munching. A look of acquiescence spread across his face.

CJ was seated on one of the uncomfortable marble-gray straightbacked institutional chairs that he swore the state of Colorado ordered to keep people like him out of places like Henry's. Ten minutes earlier he had plopped down in the chair, propped his feet up on Henry's desk, and started twisting Henry's arm for help.

When he gave Henry the details of his gumbo dinner date turned to murder, his windpipe-crushing encounter with Sergeant Fuller, and the particulars of the evening he had spent nursemaiding Tyrone Polk, Henry offered CJ his usual biting critique of the way CJ earned a living.

"You muck around in a cesspool long enough, sooner or later you're bound to get a turd or two in the face."

"I know that, Henry. Right now I need some help with finding out who killed Mabel. There has to be an autopsy."

Henry could see the fire of revenge burning in CJ's eyes. "You think it was tied to the Doo-Wop Polk thing you've been working on?" He wanted to tell CJ to slow down and think before he jumped headfirst into chasing after someone who may have committed two murders. But knowing how close CJ and Mabel had been, he washed down a handful of chips with a long swig of Coke and decided to keep the advice to himself.

"Has to be," said CJ, reaching for some chips and wondering how a doctor who should know better could be slamming down a Coke and chips at that hour of the morning.

"I'll dig up what I can."

"Can you get me something before ten?"

"I'll try."

CJ bit into several greasy, shriveled chips, chewed a couple of times, then scrunched his face up. "Damn, Henry, these things are stale."

"I don't make them, CJ. I just eat them." Henry took another swig of Coke.

CJ finished chewing, swallowed, and thought about the gas he would suffer two hours from then. "One thing more: you've got a better pipeline to the police forensic lab than me. See if they'll tell you anything about that bomb that went off at Mae's. I'm looking for a connection between the bombing, LeRoy Polk, and Mabel."

Henry shook his head in disbelief at CJ's request. "Maybe I should start kissing up to the mayor so I can apply for a job as coroner. Those forensic folks aren't going to spill their guts to an ivory-tower type like me."

"Then wing it." CJ's expression was bitterly serious. It was the same kind of sober look they had exchanged each night for 364 days before they climbed into their bunks on the *Cape Star* in Vietnam.

"I'll have something for you by ten. When's Mabel's funeral?"

"Tyrone's aiming for tomorrow. Guess he doesn't want the pain to linger."

"Fast, especially with an autopsy involved. I don't think I'll be able to make it if it's that soon. Gotta go down to Durango on business."

"I understand."

Henry finished off his Coke. "I'll have the whole nine yards on how Mabel was killed and anything I can find out about the bombing for you by ten."

CJ slipped his feet off Henry's desk and got up to

leave. "Mabel was family," he said sadly, turning to walk out the door.

"I know, I know," said Henry, at a loss for words.

CJ spent the next hour and a half trying to locate Clothilde Polk. His first stop was the new Stax of Wax construction site, but the only people there were early-bird construction workers playing grabass and milling around drinking coffee in the bright mile-high morning sun. He went inside, calling out for Clothilde as he stumbled through a maze of construction materials to the back of the building, where the pallet of drywall had slammed to the floor during his first visit. Along the back wall a temporary office area was partitioned off, with a couple of desks and some chairs jammed inside. One desk was piled high with building invoices, bank statements, canceled checks, and memos to regulatory agencies complaining about the shoddy work of electricians, plumbers, and carpenters. The other desk was littered with invoices for record-store stock and purchase orders for cases of CDs, record albums, and music videos and tapes. CJ looked around for any sign that might tell him when Clothilde planned to return. When he couldn't find anything, he called her at her rented townhouse in Cherry Creek. This time he didn't even get an answering machine, just fifteen long, high-pitched rings. He was beginning to wonder why it was that every time he needed to talk to Clothilde Polk, she was nowhere to be found.

He also wondered if Clothilde knew about Mabel's murder, and decided that because of Tyrone, by now she had to. Frustrated, he gave up on trying to connect with Clothilde and headed back home to pick up Billy DeLong for their trip to Pueblo.

Billy was standing at CJ's second-floor kitchen window, curtains parted, staring down at the driveway below. He looked like a caged animal as he watched for the Bel Air's return. The thing that Billy hated most about coming to Denver from his mountainside cabin outside Baggs, aside from the fact that he always developed a ringing sensation in his ears that lasted for a month, was the closed-in feeling that descended on him as soon as he hit Denver's western suburbs. It took him weeks to shake the claustrophobic feeling once he was back in Baggs.

CJ took the back stairs up to his apartment two at a time, noticing in his haste that Julie hadn't gotten to work yet.

Before CJ could get in the back door, Billy was pressing information on him like the town crier. "Henry Bales called about fifteen minutes ago. He said to tell you sometimes things move faster than you expect. I wrote down what he had to say, word for word." Billy handed CJ a page of notes that only a handwriting expert could have deciphered.

CJ stared at the page, shaking his head. "I can't read your chicken scratch." He handed the paper back to Billy.

"Maybe you need glasses." Billy rattled the paper and brought it up to within inches of his one good eye. "I'm quotin', now. Mabel was killed by a single incisive wound to her neck with a knife that severed her left carotid artery. Something real sharp, maybe even a scalpel. Henry said it would've been one hell of a shot even for a surgeon. Accordin' to him she lost nearly three units of blood."

CJ's eyes narrowed as he rolled his tongue around his lower lip, a nervous habit from childhood that surfaced whenever he was angry and perplexed. It made sense that whoever had killed Mabel had done so hit-and-run-style while she was listening to gospel music. "What about the bombing at Mae's? Did he say anything about that?"

"Sure did." Billy checked his notes. "Said he couldn't find out much about the bomb itself, but his source thinks it was triggered by a remote usin', I'm quotin' again, high-nitrogen-content igniter."

CJ rubbed his chin. "Think it would take a demolitions expert to know about stuff like that?"

"Well, a dumbass cowboy like me wouldn't know how to do it."

CJ sat down and thought for a moment. He had two murders on his hands, and both seemed to require a working knowledge of medicine. His prime suspects were the increasingly elusive woman who had hired him and a long-armed demolitions expert and mobster he had yet to meet. He thought about what Clothilde would have had to gain by killing her father and decided once again that Clothilde had to be holding something back. Behind her mournfully sexy eyes and Southern drawl, he suspected that Clothilde was probably capable of murder. He didn't have to think so hard about Johnny Telano. He was pretty sure Johnny Telano had killed before. He had no idea whether any of LeRoy Polk's Chicago connections had the knowledge to pull off a bombing, or if they had any specialized medical knowledge. He looked up at Billy, who was standing in the middle of the room, stuffing the message he had taken from Henry Bales into his shirt pocket as if it were a coded CIA transmittal. CJ decided that he had done enough Doo-Wop Polk investigation for the morning. "I called Mavis on the way back home. She's got one hell of a breakfast waiting. On the way over to her place you can tell me why you've got a damn answering machine."

"Simple," said Billy. "I've been turnin' my silver-smithing hobby into a business. Gotta be there for the customer."

"Makes sense," said CJ, surprised at Billy's entrepreneurial skills.

As they headed for the back door, CJ looked over at Billy inquisitively. "That igniter Henry was talking about—where do you think a person could rustle some up?"

"Don't know, but I'll think about it," said Billy, bounding down the back steps.

Twenty-one

Southeastern Colorado, known affectionately as the emerald of the plains, is a picturesque slice of the American West where rolling green hills rise alongside the Arkansas River and crystal-blue lakes, reservoirs, and canyonlands still exist, somehow having managed to escape the late-twentieth-century rush to pave the planet. Not nearly as mountainous as the midstate spine of the Rockies with its imposing snowcapped fourteeners, southeastern Colorado has more in common with the Kansas plains than Aspen, and its less rugged but equally dramatic mountains have a quiet, lonesome, bucolic majesty all their own. But like the rest of the state, Colorado's southeastern corner was suffering through a drought that had produced six months of 1930s dust-bowl conditions, and the emerald of the plains was looking more like a moonscape than a paradise.

As CJ and Billy knifed their way along I-25

through a dust storm that had materialized out of
nowhere seventy-five miles south of Denver, just past
Colorado Springs, CJ began to wonder if they had
picked the wrong day to go to Pueblo and visit Larry
Hampoli.

Pueblo, a city of one hundred thousand situated at
the intersection of I-25 and U.S. Highway 50 and the
largest city in the sparsely populated southeast corner of
Colorado, started out as a hunting crossroads for the
Ute, Apache, Comanche, and Cheyenne tribes. Pueblo
has seen its share of economic boom and bust, trans-
forming from trading post to railhead to government
seat and finally emerging as a steel town during the
1940s. The city once had rolling mills that rivaled those
of Pittsburgh and Gary, Indiana, but in the 1980s the
steel industry died, almost destroying Pueblo's economic
heart and soul. Somehow Pueblo managed to survive,
and the city was now busy playing economic catch-up.

During the steel bust, Lawrence Hampoli had been
smarter than most of his business counterparts and had
shifted his criminal activities from labor union organiz-
ing and gambling to more esoteric and financially re-
warding white-collar crime. Bespectacled and balding,
with cherubic cheeks and an actor's dramatic flair, Hampoli could curse out associates until their ears burned or
just as easily pontificate professorially to anyone who
would listen. He had a passion for horticulture, winning
the city of Pueblo's Rose Society competition for the
past five years. For two decades he had operated out of a
jumbled mess of a secondhand store where a quarter

could still buy a rusty pair of pliers and $10 could se-
cure a repairable hedge trimmer with a broken switch.

Over the years, Hampoli's building on Canal Street
had survived two fires, a suspicious bombing, and an in-
festation of termites. He called the place Hampoli's
Castings and Cast-Offs and seemed to savor the fact
that his store, with its eclectic collection of odds and
ends and its location in the center of Pueblo's racially
mixed steelworkers' neighborhood, bolstered his reputation as an eccentric.

The last thing CJ had slipped in his pocket before
he and Billy had headed for Pueblo was an index card
with Hampoli's business address scrawled across it. CJ
was toying with the card, snapping back the edges, and
juggling a thermos cup full of piping-hot coffee when
they hit the desiccated outskirts of Pueblo.

"Place looks like it's been in a forest fire," said Billy,
cruising one-handed, three fingers leisurely draped over
the crest of the steering wheel. He was busy smacking on
a five-stick wad of sugarless gum. "Betcha it hasn't rained
here in a year."

"Six months, to be exact," said CJ, wondering how
much energy Billy was expending massacring the gum
wad. For most of his adult life Billy DeLong had been
an alcoholic. But eight months earlier, when he and CJ
had nearly gotten themselves killed in a shootout with a
group of environmental extremists at a remote Wyoming
ranch, Billy had sworn off alcohol. Now he consumed
five packs of gum a day as a substitute. Diabetes had
cost him the sight in his right eye, and although he never
admitted his age, CJ guessed he was somewhere in his

late fifties. He was an obstinate, wiry, tough-as-nails, opinionated cuss and one of the best old-time cowmen in the state of Wyoming. Since that first Wyoming job, Billy had backed CJ up on half a dozen other bounty-hunting excursions, and they had developed a strong loner-to-loner kind of bond.

In addition to his cowman skills, Billy was a talented silversmith. On his trips to Denver he never failed to bring Mavis Sundee one of the handmade pieces of silver jewelry he fabricated during the long Wyoming winters, and like a wise older brother he never let an opportunity pass to remind CJ that good women like Mavis needed pampering. Still furiously smacking on his gum, Billy accelerated around a semi.

CJ eyed a twelve-pack of unopened gum resting on the transmission hump. "If you don't quit killing that gum, Billy, I'm gonna toss the rest of your stash out the window."

Billy glanced in the rearview mirror to make sure he had cleared the semi and stopped chewing. "You know, CJ, sometimes you're too damned uptight. A man switches from polishing off a fifth of rum a day to enjoying a couple of sticks of gum and you give him grief. Hell, if I was white they'd run me for president."

CJ smiled, knowing how difficult Billy's transition from booze had been, and decided to drop the subject. They sped past the first three Pueblo exits until the remnants of the old CF&I steel mills rose into view. Only partially disassembled blast furnaces, blackened coke ovens, and rusting overhead cranes remained. "Turn off at Indiana; it's the next exit, then right on Spruce till you get to Canal." Billy slowed to forty-five and eased the pickup onto the off-ramp. Somewhere between thirty-five and forty the truck's front end began to shimmy.

"Damn." CJ grabbed the coffee thermos, capping it.

"Been meaning to get that front end fixed." The vibrations didn't stop until Billy slowed down to twenty-five.

Indiana Avenue was a narrow, pothole-filled thoroughfare that incised its way into the grimy ethnic bowels of Pueblo. Soot-covered houses, blackened from years of serving as the backdrop for open-hearth furnaces and coke ovens, dotted the landscape. On nearly every corner was a grocery store whose dirty windows touted ethnic delicacies, from half-slabs of ribs to pickled artichoke hearts, homemade angel-hair pasta to flan. Bars and bungalows filled the spaces in between. Only a few people were outside on the sidewalks, all looking as if they'd rather be somewhere else. Their faces ranged from tired to disapproving to just plain worn out. Children were nowhere to be seen.

Surprised at the city's dingy appearance, Billy turned north onto Spruce Street and then onto Canal. "One thing for sure, this ain't no playground for the rich and famous. What's that address again?" he said before starting back in on his gum.

"Four forty-five."

"Nothing but *F*'s." Billy shook his head. "I don't like it."

CJ laughed. "Your West Indian genes are showing, Billy. We ain't dealing with your ancestors' island kind of voodoo."

"Guess not," snapped Billy defensively. "These are your cultured European types who take blood oaths and drive around with bodies in their trunks." He slowed to a crawl, checking out the odd-numbered addresses along the west side of the street.

CJ shook his head, amazed that a man whom he had seen shoot the head off a rattlesnake from fifteen yards with an unscoped forty-year-old bolt-action .22 and disarm bond skippers twice his size with a well-placed knee to the gut would let Caribbean island superstition and half-century-old images of mobsters from the silver screen cloud his reasoning.

Hampoli's building stood out from everything around it like old-growth trees in a new-growth forest. Three stories high and the salmon color of Colorado River basin sandstone, the building radiated in the noonday heat. A twenty-by-twenty-foot flaking advertisement for Red Man Chew covered most of one side of the building, and a sign spelling out HAMPOLI'S CAST-INGS AND CAST-OFFS in Old English script formed a quarter-circle arch over the advertisement.

Billy parked in front of the building behind a black Camaro with license plates that read TEL NO 1. "Biggest thing on the damn block." He scrutinized the building's entrance and the Camaro before looking back down the street for potential problems and shutting off the truck's engine. "Should we pass ourselves off as customers or pretend we're cops and kick down the front door?" He whistled a couple of bars of the theme from *Hill Street Blues.*

"Neither," said CJ, who had turned stonefaced to

let Billy know it was time to get serious. "I've got a feeling they'll know who we are."

They exited the truck at the same time, and the truck's springs groaned loud enough to be heard half a block away. "Springs need fixin' too," said Billy, smiling.

As soon as they walked inside the building, CJ realized that he had entered what had to be the largest refuge for junk and garage-sale leftovers he had ever seen. Hundreds of bins filled with socket wrenches, doorknobs, pliers, and faucet handles in porcelain, brass, copper, and stainless steel dominated the surprisingly airy seventy-five-square-foot room.

With a collector's eye, CJ wandered around the store in amazement, enjoying the hodgepodge and clutter. Billy followed, feeling trapped in the maze of junk. CJ could have spent hours browsing, searching the cluttered shelves and bins, hoping to find a priceless piece of Americana. But he was on assignment, and he knew his own collector's passions would have to take a back seat.

When he finally stopped his wandering to examine a wooden milk carton overflowing with old ink bottles, a rotund, pear-shaped little man wearing an acid-stained shop apron and a faded chambray shirt that looked ready to disintegrate with one more washing walked up to him. "Need some help?"

Billy had picked up a pair of rusted barbed-wire stretchers. He was so busy checking the ratchet strength that he didn't hear the question.

"We're looking for Lawrence Hampoli," said CJ, caught off guard as he rolled a fifty-year-old Levinson's Blue Black Writing Fluid bottle between his palms.

The man in the shop apron frowned. "For what?"

"Business."

"You two selling something?" His question was directed to CJ, but he was looking at Billy.

"No," said CJ.

"Larry ain't here." His answer sounded rehearsed, as if he repeated it dozens of times a day.

CJ decided to be direct. "We need to see him about Doo-Wop Polk." He looked at the man for some hint that he recognized the name, but saw none.

The man shrugged his shoulders beats-me fashion as another man with the knowing look of an eavesdropper moved from around the corner of a ten-foot-high bookcase filled with bins of garden tools. "Perhaps I can help." The newcomer motioned for the man in the apron to head back to the front of the store.

The first thing CJ noted about the eavesdropper was that his earlobes sprouted bushy tufts of uneven hairs and his hands hung nearly to his knees. "You can if you're Lawrence Hampoli." He knew the man was far too young to be Hampoli.

The man leaned back against the bookcase. "I'm Mr. Hampoli's business associate, Johnny Telano. And you're . . ."

"CJ Floyd." The split-second look of recognition on Telano's face told CJ that Telano had heard his name before.

Telano turned his gaze to Billy, who was still fidgeting with the uncooperative wire stretchers. When Billy realized that Telano was waiting for him to introduce himself, he stopped chewing his gum long enough to say, "DeLong."

Pokerfaced, Telano hesitated momentarily, running Billy's name and face through his head. When nothing clicked, he finally said, "Follow me: Hamp's out back," leading them past shelving brimming with handheld band saws, Vise-Grips, drywall tape, and linoleum knives. When they reached the metal fire door in the back wall, CJ caught a glimpse of a wooden bucket filled with dozens of carpenter's levels surrounding a prosthetic leg.

Johnny Telano noted the look of surprise on CJ's face and smiled. "We deal in anything used." He ushered CJ and Billy through the back exit into the most beautiful botanical garden CJ had seen since his first R&R in Thailand. Rock gardens filled with petunias, chrysanthemums, dahlias, irises, and roses along with clusters of geometrically perfect miniature shrubs covered the quarter-acre yard as it sloped downhill toward the next street. A cobblestone walkway led to two large ponds in the middle of the yard. One featured a waterfall, the other an eight-foot-high water spout. Honeysuckle and forsythia rimmed the perimeter of the yard, masking an eight-foot-high privacy fence. Near the fence a family of mallards basked in the sun on a patch of Bermuda grass.

Lawrence Hampoli was busy pruning a curtain of ivy that extended along the entire back wall of the building. When everyone was within earshot, Hampoli looked up as if he had just received an offstage cue. "Uncooperative vine, this English ivy, always sprouting new leaves and throwing things into asymmetry." He snapped his shears closed, and a tendril of ivy dropped to the ground.

Johnny Telano waited to see if Hampoli was going to continue his pruning. It wasn't until Hampoli laid his shears down in a patch of periwinkle that Telano spoke up. "You've got some people here to see you about LeRoy Polk."

Without looking the least bit surprised, Hampoli surveyed Billy and then CJ. His gaze moved from the gash above CJ's eye back to Telano. "From?"

"Denver," said CJ, answering for Telano, to whom the question had been directed, and at the same time checking out the pruning shears to see if they were open or closed.

"Ah, I love the Mile High City. Understand you're having one hell of a drought." Hampoli looked proudly around his yard to emphasize the fact that he hadn't been affected.

"Yeah," said CJ, eager to dispose with the chitchat.

"Terrible things, droughts; they suck the lifeblood out of everything."

"Doesn't look like you're having a problem."

Hampoli laughed. It was the insipid cackle of someone well connected. "I'd never let my flowers die, Mr. . . ."

"Floyd."

Hampoli looked at Billy. "And . . ."

"DeLong."

"Good." Hampoli noted that Billy and CJ had offered only their last names. "I like to learn about a person as the relationship develops. I'm not big on lengthy introductions." He looked at Johnny, and then cast a glance toward the center of the yard. Telano immediately started down the walkway toward the two ponds.

"Why don't we have a seat." Hampoli wiped his sweat-peppered brow with the back of his hand and headed for the shade of a twenty-foot-high Colorado blue spruce just to the left of the ponds. CJ and Billy followed. Two crescent-shaped concrete benches sat in the tree's shade. Hampoli took a seat at one end of the first bench he reached, his back to the waterfall. CJ and Billy sat down on the bench next to him. Johnny Telano remained standing, behind and just to the left of Hampoli. CJ looked at Billy, adjusting his butt on the bench, and realized that Billy was still gripping the broken wire stretchers in his right hand.

"Always something you need, isn't there?" said Hampoli, looking at the wire stretcher before crossing his legs and clearing his throat. "Now, about Doo-Wop Polk. How can I be of help?"

CJ decided to be blunt. "Mr. Polk was murdered a couple of days ago up in Denver. His daughter asked me to look into it."

"So you're PIs." Hampoli's tone of voice was accusatory.

"No."

"You're not cops," said Hampoli, his brow wrinkling along the edges of an unflattering hairpiece.

"I'm a bail bondsman."

Hampoli and Telano looked at Billy almost simultaneously. When Billy didn't answer, Hampoli turned back to CJ. "Rough business cutting bonds, Mr. Floyd.

My cousin did it for a while until a Filipino client of his cut off his arm. Of course, he was a bounty hunter too," said Hampoli sarcastically.

CJ ignored the bait and looked Hampoli straight in the eye. "I'm not here to discuss job descriptions. Polk's daughter says you might have had a reason to kill her father."

The muscles around Hampoli's eyes tightened and his nostrils flared as he sat up ramrod straight. "His daughter's wrong, Mr. Floyd."

Johnny Telano shot Hampoli a glance that said, *Can I step in now?* Hampoli's steely glare told him to sit tight. "Ms. Polk seems to have fed you a line, Mr. Floyd. Did she also tell you that her father was a thief?" He paused, looking back at Johnny Telano as if he needed to assure himself that Telano wasn't about to do something foolish. "I don't suffer people who steal from me very long, but murder old Doo-Wop Polk, that would have been too harsh."

Hampoli's condescending tone told CJ that at sometime in his life LeRoy Polk had played serious step-and-fetch-it for Hampoli. CJ looked back at Telano and sensed that his insides were churning while he stood at parade rest, waiting for Hampoli to signal the punishment he would be meting out for their intrusion.

"What did old Doo-Wop Polk steal?" said CJ, thinking back to how quickly his impending poverty and Clothilde's exotic beauty had made him say yes to a job offer without so much as a second thought about whether she might be feeding him a line.

Hampoli snickered, and the front of his toupee jiggled. "Hope you don't always take your jobs on blind faith, Mr. Floyd." Then, sensing that he and CJ had played cat-and-mouse long enough, he uncrossed his legs, vigorously shaking his right leg before putting it down. "Tapes, Mr. Floyd, tapes. Doo-Wop stole some irreplaceable and very valuable studio recordings that belonged to me."

"I'm listening," said CJ.

"During the 1950s old LeRoy was what we in the record trade used to call an outtaker. He'd rent studio time on the cheap and tape songs for anybody who'd pay him the studio fee plus a ten percent commission. He recorded in the wee hours of the morning when no one else was using the studio in order to save everybody in-volved a bundle. He wasn't union, and every artist he recorded was colored. Simply put, LeRoy was a freelanc-ing scab. But he was one hell of a mixer, and he built him-self a reputation by producing high-quality tapes that were marketable, and he did it for next to nothing."

Hampoli pulled a delicate-looking white mono-grammed handkerchief from his pocket and wiped his brow before continuing. "What he didn't tell those of us who had performers under contract was that while he was doing his tapings, he always kept a few of the warmup songs—songs that would never see the light of day—for himself. Since he was only taping colored recording artists, and nobody in the mainstream business really cared about the colored market back then, he could get away with it." Hampoli's last statement was punctuated with aggravation.

CJ had shot Billy a *we better watch our asses* kind of look the second time Hampoli said *colored*.

Billy caught the signal and tightened the grip on his wire stretchers.

Hampoli didn't take notice of either communication. "It turns out that old LeRoy was either smarter or a whole lot luckier than most outtakers. He had one hell of an ear for music, and what he ended up with years later was a stockpile of master recordings by some of the most famous rhythm and blues stars in rock and roll history. There's a collector's market out there that makes those tapes quite valuable, not to mention the redistribution dollars." Hampoli's recount of how he had been ripped off had him sweating. He patted down his brow again.

"Nobody caught on to his scam?" asked CJ, hoping to extract more information.

Hampoli took special delight in what he said next. "Like I said, back then it was the cost of doing business, and if you weren't a major recording studio and you wanted to get yourself some real unadulterated R&B, you needed a shill. Sort of like the way universities recruit colored kids to play college sports today."

CJ watched Johnny Telano's face broaden into a *gotcha* kind of grin. "What's one of those outtake tapes worth?"

"Not *those* tapes, Mr. Floyd, *my* tapes. I don't know their true value because I don't know how many of them there are, and besides, it's none of your business."

"Were they worth enough for you to clock old Daddy Doo-Wop out?"

Johnny Telano fidgeted, rocking back on his heels.

A look of exasperation that said *please let me do something to shut this asshole up* spread across his face.

Hampoli didn't flinch. "I will tell you this: LeRoy Polk had more enemies than friends."

"I know about Juney-boy Stokes and Roland Jefferson and Jefferson's wife, Willette," said CJ.

"Then you must know that even after Willette and Roland were married, LeRoy was still poking her on a regular basis, and as for pathetic old Juney-boy, LeRoy not only stole his records and his royalties, he drove the poor misdirected, confused creature into having a sex change and eventually trying to take his own life. You knew LeRoy's libido ran on AC and DC current, didn't you, Mr. Floyd?"

Mabel had mentioned LeRoy Polk's sexual proclivities, but she hadn't really spelled things out, and Clothilde had flat-out omitted to say anything.

Noting the look of surprise on CJ's face, Hampoli couldn't resist offering CJ one more piece of unsettling news. "Juney-boy had his sex-change operation right down the road from here in Montcliff, about fifteen years ago. It's the sex-change capital of the U.S., in case you didn't know it. Poor thing even came up here to Pueblo to show me what modern surgery and a barrel full of hormones can do. He looked like a linebacker in drag."

"Where's Stokes now?" asked CJ, thinking ahead, trying to come to grips with which way to move his investigation.

"I never saw him again after that. He could be

dead. I know that he tried to kill himself once. Took a bunch of sleeping pills. It made the Pueblo papers."

"You seem to know a lot about what went down in Chicago's R&B world outside the business of making records," CJ said, noticing Billy taking the whole conversation in bug-eyed, as though he had just tuned in to an X-rated movie.

Hampoli broke into a lecherous, self-satisfied grin. "Always preferred the dark side of town, myself."

"Did you know Mabel Pitts?" said CJ, trying to mask the sorrow in his voice.

"Sure. She was LeRoy's first wife. Nice lady."

"She was murdered in Denver last night. Don't suppose you were up there poking around the dark side of town, by any chance."

Hampoli looked at Johnny Telano, back at CJ, and then at his watch. "Your time's up, Mr. Floyd. I need to get back to my pruning."

A look of satisfaction spread across Telano's face. "Let's go. Show-and-tell's over." He quickly walked around behind CJ and Billy. "Move it."

Neither CJ nor Billy budged. "I can understand Juney-boy Stokes and even Roland or Willette Jefferson wanting to settle things with LeRoy Polk, but why would they want to kill Mabel?" said CJ.

Hampoli ignored CJ, got up, and walked away. When CJ stood up to follow him, he suddenly felt the unmistakable nudge of a gun barrel against the back of his neck.

"Get the fuck out of here." Johnny Telano nodded for Billy to get up too as he shoved the barrel of his Colt

into CJ's neck and started ushering him toward the door
they had come through earlier.

When Billy tightened his baseball-slugger's grip on
the barbed-wire stretchers, CJ sent him a sideward glance
that said, *I wouldn't do that, Billy.*

Telano caught CJ's body language. "Drop that fucking thing, Uncle Remus, or I'll blow the snot out of your
head."

Billy relaxed his grip, and the wire stretchers fell to
the ground.

"You're two shines with balls, I'll give you that, but
you're out of your league down here. Don't come back."

Telano gestured for Billy to catch up with CJ, and
they headed toward the exit with Telano's Colt aimed
squarely at CJ's back. At the doorway CJ hesitated and
looked over at Billy. "Guess you'll have to buy your wire
stretchers somewhere else."

Billy didn't respond. He was frowning, cursing
silently under his breath, and gritting his teeth into his
wad of gum because there was nothing he hated more in
the world than losing face and being called a shine.

Twenty-two

Johnny Telano ushered CJ and Billy out the front door of Hampoli's Cast-Offs and watched them drive away. They had no way of knowing that the pear-shaped man in the shop apron had slapped a homing device beneath the right rear wheel well of Billy's truck in order to track their movements. Johnny spent the noon hour at an abandoned CF&I steel company ingot millyard burning rats. A week earlier he had spent another noon hour in the same millyard, locating the rodents' holes and tagging each one with orange iridescent paint. Burning rats was a game Johnny Telano loved dearly. It always gave him an adrenaline rush, as if he were directing a moon rocket launch. He had started burning rats as a teenager on a dare from other neighborhood kids: *Bet ya gorilla can't burn rats.* His torching methods had been honed to perfection over the years. He would plug the rodents' exits with rags, pour gasoline down their holes, light a match, and hover over the opening with a shovel, smashing the rats as they scurried for their lives.

Johnny never burned rats alone. He always called one of the half-dozen cousins he had grown up with to invite them beforehand, then nervously paced rodent territory in a frenzy of anticipation until his relative arrived. Most often it was Adolphus or Leon Mortelli, one of his mother's brother's boys, burly young men who usually sported manure-splattered overalls and who enjoyed driving the twenty-five miles into Pueblo from their parents' farm as a break from the monotony of raising pigs. Leon was his partner for the day. They started their killing slowly, missing as many rats as they hit, but soon, blood-bonds between them and a twelve-pack of Bud were enough to synchronize the sounds of the business ends of their shovels as they slammed against the earth over and over, sending rodent after rodent to its death.

As the broken bodies of rats began to pile up around a hole, Johnny and Leon kicked at the dirt in unison, a choreographed exclamation mark to their success at inflicting pain. Finally, when no more rats came out, they crouched in a long pause, tired from killing, frustrated that the game was over.

They watched the restless, flickering gasoline flames as they toyed with rat carcasses with the toes of their shoes. Johnny looked at his watch and said, "Next week should be better. I've already marked the holes."

Leon grinned, turning to leave.

Johnny grabbed his cousin's meaty arm, holding him back. "But right now I need your help with a bigger job," he added, eyeing the eighteen-wheeler Leon had driven up in. He smiled broadly as they headed toward the semitrailer filled with livestock.

When Johnny returned to Hampoli's, Hampoli was seated out back on the bench next to the waterfall, surveying his handiwork. "Look okay to you, Johnny?" he said, framing the perfectly manicured wall of ivy viewfinder-fashion between his forefingers and thumbs.

Johnny glanced at the wall. "Beautiful."

Hampoli cocked his head from side to side, unable to resist different views of his masterpiece. His earlier impeccable English had disappeared. "I told you that fucking dead coon was gonna end up causing us trouble, Johnny. I pegged it from the start." He sniffed the air. "I smell gasoline. You been out burning goddamn rats?" He shook his head in disgust.

A smile spread across Telano's face. "Don't worry about this thing with Polk. I'll handle it, that Floyd character and his one-eyed Jack."

"I'm not worried about those two dipshits," said Hampoli, finally turning his attention from the wall. "I'm concerned about this Polk thing working its way south down the interstate from Denver to my front door. I've already got enough problems with an ex-wife giving the Pueblo cops daily recitation. I don't need some Denver bluebelly coming down here deciding to make his career off of me."

Telano pulled a handkerchief from his pocket, sat down on the bench next to Hampoli, and dusted off his shoes. "You're sweating over nothing, Hamp. Bureaucracy's on our side. That Juneteenth bombing's got half of Denver's cops sniffing around every nook and cranny for mad-bomber types. It'll be weeks before anybody up there decides to take a hard look at what happened to some burned-out DJ."

Hampoli leaned back, hands behind his head, and considered Telano's assessment. "Maybe so," he said finally, sounding as if he were trying to convince himself.

"What about that Floyd guy and his runt?" asked Telano.

Hampoli looked surprised at the question. "You're tailing them, aren't you?"

Telano nodded.

"Stay on their asses. Put a shooter on them if you have to. Maybe they'll lead us to the tapes." Looking disappointed, Hampoli pulled his hands down from behind his head. "I was expecting you to find the damn tapes when you were up in Denver nosing around Mabel's."

Telano looked at Hampoli sheepishly. "I told you—"

"Piss on what you told me, Johnny. Excuses are for losers. The bottom line is, I still don't have my tapes."

Johnny Telano didn't like being cut off by anyone, not even Hampoli. It was a sign of disrespect. It reminded him of the days when kids used to call him gorilla. He shoved his hands in his pockets, rolled his tongue around in his cheeks a couple of times, fighting back the urge to respond, and finally looked off into space.

Hampoli watched Telano's eyes. They always told him how far to push. To make amends for cutting Johnny off, and to make sure that Johnny wouldn't mope around feeling wounded for a week and maybe poison a few of his exotic plants, he decided to toss him a bone.

"Tell you what. You can dog that Floyd guy's ass, share the confessional booth with him if you like, or mummify his nuts. Just bring my tapes back."

The cold, blank stare on Johnny Telano's face didn't change.

Shouldn't have pushed him after he's been out burning rats, thought Hampoli. "And remember, it's the tapes I want, Johnny. I don't need some Viet Cong bridge blown up."

Johnny Telano responded with a sly, casual smile. He was still moping, but he had what he needed: permission to deal with CJ and Billy any way he wanted. He planned to settle up with them without the need for anything as dramatic as explosives. After all, it was a game not much different than killing rats.

A semitrailer packed with cattle headed for a feedlot sped past the phone booth CJ was sharing with a dead cat, an army of flying gnats who all seemed to be seeking refuge in his eyes, and a carpet of discarded Styrofoam cups laced with tarry goo. CJ was hastily thumbing through the yellow pages. The nauseating aroma of fifty nervous bovines with loose bowels waffled its way into the phone booth. CJ's nostrils flared and his nose turned up in disgust as he wondered why anyone would ever complain about the smell of one of his cheroots.

From the time he and Billy had been escorted out of Hampoli's at gunpoint until they finally found a phone booth with yellow pages that listed not just Pueblo but also Montcliff businesses, Billy had been bellyaching. "I should have coldcocked the bastard with them wire stretchers."

"And ended up getting us killed?" said CJ for the

tenth time, hoping that Billy would finally drop the subject. Billy stood just outside the open phone booth, frowning. He still had the strength and agility of a man half his age; he had managed cattle ranches with more grazing acreage than the city of Denver; he had been stomped and skewered by half a dozen angry bulls; and for years he had existed on not much more than hardtack and rum. CJ knew that in almost any other circumstance Billy would have taken Telano's head off with the wire stretchers.

"SOB reminded me of a gorilla," said Billy. "Did you check out those long, hairy arms of his?"

CJ nodded, but he really wasn't thinking about Johnny Telano. He was mulling over something Clothilde had said during their Juneteenth meeting at Rosie's garage, something about Juney-boy Stokes that had been gnawing at him ever since they left Hampoli's. "He would have killed Daddy," had been her exact words. Maybe Juney-boy had done just that. CJ certainly wasn't going to take Hampoli's story about Juney-boy being suicidal as gospel until he checked it out for himself.

The thing that didn't make sense was why Juney-boy hadn't come after LeRoy Polk earlier. Maybe his sex change had temporarily made him change his mind about LeRoy, and if he still lived in Colorado, maybe LeRoy's move to Denver six months earlier had pushed him back over the edge. Hampoli had implied that LeRoy Polk and Juney-boy had been involved in a sexual relationship somewhere along the line. Homosexuality and bisexuality were things CJ could understand, but changing your sex was something from a different world.

"Ever been to Montcliff?" said CJ, looking up at

Billy after finally finding what he was looking for in the yellow pages.

"No."

CJ pointed south through the filthy phone booth window. "You're headed there now."

Billy shrugged. "Okay by me as long as I don't run into another hairy gorilla."

CJ ran his finger down the one-page listing of Montcliff PHYSICIANS & SURGEONS, stopping at the name *Maurice Sinclair*. It was a name he had heard before. A few years earlier a cross-dressing male prostitute whom CJ bonded out of jail once or twice a month had told CJ that he was thinking about a sex-change operation. He had even gone so far as to ask CJ if he could use him as a psychological reference. Ultimately the man had disappeared, but CJ remembered the name of the doctor he had mentioned so often, Maurice Sinclair. Juggling the open phone book on his knee, CJ stuck his hand out of the phone booth. "Hand me some change, would you, Billy?"

Billy dug a handful of change out of his pocket and dumped it in CJ's hand. When the sweetest-sounding operator in the world came on the line asking for money, CJ pumped $1.45 worth of coins into the slot. After half a dozen rings another woman pleasantly answered, "Dr. Sinclair's office."

Trying his best to sound like a patient in need of help, CJ said, "I'd like to speak to Dr. Sinclair about an operation."

"Do you have a referral?"

Realizing that her question was probably the first tool the office staff used to screen out kooks, CJ answered "Dr. Henry Bales, from Denver," hoping that she didn't have a list of Colorado physicians at her fingertips. It would have been difficult trying to explain why he was being referred for sex-change surgery by a pathologist.

There was a momentary pause. "Our initial consultations are five hundred dollars, and we will require a comprehensive psychological evaluation that can take months."

"Can I come by today?"

There was a longer pause. "How about three o'clock? May I have your name and a phone number where you can be reached?"

Surprised at how quickly an appointment was available, CJ stumbled over both requests. "Ah . . . CJ . . . Floyd, ah . . . 555-3311."

This time he was put on hold for close to three minutes. When the receptionist came back on the line, she sounded much more abrupt. "The doctor will see you at three. Please be prompt."

CJ stood speechless, wondering whether same-day service was the rule of thumb when it came to the sex-change business. He checked his watch. Montcliff was sixty miles away, which meant that he and Billy had an hour to kill. "Thanks."

"You're welcome," said the receptionist.

CJ cradled the receiver in his left hand and kicked at the dead cat's torso before hanging up. A rib poked through the scraggly fur, scratching his shoe. CJ curbed his urge to kick the cat again and turned to Billy. "Ever thought about having a sex change, Billy?" He hoped that Billy had finally gotten over being insulted at Hampoli's.

Billy grunted "No," eyes to the ground.

Billy's demeanor told CJ that Johnny Telano and Lawrence Hampoli had made themselves an enemy for life. "Tomorrow's another day, Billy."

Another cattle trailer and a string of campers whizzed by before Billy finally looked up. CJ realized that Billy had finally shelved the Telano encounter when he said, "Sex change? Are you crazy?"

Twenty-three

Montcliff, Colorado, is a windswept Victorian and adobe city of eighteen thousand, a onetime rough-and-tumble silver mining town. Nestled along the banks of the Cucharas River and just fifty miles from Colorado's southern border, Montcliff is also home to the world's second-largest known meteorite. Former home to the likes of Kit Carson, Bat Masterson, Billy the Kid, Doc Holliday, and dozens of turn-of-the-century silver mining robber barons, Montcliff still takes pride in being the point of origin for the celebrated but short-lived Appaloosa Trail. In the decades after Old West heroes and robber barons were king, Montcliff settled into being just another quiet, economically depressed Colorado mountain town where the residents live and work in the shadow of a tarnished splendor built by former wealth.

Montcliff has at least two other claims to fame. The city's southern border kisses the infamous Elbow Bend at

Highland Creek, where on Easter Sunday 1862 a creek-side tent city housing hundreds of gold rush prospectors went up in flames, killing fifteen men and a dozen pack horses and mules. The cause of the suspicious fire was never determined, but two days afterward, H. J. Bigalow, a prospector known for his violent temper, filed for owner-ship of three gold mining claims that ultimately made him a wealthy man.

Montcliff's other reason for being in the national spotlight is that since the end of the Vietnam War the city has developed into the sex-change capital of the West, all because of one man, Dr. Maurice Sinclair.

Sinclair opened his original surgical practice fresh out of a general surgery residency from the University of London. He chose Montcliff to set up shop because he was enamored with Colorado's climate, mountains, and Wild West lore. Something of an oddball new-age health nut, Sinclair also believed that he could live a more pur-poseful and energetic life in a town that was sixty-six hundred feet above sea level, where the body's oxygen-carrying capacity was increased tenfold over that of someone living at sea level. Sinclair began his practice doing trauma surgery on injured miners at cut-rate prices, branched out to bowel bypass operations for obesity, and after eight years in practice successfully completed his first sex-change operation on a male postal worker from Detroit. His sex-change operations now numbered in the thousands.

Sinclair's office was a former church rectory in a neighborhood dotted with small adobe houses that lined a narrow, crooked, dead-end street dominated by an abandoned brewery. Nothing about Dr. Sinclair's building suggested a medical office, and he preferred it that way because in nearly three decades as a surgeon he had had enough media scrutiny to fill several lifetimes.

During their drive to Montcliff, CJ and Billy spent most of their time discussing what they each thought might be Clothilde Polk's hidden agenda. CJ favored the idea that Clothilde wanted him to find her father's killer before the killer came after her and the pirated tapes. Billy sized Clothilde up as a money-grubber who wanted CJ running interference for her while she set up Stax of Wax.

They arrived ten minutes early for CJ's appointment with Dr. Sinclair. Since there were no signs on the building, the only assurance CJ had that he was in the right place was that the address on the building matched the one he had scribbled down from the yellow pages.

Billy stretched his legs and yawned before getting out of the truck. "Don't look like no medical office to me."

CJ was already on the sidewalk gazing up at the forestlike canopy formed by the branches of the forty-foot-high Dutch elm trees that surrounded the house. He had a cramp in his leg, and he was perspiring like a horse from too many hours of riding shotgun in Billy's air-conditionless truck. A thin wisp of a breeze arced across the yard, carrying a dry, earthy smell in its wake. As he reached back to rub at the cramp, he noticed the huge, burned-out patches of grass around Sinclair's office and thought about his own drought-damaged lawn.

On their way up the narrow walkway to the house, CJ thought about what the office of a sex-change surgeon might look like. When he swung back the heavy, Gothic-

looking front door, he and Billy found themselves staring
into a huge, airy, but still very churchlike entry. The walls
were pale blue, and the new-fabric smell of freshly installed carpet hung in the air. A three-by-five beet-red
throw rug bearing a large silver caduceus and the name
MAURICE SINCLAIR, M.D., greeted them as they stepped in.
Alcoves in the walls on either side of the entry reiterated
the building's heritage. The smoothly contoured pockets
that had once held the figures of the Christ child,
prophets, and saints now contained Indian artifacts. Billy
nudged CJ to move along. When they stepped through a
twelve-foot-high Italian archway, all remnants of church
architecture disappeared, giving way to a modern doctor's
office with a spacious waiting room. An obligatory com-
plement of chairs hugged the walls and an aseptic-looking
high-tech reception area dominated the middle of the
room. Off to one side of the reception area stood a bottled-
water and coffee alcove with a neatly stenciled sign
thumbtacked to the wall that read PLEASE BUS YOUR OWN
CUPS.

CJ walked up to the reception desk and announced
nonchalantly, "I have a three o'clock appointment to see
Dr. Sinclair." He looked around for Billy and realized
that Billy had picked up a *People* magazine from a rack on
the wall and taken a seat.

"Certainly," said the pale woman seated behind an
alabaster countertop that matched her skin tone. CJ recognized the voice as that of the woman who had made
his appointment. She looked up and smiled, displaying
stained, mottled brown teeth. "Please fill out these papers
and Dr. Sinclair will be with you shortly." She handed CJ
two preprinted forms, and he turned to walk away.

"Ah . . . Mr. Floyd, you'll need to read these as well."
She nudged three red, white, and blue pamphlets across
the countertop. The title of the red pamphlet on top was
Starting Over: Coping with Your Inner Self. "And your payment
will be in the form of?" she said hurriedly.

When CJ thought about the fact that his per diem
expenses would now include reimbursement for a sex-
change consultation, he smiled and tried to imagine the
expressions on Clothilde's and Vanetta's faces when they
saw the receipt. "Do you take plastic?"

"Visa, Mastercard, and Discover."

CJ pulled his Visa card out of his wallet, knowing
that he was already at his limit, and watched the receptionist run it through her charge-card machine.

"You can sign the charge slip on your way out." She
handed CJ the credit card and looked toward Billy. "And
the gentleman with you is?"

"Just a friend."

The receptionist gave CJ a look that told him she
was thinking, *We must learn to be honest,* and then went back
to her work.

CJ sat down and completed the information on the
forms he had been given. Both were routine medical history questionnaires without a single reference to sex-
change surgery. He returned them to the receptionist, sat
back down, and started to read Dr. Sinclair's pamphlets,
beginning with the red one. In the fifteen minutes it took
to read all three, he also had a chance to consider how he
was going to get Dr. Sinclair to discuss Juney-boy Stokes.
He never could come up with an answer, so he decided to
wing it. In reviewing the pamphlets he learned that Dr.
Sinclair was happy to see anyone for an initial consulta-

tion for what he called gender-reassignment surgery as rapidly as possible. The pamphlet made it a point to note in italics that *"eighty percent of such patients never return."* The brochure also pointed out that Dr. Sinclair's specialty was changing males to females, and although he had successfully completed gender-reassignment surgery on females, he still considered the female-to-male procedure experimental.

Most of Dr. Sinclair's patients were transsexuals, individuals whom Sinclair defined in his more technical white manual as having a gender identity disorder. Through some cruel trick of nature or nurture, they had lived their lives harboring an unshakable conviction that in reality, spirit, soul, and sexuality, they were women living in the bodies of males or males burdened with the physical trappings of a woman.

In the blue book Sinclair outlined his patient acceptance guidelines for gender-reassignment surgery, stating emphatically in the first paragraph: "It is impossible to change a person's sex since sex is determined by chromosomes which cannot be altered. Thus, again, the preferred term, gender-reassignment surgery, must be adhered to." Sinclair's standard preoperative guidelines followed a rigid protocol: "The patient must live full time for a year as a member of their new gender, undergo nine months of presurgical male or female hormonal therapy, and submit to a year of psychological counseling and group therapy with a second thorough psychological evaluation two weeks prior to surgery." The last page of the blue booklet noted that the cost of gender-reassignment surgery could run as high as $25,000, and insurance rarely covered any portion of the pre- or postoperative procedures.

CJ was staring at the $25,000 figure, wondering how Sinclair's patients came up with that kind of cash, when the receptionist walked up to him. "Dr. Sinclair's available to see you now."

"I'll stay here," said Billy, scrutinizing the pale, rail-thin receptionist and trying to determine whether she might ever have been one of Sinclair's patients.

CJ followed the woman through an archway and down a hall to the right of the reception area directly to the wide-open door of Maurice Sinclair's office. Sinclair was seated behind a massive walnut desk with a green in-laid leather top. Two open French doors occupied most of the wall behind him, and four bookcases overflowing with books occupied every square inch of wall space to his right. The remaining walls were filled with pho-tographs of Sinclair either big-game hunting or shaking hands with or hugging people that CJ suspected were his patients. CJ found it interesting that except for the wall behind his desk, Sinclair's face was prominently featured on every wall in the room.

Sinclair stood up as soon as CJ walked in. He was a slim man in his early sixties, just under six feet tall, with a closely cropped military-style haircut, a long, fragile-looking nose, and a thin, arching mustache that looked as though it had been sketched on with an eyebrow pencil. He looked briefly at the papers on his desk before ex-tending his hand to greet CJ. "Mr. Floyd, welcome to Montcliff."

Sinclair's accent was a strange mixture of formal British English and Western drawl. He walked around to the front of the desk and leaned back on its edge. "Please have a seat." He motioned to a large burgundy wingback just beneath a photograph of him and another man in hunting garb, cradling the head and neck of a 250-pound antelope.

CJ sat down, adjusting his bulky frame in the under-sized wingback. Seeing that CJ was as comfortable as he'd get, Sinclair spoke up. "I understand you are looking for some help." His tone of voice was empathetic.

CJ's decision to come to Montcliff had come on the spur of the moment, and he hadn't really thought through how he was going to tell Sinclair that he really wasn't there for gender-reassignment surgery, just as he hadn't determined how he was going to explain to Sin-clair that he wanted him to breach patient confidentiality and tell him about a patient of his who may have tried to commit suicide fifteen years ago. He didn't know whether Sinclair encountered imposters every day or not. For all he knew, Sinclair had a button on his phone that speed-dialed the police. He finally decided that since he had gotten this far on the basis of insincerity and guile, he might as well try making a stab at the truth. "You're right about needing help, but it's not what you think." He took a deep breath and waited for Sinclair's reaction.

"I didn't suspect you needed my services. Your health history's as clean as a whistle, except for smoking, of course." Sinclair shook his head disapprovingly. "On top of that, very few of my patients could have resisted the opportunity to embellish the request for family and social history on my medical history forms. When my re-ceptionist gives them two pages to fill out, she usually gets back four. So you see, you hardly fit the profile. But in my business, since I can't take the chance of missing the opportunity to help even one lost soul, even when my receptionist or I suspect an imposter, we expedite all consultations. So much for protocol, Mr. Floyd. Now, what's your angle?"

Sinclair's British accent was becoming more pronounced the longer he talked. Since honesty suddenly seemed to be the order of the day, CJ decided to be direct. "I'm trying to find out if you performed a sex-change operation on a man by the name of Juney-boy Stokes. It would have been about fifteen years ago."

Dr. Sinclair smiled briefly before turning stone-faced. "I'm guessing you're a private eye, Mr. Floyd, because you're far too naive to be a disgruntled lover or newspaper reporter, and you're certainly not from one of my doubting-Thomas colleagues in the medical community or the police." He paused and shifted his weight on the edge of his desk. "Nonetheless, whatever your profession, I'm sure you are aware that the doctor-patient relationship remains privileged and confidential. By the way, we don't call them sex-change operations. Gender-reassignment surgery is the name I prefer." Sinclair's accent had turned resoundingly British and very upper crust.

Realizing that he wasn't going to get a thimble's worth of information out of Sinclair about any of his patients, CJ decided to try another tactic. "Your literature says you've performed close to a thousand gender-reassignment surgeries. Ever run into any problems in patient selection?"

"We have to be careful to avoid schizophrenics and the occasional transvestite who's simply a cross-dresser and falls into some peripheral gray transsexual area, but I've seen so many true transsexuals that I can almost count on my being one hundred percent correct in my assessment when they walk through the door. I was with you, wasn't I?"

"Sure were." CJ could tell that Sinclair had answered the question before. He smiled, knowing that he had struck the vein he was mining for. A boastful surgeon's ego in need of further tweaking. "Ever made any mistakes?"

Sinclair frowned, sidestepping the question. "If there is ever any insecurity on the part of my patients, up to and including the night of surgery, I don't operate. Any second thoughts, we cancel." His tone was abrupt.

"Ever been asked to undo a surgery?"

Sinclair's frown turned into a scowl. "I'm not sure what you're after, Mr. Floyd, but you should know that my practice record is impeccable. In answer to your question, I have only been asked to reconstruct a case once, and that was a case where I hadn't done the original surgery."

Sinclair's defensive posture made CJ remember something his uncle had always said about people with Texas-sized egos: *Strum a common fiddle just right, and it could end up singing like a Stradivarius.* It bothered CJ that Sinclair had just called someone a *case* instead of a patient. It sounded too assembly-line. He decided it might be wise to have Henry Bales take a closer look at Dr. Maurice Sinclair. "Sounds to me like you've got a one-crop economy here," said CJ, deciding to take one last shot at Sinclair's ego.

Incensed, Sinclair responded, "I get as much work as I do because I'm good, my rates are reasonable, and I have a following. I don't know what your game is, Mr. Floyd, but I've been as cordial as I know how. I wish you success in your mission, but right now I have to return to my patients." He stood up from the edge of his desk. When he did, CJ noticed an ivory ashtray on the desktop behind him. "Are you a smoker?" asked CJ, digging in his vest pocket for his pack of cheroots.

"I'm not," said Sinclair, following CJ's eyes to the ashtray. "That ashtray was a gift from one of my patients. It's ivory."

CJ started wetting down the tip of his cheroot.

"I'd appreciate your not lighting that thing up until you're outside the building. This is a medical facility."

"What do you think, Doc? Should I try Nicoderm patches?"

"They work quite well, in my experience. I'd give them a whirl if I were you."

"Maybe I will," said CJ, turning to leave. Sinclair's support for smoking intervention didn't make him a killer, nor did the ashtray on his desk, but they were food for thought. As he left Sinclair's office, CJ thought that he had seen, heard, and done just about everything in twenty-five years of bail bonding and two tours in Vietnam, but he realized that he had stepped into a strange new world. A world where red, white, and blue brochures and an egotistical surgeon were kings and the intricacies of having your Adam's apple shaved, your penis debulked, or your pectoralis muscles turned into breasts were the order of the day.

When CJ got back out to the waiting room, Billy was reading Sinclair's blue brochure. A sandy-haired man in a wrinkled brown suit and kelly-green tie was seated two chairs down from him, fidgeting with the crease in his trousers. He looked up nervously as CJ appeared. CJ smiled sympathetically as he watched the man thumb through the red brochure. He wondered how long the demons inside the man had been chasing him before he had decided to come to visit Maurice Sinclair.

Billy started to place the blue pamphlet on the end table next to him but thought better of it and rolled it up and stuck it in his back pocket. He stood up, shaking his head in disbelief. "Terrible thing to have something always gnawing at you like that."

The man in the brown suit nodded in agreement, although Billy's comment hadn't been directed to him. Before Billy had a chance to say anything else, the receptionist who had first greeted them walked up. "I need you to sign your credit-card slip back over at the front desk." She sounded as if she expected CJ to bolt out of the room, and the look of disapproval on her face told him that Dr. Sinclair had already informed her about the impersonation.

CJ stepped up to the reception desk, signed the credit card slip, pocketed the receipt, and headed for the door. Billy followed a couple of steps behind, looking back at the man in the brown suit, who was now frozen in concentration, reading the white brochure.

By the time CJ and Billy reached Colorado Springs on their trip back home, the thunderheads that had promised showers earlier had drifted across the Palmer Divide, disappearing into a hazy fog that blanketed the summit of Pikes Peak. An impromptu stop at the home of Lawrence Hampoli's ex-wife near the Pueblo country club on their way from Montcliff had produced nothing but a couple of hyperexcitable border collies who barked at them from the time they pulled up in front of the ad-

dress Julie had given CJ until they pulled away. CJ left his
card in the mailbox with a note for Carol Hampoli to call
him about Juney-boy Stokes. Given her track record with
the police and the press, CJ figured that if she had any
dirt that involved Hampoli and Juney-boy she'd contact
him fast enough.

CJ was thinking about the odds of Carol Hampoli
ever calling, notching his chances as seven in ten, when a
swarm of drought-precipitated early-summer grasshop-
pers slammed into the windshield. The resulting noise reminded CJ of semiautomatic gunfire. Blinded, Billy began
pumping the brake as if it were a stirrup. "Son of a
bitch." A thick yellow gelatinous goo began working its
way down the windshield. Billy slowed the pickup to
twenty, eased off onto the shoulder, and flipped on the
windshield wipers. Suddenly he caught a glimpse in the
rearview mirror of a semi barreling down on them.
"Jump the fuck out!" he screamed to CJ.

When CJ didn't respond, Billy shoved him against
the door, thanking God for the truck's faulty hinges and
worthless locks as they both went sprawling out onto the
asphalt shoulder. Instead of taking the pickup head-on,
the semi's driver kissed the truck's back bumper, sending
the pickup careening several hundred feet down the
shoulder in a series of rollovers.

The semi barely slowed down after the collision, and
in a matter of seconds the driver had the diesel engine
revving as the big rig's livestock trailer fishtailed three or
four times and disappeared over a rise.

CJ had landed awkwardly on his right shoulder with
the impact of a sledgehammer. Billy, who had taken the
tumble no more deftly, ended up landing on his behind,

and he was now sitting up Buddha-like, watching the semi's taillights trail off beyond the rise.

"You okay?" asked Billy, for the moment unwilling to move.

CJ's shoulder was shooting pins and needles. "I'm still breathing, but I don't think I'll be playing tennis at the country club for a while."

Billy finally stood up. When he realized that all his body parts were still in place, he walked over to CJ. As he helped CJ up, he noticed that CJ's vest was knotted up around his neck, most of his chambray shirt had been ripped away, and all the skin from the middle of his right bicep up to his shoulder blade was either covered with blood or peppered with asphalt.

CJ was shaky as a toddler. "Did we piss some cattleman off?"

Several cars had now pulled off onto the shoulder, and a blond man in a Colorado Rockies cap came running up to help. "You two all right?"

"Tell you in a minute," said Billy, heading down the shoulder toward his pickup.

The man and CJ trailed along. When Billy reached the pickup, which had landed right side up, he began looking for the point of impact. He quickly found it.

CJ and the Samaritan stood dumbfounded while Billy dug around the pickup's rear bumper. He eventually pulled out a clump of brown goo from between the tailgate and the left rear bumper.

"Porkers," he said, sniffing at his hand and frowning. "The fucker was haulin' pigs." Billy slammed what CJ now realized was a clump of pig shit to the ground, walked over the edge of the shoulder, and began wiping off his hand in the nearby grass. "Porkers," he repeated, continuing to wipe off his hands.

There wasn't a hint of wind, and the ice-blue Colorado sky was cloudless and starless when CJ and Billy crossed the seven-thousand-foot Palmer Drive over Monument Hill and dropped back into the Front Range basin in their rented Corsica. It had been nearly four hours since their encounter with what they now knew had been a Kenworth rig hauling a trailer full of pigs. Both CJ and Billy were strangely silent. There were no sounds of chewing gum. CJ's head was pressing into the grease-stained ceiling of the car. He slouched down, trying to get more comfortable, as Billy pushed the Corsica up to eighty.

The only injury Billy had sustained in his barrel roll from the truck was a strained right hip that barely had him limping. He had popped a couple of the half-dozen aspirin he always kept in his wallet, refused the medical attention that had been offered at the Colorado Springs Penrose Hospital ER, and told CJ on their way out of town that he had never trusted hospitals or doctors because they both always smelled too much like freshly cleaned urinals.

CJ had a minor but exquisitely tender Class I shoulder separation. He hadn't realized until an hour into their ER visit that the scabbed-over knuckles of the right hand he had injured in a tussle with a bond-skipping Evan Picone booster three weeks earlier had turned into open wounds again. After his shoulder and hand were X-rayed and treated, he and Billy were escorted into a sterile-looking hospital conference room for a forty-minute audition with a Colorado State Patrol policewoman. The bright-eyed, baby-faced, straight-arrow-looking officer, who looked as if she had just graduated from the state police academy, was well mannered and professional, and most of her questions about the hit-and-run accident were directed at helping her facilitate what she kept calling the "law enforcement capacity of the Colorado State Police." Her questions had been repetitious and seemingly endless. She quizzed Billy about his driving record and whether he wore glasses. She wanted to know whether either of them had been drinking or if they had been drag racing, playing chicken, or had purposely cut the truck off. The last question had so ruffled Billy's feathers that he blurted out, "Cut him off, shit, the son of a bitch ran right up our ass."

She had ignored Billy's outburst, asking him how fast he had been driving, where exactly they had been hit, and how long before impact he had seen the other truck. When she asked Billy why he had jumped out of the pickup, Billy came unglued, shouting, "To keep on breathin'." The officer smiled briefly before boring back in with a series of questions about whether CJ and Billy were anti-trucker, anti-beef, or anti-pork. When Billy said "No," CJ thought about the encounter he and Billy had had with the group of anti-cattle-industry radical environmentalists the year before but quickly put the thought behind him, knowing that all of those people were either dead or in jail. The session ended with the officer closing her notepad, offering an official-sounding "Thank you, I'll be in touch," and leaving CJ and Billy wondering who had been victimized.

While Billy had sat mumbling to himself, still angry

at the officer's questions, CJ was thinking about a question the officer hadn't asked: how in the hell was the Kenworth's driver tethered to either Lawrence Hampoli or Johnny Telano?

They had left the hospital in a courtesy van from the rental car agency with Billy lamenting the death of his truck and CJ popping a couple of five-hundred-milligram Vicodin as he tried to get used to breathing with an A-C strap that felt like a corset wrapped around his shoulder and chest.

Billy eased off the accelerator when he thought he saw the headlights of a state patrol car approaching from behind. When the car shot past him out of the night, Billy shook his head, disappointed that he had ever slowed down. He had been silent, deep in thought, ever since they started up the divide. Something had been bothering him ever since they left Colorado Springs. In fact, it had him feeling edgy. A couple of sticks of gum would have helped, but his stash was with the remains of his truck. "Ever shovel pig shit?" he said to CJ out of the blue.

"No. Dog shit, bird shit, even cow manure when I was young, but pig shit—never had the honor."

"It has a real runny consistency and one hell of a characteristic smell. Never really hardens up like the stuff from a cow. I smelled it the instant I bailed out of the truck. Like it was hangin' there waitin' for me to take a whiff while I am barrelin' through the air."

CJ knew that Billy was headed for a point, and he also knew that if he gave Billy enough storytelling room he might not get there until morning. "How about taking a shortcut to where you're headed, Billy? It's been a hell of a long day."

Billy glanced over at CJ, who was obviously hurting, hunched down in his seat like some clown in a miniature car at the circus, and decided to take CJ's advice and make his point. "Remember when you asked me the other day about where you could get igniter to set off a bomb?"

"Yes."

"Well, the pig shit got me to thinkin'. If you know what you're doin' you can turn the stuff into an explosive."

CJ eased up in his seat until his head produced a cannonball-sized indentation in the ceiling. "You sure?"

"As sure as this car's doing seventy-five," said Billy, glancing down at the speedometer. "As sure as I've seen barns with too much manure packed around 'em go up in flames."

"How come you didn't mention anything about it the other day?"

"Why would I? I figured you were dealing with some high-tech psycho, not some whacked-out trucker haulin' pigs."

CJ slouched back down in his seat and ran Billy's theory through his head. If the bombing of Mae's had been a warning, then their encounter with the Kenworth had probably been a bungled murder for hire. He didn't know if the series of love taps were all coming from the same person, but he knew that somebody out there had made his point.

Confident that no more state patrol cars were lingering behind him, Billy nudged the gas pedal to the floor,

pushing their speed up to eighty-five. As they rounded
the quarter-mile-long curve just beyond the high-priced
development of Surrey Ridge, the sprawling lights of
Denver came into view. The Front Range glow made CJ
think about his night on Lookout Mountain, and it reminded him that the next morning he had to attend
Mabel's funeral.

Twenty-four

Mabel Pitts was buried on the hottest June 22nd ever recorded in Denver. The temperature had reached ninety degrees by ten-thirty, when two gleaming black Hubble's Mortuary limousines and the gunmetal-gray hearse carrying Mabel's body parked in front of the Mount Carmel Baptist Church. When CJ arrived fifteen minutes later he was sweating and out of breath. He had disregarded the A-C strap he had been given at Penrose Hospital, deciding he'd rather endure pain than immobility.

Billy DeLong had declined to come, saying that funerals always gave him diarrhea, so CJ entered the nearly packed 350-seat church alone. Right away he spotted Winston Dunn and Sergeant Fuller at the back of the church and realized that they weren't there simply to pay their respects. Fuller and Dunn didn't see him as he stepped behind one of the bulky twelve-foot-high pillars supporting the church balcony. Remembering the words of his uncle, *It's always better to be the looker than the lookee*, CJ settled up against the highly polished Philippine mahogany and caught his breath.

Mavis Sundee caught a glimpse of CJ trying to position his 220-pound bulk behind the pillar and headed for him. She sneaked up beside him and planted a kiss softly on his cheek. "Playing hide and seek?"

"No." He nodded toward Fuller and Dunn. When Mavis saw Dunn, who she knew had put the word out on the street that she and Willis may have blown up Mae's themselves for the insurance, her face turned cold and she snuggled up against CJ as if she needed protection.

After arriving home from Pueblo the previous evening, CJ had dropped Billy off at his place and spent the night at Mavis's, explaining to Billy that he needed a break from his timber-rattling snoring. He had showed up at Mavis's feeling like a scalded dog, and it took him fifteen minutes to calm her down and explain to her why he looked like a mugging victim. He had to promise Mavis in almost a blood oath that he was going to start acting his age before she caved in and gave him permission to soak his battered body in her whirlpool bathtub. She didn't tell him the specifics of Mabel's funeral arrangements until he had soaked for a half-hour. He dragged himself to bed an hour later and propped his injured shoulder up on a levee of goose-down pillows that Mavis had positioned down the middle of the bed. He fell asleep with her head cradled in the curve of his other arm, wondering why she continued to put up with him.

The double dose of Tylenol 3 that CJ had popped while he was in the whirlpool made him sleep so soundly that he didn't hear Mavis get up to leave for the church. When he did get up the piney scent of the herbal shampoo Mavis used still clung to his chest. He headed for another thirty minutes in the whirlpool, not realizing that Mavis had left two seven-grain cinnamon rolls, a carafe of orange juice chilled on ice, and a pot of decaf out for him until he wandered into the kitchen, cheroot in place, looking for a match.

CJ took Mavis's hand, squeezed it, and leaned into the pillar as he scanned the crowd. He thought about how reassuring it had been to have Mavis next to him all night, and he felt guilty about telling her that he and Billy had been involved in a minor accident instead of admitting that someone had tried to shove them both to the other side of life.

"How's the shoulder?" asked Mavis.

"It's stiff, but it's not as sore as it was last night." To prove his point, CJ tried unsuccessfully to raise his arm above his waist.

Mavis smiled at his effort. "After the services, try my whirlpool again. I've got to circulate and hand out programs. See you after the service." She nodded toward Dunn and Fuller, who had now been joined by Vernon Lowe.

CJ scanned the rest of the church and spotted Tyrone Polk seated in the second pew next to Clothilde. Given the fact that Clothilde kept insisting that either Tyrone or Mabel had killed her father, he wondered why she was there. Knowing how loose she had been with the truth and how Mabel had insisted on calling her a black widow, CJ wouldn't have put it past her to show up simply to gloat. CJ moved down the center aisle of the church toward where they were seated. He spotted Dittier Atkins and Morgan Williams halfway down the aisle, nodding as he walked by. He stood at Mabel's open casket with his eyes locked on her face, mouthed "God bless you" softly, then turned, and walked back to Tyrone and Clothilde's pew. He slid in next to Clothilde and looked back for Mavis, who had disappeared into the foyer. Only then did he realize that Sergeant Fuller and Winston Dunn were watching him.

"Glad you could come," whispered Tyrone, reaching across Clothilde to shake CJ's hand.

Before CJ had a chance to answer, Clothilde, whose only reason for attending the funeral had been to keep an eye on Tyrone, said, "Any new leads on who else helped kill my father?" Her eyes darted straight toward Mabel's casket.

Trying to remember that he was in church, CJ held back from saying what he was thinking. "I went to Pueblo yesterday and talked with Hampoli. Why don't we discuss it after the service?" His dislike for Clothilde Polk had come to a boil.

"We're in the first limo; you can ride with us."

"First limo." CJ slipped out of the pew, walked back up the aisle, and slid into a seat next to Morgan and Dittier, glad to be separated from Clothilde.

Morgan patted CJ on the shoulder sympathetically. "Mabel was good people. You gonna be trackin' her killer?"

CJ nodded and then looked back to see if Fuller and Dunn were still watching him. They had disappeared.

"Me and Dittier think it was somebody from one of them gangs."

CJ was in too somber a mood to discuss Mabel's murder, but he suspected that Morgan's gangbanger theory was way off the mark. "You find Geronimo yet?" he said, changing the subject.

"No. Been like lookin' for a ghost. I'm close to givin' up."

Dittier eyed Morgan dejectedly and began shaking his head rapidly back and forth in protest. He was still protesting when the church's organist began hammering out a powerful rendition of "What a Friend We Have in Jesus" and Reverend Buford Grimes, the Mount Carmel pastor, walked in to begin the service.

An hour and ten minutes later the service ended. The active pallbearers, six men Mabel's age, carried the weight of her coffin down the church's center aisle to the front steps, where three hefty men from the mortuary took over. CJ checked the program, smiling at the fact that he was listed under his full name, Calvin Jefferson Floyd, as an honorary pallbearer.

Outside the church a crowd of people milled around, waiting to be assigned to limos and the long string of cars in the funeral procession. CJ had knifed his way through the crowd toward the first limo when Vernon Lowe rushed up, out of breath, to meet him. "Watch your rear, CJ," Vernon said in a near whisper. "Sergeant Fuller and Dunn are about to stick it to you." Vernon looked around to make sure Fuller and Dunn hadn't heard him. "They're saying that maybe you and that Polk woman set both her daddy and Mabel up." Vernon paused, noting the puzzled look on CJ's face. "Insurance, CJ, insurance. That old dustbag of a disc jockey had a pot full of it. I figured you knew that."

CJ's eyebrows arched upward as they always did when he felt he had missed the obvious. As many insurance fraud investigations as he had been a part of, and as often as he dealt with insurance companies as a bail bondsman, he had missed the insurance connection altogether. "Who told you so?"

"Dunn."

"Why'd he decide to confide in you?"

"Don't know. He and Fuller just stopped me while I was lookin' for a seat and asked me did I know where you were the day I did the autopsy on LeRoy Polk. Then they asked me if I knew that Polk and Mabel had been married. When I didn't have an answer for the second question they hammered me for a few more minutes with questions about you and Clothilde. That's when they told me about the insurance."

CJ wasn't certain whether Fuller and Dunn actually did think that he and Clothilde had conspired to kill her father and Mabel, but he suspected that they had goaded Vernon into delivering their message in hopes of monitoring how he responded when Vernon broke the news. He was certain they were still around somewhere, but when he looked through the crowd he didn't see them.

"They even claimed you may have blown up Mae's," said Vernon.

"They're idiots, Vernon."

"No need to convince me. Just thought you'd like to know."

"Appreciate it."

Vernon looked back at the line of cars, then at the

strange way CJ was holding his shoulder. "What's with the shoulder, home?"

"Nothing, just a strain."

"Good; gotta catch my ride."

"Later." CJ watched Vernon disappear in the crowd. He had the sinking feeling that Fuller and Dunn were conveniently situated where they could watch his every move the same way he had watched theirs earlier. He made his way through the crowd, shaking hands, trying to avoid getting his shoulder jostled, until he reached the first limousine. He tapped on the rear window. The doleful, low-pitched mechanical hum of the electric window descending reminded him that he was at a funeral. Tyrone opened the door, red-eyed from crying. Clothilde was seated next to him, looking bored. Tyrone nodded for CJ to get in, and CJ took the limo's jump seat, facing them. The first two questions he wanted to ask Clothilde were why she had failed to mention that her father had pirated a stockpile of priceless R&B recordings, and whether she was looking forward to a big payoff from his insurance. But then he remembered something that his uncle used to tell him when he first started out in the bail-bonding business: *It ain't the fierceness of the bark that counts in a dog, it's the reality of his bite.* He decided to save his bite for a little later.

He turned to Tyrone instead. "How you doing, Tyrone?"

"Hangin' in there."

"I know it's tough." He patted Tyrone on the knee. Then he turned to Clothilde, deciding it was time to tell her he was going to Chicago and to fill her in on how his meeting had gone with Hampoli. "I'm heading for the Windy City this afternoon."

"Good," said Clothilde smugly. "No need to waste your time here."

CJ forced back a frown. "When I talked to Lawrence Hampoli yesterday, he said your father stole some rare studio tapes that belonged to him. You never mentioned any of that."

"Hampoli's a mobster. I told you that up front. And he lies." Clothilde was staring down at the limo floor.

"Then that explains why he also told me such a whopper about Juney-boy Stokes. According to Hampoli, Juney-boy wasn't real happy with the set of sex chromosomes he was handed out. In fact, Hampoli claims he disliked the resulting equipment so much he had it rearranged. He says Juney-boy's a woman now."

"First I've heard of it," said Clothilde with a shrug.

Tyrone was suddenly all ears. "Mabel said something to me about that Stokes guy the day she was killed. Said if anybody had reason to kill my father it was him. That's what I was trying to tell you the other night at the Empire Lounge."

CJ adjusted himself in the seat as he listened to Tyrone's revelation. His shoulder nudged the limo door, but when he grimaced in pain, neither Tyrone or Clothilde seemed to notice. "Hampoli claims Stokes had a sex change and ended up trying to kill himself. Know anything about that?" He looked at Tyrone and then Clothilde for a response.

Tyrone shook his head.

"So?" said Clothilde.

"So if Stokes is still alive he may have killed your father and Mabel."

"Makes sense," said Tyrone meekly.

Clothilde shot Tyrone a *who asked you* raised-eyebrow stare before turning her attention back to CJ. "Mabel's not my problem, or yours. You're being paid to find out who killed my father. As for Juney-boy Stokes, I don't believe in ghosts."

CJ had finally had his fill of Clothilde Polk. He leaned forward until his face was within inches of Clothilde's. "Mabel Pitts is my problem." A few errant drops of spittle hit Clothilde in the face. "And so's your lying. Everything you've told me's been a hundred and eighty degrees from the truth. I came close to getting killed yesterday because of you, and guess what, my sweet manipulative sister, I've finally reached my limit." CJ pulled out a loose cheroot from his coat pocket, slipped it into his mouth, and clamped down on it. "I don't have to go to Chicago, and I sure don't have to keep shilling for your lying bourgeois ass." He sat back in his seat, fumbled for his lighter, and lit up his cigar. "It's up to you," he said, blowing smoke in Clothilde's direction.

"The only thing I wasn't truthful about were the tapes," said Clothilde defensively. "And Hampoli's wrong. Those tapes belonged to my father."

"Chicago or not?" asked CJ.

"Does a thousand-dollar bonus answer your question?"

CJ took a long drag on his cheroot. "How many tapes are there? And what are they really worth?" he said reluctantly.

"Three tapes altogether, with maybe forty songs, and I'd guess that marketed as newly discovered R&B gems in the form of albums, compact discs, and forty-fives they'd be worth half a million, maybe a million. To collectors they might bring even more."

"Any big names on the list?"

"As big as you can get, including folks that became some of Motown's biggest stars."

CJ's eyes ballooned. "Big enough for me. Hope you've got them under lock and key."

"They'd have to kill me to get them," said Clothilde, looking over at Tyrone.

"The way things are going, you might get your wish," said CJ. "But if you ask me, it sounds like this whole mess is gonna end up in court."

"Thieves stealing from thieves," said Tyrone, delighted to hear CJ's assessment.

Clothilde had backed down for CJ, but she wasn't about to acquiesce to Tyrone. "The only one who's going to end up in court is you, Tyrone. You'll be seeing the inside of a courthouse long before me."

The muscles in Tyrone's face went slack. He was about to say something in rebuttal when the limo driver swung open the front door, cutting him off. "Everybody here?"

After a long moment of silence, Clothilde said, "Yes."

"Okay," said the driver, getting in and slamming the door. Seconds later two motorcycles pulled up alongside the limo. CJ never heard the limo's engine turn over. All he felt was a forward surge, and he heard the high-pitched whine of motorcycle sirens as they pulled away. Clothilde and Tyrone were silent during the short ride to the cemetery, preferring instead to exchange hateful stares.

*   *   *

Mabel Pitts had a placid, uneventful interment in ninety-nine-degree heat. The crowd at the cemetery was about three-quarters of the one at the church, and only a few people remained milling around after the brief graveside ceremony. Tyrone stayed until Clothilde screamed at him that their limo was ready to leave. CJ opted to ride back with Julie and Mavis after telling Clothilde that he'd get back to her as soon as he returned from Chicago and instructing her to call Julie immediately if anything out of the ordinary happened. In an act of repentance, Clothilde told CJ about Sergeant Fuller and another policeman, whom she kept referring to as a stringbean-looking cop, interrogating her for an hour about the Juneteenth bombing and her father's murder. She didn't tell CJ that two days earlier she had also given the police and the DA a packet of papers that tied Tyrone to a construction materials money-skimming scam. When Clothilde's and Tyrone's limo pulled off, only Julie, CJ, and Mavis were left at Mabel's graveside.

Melancholy and pensive, with ribbons of sweat working their way down both temples, CJ kicked a softball-sized chunk of dirt away from the open grave. "Have Morgan and Dittier take some time off from looking for Geronimo and keep an eye on Clothilde," he said to Julie. "She doesn't know it, but she's in way over her head."

"Will do," said Julie.

"And ask Henry Bales to run a check on this guy's medical license for me, including any abnormal bleeps in his peer-review profile." CJ pulled his checkbook out of his coat pocket and scribbled the name *Maurice Sinclair* on the back of a deposit slip, grimacing in pain the entire time he was writing.

"Watch your backside, CJ," said Mavis as CJ handed Julie the slip.

"That's Billy's job." CJ smiled, trying to mask pain that was now obvious to Julie and Mavis.

Mavis decided against retreading any more of the ground that always seemed to send their relationship into a tailspin. "They're discharging Daddy from the hospital this afternoon," she said, changing the subject, hoping that her plea hadn't fallen on deaf ears.

CJ was happy about Willis's release, but he knew that Willis was just hot-tempered enough to start where he had left off in his challenge to the monorail. "Keep Willis at home."

"I'll do what I can, but he's just as stubborn as you."

CJ ignored Mavis's double meaning. In the distance he heard the throaty roar from the diesel engine of a backhoe starting up. He watched a feathery plume of black smoke rise from the backhoe's exhaust and wondered how many graves the driver dug every day. Tears welled up in his eyes. He kicked the dirt in front of him, and a few clumps of loose soil skipped across the ground and rolled into Mabel's grave.

Mavis started to lock her arm in CJ's. When he flinched she remembered to move around to the other arm.

"What happened?" asked Julie, watching CJ's response.

"I got hit by some pigs." He wrapped Mavis's arm in his. As they walked away from the grave he repeated the details of his and Billy's accident. But this time he told Mavis the truth. It scared her enough that she tightened her grip on his arm. At Julie's car CJ hesitated and looked

back one last time toward Mabel's grave. Then they left
the cemetery in a rush, never realizing that they were being
followed by an unmarked police car carrying Sergeant
Fuller and Winston Dunn.

Fuller was jammed behind the wheel of the air-
conditionless Ford, sweating like a pig. Dunn was nursing
a can of Dr Pepper. "Think Floyd really had something to
do with that bombing?"

"What I think doesn't matter. We're running damage
control, or didn't the mayor make that clear?" Fuller knew
that Dunn had made a visit to the mayor's Turkey Creek
Canyon ministorage. He had been there himself.

Dunn swirled his Dr Pepper around in the can.
"There wasn't a word of criticism about monorail or
Wiley in the papers today. I checked every column."

"Ever heard of tomorrow?" asked Fuller, knowing
that the mayor hated his staff calling him by his last name.

Dunn took another sip of Dr Pepper, keeping his eye
on Julie's red Honda. "That secretary of Floyd's drives like
a bat out of hell." He smiled to himself. "Have you ever
noticed the sweet little ass on her?"

Fuller didn't answer. He had a first and second mortgage, two teenagers ready for college, a wife with a back-
woods Blue Ridge Mountain jealous streak, and a pension
he planned on collecting. "Zip it up, loverboy, or haven't
you heard, Floyd protects her like she was his little sister."

"Just thinking out loud."

"Think about not letting any of this Juneteenth shit
stick to the mayor, and maybe you'll stay employed," said
Fuller, accelerating to keep up with Julie.

Dunn dropped his empty can on the floor, stroked

his chin, and thought about how much he really needed his job.

CJ moped around Mavis's house for most of the rest of the day until Mavis talked him into finally leaving for an early supper at Poppa Loomis Kinnard's Bar-B-Q. He mumbled through the meal, picking over his food before reluctantly ordering dessert. After a sip of coffee and a bite of sweet-potato pie he grumbled, "I ain't in the mood. Let's head home." He dropped Mavis back at her house with an apology, reminded her he'd be going to Chicago in the morning, and headed home listening to a doleful-sounding Ironing Board Sam tape he hadn't played in years, preparing for what turned out to be one hell of a fretful night's sleep.

Twenty-five

Jungle Jim Huerra's immaculate, hand-waxed, orange-and-white Metro taxi turned off I-70 onto Peña Boulevard on the last leg of a twenty-three-mile cab ride from Rosie Weaks's garage, where CJ had left the Bel Air for an oil change, to the new Denver International Airport. Huerra had earned his nickname during a three-year stint as a heavyweight on the pro wrestling tour because he liked to jump from the ropes and land on his opponent's neck. He had gambled away most of the money he had made except for the $6,000 he had used to make a down payment on his three cabs. Air fresheners shaped like Christmas trees were tucked into individual plastic holders that had been stitched in a row to the back of the driver's seat. The suffocating scent of pine filled the car. CJ and Billy sat silent in the backseat.

"The whole airport's a goddamn boondoggle," said Jungle Jim, a freckle-faced, brown-skinned Chicano. He glanced back for a response, something he hadn't gotten from CJ or Billy since CJ had uttered "DIA" as he and Billy slid into the backseat from opposite sides of the cab.

"Three and a half billion dollars pissed away in the wind." Jungle Jim, punctuating his point, slapped his hand down on the front seat just as DIA's surrealistic main terminal rose in the distance from the desiccated Colorado plains, looking like a mammoth white revival tent sitting in the middle of a desert.

Jungle Jim continued his indictment. "Damn politicians don't know a thing about business. But then, they don't have to pay no bills. Take my business, for instance. I've got three of these cabs running twenty-four hours a day. Every one of 'em's the kind of rolling stock I'd want to ride in myself. Ain't a better set of cabs in the state." He paused, hoping for some thread of positive reinforcement from the back, but instead all he got was silence. CJ was busy trying to figure out how to approach Roland Jefferson when they got to Chicago, and Billy was still thinking about who might have tried to flatten them both with a Kenworth. Their silence didn't stop Jungle Jim. "We all pay the piper in the end. Me, I got drivers, repairs, gas, oil, not to mention new rubber. Don't nobody but politicians get a free lunch."

Jungle Jim whisked past what had once been a wheat field, where now a bevy of rickety old hay wagons, plows, and several rusted-out John Deere tractors stood, the result of an art-in-public-places mandate.

Jungle Jim attacked the assemblage with a vengeance. "Can you believe they paid somebody a hundred and sixty-five thousand for that junk?" He pointed back at the collection of farm implements. "I could have gotten them acres of the shit for free."

Jungle Jim took the exit ramp to the western terminal, finally slowing down as he approached the United section. He stopped abruptly at the fifth skycap station, gave the man a wink of recognition, and announced with true capitalistic flare to Billy and CJ, "Forty-five bucks."

CJ handed him a fifty while Billy collected their luggage from the trunk. "Keep the change."

Jungle Jim pocketed the fifty, jumped back in his cab, and eased away while Billy stood curbside trying to guess the number of times Jungle Jim ran through his anti-DIA spiel every day.

CJ and Billy entered the terminal pondering vastly different things. While CJ was busy thinking about how to deal with Roland Jefferson and maybe even locate Juney-boy Stokes, Billy was concentrating on whether the Colt .45 he had packed in his duffel bag would make it through airport security.

When their 737 landed at O'Hare three hours later, Billy's question had been answered and CJ had decided that as soon as they checked into their hotel they'd pay a visit to Roland Jefferson's house. Their South Side hotel was just off the Stevenson Expressway at 31st. Situated along the fringe of the Illinois Institute of Technology neighborhood, the hotel had been given a rave recommendation by Charlene Gentry. When CJ saw the drab brown, seedy-looking six-story building, with its faded white, pigeon-dropping-stained front awning and the collection of beer bottles in the gutter out front, he suspected that Charlene's memory of what Chicago's South Side hotels had been like when she was in nursing school had also eroded with time. He was pleasantly surprised, however, when he stepped inside the building to find an intimate, bright, refurbished lobby, pleasant people behind the front desk, and a tiny gift shop that he later found out carried the special brand of Durham, North Carolina—packaged cheroots he loved. As they checked in, no one at the registration counter seemed to pay any attention to their cowboy boots or their Stetsons.

When CJ and Billy reached their stuffy, unpretentious fourth-floor room, the message light on the phone was blinking. Billy tossed his duffel on the floor and his sweat-stained Stetson on one of the room's twin beds and walked over to open a window while CJ checked the message. Billy opened the window to a stream of humid air, immediately closed it, and looked for a thermostat to crank up the air-conditioning. He located the thermostat just to the left of the window and lowered it to 65 degrees.

CJ had finished listening to the phone message when Billy turned away from the window and the view of the parking lot and Dunkin' Donuts below.

"What's up?" said Billy, taking a seat on the edge of the bed closest to the window.

"Strange, real strange. Julie says Henry Bales checked out our sex-change magician, Dr. Sinclair. Seems as though he's never had a malpractice suit brought against him in his life. But according to Henry, he had a string of complaints to the medical peer review board from a patient several years back. The patient's name was Juney-boy Stokes. She also said Hampoli's wife called and said if I leave any more business cards in her mailbox she's callin' the cops."

"So much for your women scorned angle," said Billy. He picked his oil-stained duffel bag up off the floor and set it on the bed. "Think Stokes is alive?" he asked, rummaging through his duffel.

"I'm not sure. Right now I'm guessing he is."

Billy pulled a metal box the size of a large shaving kit out of the duffel bag and laid it on the bed.

CJ sat down on the other bed and opened the overnight bag he had tossed there earlier. He pulled out a map of Chicago and spread it out with a grunt, trying to ignore the pain in his shoulder. "According to Charlene, we can catch a cab up to Jefferson's." He ran his index finger along the Stevenson Expressway to South Cottage Grove Avenue where it intersected 47th a few blocks from Roland Jefferson's address on south Kenwood. "Shouldn't be more than a three-minute ride." When he looked up from the map, Billy had opened his box. CJ's eyes narrowed and his forehead wrinkled as he watched Billy pull a Colt revolver out of the metal box. CJ didn't know how many antique Colts Billy had, but he was aware of at least five: two Civil War Avenging Angels, a battered old army piece, an 1873 navy Peacemaker, and the .45 frontier six-shooter Billy was holding, the gun that reportedly won the West.

"Damn it, Billy, are you crazy draggin' that thing through airports? You're gonna have the FBI on our asses."

"Can't hit what you can't see," said Billy, laying the gun on the bed. He nodded at the metal box, adding, "Lined it with lead myself, using melted fishing sinkers and Krazy Glue. Left just enough unlined pockets for my shaving stuff. I expect it looks just like a shaving kit when it passes through those airport X-ray contraptions."

CJ shook his head in disbelief. Sometimes he wondered if Billy hadn't been hanging off the side of his Wyoming mountain too long. "Check that thing the way you're supposed to on our way back. If you don't, I'm leaving your gun-toting cowboy ass right here in Chicago."

Billy frowned and put the gun back in the box. He had backed CJ up on half a dozen bounty-hunting jobs, including one where they had to track down a four-hundred-pound sumo wrestler wanted on a Mann Act conviction. In order to subdue the wrestler when they found him living in the Utah desert in a hut made of cardboard boxes and kitchen-floor linoleum, CJ had had to use Billy's 30.06 as a club instead of a rifle. CJ hadn't complained about the handiness of the weapon Billy had smuggled through the Salt Lake City airport then, so he had a hard time understanding CJ's concern now.

They spent the next few minutes unpacking. It wasn't until CJ was hanging his pants in the closet, inhaling the strangely odd mixture of pine tar, mothballs, and cedar, that he realized Billy hadn't moved to hang anything up. CJ adjusted the lucky calico riverboat gambler's vest he always brought along on trips on a hanger. "Traveling pretty light, aren't you, Billy?"

"Don't plan on stayin' too long." Billy tucked a rumpled chambray shirt and a change of underwear into a bureau drawer.

CJ shut the closet door and patted down his pockets to make sure he had the key to the room. "Ready to rock and roll?"

Billy eyed his .45. "Should I bring Bertha along?"

"I don't think so. Everybody tells me Chicago's a peaceful enough town."

Billy closed the metal case reluctantly and slid it under the bed.

By the time they got to Roland Jefferson's house, CJ knew that nowhere in this lifetime or the next would he ever take another Lake City cab. Their driver smelled like a brewery, the only speed he seemed to know was sixty, and CJ swore that their three-mile trip had turned into ten.

Roland Jefferson lived in the end building of an orphaned but well-maintained cluster of eight rowhouses that remained in the 4300 block of Kenwood. The rowhouses were surrounded in every direction by vacant lots filled with automobiles up on cinder blocks, trash, and weeds. In the lot next to Roland's house someone had been barbecuing on a set of blackened bedsprings, and the remnants of the charcoal and burned ribs still clung to the metal.

"Damn," said Billy, exiting the cab behind CJ. "Ain't seen nothin' this ugly since Korea."

"Pretty bad," said CJ. He paid the driver as he surveyed the neighborhood.

"Thanks," said the driver, who was already gunning his motor, preparing to get back up to speed.

CJ stood on the sidewalk looking up at the modest rowhouses, double-checked the address, and started toward the door with Billy trailing behind. CJ rang the doorbell four times before Willette Jefferson answered. He had called ahead from their hotel lobby, posing as an insurance salesman, and asked for Mr. or Mrs. Jefferson to make sure someone was home. A polite woman had answered, confirmed who she was, and immediately declined any interest in insurance. It always amazed CJ how quickly some people gave out their names over the phone.

"Who is it?" asked Willette, peering through the door's diamond-shaped peep-hole.

Realizing that she was watching them, CJ smiled at the door self-consciously. "CJ Floyd. I'm trying to locate Roland Jefferson."

"He's not in."

"Can you tell me where to find him?" said CJ politely, imagining a frail, frightened woman cowering behind the door.

"No."

Politeness hadn't gained him admittance, so he moved on to plan B. "I'm here with my partner from Denver; we're friends of Mabel Pitts."

The deadbolt tumbled back, and the front door swung open just far enough to reveal a heavy-duty chain lock and the shadow of Willette Jefferson's face. "Why do you want to see Roland?" She eyed CJ and Billy suspiciously. "And how do you know Mabel?"

"Mabel sort of raised me."

"How's she doing?"

"She's dead," said CJ, hoping that the terse piece of information would make Willette eager to find out what had happened to Mabel.

Willette gasped and covered her mouth. "You two cops?" she asked finally. "I hear cops out West dress real strange." Her eyes shot up to CJ's Stetson.

"No, just friends of Mabel's."

Willette hesitated before unlatching the chain and swinging the door back fully. Far from frail, she was an aging, statuesque, green-eyed beauty. "Come on in."

As they followed her into the house CJ noticed that she had a ballerina's gait. He pegged her to be in her late fifties, early sixties tops, and from the firm look of her body he suspected she worked out every day. When they reached a sparsely furnished family room, Willette turned around quickly as if she expected to catch CJ and Billy watching something they shouldn't. She remained standing, never offering them a seat.

"My friend here's Billy DeLong," said CJ, trying not to let his gaze stray from Willette Jefferson's face. "Like I said outside, I'm CJ Floyd. You must be Willette."

"Good guess." It was said coldly enough for CJ to wonder if he might not need another Mabel reference. But this time Willette beat him to it. "What happened to Mabel?"

"Someone stabbed her."

Willette winced before a painful look of sorrow blanketed her face. "Mabel and I did a couple of semesters of college together. Believe it or not, we were both going to be doctors. Women ahead of our time. But we only lasted a year before men started to worm their way into our lives."

It surprised CJ that Willette would be so candid with strangers. He suppressed his urge to ask if one of the men she was referring to had been LeRoy Polk. "So you tossed medicine aside for men?"

Willette frowned, preferring her description to CJ's. She seemed to anticipate what was coming next. "I know what happened to LeRoy. That's why you're looking for Roland, isn't it?"

"Partially; we're also looking for Juney-boy Stokes."

"Is that poor lamb caught up in LeRoy's murder

too?" Willette caught herself and raised her hand to her mouth when she realized how incriminating her statement sounded for Roland. "I didn't mean it to sound as though Roland's involved."

"I understand," said CJ, recognizing that if he was going to have any chance of finding either man he needed to keep Willette talking. "Is there any chance we might be able to catch up with Roland today?"

Willette thought about CJ's question for a moment. "He might be at Gipson's, over on Record Row."

"I'm not familiar with it."

"Gipson's," repeated Willette with emphasis. "The place is about all that's left over from Chicago's rhythm and blues recording industry heyday. Roland used to own the place when it was Turnstyle Records. He and a bunch of old-timers like to hang out there and reminisce."

"Did he own Turnstyle with LeRoy Polk?"

A hint of impatience crept into Willette's voice. "You'll have to ask him that yourself, Forty-ninth and Cottage Grove. It's easy to find."

"One last question. Was Daddy Doo-Wop straight?"

"If you mean was he gay, no, he wasn't."

"What about bisexual?"

"I wouldn't know."

Suspecting that he had run out of passwords, CJ nodded to Billy that it was time to go, and they followed Willette back down the hallway to the front door. "Thanks for your time." As they stepped back out into the sticky Chicago afternoon, a southeasterly breeze had kicked up off Lake Michigan and the red iron-ore haze from northern Indiana's steel mills hung in the air.

Willette looked up into the curtain of pollution and

smiled as if it had come to rescue her. "Good luck in finding out who murdered Mabel." As she turned and closed
the front door, CJ couldn't help but notice that she hadn't
wished them luck in finding LeRoy's killer.

As they walked down the steps, CJ pulled the map of
Chicago out of his back pocket and handed it to Billy.
"Fold this thing out for me, Billy, my shoulder's giving me
fits." He reached in his vest pocket, slipped out a couple
of Motrin, and popped them both.

"How the hell can you do that without water?" asked
Billy, folding open the map in front of them.

"Practice." CJ forced back the urge to belch. He located Cottage Grove, noting where it intersected 49th.
"Looks like it's about six blocks west and a couple blocks
south. You up for hoofin' it?"

"Damn straight. No more Chicago cabs for me."
Billy refolded the map and stuffed it in his back pocket as
they started walking down the strangely quiet street toward Cottage Grove. Billy was the one who heard the car.
Later he would tell CJ that the sound of the car's engine
revving made him think that their earlier tipsy cab driver
was returning until he looked back and saw a dark green,
late-model Buick bearing down on them. He shouted to
CJ, and they dove for the ground. The three quick pops
from a .38 were masked by the sound of the car's whining
engine and the guttural roar of dual glass-packed mufflers.

The Buick was a block and a half away before either
of them looked back up from the crumbling sidewalk they
were hugging.

"Shit," said CJ, reaching to make sure that his injured
shoulder hadn't popped out of place. "Did you get a plate
number?"

"Hell, no," said Billy.

"Buick?"

"Century," Billy said with certainty.

"Green."

"Yeah."

"What did you make of the cannon?"

"Small-caliber. Probably a .38. Nothin' bigger." Billy stood up and started dusting himself off. His shirt was ripped open from his silver Hopi belt buckle to the right shoulder. The only thing he could think of at the moment was that he had at least had the good sense to pack another shirt.

CJ got up, moving slowly, his eyes locked on the rip running down the front of Billy's shirt. "You okay?"

"Didn't piss my pants."

"Me neither," said CJ, glancing down to make certain.

The breeze that had been blowing earlier suddenly died, and the air became desert-morning still. CJ looked around at the vacant lots surrounding them and back up the street toward where the Buick had disappeared. The same eerie silence had returned. He glanced at the vacant lot to their right. "The lead's probably out there somewhere. Wanna take a look?"

"Nah," said Billy. "What's the use?"

"Think you're right."

"Could have been gangs, in a neighborhood like this," said Billy.

"Or a close Chicago connection of Lawrence Hampoli's. Maybe even Roland Jefferson, or Juney-boy Stokes," said CJ. They dusted themselves off and CJ checked his shoulder again before they started walking toward Cottage

Grove. This time their pace was brisker, and every so often they glanced over their shoulders to make certain there were no more green Buicks approaching.

"Hope Jefferson's at this Gipson place. It'll save us a hell of a lot of time," said CJ as they turned onto 49th Street.

Billy wasn't thinking about Roland Jefferson or saving time. He was thinking about the battery of insults and assaults that he had suffered in the past two days. His life had been threatened by a second-rate mobster, he had spent an afternoon reading the propaganda of some sex-change quack, he had been run off the road by an eighteen-wheeler and nearly killed, his truck was totaled, and now someone had tried to pepper him with a .38 from a speeding car. The only things on Billy's mind at the moment were that he and CJ had better start winning a few battles and that he was damn sure going to dig out his Peacemaker as soon as he got back to the hotel.

Twenty-six

Tyrone Polk had been claustrophic ever since a Hell Week fraternity hazing during his second year of prepharmacy studies at Purdue, when his future frat brothers had taken him and six other blindfolded pledges to a Lafayette, Indiana, suburb, locked them in what they were told was a meat locker, poured a pint of Karo syrup into each pledge's hair, slipped stocking caps over their heads, and shackled them to drainpipes. In reality they had been locked in a thirty-by-thirty-foot storage room at a cardboard-container plant that had been stocked with enough hundred-pound blocks of ice to generate the sub-freezing temperatures and life-threatening scare their brothers desired. It had taken Tyrone and the others over two hours to free themselves and make their way the seven miles back to their dorms with stocking caps still plastered to their heads. Ever since, Tyrone had harbored a deep-seated fear of cramped quarters and a hatred of the cold. So when he was dragged out of bed by two very eager Denver policemen the same morning that CJ and Billy left for Chicago, handcuffed, taken to jail, strip-searched, fingerprinted, and locked in an over air-conditioned, 55-degree, ten-by-ten-foot jail cell on charges of receiving stolen goods, construction fraud, and forgery, all the worst fears of his life were rekindled. The charges had been levied by the Denver DA's office on the strength of a ream of incriminating documents given to them by Clothilde Polk's lawyer, who had demanded that Tyrone be arrested. Tyrone had been shivering in the 55-degree chill all morning with his stomach in knots and the veins in his temples pounding. He was past trying to figure out why Clothilde would have done this to him, and he was busy contemplating what to do next.

Tyrone was pacing the cell, hugging himself and trying to stay warm, when a burly policeman in official departmental summer-issue dark blue shorts and a matching crewneck shirt walked up to the holding cell. "Polk, you get to come with me." He unlocked the cell with a magnetic key card and motioned for Tyrone to step out. "You must know somebody special to spring you on a PR bond this fast." Tyrone smiled and walked with him stride for stride down a long, wide block of empty cells, hoping that wherever they were headed would be warmer. Halfway down the cell block a body-wrenching shiver shot through Tyrone. The policeman watched unsympathetically as Tyrone lurched. "Gets hot in these holding areas with all that body heat; sometimes these cells get stacked up ten people deep. We like to keep the temperature down around sixty." He led Tyrone through a heavy metal door that required the use of two magnetic access cards and into the light and warmth of a room where Tyrone's attorney was completing papers for his release. Several other people were in the room. Tyrone knew only that his attorney's name was Clyde Bodine, that he worked for a firm that specialized in negotiating sweetheart contracts with the city, and that LeRoy Polk had retained the firm to grease the skids for his Stax of Wax project.

Tyrone looked at the officer who had escorted him out. "Which one's Bodine?"

The policeman pointed to a tall, casually dressed black man standing in the corner talking to a clerk. Tyrone rushed over to the man. "You Bodine?"

"Yes."

"Can you let me have a quarter? I'm Tyrone Polk."

Bodine, a seasoned attorney who had just about seen it all, seemed unfazed. He reached in his pocket and handed Tyrone a quarter.

"Where's a pay phone?"

"Over there, on the far wall. Who do you need to call?"

"None of your business."

Bodine shrugged and coolly went back to completing his paperwork.

A woman with a lacquered, six-inch-high Texas tease beehive hairdo hung up the phone as Tyrone approached. She sidestepped Tyrone as he grabbed the receiver, dropped the quarter in the coin slot, and dialed his number. Still a bit claustrophobic, he waited nervously for someone to pick up on the other end. On the fourth ring, Julie Madrid answered.

"I need to speak to CJ; this is Tyrone Polk. It's urgent." He started shivering again as soon as he finished the sentence.

"He won't be back in the office until tomorrow," said Julie.

Tyrone's teeth started chattering. "What time?"

Julie looked at the copy of CJ's itinerary on her desk. "I'd say about five," she said, knowing that she would be working late the day he got back, as she always did after he'd been out of town.

"I'll be there," said Tyrone.

"Can I tell him what it's about?"

"I'll tell him myself. But if he beats me there, just say I need him to help me settle a score with Clothilde."

Twenty-seven

Aside from the fact that the building was brick rather than concrete and square instead of round, Gipson's Original House of Chicago Soul had the forbidding camouflaged look of a World War II German bunker as it stood gasping for life in the middle of a block of boarded-up buildings that had once been the heart of Chicago's Record Row. The windows of the drafty old building were covered with a heavy-gauge green-tinted plastic all year round in constant preparation for Chicago's notorious November-through-February wind known as the hawk. The plastic filtered the light from the inside down to an anemic forty-watt glow that told the casual onlooker that nobody was home. But as the last outpost of Chicago soul, Gipson's teamed with activity day and night.

"Looks deserted to me," said Billy, peering into one of the windows, trying to see through the plastic.

CJ ignored Billy's grade school attempt to see what was happening, and before Billy realized it, CJ was through the front door. As he rushed to catch up with CJ, Billy noticed the ratty, weather-beaten, bullet-hole-riddled sign above the door that read WING GIP-SON'S: THE ORIGINAL HOUSE OF CHICAGO SOUL, and he wondered if going inside would subject him to another life-threatening situation.

The same woman who had greeted Roland Jefferson the day after his trip to Denver met CJ and Billy, but instead of sporting go-go boots and hip huggers, she was now wearing 1955-style Capris and a heavily starched low-buttoned cotton blouse with a Rorschach-ink-blot-like mustard stain above the right pocket. "Help you gents?" she said warmly, recognizing Billy and CJ as first-time visitors to Gipson's but potential longtime customers.

"We're looking for a couple of brothers we're told hang out here, Roland Jefferson and Juney-boy Stokes," said CJ, making certain to mention both men.

"Can't help you with either, but five'll get you ten Wing probably can. Follow me, I'll give you an introduction."

CJ wondered why the woman was being so helpful until he remembered that everyone in the world didn't spend their life dealing with bottom-feeding criminals hopscotching their way around the law. It was more likely that the woman thought he and Billy were part of the extended family of rhythm and blues old-timers and nostalgia buffs she dealt with every day.

They followed the woman down a wide, dimly lit corridor where hundreds of photographs of rhythm and blues legends hung on the walls. Billy kept up with her, but CJ slowed down to gawk at the photos and the frequent detailed inscriptions written on them. He could almost hear Daddy Doo-Wop Polk's jive-talking machine-gun rat-a-tat introductions to their songs. He eased past photos of Kenny Fullett, the Sequins, and the Cordaires, remembering every one of the Cordaires' names: Ulysses "Chubby" Renfroe, Henry Williams, Jr., Dickey Thomas, Tony Racine, and the big brown-skinned brother who sang baritone, Housted. He stared at yellowing photographs of some of the most famous names in rhythm and blues in their youth and came to a dead stop at the sepia-toned photo of his favorite singing group, Mystique, the Gary, Indiana, group that recorded "Dream On." He was staring at the inscription Sammy Cales, Mystique's lead singer, had written on the photo—"To Ellisteen, We got it going now, Baby. See you in Chicago"—as if he expected Sammy to break into some 1950s glide-step choreography, when Billy came back to get him. "Come on, CJ, we're here on business." Startled, even a little embarrassed, CJ followed Billy past dozens of additional photographs until he stepped down a filthy white-shag-carpeted incline and entered a room that was thick with smoke. Ruby red and avocado vinyl booths lined the walls, and 1950s-style tables with pink-and-silver-flecked two-inch-thick formica tops dominated the center of each booth. Four huge jukeboxes, a Rock-ola, a Seeburg, and two Wurlitzers, names that once dominated the American jukebox industry, occupied the four corners of the room. A full-service bar sat along the wall between the Wurlitzers, where two aging waitresses in straight, tight-fitting, unpleated skirts were waiting for their drink orders. Jerry Butler's classic ballad "For Your Precious Love" was playing on the Rock-ola.

Most of the booths held three or four people, and as CJ scanned the haze, he realized that there wasn't a single booth that was unoccupied. He looked around the room a second time to get his bearings, since experience had taught him that in times of war and peace, whenever you enter new territory, you always look for a second rabbit hole out. He located an exit just to the right of one of the Wurlitzers and nudged Billy. They had shared enough bounty-hunting assignments for Billy to know what the nudge meant.

A wiry little man in Levi's and black high-top Converse All-Star shoes came up to the woman who had escorted them into the room and whispered something to her that CJ couldn't make out. When she turned to respond to the man, CJ counted the people in the room. There were just over thirty: some engaged in a steady buzz of conversation and clinking of glasses, others just sitting back enjoying the music. Something about the customers struck CJ as odd, and it wasn't until Jerry Butler had finished singing and a gray-haired woman who looked to be in her late sixties got up from one of the booths and walked over to feed the jukebox that CJ realized what it was. Everyone in the place was a senior citizen.

Finished with her conversation, the hostess turned to CJ. "Wing's sittin' in the last booth over there by the Rock-ola. Come on, I'll introduce you."

Louis "Wing" Gipson, the man who had met Roland Jefferson after Daddy Doo-Wop Polk had been murdered, was sitting in a booth alone, lip-synching to the Dells' romantic R&B classic "Oh, What a Night." A freshly prepared rum and Coke sat in the middle of the table. From three feet away Billy caught a whiff of what had once been his favorite libation, and he immediately reached into his pocket and popped a couple of sticks of gum.

"These two brothers need to speak with you," said the woman in Capris, smiling and interrupting Wing just as he started to take a sip of rum and Coke. After a half-swallow, he put the tumbler back down. "If you're lookin' for money, I'm fresh out." He inched up in his seat, reached in his right pants pocket, and pulled it inside out. When he did, the stump of his amputated left arm started to gyrate. Wing grinned, patting the stump. "Always does that when I'm sittin'. Doctors say it's an involuntary reflex. Wish I could get my Johnson to do the same thing." He stared at CJ's and Billy's Stetsons, Billy's torn shirt, and then down at their boots. "What you two cowboys want?"

"We're looking for Roland Jefferson and Juney-boy Stokes," said CJ.

"They ain't got no money either. I can vouch for that."

"We're not out to collect on bad debts. We're trying to see if they can help with a case in Denver."

Wing put down his drink, suddenly fully engaged. "I should have known it from the Wild West getup. You're lookin' for who murdered Doo-Wop Polk." He paused and took another sip of Coke. "You two got names?"

"CJ Floyd."

"And Billy DeLong," chimed in Billy between smacks of gum.

"Clothilde Polk hired me to look into what happened to her father."

Wing broke into a close-to-toothless grin. "What happened, my ass. The cocksucker was murdered. I'm surprised that that stuck-up little sexpot daughter of his would even care. She spent most of her life suckin' LeRoy dry."

Every time CJ turned a corner he got another reaffirmation that Clothilde was a whole lot different from the way she had presented herself to him at first. "Think she could have killed him?"

"Accordin' to how the *Defender* said he died, yeah. She wasted a shitpot of LeRoy's money screwing around. I'd wager she could have done it."

It still didn't make sense to CJ that Clothilde would have hired him to find a phantom killer unless she had some convoluted plan to involve him or use him as a patsy to track down a bunch of tapes she really didn't have. He remembered what Vernon Lowe had told him at Mabel Pitts's funeral about Winston Dunn and Sergeant Fuller looking into the possibility that he and Tyrone may have killed LeRoy and decided that as bizarre as it may have seemed, maybe Clothilde did have a plan.

CJ turned his attention back to Wing. "Mind if we sit down?"

"Be my guest."

As he and Billy slid into the booth across from Wing and his rum and Coke, Billy popped another stick of gum. One of the waitresses who had been standing at the bar earlier came over to take their drink order, but CJ waved her off, not wanting to add to Billy's tension. "What do you know about LeRoy's other kid, Tyrone?"

"Not much, except his mother's a good lady. He lived here on the South Side most of his life, but you wouldn't have known it. LeRoy kept him out of sight—in them mostly white schools."

CJ thought about whether he should tell Wing that Mabel was dead and decided against it, reasoning that Wing might be a lot more talkative if he thought only one person had been murdered.

"Do you know if Tyrone had any knowledge about explosives or any background in medicine?"

Wing cocked one eye suspiciously. "Beats me."

Wing's quick response bothered CJ. He thought about why he had been so lackadaisical about pursuing Tyrone's background until he remembered that Tyrone was Mabel's son. He sat back in the booth, wondering what he might have missed about Tyrone. "Let's get back to Roland Jefferson and Juney-boy Stokes," he said finally.

"Let's," said Wing. "That's if you're buyin' the drinks."

"My pleasure." CJ eyed Billy, daring him to reach for another stick of gum.

Wing chugged the rest of his rum and Coke and held his empty glass up in the air for the waitress to see. He wiggled it around several times to get her attention. "First off, I ain't seen Juney-boy in years, not since he went from being Juney-boy to callin' hisself June. Shame, if you ask me. The son of a bitch had the finest voice you ever heard. Could've made it big."

"June?" asked CJ, stringing Wing along.

"The man had a sex change. Had it done out your way in Colorado. I figured you'd know that." Wing grimaced and grabbed his crotch as though he could feel the pain of Juney-boy's surgery.

"When was that?"

"I'm thinkin' fifteen years ago or thereabouts, close to when LeRoy quit pokin' him in the butt." Wing smiled at the waitress who had just walked up to the booth with his fresh rum and Coke. "Don't tell me you didn't know that LeRoy liked dippin' his wick into more than one kind of well. Hell, everybody on the South Side knew that."

CJ watched Wing finish a third rum and Coke in two swallows. "What made LeRoy back away from his relationship with Juney-boy?"

"I ain't sure, but my guess is it had somethin' to do with the fact that LeRoy had pinched the rights to most of Juney-boy's songs and white folks were knockin' on LeRoy's door, throwin' money at him for the rights to rerecord 'em. Guess LeRoy didn't want to share the proceeds. Pity, all his life poor Juney-boy never seemed to get what was comin' to him. His momma dressed him like a girl till he was seven; LeRoy ripped off the rights to his records; he never knew whether he was fish or fowl; and LeRoy could talk the poor confused bastard into anything."

"Even a sex change?"

Wing thought hard about CJ's question before taking another swig of his rum and Coke. "I'd book even money on it."

"Sounds to me like LeRoy Polk stole something from just about everybody he ever knew. Who'd he clip the worst?" asked CJ. Wing waved him off with his stump and glanced at the Seeburg as the classic rhythm and blues ballad "Anyday Now" began its sad, enticing, three-minute-fifteen-second tale of damaged love. Wing didn't look back CJ's way until Chuck Jackson was halfway through his second lamenting refrain. Suddenly Wing was singing along, lost in another time until the record ended.

"Helped produce that one myself. Never let it spin without chiming in. As for your question about LeRoy, I'd say he screwed everybody about the same, but I always loved the way he stuck it to Larry Hampoli and his fuckin' red nickel crew. Back in the fifties in the black joints like this we was supposed to give Hampoli a double cut of the money from the music played on the jukes by makin' customers use special red-striped nickels that only paid the owner half their face value." Wing nodded toward the Rock-ola. "LeRoy figured out a way to rig the jukeboxes so the music would play whenever the owner wanted without dropping in the nickels. Like I said, I wouldn't say he screwed Hampoli more than anybody else, but I loved the fact he did."

"Did he ever stick it to you?"

"Yeah, but that was thirty-five years ago. Don't matter now. He sold me a piece of that record company of his, Stax of Wax. A piece that really didn't exist. I only bought in at five percent. Some folks bought in a lot higher."

"Like Roland and Willette? Think either one of them could have been pissed off enough to kill LeRoy?"

Wing hesitated before answering. "Back in the old days, maybe, but not now." He finished off his drink and waved at the waitress for another.

At the rate Wing was polishing off drinks, CJ figured he needed to wrap up their conversation before going broke. "Word is LeRoy pilfered a bunch of unreleased golden oldies by R&B legends from Hampoli, and they're now worth a fortune."

"I've heard that too," said Wing. "Fuck if they are. If they were, LeRoy would've met his maker a lot sooner than a few days ago."

The waitress brought Wing another drink along with a fresh coaster and two cocktail napkins. As she placed them on the table, she gave him a look that said, *Don't you think you've had enough?*

Wing ignored her. Before taking a sip he reached in his shirt pocket and pulled out a couple of red-striped nickels. "Do me a favor." He handed the coins to Billy. "I'm feeling a little too frosted to negotiate the room right now. How about droppin' these in the Rock-ola over there and punching in D5 and D11?"

Billy got up and headed for the jukebox, happy to get away from the smell of rum.

"You wouldn't have killed LeRoy yourself?" asked CJ, pressing to finish his questions before Wing became incoherent.

"Son of a bitch wouldn't have been worth it." Wing was starting to stumble over his words.

"Then I'm back to my first question. Got any idea where I can find Roland Jefferson?"

"Ain't seen him for a couple of days. I'd say he's hidin'."

"From who?"

"You would be my guess." Wing stared across the table, trying to focus on the spot where Billy had been sitting. Then, realizing that Billy had left, he looked around the room until he spotted him. "Him too." He nodded toward Billy.

"Don't know why he'd be ducking us."

" 'Cause he was in Denver the day LeRoy died."

CJ's eyebrows arched into perfect V's.

"Gotcha there, didn't I, cowboy?"

"Did his wife know he was in Denver?" asked CJ, trying to gauge Willette Jefferson's potential involvement.

Wing looked at CJ as if he were half sloshed. "Hell, yeah."

His answer made CJ start thinking. Maybe Willette had steered them to Gipson's knowing that Roland wouldn't be there, or maybe the hostess had directed them to Wing at Willette's request so they could hear him spout off about why everyone in Chicago had a reason to kill LeRoy Polk. CJ looked up as Billy slipped back into the booth. "A Casual Look," one of the songs Wing had asked Billy to punch in on the jukebox, began playing. This time CJ hummed along with the lyrics.

"See you know that one," said Wing.

"One of my favorites when I was a kid."

"I like a man who's into music." He pulled two more red nickels out of his shirt pocket and handed them to CJ. "Anytime you're in Chicago, you're welcome to drop in here and use 'em. You'll always get 'em back before you leave. That way you get to hear the music for free and forever."

"Thanks." CJ pocketed the coins. "One last thing. You wouldn't know anyone with a green Buick who likes to take potshots at pedestrians?"

"Can't say I do. Why?"

"No special reason," said CJ as he and Billy stood

up to leave. He tossed a twenty on the table for Wing's drinks.

A sad look crossed Wing's face as if he were about to say good-bye to a couple of lifelong friends. "Keep on truckin'." He transitioned into lip-synching to "A Casual Look" as he rolled what was left of his rum and Coke around in his glass.

When CJ and Billy reached the ramp with the filthy shag carpeting, the woman who had greeted them was standing at the bottom of the incline. "Did Wing fill you in on what you wanted to know?"

"Pretty much," said CJ.

"Good. Did he offer you any red nickels?"

"He sure did."

"Hang on to them. They'll be valuable one day. You can tell folks they were given to you personally by Louis 'Wing' Gipson, one of the movers and shakers behind Scat Back Records and the original sound of Chicago Soul."

"How'd he lose his arm?" asked Billy, who had been wanting to ask the question since first meeting Wing.

"In Korea." The woman turned to her right and pointed to a small framed object on the wall that CJ had missed earlier.

Billy leaned down to take a look and turned back to CJ, wide-eyed. "Silver Star."

"Wing was an ordnance NCO and machine gunner during the battle for Hill 351 in Korea; only two people left that place alive," said the woman proudly. "You probably know it as Pork Chop Hill."

CJ bent over to take a good look at the medal. "Learn something new every day," he said, starting up the ramp. He and Billy both stopped at the top of the ramp as the sound of a new jukebox tune began playing in the background.

"That's DII," said Billy.

As the mellow sound of another Jerry Butler tune, "Make It Easy on Yourself," worked its way up to where they were standing, CJ looked back down the ramp feeling as though they had just passed through some strange musical time warp.

Twenty-eight

Two days before actual surgery, Maurice Sinclair always walked his patients through a dry run of their gender-reassignment procedure that included everything from discussing the details of how induction anesthesia would be performed to providing them with a videotape of the actual surgical procedure. He had developed the protocol because he was the kind of man who didn't like being second-guessed or having loose ends. Part of the dry run also included surgically draping his patient operating-room—style and briefly having them assume the uncomfortable position they would be in for their nearly three hours on the operating table.

Gregory Borden, a delicate, five-foot-ten, thin-boned bird of a man, had had a gender-identity problem for as far back as he could remember. Eighteen months earlier he had walked into Dr. Sinclair's office looking for help. Two weeks later he was on the road to gender-reassignment surgery. He had lived as a woman for nearly a year, taking enough estrogen to develop normal-sized female breasts and atrophy his testes and prostate, and he had undergone so much counseling that he now knew the psychologist's questions before they were asked. But it had only been in the past few weeks that he had been comfortable with giving a dwindling number of friends and family members notice of his surgery date. For Gregory Borden, the final hours before the end of his lifelong agony were now at hand.

Gregory sat up from his reclining position on Dr. Sinclair's examining table, waiting for the videotape of the procedure he would undergo to appear on a TV monitor above his head. It was six-thirty P.M., and he and Dr. Sinclair were alone in the examination room. Gregory was still dressed in a hospital gown from Dr. Sinclair's final presurgical examination and a draft from the air-conditioning vent above his head had him shivering. For months Dr. Sinclair had told him what to expect. That his reconstructed vagina may not appear as perfect as he had envisioned. That he was going to have to endure the discomfort of an indwelling catheter for several postoperative days and that hot sitz baths would be a daily routine for weeks after the surgery. Dr. Sinclair had also emphasized that sexual activity would be out of the question for two to two and a half months after the procedure.

Dr. Sinclair stepped over to the monitor, adjusted it, and punched up the videotape on the VCR. Then he stepped back and patted Gregory on the shoulder reassuringly as the tape began. The entire three-hour surgical procedure had been edited down to fifteen critical min-

utes that Dr. Sinclair considered essential viewing for his
patients. There were five minutes of presurgical proce-
dures and Hollywood voice-overs before the narrator announced, with the graphic surgical procedure now filling
the screen, "A U-shaped skin incision will be made so
that part of your scrotum will be used to form a pocket
that will eventually become the posterior or back portion of your new vagina. You should be aware that there
will be some bleeding. Your testes will be pulled down-
ward along with the spermatic cord, which will be
clamped, amputated, and tied off." Gregory Borden grimaced, giving Dr. Sinclair a helpless look when the spermatic cord was severed. It was the only time during the
entire fifteen-minute videotape that he flinched.

Dr. Sinclair took Gregory's right hand in his own,
patting it reassuringly as the video continued. "The re-
mainder of the scrotum will become the anterior or
front part of your new vagina. Following the scrotal reconstruction, your penis will be denuded of its skin, the
urethra dissected out and redirected so that you can uri-
nate, and a small portion of the tip of your penis will be
used to form a new clitoris. After that a suitable vaginal
cavity will be constructed to the depth of your residual
prostate."

Gregory's eyes stayed glued to the videotape. It was
strange how actually seeing the surgery brought home to
him for the first time that he would be losing a part of
himself. But it was a part he never should have had; an
unnecessary appendage, which had constrained what he
should have been all his life, a woman. Recalling the tor-
ment he had lived with for thirty-two years, he knew
that he was doing the right thing.

Except for the voice on the tape, the room was silent as the final phases of the vaginal reconstruction procedure were illustrated. Gregory continued to stare at the monitor for several minutes after the videotape ended.

"Any questions?" asked Dr. Sinclair when he felt Gregory was ready to respond.

"No." Gregory Borden's voice had an urgent *let's get this done* ring.

"Then you should probably get out of that gown and get dressed now," said Sinclair, moving to leave the room.

Gregory walked over to where his clothes were hung and pulled a boldly patterned floral blouse from its hanger. Dr. Sinclair stopped and turned back to Gregory. "You know that if you have any questions I'm available twenty-four hours a day, and if you choose not to have the procedure, I will clearly understand."

Gregory's cheeks had flushed. "I've prepared for this too long to turn back now, Doc. It's in your hands now."

Dr. Sinclair opened the door just wide enough to exit. "I'll be in my office if you need me. The tape is yours to keep." He offered Gregory a final smile of reassurance, then disappeared from the room.

Five minutes later Gregory Borden was gone, leaving Dr. Sinclair alone in his office, seated behind his desk in the supple leather chair a grateful patient had given him. He was finishing up some dictation after a long twelve-hour day. He had turned off the office air-conditioning to allow a soothing evening breeze in through the partially opened French doors behind him. He was in the midst of dictating his final presurgical progress notes on Gregory Borden when he decided to have a glass of iced tea. As he got up from his chair to head to the small refrigerator in the far corner of the room, he glanced at a letter from the peer-review committee of the state Board of Medical Examiners that he had received the previous day. The letter stated that there had been a recent inquiry into the level of medical and surgical care he had afforded a patient named Juneyboy Stokes in a case of gender-reassignment surgery fifteen years earlier. Protocol required that whenever such cases were reevaluated by peer review, the physician involved had to be notified in writing and by certified mail. The drab green postal service certified mail sticker on the back of the letter he had signed had remained on top of a pile of papers on his desk, gnawing at his subconscious all day. He suspected that the inquiry had been generated by the snooping bail bondsman who had visited him, CJ Floyd.

He had just stepped around the edge of his desk on his way to the refrigerator when the report of a rifle startled him, and he looked back toward the open French doors, where the sound had come from. As he did, a second bullet, which he would later learn came from a 30.06 high-powered rifle, shattered a pane of glass in one of the French doors, vibrated several others into cracking, and lodged in the two-inch-thick permaplaqued certificate of surgical residency hanging on the wall in front of his desk. It took him a few seconds to realize that someone was shooting at him. He jumped away from the doors, out of the line of fire, wondering if after all of these years one of his patients had finally leaped off the edge of sanity. Panting loudly, he eased back flush against the wall behind his desk and slipped down into a crouched, airplane-crash position, arms over his head, hoping that there wouldn't be any more shots. When he finally summoned up the nerve to reach over and close the French doors, he realized that the back of his shirt was wet. He scooted back to his position of safety against the wall and let out a sigh, thinking *Why the hell would anyone be shooting at me?* when it hit him that the shooting, CJ Floyd's visit, and the certified letter had to be tied to the reason. With his back to the wall and his legs spread out beneath the desk, he began running the names of patients who might have reason to want to kill him through his head. Juney-boy Stokes's name kept recurring. Clearing his head with a quick shake, he tried to remember if he had kept the bogus request for consultation that CJ Floyd had filled out in his office. He finally mustered up the courage to stand up. He inched his way around his desk, out of any line of fire through the French doors, grabbed the certified letter off his desk, and reread it.

After reading the letter three times, he decided that no amount of patient confidentiality was worth getting killed. He ducked back down to the floor and crawled in front of his desk, past the French doors, and out of his office. Once he was in the hallway, he rushed to the patient records area, pulled out the file drawer marked D through F, and rummaged through the records until he found a chart labeled FLOYD, CJ. The chart was sealed with a piece of red tape, and a stamp on the jacket read "Account Paid in Full, No Longer a Patient of Record." He popped the seal, pulled out the history form, and ran his fingers across the top of the sheet looking for a phone number. When he saw the number, his pulse slowed for the first time since the shots. He sat down on the edge of the reception desk to dial the number, thanking his maker that he kept the records of all his patients, imposters or not. He was, after all, a man who abhorred loose ends.

Twenty-nine

After leaving Gipson's, CJ had rented the only car left at the discount rental agency down the street from the hotel, and he and Billy spent most of the rest of the day looking for Roland Jefferson at the list of South Side rib joints, dimly lit bars, and sleepy jazz clubs the hostess at Gipson's had told them Roland frequented. After six hours of searching they came up empty-handed, but during their canvass they turned up a couple of old-time Chicago rhythm and blues artists and a DJ who had worked with Daddy Doo-Wop Polk during the fifties. The DJ confirmed that LeRoy had ripped Larry Hampoli off by stealing "a shitpot full" of what were now extremely valuable unreleased recordings. "Didn't nobody but brothers know about it back then," the DJ had emphasized.

When Billy told the old DJ that they had been shot at just down the street from Roland Jefferson's house, the man laughed, showing a mouth full of red, inflamed, toothless gums, and said, "Hampoli's got connections that stretch from here to California. He probably put a shooter on your ass just to see if you'd mess your pants."

LeRoy Polk's friends also confirmed one other thing. Juney-boy Stokes had been a sexually confused and tormented human being who had vacillated between being heterosexual and bisexual all his life.

They dragged back to their hotel just after sunset, dog-tired from navigating an unfamiliar city in their second sardine-can-sized car in two days. The message light on the phone was blinking again. CJ picked up the receiver and punched in the code for voice mail. Julie was on the other end with a message that sounded especially rushed. "It's getting real dicey here in Denver. Tyrone Polk called, said he'd catch you tomorrow. Clothilde called about four and said someone broke into her apartment and trashed it. Claims they were looking for some old R&B tapes. She said to tell you she was going to be staying at her bookkeeper's tonight and for you to call her as soon as you get back in town. I've got the number she'll be at. She sounded scared, CJ." There was a long pause before Julie added, "Rosie says the Bel Air's done and he'll pick you up from DIA. Don't you and Billy scarf down too many of those Chitown Vienna sausages. See ya."

CJ hung up the phone wondering if he hadn't picked the wrong place to look for LeRoy Polk's murderer, but it troubled him even more that he might also be searching in the wrong place for whoever had killed Mabel.

He stretched out on the bed, second-guessing himself as he watched Billy polish off the cold double cheeseburger he had stashed in his duffel when they had stopped to eat earlier in the day. CJ kicked himself for not also ordering a burger to go.

The next morning they staked out Roland Jefferson's house. The *Tribune* was still wrapped in a rubber band on the front porch when they showed up, and when Billy checked the mailbox, mail from the previous day was still inside. Three hours later neither Roland nor Willette had appeared. CJ's concern about having enough time to return the rental car and make it to O'Hare and Billy's constant complaining about feeling like a sardine brought the surveillance to an end.

CJ ran ten to fifteen miles over the speed limit all the way back to O'Hare, only to find out when he got there that their flight was thirty minutes late. In their haste CJ had forgotten about Billy's gun and his promise about leaving Billy behind. Billy hadn't. He rushed ahead of CJ, slapped his duffel on the screening belt with a loud thump, and quickly slipped through the metal detector.

CJ grimaced in anticipation, but Billy's duffel passed through the X-ray screening as swiftly as Billy had eased through the metal detector. As they gathered their bags on the other side, Billy was grinning from ear to ear.

When they reached their departure gate it was packed with business travelers, vacationers trying to get a jump on summer, and two women's field hockey teams. Every seat in the waiting area was occupied.

"Think I can buy a shirt that says Cubs in one of those shops we passed?" Billy was rocking back and forth on the heels of his boots like an excited kid.

"It's a good bet," said CJ, checking out the standing-room-only situation and thinking about how long it was going to take them to deplane on the other end.

"I rooted for the Cubs when I was in the service," said Billy, explaining a sports enthusiast side of himself that CJ had never seen. "I'm gonna head on back and see if I can't find a shirt. Be back in a minute."

Billy hadn't been east of the Colorado state line in years, so CJ suspected that the enticements in the concourse shops would keep him occupied for the time they had to wait. "Don't end up missing the plane."

"Not a chance. Blue skies and sunshine are my thing, not skyscrapers and soot." He tipped his hat to a woman carrying a couple of shopping bags filled with designer boxes, danced around her with an "Excuse me," and headed off down the concourse.

CJ stepped over to a spot that had opened along the concourse railing and leaned back against the polished chrome. For the first time in nearly two hours he finally had a chance to catch his breath. He suddenly wanted a cheroot as badly as he had wanted one in years. But more than that he wanted to put the Daddy Doo-Wop case behind him.

He sank his weight into the railing as he tried to determine how close he was to getting his wish. His first assumption had always been that whoever had murdered LeRoy Polk had some background in medicine. He didn't have any reason to change his mind. His second assumption about the murder was that, contrary to what Denver's two newspapers continued to report, the Juneteenth bombing had nothing to do with the monorail issue, Mayor Wiley, or Willis Sundee. The bomb had been meant for him or Clothilde. Finally, there were the pirated

R&B tapes. Everybody and their mother seemed to know that Daddy Doo-Wop had stolen them. If so, why all the recent fuss?

CJ was about to run through the possible links between Mabel's murder and LeRoy Polk's when a counter agent with a raspy, irritating, I'm-in-charge kind of voice called out, "Flight 931 to Denver is now ready for boarding."

CJ looked down the concourse for Billy, remembering with some uneasiness that Billy had wandered off with a .45 in his duffel. Billy didn't return until the last boarding call five minutes before takeoff. He was carrying a shopping bag filled with half a dozen official National League Chicago Cubs uniform shirts from the 1940s, 1950s, and 1960s.

"Cuttin' it pretty close, Billy." CJ eyed Billy's bag as he headed toward the jetway.

"Replacements for the shirt I ripped to shit. And you can charge 'em to your client, Clothilde Polk," said Billy, grinning broadly.

CJ and Billy talked baseball for the next hour and a half, and CJ's thoughts didn't return to Mabel until their pilot announced that they were making their initial approach to DIA. When CJ looked out the window at the parched wrapping-paper-brown wheat fields of Colorado's eastern plains, wondering how much longer the state was going to have to endure a drought, he remembered something that Mabel always used to say about predicting the weather: *When my left hip joint starts screaming bloody murder twenty-four hours a day, that's a notice to tell me it's gonna rain like hell.* CJ sat back in his seat, wishing that he had a similar tried-and-true method for finding her killer.

As the 757 descended, CJ could see dark funnel-shaped clouds of topsoil swirling around in the wind. Billy leaned over him and looked out the window at the whirling dust devils. "Think it's safe to land?"

"As safe as walking down a Chicago street."

Billy sat back and nudged his duffel with the toe of his boot. "All that goes around comes around." A few seconds later the plane's wheels touched down with a screech. Billy nudged the duffel one more time for good measure just as the pilot reversed the big engines.

Forty minutes later Rosie Weaks pulled up to his garage in his one-ton dually, with CJ in the front seat chomping at the bit to pick up the Bel Air and head home and Billy in the backseat still nudging his duffel with his toe. Rosie's nephew Darryl Gentry and Sweet Roy Cummings were in the first service bay working on a beat-up 1961 Electra 225, putting the final touches on the rewiring job Darryl had told CJ about earlier.

"What's up?" said CJ, watching Sweet Roy unscrew the car's driver-side door panel as Darryl looked on so engaged that he glanced up only briefly to nod hello.

"Your world, CJ," said Sweet Roy.

Sweet Roy had been a pimp until his drinking got to the point where he could no longer take care of himself or his ladies. Now he lived up three dark flights of stairs above a dairy and survived on a part-time job hosing down milk tankers. He was also a journeyman electrician, but no one would hire him because the alcohol had made him mistake-prone and undependable. The name Sweet Roy had been acquired because of his good looks and persuasive ways with women. Rosie called him the snake charmer and claimed that he would never kick his drinking habit until he got comfortable with himself deep down inside. For some people the penalty for being born pretty was worse than the penalty for being born black, according to Rosie.

Sweet Roy carefully teased out the upholstery in the door panel, revealing a maze of red and white wires. He began tugging, cutting, and then splicing the wires so quickly that even CJ was amazed at his deftness.

"Just pretend they're nerves, Darryl, running around inside of you. We've all got wires like these, you know. They just ain't color-coded. Cut one, like this one here, and things don't work. Now check the power-lock button. I guarantee it won't work." He pushed the button to demonstrate.

"Splice it, like this, and it works. Now try it." The lock clicked into place. "Slick as glass, ain't it?" said Sweet Roy. "I tell you, I could have been a brain surgeon with these hands, sweet-talking all those nurses and every day taking home a pocketful of money."

Sweet Roy's remarks and Darryl's fascination made CJ suddenly think of something he hadn't considered about LeRoy Polk's murder the entire time he had been dogging suspects halfway across the country and back. Something about medicine and on-the-job training that would gnaw at him the rest of the night.

He settled up with Rosie, who was in the back with Billy getting the den ready for an evening of gambling. "Let's go, Billy." CJ sensed from the look on Billy's face that he would rather stay and try his gambling luck, but Billy followed him anyway. On the way home, CJ plopped in a B. B. King tape and thought about the difference between real blues and R&B. He pulled into his driveway on Bail Bondsman's Row, and he and Billy jumped out of the car and were heading for the back steps to his apartment when Julie came running down the driveway.

"You've got someone waiting for you in the office." Julie sounded out of breath.

"Can it wait? I'm beat," said CJ.

"Don't think so; it's Tyrone Polk."

CJ shook his head in disgust and tossed Billy the keys to the apartment. "Catch up with you later."

"He's been in my office over an hour, nervous as a cat, waiting for you and bitching about Clothilde having him arrested and put in jail."

Julie's announcement reminded CJ of how hungry he had been for a cheroot. As he followed her back to the front office door, he reached in his vest pocket for one and realized he was out. When he thought about how Mavis had been pestering him recently to stop smoking, he figured that maybe it was just as well.

Thirty

Tyrone Polk was sitting in Julie's cramped little office alcove, elbows on the back edge of her desk, supporting his head with both hands and looking for all the world like a man who was carrying the weight of a lifetime of transgressions on his back.

When CJ walked in, Tyrone jumped up as though a firecracker had just gone off. Everything about him was out of character. His clothes were wrinkled, his hair was uncombed, and he had a sour, unbathed kind of look. "I can't believe she had me arrested." The words came out in a rush.

"Hold your horses, Tyrone. Start at the beginning of the movie. I don't like coming in on the middle. Let's go in my office."

Tyrone took a deep breath, exhaled in a series of splutters, and followed CJ into his office. CJ shut the door just as Julie came back in from outside.

"Clothilde had me thrown in jail yesterday. I almost died. I still don't have my bearings. She knows I can't stand being cooped up. She told the DA and the cops I was skimming construction loan money and stealing building materials from the construction site at Stax of Wax."

CJ took a seat behind his desk, leaving Tyrone standing forlorn-looking in the middle of the room. "Were you?"

Tyrone looked at CJ as if to say, *I don't need to prove my innocence to you.* But instead the words "I wasn't taking anything that didn't belong to me" rushed out.

"Then you're home free."

"That's not what my lawyer says. He claims Clothilde's gonna take it to trial."

"Then you better muster up a defense," said CJ. He would have been more sympathetic, but Tyrone's response had sounded too much like those he got from the street thugs and armed robbers he posted bond for every day.

Sensing that he wasn't going to get the kind of sympathy from CJ he had expected, Tyrone decided it was time to move beyond his problems with Clothilde. "Clothilde's small potatoes. I'm here about something else."

He sat down in a lumpy short-legged chair and took another deep breath. "The last laugh's gonna be mine." There was a Mona Lisa smirk on his face.

"You know those stolen tapes Clothilde's been screaming about? Well, that know-it-all little witch is about to get the surprise of her life, because Mabel had a set of the tapes too. It'll roast Clothilde's ass when she finds out. I need you to go to Mabel's house with me and help me find them." Noticing the look of hesitation on CJ's face, he added, "I'll pay you a thousand bucks. Shouldn't take more than fifteen minutes. I've got a pretty good idea of where they are."

CJ was still trying to come to grips with the fact that he was seeing a reincarnated Tyrone. A thousand dollars for fifteen minutes' work sounded inviting, and he was about to jump at the offer when his conscience got the better of him. "Can't do it, Tyrone. I'm working for your sister. There's a conflict. Besides, why didn't you tell me about the duplicates before?"

"Half-sister, and it's no more a conflict than her having me thrown in jail. As for not telling you about the tapes, you left town before I could."

"How do you know there's another set of tapes?" said CJ, ignoring Tyrone's weak excuse.

Tyrone stood up and started pacing the room. "Mabel told me about them a couple of days before she was killed. She said that if Clothilde had a set, so should I. I never got a chance to talk to her about the tapes again before she died. After she was murdered the cops sealed off the house. I don't want to stand here arguing with you, CJ. I know there's other bondsmen right here on Delaware Street who can use a quick thousand. You in or out?"

"Out until I talk to Clothilde." It was all CJ could do to keep from laughing at Tyrone trying to sound tough. He wondered what Tyrone would actually do if he was forced to deal with Cicero Vickers, the crafty, well-heeled bondsman next door who had gotten that way by having people like Tyrone for lunch, or Herman Currothers, two doors down, who thought all black people had defective genes. A few hours earlier CJ had been questioning how central the pirated tapes were to Mabel's and LeRoy Polk's murders. Now it sounded as if they were the nucleus.

"Tell her, smell her, promise her a child, makes no nevermind to me. But do something fast because in five minutes I'm out the door," said Tyrone.

Tyrone's new thunderball attitude had CJ worried. During Vietnam he had seen too many namby-pamby types like Tyrone turn into loose cannons. Shaking his head in disbelief, he reached for the intercom and buzzed Julie. "What's that number for Clothilde?" Julie gave him the number, and he quickly dialed it. The phone rang half a dozen times before Vanetta answered with all the enthusiasm and charm of a sweatshop employee.

"CJ Floyd. I need to speak to Clothilde."

"She's not in. Can I take a message?"

"When do you expect her back?"

"Don't know. She left about thirty minutes ago on her way to the construction site to pick up some papers."

CJ tried to decide whether to have Vanetta pass his message on to Clothilde. He pictured Vanetta flipping through the company checkbook, determining who would get paid and who wouldn't, as if she were Santa deciding who had been naughty and who had been nice, and it made him feel as though he were about to be punished. "Just tell her I'm headed out with Tyrone," he said finally, trying to take the edge off his guilt with a message that skirted the truth.

"Fine," said Vanetta, banging down the receiver.

Before CJ could get back to putting a damper on Tyrone's charge up San Juan Hill, Julie buzzed him.

"Dr. Maurice Sinclair's on the line, says it's urgent.

It's the third time he's called today. I didn't get a chance to clue you in earlier because of Tyrone."

"Put him through." CJ shot a glance Tyrone's way. "And Tyrone, sit the hell down."

Tyrone ignored him and continued pacing.

The phone rang twice before CJ picked it up. "Floyd," answered CJ, trying the best he could to sound in control.

Maurice Sinclair's voice sounded thready and distant. "I've been trying to reach you all day."

"Just got back from Chicago."

There was a long pause before Sinclair responded. "I think you should be aware of something I didn't mention to you while you were in my office the other day."

"I'm listening." CJ was prepared for anything, even the possibility that Juney-boy Stokes was sitting in Sinclair's office with a third set of pirated tapes.

"It's about Juney-boy Stokes."

"Yeah," said CJ, wondering why Sinclair seemed to be stalling.

"I performed gender-reassignment surgery on him about fifteen years ago. Don't get me wrong, now. There was a good surgical result. One of my best."

Don't pat yourself on the back too much, thought CJ.

"But . . . ah . . . operating on him was a mistake."

"How's that?"

Sinclair continued, close to stuttering. "Remember when I told you about being able to spot a transsexual on sight?"

"Yeah. Struck me as pretty high and mighty."

"Well, ah . . . Stokes fooled me."

"Meaning?"

"I don't think Juney-boy was transsexual at all. Looking back on it, I'd say he was a . . . just bisexual . . . and terribly confused."

"And the difference is?" said CJ, who was determined to make Sinclair spell things out in black and white.

Dr. Sinclair was breathing heavily into the phone, close to hyperventilating. "The surgery wasn't a necessity," he said hesitantly. "Juney-boy wasn't a woman trapped in a man's body, as he led me and several psychologists to believe during all his presurgical visits. He was just one hell of an actor and a very confused, easily manipulated, and psychologically damaged man. Someone capable of passing himself off as a transsexual because at the time that's what he needed to pretend to be. I'm sorry to say he tricked me."

It wasn't difficult for CJ to understand Sinclair's conclusion, just hard for him to swallow the fact that a man as cocksure of himself as Sinclair could now claim that he had been tricked. He thought back to Sinclair's red, white, and blue brochures, recalling that he hadn't seen any disclaimers about putting patients back together or refunding their money in case of a mistake. "What you're saying is that you fixed something that didn't need fixin', right?"

Sinclair ignored CJ's question until there was a sudden crack of static on the line. Then, sounding very frightened, he blurted out, "Last night someone took a shot at me with a high-powered rifle. I'm sure it was Stokes."

"Where?"

"At my office."

CJ stopped tracking Tyrone's movements and sat back in his chair, trying to sort things out. He was faced with a possible conflict of interest in fulfilling his obligation to Clothilde if he helped Tyrone, and now he had to determine how Maurice Sinclair's minor surgical error had figured in LeRoy's and Mabel's murders. "I talked to a guy named Hampoli in Pueblo who said Juney-boy might be dead."

"I don't think so," said Sinclair.

"Have you told the cops about being shot at?" asked CJ, looking back up for Tyrone.

"I have, and I've given them all my records related to the case, including Jarrett Stokes's file and yours."

It was the first time CJ had heard anyone call Juney-boy by his real name. "Then you are a model citizen, Doc. Question is, what do you want from me?"

"Two things. I want you to keep Juney-boy . . . ah . . . June, away from me, and I don't want you making any more complaints to the state medical board."

CJ sat forward in his chair, recalling that Wing Gipson had called Juney-boy June as well. "I can't help you with the first request. As for the second, I'd recommend you speak to your patient, Mr. Stokes."

"Then we're done with this conversation," protested Sinclair. "I wouldn't know where to begin looking for Stokes, and I certainly don't intend to talk to someone who's trying to kill me. I think the police need to handle this."

"Guess so," said CJ. He was about to ask Sinclair if he had Juney-boy's last known address, but Sinclair slammed the phone down before he could. *Have a pleasant day playing God,* thought CJ as he hung up. He pushed the chair away from his desk, still puzzled about why Sinclair would think that he and Juney-boy Stokes were in cahoots. But before he had a chance to consider the question, Tyrone was back in his face.

"You in or out? If you say out, then I'll know Clothilde's money means more to you than Mabel."

"Dammit, Tyrone, you're pushin' the wrong fuckin' buttons." CJ stood up, using every ounce of willpower he had to control his temper.

"It's your call," said Tyrone, softening his tone, aware that he had said the one thing he needed to say to move CJ off the dime.

CJ tried to think up reasons not to go with Tyrone. When he couldn't, he finally stepped around his desk and said, "Let's go."

He stopped at Julie's desk on the way out. Billy had come downstairs and was helping Julie rearrange the papers on her desk so that she could make room for a couple of pizzas that had just been delivered.

"Piping hot," said Julie. "Two for one, just like they advertise on TV."

CJ opened one of the boxes and grabbed a slice of pizza to go. "I'm headed out. I think you should come along too," he said to Billy.

Billy hastily wrapped a slice of pizza in a paper towel that Julie handed him as they both looked up and realized that Tyrone was already outside. CJ looked pleadingly back at Julie as he headed for the door. "Need you to work a little longer. Call Dr. Sinclair back and ask him how many complaints he had over the years from the State Board of Medical Examiners concerning his treatment of Juney-boy Stokes. Then call vital statistics down at the Department of Health and see if they have a record of a Jarrett Stokes ever having died. We'll be at Mabel's."

Julie looked at her watch and realized that CJ's Chicago trip had him out of synch. "It's almost eight o'clock. The bureaucrats down at state health are long gone."

"Damn. Then call Henry Bales and ask him to fire up that Front Range Pathology Consortium computer of his and search the records over the past fifteen years for an autopsy on any suicide victim named June, Jarrett, or Juney-boy Stokes." CJ headed out the front door with Billy trailing. "As soon as you get something, call me at Mabel's."

Julie gave CJ a look of concern, the special one she reserved for the times when she knew he was headed for trouble. "Okay," she said, teasing off a slice of pizza.

Tyrone had pulled his car off the street into the driveway and was gunning the motor. When CJ opened the door on the passenger's side to let Billy slide in the back, Tyrone slipped the gearshift into reverse and dropped a bomb that let CJ know the real reason he had been so interested in his help. "Before we take off, I guess I should tell you somebody in a black Camaro's been following me all day."

Billy was out of the backseat and back on the driveway in one fluid motion. "Telano," he said, frowning.

"My guess," said CJ. "I wouldn't want someone slipping up behind us and popping a cap in my ass. Why don't you follow us in my Jeep. It's in the garage." CJ turned from Billy and gave Tyrone the distrusting look he reserved for clients who withheld information from him. He was about to get in the car when he suddenly remembered the feel of the barrel of Johnny Telano's gun on his neck. "Hold it, Tyrone, I need to get something out of the garage." He ran into the garage and pulled the empty five-gallon paint can that held his holstered .38 out of one of the cabinets above his cluttered workbench. When he tried to pop the can's lid with a screwdriver, he realized that he didn't have the strength to hold the can still with his injured arm. He dropped down on his knees, clasped the can between them, popped the lid, and pulled out the loaded snub-nosed gun. He unbuckled his belt, slid the holstered gun onto it, and slipped the holster around to the small of his back, grimacing in pain the entire time.

When CJ got back outside, Billy was coming down the steps from his apartment carrying his duffel. There was no need for CJ to ask why. "If you see the Camaro, give it some room. I want you to be the one bringing up the rear," CJ called out to Billy.

Billy nodded without saying a word.

As CJ jumped in Tyrone's car, he felt the kind of shooting pain in his shoulder he hadn't felt all day. "Shit," he said, reaching across his body with his left arm to close the door.

"What's the matter?" asked Tyrone.

"Just a sore shoulder with a mind of its own."

Tyrone backed down the driveway as CJ watched Billy, duffel draped over his shoulder, disappear into the garage.

Thirty-one

By the time CJ and Tyrone reached Mabel's the sun had set and a blanket of clouds had moved across the Front Range into the city. All the way over CJ had to keep reminding Tyrone that Billy was following them, and if they didn't want to lose him, Tyrone needed to slow down. Tyrone would slow down for a few blocks until his adrenaline got the best of him, and then speed back up. When he turned onto California, dinging the curb and nearly taking off a hubcap, CJ reached over and grabbed his arm. "Slow the shit down." Tyrone responded by making a U-turn midway down the block and sliding to a stop in a curbside layer of sand and gravel that had been in front of Mabel's since winter.

Across the street, Rufus G. Tibbits Memorial Park was as quiet as CJ had seen it in months. He wondered why until he remembered that Rosie's den was open for business. It had always baffled CJ that the loiterers, drifters, dopers, and street thugs who called the park home and never had a dime when it came to him bailing them out of jail always seemed to be able to find a few dollars to gamble.

Tyrone was out of the car. "I've got a key."

"Cool it," said CJ, looking up at the house, trying to determine if there was any activity inside. When he was satisfied there wasn't, he and Tyrone headed for the house. As they walked up the sidewalk CJ felt a renewed sense of loss.

Tyrone fumbled with the key to the front door until the deadbolt finally clicked. He pushed the door open and they walked inside to the musty smell of a house that needed airing.

Tyrone turned on a light and took a couple of steps down the hallway before he realized that something was stuck to his right shoe. "Hold on." He looked down and realized that a six-inch strip of yellow police crime-scene tape had stuck to his heel. "Shit." He reached down, unsnarled the tape, squeezed it into a knot, and tossed it aside.

"It's stuffy in here," said Tyrone, moving toward the kitchen. When he passed the living room where Mabel had been murdered, he sped up.

CJ hesitated at the living room entry, remembering all the good things that had happened to him in Mabel's house. He reached around the corner into the living room and flipped on the light switch. The room looked the same as it always had except for the absence of Mabel's cumbersome reel-to-reel tape recorder, her tape deck and mountains of gospel tapes, and the chair she had been murdered in. CJ knew that the missing

things were probably jammed into some police evidence
locker downtown. He looked at the empty spot where
the chair had been and thought about the nearly three
units of blood that Henry Bales had said Mabel lost
while she sat bleeding to death in her living room. He
then thought about what Henry Bales had said about
her carotid artery being severed, possibly with a scalpel.
As he looked around the room for something that
would soften his sorrow and rekindle the pleasant memories of the past, he heard a series of loud thuds from
the kitchen. He reached for his .38 and spun around.

"I need some help," Tyrone called out in a muffled
voice from the kitchen.

It finally hit CJ that Tyrone was a man on a mission, more interested in finding a bunch of pirated
forty-year-old rhythm and blues tapes than in finding
out who had killed his parents.

In the kitchen Tyrone had turned on every light,
opened all the cabinet doors, and placed most of the
drawers on the floor. CJ watched, dumbfounded, as Tyrone moved from cabinet to cabinet, pulling out canned
goods, condiments, notebooks of handwritten recipes,
and even the miniature syrup bottles Mabel had collected over the years. When he couldn't stand to watch
Tyrone rip apart Mabel's kitchen any longer, he walked
over to him and grabbed him by the arm as he was
about to toss one of Mabel's recipe books for berry pies
into the sink. "Toss one more thing and I'll break your
arm." He squeezed until Tyrone wrenched out of his
grip, rubbing his arm in pain.

"Okay, okay."

CJ knew Mabel's house as well as he knew his own,

and he had an inkling of where Mabel would have stashed something she considered important. Rather than have Tyrone continue to tear the house apart, he said, "I think we should go down to the basement. But if you so much as move a paperback book out of place without my okay, it'll be your head you're rubbing."

Tyrone shrugged his shoulders, feigning toughness. "Okay by me; doesn't look like we're going to turn anything up here."

When they turned to go downstairs to the basement, CJ noticed several broken jars of canned tomatoes near the door to the canning pantry that he had helped Mabel line with cedar thirty years earlier. Tomatoes had been tracked everywhere. He turned to tell Tyrone to clean up his mess, but Tyrone was already halfway down the steps.

Johnny Telano had pulled his Camaro with the TEL NO 1 plates up to the curb on the Tibbits Park side of California half a block down from Tyrone, making certain not to kiss the curb and scuff his $400 Michelins. Tyrone and CJ had been inside Mabel's for twenty minutes, and it was finally dark when he climbed out of the Camaro and headed for Mabel's house. He was several steps beyond the front bumper, thinking about how to dispose of CJ's and Tyrone's bodies if he had to kill them, when he felt the cold barrel of Billy DeLong's Peacemaker lodge itself in his left ear. He froze instantly, not wanting to risk another step, wondering how someone had been able to sneak up on him so easily.

Billy shoved the barrel a little harder just for effect.

"If it ain't Brer Rabbit, and driving a Camaro. Now, don't that take the cake?"

Telano remained silent.

"Think I'm gonna do the escorting this time," said Billy. "First thing I want you to do is fish the keys to that black rocket of yours out of your pocket and hand them to me real slow."

Telano reluctantly handed Billy the keys. "Lucky for you you're good at dodging semis and that my people in Chicago missed poppin' your ass."

"Real lucky," said Billy, pocketing the keys. "Next, I'm gonna pat you down. If you move, I'm gonna blow whatever brains you got over into the park." Billy wasn't sure where Telano kept his gun, but he was certain he was carrying one. He reasoned the gun would have to be holstered either under his shirt in the small of his back, in a leg holster, or in a pants pocket. Enjoying the fact that the long-barreled Peacemaker gave him leverage to move around while still keeping the gun snug in Telano's ear, Billy moved his left hand across Telano's pockets and around to the small of his back without finding anything. He was two-thirds down Telano's left leg when he struck paydirt. "What's this here? Hope it's not a tumor." He pulled Telano's trouser leg up, slipped a leg holster down to the top of Telano's shoe, and unholstered a Colt. He straightened up from the half-crouch he was in and slipped the gun in his pocket. "I know you're partial to big rigs and pigs, but since I don't have one here right now, I'm gonna let you snuggle up in your Camaro," said Billy. Seething with the knowledge that Telano had orchestrated the hit and run on his truck and the drive-by shooting in Chicago, he cocked the hammer back on his .45. "If you give me so much as a wiggle, you're gonna hear the other side of this hammer. Now, I want you to back your low-slung, gorilla-looking, underworld ass around to the trunk of that phallic symbol of yours." As they passed the Camaro's front door, Billy reached in his pocket and fumbled with the key remote until the trunk lid popped up. Telano turned his head to the side, ready to protest, but thought better of it when he felt another nudge in his ear.

"Slip in and get comfy," said Billy, knowing that if Telano was going to do anything, now was the time. He was surprised at how quickly Telano stepped up over the bumper and into the trunk, squatting down like he was going to take a dump inside. "Roll on your side," said Billy, pulling the Colt out of Telano's ear before shoving his head down to the carpet and slamming the trunk. He didn't know how much trouble Telano was going to have breathing inside, but he figured he owed him for calling him an Uncle Remus, ramming a gun in CJ's neck, totaling his truck, and orchestrating the target practice episode outside Roland Jefferson's house in Chicago. Billy decided they were just about even. Since he didn't know how much longer Tyrone and CJ were going to be inside Mabel's or if Telano had called for backup, he decided that the best thing to do was wait things out in the Camaro.

When he opened the door to get in behind the wheel and saw what Johnny Telano was carrying around with him on the front seat, Billy whistled in surprise. Sitting on top of what he suspected was state-of-the-art eavesdropping equipment was an Uzi 9mm. *That fucker really is crazy,* thought Billy. He pushed the Uzi aside to get a better look at Telano's bugging paraphernalia, suspecting that Telano must have been listening to them ever since their trip to Pueblo. He wondered who else Telano had tuned in to. After a few minutes of fumbling with the dials on what looked like a stereo receiver and thinking about how he was going to afford a new truck, Billy sat back in the driver's seat to wait for Tyrone and CJ to finish up their business inside Mabel's.

Thirty-two

CJ was down on one knee on the basement floor, refolding the last of the two dozen quilts he had taken out of an antique carpenter's chest he knew Mabel used for storing her most precious possessions. It had taken him a while to complete the job because of his bad shoulder. "No tapes in here," he called out to Tyrone, who was across the room searching through a wall of built-in bookcases filled with cookbooks, romance novels, black memorabilia, and Western knickknacks.

Tyrone was carefully placing everything he removed from a shelf in its own special area on the floor so he could return it to its proper place without incurring CJ's wrath.

"Anyplace else you'd think she might have stashed them?"

CJ thought for a moment, but he was feeling so guilty about going through Mabel's things that he couldn't focus on where she might have hidden the tapes. In addition, his mind kept wandering back to the phone conversation he'd had with Maurice Sinclair. Sinclair's demand that he keep Juney-boy Stokes away from him still hadn't made sense.

"What do you know about Juney-boy Stokes?" said CJ, folding up the second of Mabel's Colorado State Fair–prizewinning zigzag log cabin quilts.

"Only that he was an R&B singer, and he and my father worked together back in Chicago."

"Anything else?"

"Other than hearing folks say he was gay, that's about it."

CJ thought about all the labels people had hung on Juney-boy. Although the consensus was that he was sensitive and talented, with a voice from God, everyone seemed to need to pigeonhole him in some sexual-preference box. CJ folded the last quilt and laid it in the chest, wondering if his own idiosyncrasies caused the same reaction in people.

"Think I've found something!" screamed Tyrone, stacking the last of a shelf of tall, three-inch-wide cookbooks into two neat piles on the floor. Lined up on edge behind the books, flush against the wall, were three studio-style open-reel tapes. "Got 'em, got 'em right here!" Tyrone took the spools off the shelf, slipping each one over his hand and onto his right arm. He spun each spool around as it slipped down to his elbow.

CJ walked over to Tyrone, judiciously avoiding the stacks of cookbooks.

Tyrone held his free arm up in triumph. "I knew they were here. I knew it. There's another reel-to-reel tape player down here. Let's listen to one." Tyrone slipped the first reel back off his arm and set it on a shelf.

For CJ the tapes only reinforced the fact that Mabel was dead. "Don't press your luck, Tyrone," said CJ, thinking about whether Johnny Telano was still on Tyrone's tail. "You got what you came after; let's go."

Tyrone gave CJ the aggravated look of a child who had just been disciplined. "My mother and father are dead because of these fuckers. I want to hear what the hell's so special about them."

It was the first time CJ had heard Tyrone express any concern about Mabel since they had walked in the house. He glanced at his watch. They had been there just over half an hour. Billy hadn't made an appearance, and Julie hadn't called with the information he had asked her to get from Henry Bales. Although he had a sagging feeling that something could still go wrong, he figured he owed Tyrone a chance to listen to at least one tape. "Make it fast, Tyrone."

Tyrone slipped the other two spools off his arm and stacked them on a wobbly table near the stairs next to an old reel-to-reel recorder covered with dust. He retrieved the first tape from the shelf, inspecting the faded blue sticker on its side. Several song titles with the names of the recording artists had been neatly printed on the sticker and numbered one through eleven. "You're not gonna believe this, but the first song on here's by Juney-boy Stokes. 'Lonely Teardrops.' "

CJ remembered the song as a smash Jackie Wilson hit that had spent half a year at the top of the R&B charts. He remembered his uncle playing it all day long for months. "Lonely Teardrops" had even seemed to make his uncle cut down on his drinking for a while.

Tyrone teased a lead of tape off the reel gingerly, hoping the fragile thirty-five-year-old tape wouldn't crack away in his hands. He had managed to ease out close to half a foot when the wall phone above the tape player rang. It startled him so much that three inches of tape broke off in his hands. "Damn," he said, starting over.

CJ stepped over to the phone and answered it. "Yeah."

"It's me."

CJ recognized Julie's voice on the other end of the line. "What've you got?"

"No state bureaucracy's working overtime, that's for sure. But Henry was still at his lab. It took him a while to turn up something on Jarrett Stokes, but he did."

"I'm all ears."

"He's dead, all right, and it was suicide. The autopsy was done in Denver fourteen years ago. But his death certificate lists him as Jarrett, not June."

CJ was disappointed. Julie hadn't told him anything he hadn't suspected except that as far as the state of Colorado was concerned, sex-change or not, they had autopsied a man named Jarrett. "Anything else?"

"Nothing much. Henry said the poor man stuck a gun in his mouth and pulled the trigger. Took off most of the top of his head."

"Damn," muttered CJ.

"There was one final thing," said Julie. "I'm not sure it makes a difference, but Juney-boy wasn't using the name Stokes when he died. According to Henry, he was calling himself June Ebson. His daughter's name was typed in as next of kin on the autopsy report: Vanetta Ebson."

CJ tightened his grip on the receiver until his fingers felt numb. "I'll be damned." Instead of feeling a sense of closure, he felt bitter and sad: bitter because he had lost Mabel and sad because he suddenly remembered what it had been like growing up in the shadow of an alcoholic uncle whom everyone whispered about behind his back. He had no idea what torments Vanetta had suffered as the daughter of a confused 1950s R&B star, but he was pretty sure the demons she had to be battling were products of Juney-boy's lifelong attempt to define himself sexually, and he suspected that Vanetta had been hearing whispers all her life.

The recent complaints that Dr. Sinclair had insisted CJ had made to the state Board of Medical Examiners now made sense. They had come from Vanetta. He thought back to the stack of complaints to state licensing agencies he had seen on what he now realized was Vanetta's desk two days before he left for Chicago. He should have recognized the pattern of a brooding complainer then.

Julie finally interrupted CJ's thoughts. "Need anything else?"

"No, just thanks for staying late," said CJ, relaxing his grip on the receiver.

"Humor me in my next paycheck," said Julie, hanging up.

The line clicked off just as Juney-boy Stokes began his rendition of "Lonely Teardrops." CJ immediately understood what Wing Gipson had meant about Juney-boy having a once-in-a-lifetime voice. The song started out in an understated, satiny, midrange natural vibrato with an undertone of sweet sexuality, then rose to the pulsating, tantalizing level typical of 1950s male gospel, and finally transitioned to its pleading, emotional refrain, a musical universe away from Jackie Wilson's original frisky song of lament.

CJ and Tyrone sat mesmerized, caught up in the penetrating, melodic voice of Juney-boy Stokes. When the song ended, they looked at each other, speechless. *Jerry Butler, Sam Cooke, and Jackie Wilson, all wrapped in one,* thought CJ.

A second song began to play, but CJ couldn't get the sound of Juney-boy Stokes out of his mind. It wasn't until the song ended that he walked over to the reel-to-reel and turned it off. "You can listen to that later, Tyrone. I think we've just about worn out our welcome here. This place is one blink past being an official crime scene, and you've had somebody tailing your ass all day long. It's time to split. Besides, I think I've figured out who killed LeRoy and Mabel."

Tyrone's eyes widened. "From listening to a song?"

CJ thought back to the intensity he had seen on Darryl Gentry's face as he had watched Sweet Roy wire the Electra. "No, from understanding the pain that fuels revenge and finally realizing that instead of searching for a killer with a background in medicine and explosives, I should have been looking for someone driven enough to want to learn to kill."

CJ's revelation had Tyrone confused and a little spooked. This time he didn't argue about wrapping things up. He slipped the tape off the reel-to-reel, retrieved the other two spools, tucked them under his arm, and looked at CJ. "We're out of here." He headed up the basement steps, cradling the tapes under his arm protectively. Two steps from the top of the stairs, Tyrone stopped so short CJ almost ran into him.

"What's the matter?"

When Tyrone didn't answer, CJ moved up a step. Peering over Tyrone's left shoulder, he had an unobstructed view of the landing above, where Vanetta Ebson was holding a 9mm Glock inches away from Tyrone's nose.

Thirty-three

The only thing CJ could think of as he watched how comfortable Vanetta looked holding the Glock was how badly he had miscalculated the odds of successfully completing his job for Clothilde Polk. Eight in ten now seemed like one hell of a stretch.

"Tyrone, turn around and back up the steps out of that hole." Vanetta's voice had a drill sergeant's edge. "Floyd, stay where you are." She stepped around the corner back into the kitchen, out of CJ's view.

CJ reached for his .38, but Vanetta was way ahead of him. "If you're armed down there, you should know that the first person you're going to get a good shot at is Tyrone. He's standing with his back to me whimpering like a lost puppy. I'm betting he's praying you don't come out of that cellar shooting. Tell him, Tyrone." She nudged the Glock into the base of Tyrone's skull.

"She's telling the truth, CJ."

"Now, how about tossing whatever toy you're packing up here to me, and don't fool yourself into thinking I don't know what I'm doing. I know plenty about firearms and how to use them."

CJ thought about heading back down into the basement and calling the police, but he knew that if he tried, Vanetta would probably kill Tyrone. A bull's rush up into the kitchen would be stupid and likely to get everyone killed. He was trying to conjure up another alternative when Vanetta said, "I'm waiting."

CJ thought a little longer before deciding that if he left the basement unarmed, the odds wouldn't be even, but at least it would be two against one. He tossed his .38 up into the kitchen, hoping that he had made the right decision.

"Good boy." Vanetta stepped over and picked up the .38, her own gun still trained on the back of Tyrone's head. She released the .38's magazine and shook the cartridges to the floor. "Now come on up," she ordered, dropping the .38 into an open canvas bag on the cooktop island beside her.

CJ stepped into the light of the kitchen, expecting to encounter a desperate, unstable woman teetering on the brink. Instead he saw the same well-groomed, slender, bespectacled bookkeeper he had first encountered at Stax of Wax.

"Drop those tapes in the bag on the cooktop, Tyrone. Floyd, you stay put."

Shaking noticeably, Tyrone did as he was told.

Once the tapes were safely in the bag, Vanetta looked relieved. "I've been watching this place off and on, waiting for the cops to leave and for Tyrone to show up for the past two days. I only live three blocks away. When you called for Clothilde and said you were heading out with Tyrone, I figured the chickens were finally coming home to roost. It's a good thing you came along. Tyrone kept looking in all the wrong places." Vanetta gave CJ a broad winning-gambler's smile. "One place he should have looked closer was that pantry upstairs. He would have gotten one hell of a surprise." Vanetta reached over and patted her tomato-stained bag. "Anyway, I've got what I came for."

"How'd you know Mabel had a duplicate set of tapes?" asked CJ, gauging the distance between the two of them.

Vanetta looked at him as if he were speaking to a wall.

Tyrone answered instead. "Clothilde knew. And if she knew, so would her shadow." His voice was low-pitched and thready.

"I had to put up with sniffing up that prissy bitch's ass and pretending to be chickenshit for too damn long. Why else do you think I would have played lapdog to her or that father of hers unless I expected it to pay off in the end? I was hoping to blow her head off at June-teenth, but I missed."

CJ thought about his next move and decided the best thing to do was keep Vanetta talking. "You can't keep killing people over those tapes."

Vanetta's eyes misted over, and the veins in her neck bulged. "You heard my daddy sing. You heard his voice. He was a fragile man, confused about who he was all his life. He even went back to using my mother's maiden name, Ebson, in the end. Doo-Wop Polk took advantage of his confusion. He stole his voice away from the world and turned him into a freak."

"What about Maurice Sinclair?" said CJ.

Vanetta rolled her eyes. "Sinclair was just a mechanic. I should have put a rifle bullet in him the other night down in Montcliff when I had a chance. I've seen those hideous sex-change brochures of his, and I've had fifteen years to memorize the sex-reassignment video he gave my father. A pornographic piece of shit he's still passing out to patients like candy." Vanetta paused, and the pained look on her face developed into a smile. "You might say the images on that videotape sparked my interest in medicine. You can't imagine how that tape helped me to prepare myself for what I had to do."

CJ hadn't seen the tape, but considering the ways in which LeRoy Polk and Mabel Pitts had died, CJ knew that Vanetta had learned her lessons well.

"Time to go," said Vanetta. There was a hint of finality in her voice as she softly began humming "Lonely Teardrops."

CJ looked into Tyrone's eyes for some hint that he might make a move on Vanetta, but all he saw was fear.

"We're going to take a walk in the park. It came to me while Daddy was downstairs singing. Floyd, turn around and back over here until you're shoulder to shoulder with Tyrone. Then I want you both to do a one-eighty until you're facing the front door, walk up the hallway, and out the door. I'll be right behind you." Vanetta slung the bag with the tapes over her shoulder, backed away from Tyrone, and watched CJ follow her instructions. As they made their turn, CJ could feel Tyrone's entire body quivering. When they walked past the living room, CJ couldn't resist saying, "There was no need to kill Mabel."

Vanetta, who had started humming again, stopped and responded in an excited, high-pitched voice. "She wouldn't give me the tapes. After I sat and pleaded with her for a half hour. When she asked me if I had killed LeRoy, I panicked. Afterwards, I had to get out of there fast because some hairy-looking white guy was in the alley casing the place. I didn't even have time to look for the tapes."

When they reached the front porch, CJ stopped in his tracks, hoping that Tyrone would follow suit. His plan to keep Vanetta talking had only moved them closer to being shot, so he decided it was time to stall and hope for Billy DeLong.

"Keep moving," said Vanetta.

CJ didn't budge. Neither did Tyrone.

Vanetta stepped forward and jammed the barrel of her gun into the nape of CJ's neck. "Don't get stubborn on me, bounty hunter."

CJ still didn't move. He was busy counting off the seconds in his head. He was hoping to get to sixty, but when he felt Vanetta give the Glock a little twist, he stopped at forty-five and started down the front steps with Tyrone following in synch. When they stepped off the curb, CJ glanced up the street for some sign of Billy just as Tyrone started shaking as if he had the DTs. Vanetta stepped back and watched as Tyrone trembled through a series of shakes and gyrations that left him in the middle of the street on his knees.

"Get up, Tyrone. I'll shoot both of you right here if I have to." Her voice was shaking.

CJ finally grabbed Tyrone by the shoulders and steadied him. "Take it easy, Tyrone, take it easy."

A moment later, Tyrone's shaking ebbed. The entire episode had taken a couple of minutes.

It wasn't until they were across the street and at the entrance to the park that CJ realized Tyrone was wheezing like a bulldog. As they started down the walkway that slanted its way across the park and Vanetta said "Head straight for the fountain," CJ knew that Vanetta intended to walk them to the center of the park, where there was a fountain as noisy as a waterfall. He looked around, wondering where the drug pushers were now that he needed them.

A layer of low-hanging clouds and a misty fog had moved in, blocking out the moon, and the park seemed as dark as CJ had ever remembered. His right ear had started to plug up like it always did when there was a drop in the barometer. The forty-foot pines and massive cottonwoods that lined the edge of the walk enhanced the darkness. As they moved deeper into the park, he kept wondering where the hell Billy was. In a fit of optimism, CJ decided they still had a few things going for them; he knew the lay of the land better than Vanetta, the inky darkness could spoil the aim of any shooter, and he expected that deep down inside Vanetta was even more nervous than Tyrone.

They were thirty yards away from the fountain when CJ heard a faint rustling in a cluster of stubby, four-foot-high mugho pines to his right. He immediately thought *Billy,* as everyone stopped at once. Vanetta cautiously looked to her left and right, and CJ realized that he could hear his own excited breathing. A few seconds later he realized he could hear Vanetta and Tyrone breathing as well. Vanetta stepped over and kicked one of the bushes. There was no more movement and the only sound that resulted was the scraping of pine needles against bark. "Okay," she said, nudging CJ in the back with the Glock as they started walking again.

A few steps later, there was another noise in the bushes. This time no one stopped, and Vanetta didn't say a thing. Her head was too busy whipping from side to side in the direction of the mugho pines.

CJ swore that he could make out the outline of something larger than a fountain up ahead, but before he had a chance to consider what it might be, the blinding glare of a set of high-beam headlights flashed in his face, and he heard the high-pitched squeal of an animal.

In the swath of light, Geronimo streaked out of the scrubby mugho pines in skittish overdrive, slamming all of his 150 pounds into Vanetta. The Glock discharged twice. One bullet took an inch-and-a-half-wide bite out of the top of Tyrone's right ear. The other lifted off into the inky black Colorado sky. Vanetta landed on her right hip and screamed a second before the back of her skull slammed into the concrete walk. The sound of water rushing from the fountain and Geronimo's grunting filled the night air.

"That you, Billy?" CJ called out toward the lights.

"Yeah."

"Better come over here and help me check on Tyrone; he's on the ground vibrating like a three-stroke motor."

When Billy stepped into the path of the high beams, CJ realized that Vanetta's chance meeting with

Geronimo had been a blessing as he watched Billy swing his Winchester magnum with its telescopic lens over his right shoulder and grab the old wooden milk crate he had been using to steady it on the hood of the Jeep.

CJ knelt down by Vanetta to see if she was breathing. A trickle of blood was coming from her right ear. He ran his hand past her nose and mouth a couple of times. When he checked for a carotid pulse, he found the artery was pounding just as forcefully as his.

Thirty-four

Half a dozen police officers were busy in Tibbits Park running their final crime-scene traps while CJ and Billy sat being questioned by Sergeant Fuller about the shooting. Tyrone had been taken to Denver General Hospital, groggy and incoherent, and Vanetta had been escorted away in handcuffs, humming "Lonely Teardrops." Infuriated and feeling put upon, Sergeant Fuller had been called to the scene from the seventh inning of a Cubs-Rockies game that was tied 6 to 6 by the chief of police, who told him only that CJ Floyd had been involved in a shooting with a Juneteenth bombing suspect and he needed Fuller to haul ass over to Tibbits Park and cover the mayor's flank. "Especially since while you're busy stuffing yourself with ballpark franks, the mayor's issuing a press release outlining his modified position on monorail," the chief had said.

Clothilde had shown up briefly after CJ called her

from Mabel's to explain what had occurred. She surveyed the flurry of activity, appearing calm at first, but
the second that she saw Vanetta sitting in the back of
one of the police cars, she rushed the car screaming,
"You bitch! You bitch!" Clothilde had the door open
and Vanetta halfway out of the car with a hank of her
hair firmly in her grasp before she could be restrained.
After regaining her composure and being assured by CJ
that the duplicate tapes were safe, Clothilde made
arrangements to meet with Sergeant Fuller the next
morning in his office and left, appearing as placid as
when she had arrived, and as enigmatic to CJ as she had
appeared from the start of the case.

Fuller was in the last frustrating stages of wrapping
things up with Billy. "You could have suffocated that
Telano character, locking him in the trunk of his car
like that. We've got laws here in Denver; this isn't some
Wyoming gully wash."

Billy was feeling so wiped out from the aftermath
of nearly having shot a woman that he didn't care what
Fuller thought about his treatment of Johnny Telano. "I
had to park him somewhere; I couldn't do two things at
once. When I saw CJ and Tyrone come out of the house
headed for the park shoulder to shoulder with somebody
stickin' to 'em like glue, I knew they was in trouble. It
was a damn good thing I had Telano stashed."

Fuller notched up his pants, eyeballing CJ's Jeep.
Unsympathetic with Billy's explanation and still upset
about having to leave the baseball game, he wanted to
have the last word of the evening. "And you thought it
was okay to drive this vehicle into a restricted unmotor-
ized area?"

"The best thing I did all night was to jump that squirrelly-assed Telano on foot and leave the Jeep on the back side of the park. If I hadn't, I never would've had time to pull up here to the fountain. I was cuttin' it to the bone as it was."

"We still haven't seen a sign of any damn pig," said Fuller, still distrustful of CJ's and Billy's accounts of the events.

"Geronimo was here," said CJ. "Could be he's afraid of cops."

"I wouldn't be so cocky, Floyd. There're a lot of pieces to this puzzle that still haven't fallen in place. Although you claim that the Ebson woman blew up Mae's, we still don't know who pulled off that Juneteenth bombing for sure, and no one's erased your name off my list. I want you in my office by eight A.M., and we'll discuss it more then." Fuller turned away from CJ and waved at a traffic control officer he recognized. "Hey, Tony, come over here a minute." The traffic cop strolled over and they shook hands. After some small talk, Fuller pointed to CJ's Jeep. "What do you think about that Jeep over there occupying a pedestrian walkway in a city park?"

Without saying a word the cop walked over to the Jeep, pulled a citation book out of his back pocket, scribbled out a ticket, and slapped a hundred-dollar fine for unlawful use of a motor vehicle in a restricted area under one of the Jeep's wipers.

CJ thought about walking over to the Jeep, grabbing the ticket out from under the wiper, and tearing it up, but he recognized the difference between yanking the chain of the toilet bowl police and screwing with the real thing, so he stood at parade rest, hands behind his back, and didn't say a word.

Thirty-five

During the night a freak early summer monsoon soaker moved into Colorado on the heels of a fast-moving backdoor cold front out of the Texas Panhandle, breaking the six-month high-plains drought. The front stalled as it pushed its way into Wyoming, shrouding Denver in a low-level fog and rainforest drizzle that closed DIA, leaving weather forecasters scratching their heads in surprise and predicting that the rains would probably hang around for the rest of the week.

CJ spent most of the next morning in a damp, musty, converted broom closet of a room at the Denver Jail across the street from his office, answering Sergeant Fuller's questions. The police had searched Vanetta Ebson's Curtis Park apartment, which was just a few blocks from Mabel's, the night before and found stacks of medical textbooks and journals, including dozens of articles and brochures on the side effects of nicotine and contraindications to the use of Nicoderm patches in cardiac patients. *Gray's Anatomy, Steward's Operative Urology,* and Green and Money's 1969 treatise on transsexualism and sex reassignment were found dog-eared on the nightstand next to Vanetta's bed. The entire chapter on surgery for the transsexual had been highlighted in yellow. An aging videotape with the name JARRETT STOKES printed in black Magic Marker on the side had been found in a VCR in the living room. The officer who found the tape had turned on the VCR to watch the tape chatter and skip through a graphic depiction of penile stripping and castration that made him struggle to keep from throwing up.

Fuller kept pressing CJ to tell him whether he had had any inkling that Vanetta Ebson had killed LeRoy Polk or Mabel. "If you knew anything and didn't tell us, you're guilty of obstructing justice, or at the very least interfering with an ongoing police investigation." It took CJ the better part of an hour to convince Fuller that he hadn't found out about Vanetta until the previous evening.

Since Clothilde Polk had confirmed the night before that Vanetta had been a bookkeeper for a nursery before she was hired, the police weren't surprised to also find boxes of brochures and flyers on horticulture in Vanetta's apartment. But when they started leafing through stacks of order forms for high-nitrogen fertilizers paper-clipped to detailed, handwritten notes with lists of concoctions that didn't look at all as if they should be used on ferns, shade trees, and grasses, they became suspicious that Vanetta had manufactured something more than an improved plant food. Fuller knew that the DA's office was going to have a tough time placing Vanetta at the scene of the Juneteenth bombing, but he was a homicide cop with two murders on the front burner, so he really didn't care about the DA's problems. He seemed to enjoy the fact that CJ had overlooked Vanetta's horticultural background.

"Goddamn crazy woman's bomb could have blown your head halfway to Cheyenne, Floyd. I'd say you and that Polk woman were fuckin' lucky." He was about to blast CJ for not telling him about Juney-boy Stokes or Dr. Maurice Sinclair when a property room officer came in to tell him he needed him to check on a piece of evidence. "I'm almost done with you, Floyd. Cool your heels. I'll be back in a few minutes."

Fuller took off in a rush, giving CJ time to think about Maurice Sinclair. CJ didn't understand cross-gender identification, transsexualism, sex-reassignment surgery, or the psychological problems associated with them any better than he had the day he first visited Maurice Sinclair, so he couldn't honestly say that he understood the problem Juney-boy Stokes had lived and died with. But he did know that doctors were obliged to make accurate diagnoses and that mutilating someone and then saying *sorry* wouldn't wash with the state Board of Medical Examiners or with the kinds of lawyers who would probably press Vanetta Ebson to file a wrongful death lawsuit on her father's behalf.

Fuller was back in less than five minutes. He took a seat across from CJ, toweling grease off his hands with a damp rag. "Damn wheel bearing. Somebody used it to brain their cousin. What's your guess, Floyd? Think that Ebson woman was obsessed?"

"Can't say. I'm not a psychologist."

"Tell you what I think." Fuller leaned his rough-hewn character-actor's face into CJ's. "She was nuts. And LeRoy Polk's move to Denver set her off."

When Fuller finished with CJ, he passed him on to a couple of bomb squad cops who questioned him for another half hour before an electronic surveillance expert came in to find out if Billy DeLong, the one-eyed, gum-smacking man he had just questioned, would in fact come back from Wyoming and testify against Johnny Telano when the DA brought him up on wiretapping charges. "What did he tell you?" CJ asked.

The surveillance expert frowned. "That funerals and big cities give him diarrhea."

"I'll work on him for you," said CJ.

CJ left the jail feeling as though he had been caught up in a game of musical chairs. He walked across Delaware Street hatless in the fog and drizzle and headed up Bondsman's Row into a stiff wind toward his office. The temperature had dropped 40 degrees from the day before, hovering since midnight in the upper 40s, and although it was the middle of June the frosty chill of fall hung in the thin Rocky Mountain air. The damp weather had CJ's injured shoulder throbbing. He rubbed it, thinking about the tenacity of Mabel Pitts, and the hint of a smile formed on his lips.

A Tower Nursery delivery truck was parked in front of CJ's office. He looked at the truck, then up at the porch, where through the railing he could see Julie and Mavis on their knees. The nursery truck pulled off just as he started up the sidewalk to the house. Julie and Mavis were busy arranging flats filled with creeping buttercups, mountain gold, white rock crests, sunrose, candy tuft, and petunias.

"We're gonna have flowers in my garden out back, come hell or high water," said Julie, smiling at CJ as he walked up.

"Come on up and give us a hand," Mavis chimed in. "You might as well; all your homies got tired of waiting for you and split." She wanted to jump up and hug CJ, but years of catering to his lone-wolf personality had taught her when to strum the wires that ran to CJ's psyche and when not to. They'd have plenty of time to talk about what had happened the previous night.

CJ stepped up on the porch and glanced at the waterlogged *Rocky Mountain News* lying in one of his wicker chairs. The headline read MAYOR MOVES FOR MORATORIUM ON MONORAIL. CJ picked up the paper and read the first two columns of the story beneath the headline. "See Willis won the war," he said, smiling at Mavis.

"Just the initial skirmish. Wiley's now talking about an alternative transportation plan using light rail. He and Dunn will be back. But by then we'll have rebuilt Mae's, and Daddy will have a new strategy for Hiz Honor."

CJ laid the paper back down in the chair, primed for a new Mae's, a catfish dinner and a slice of sweet-potato pie, but he couldn't hide his disappointment that Billy had taken off before they had a chance to compare notes about their interrogations.

Julie looked up from counting the petunias in one of the flats. "Billy came back half an hour ago with ants in his pants about finding a new truck. Rosie was here with Dittier and Morgan. Billy told us about what happened last night—twice, in fact, for effect. Then they all left in that gas-guzzling crew cab of Rosie's to go find Billy a truck." Julie separated out a row of petunias. "By the way, they found Geronimo this morning sleeping like a baby in a bed of zinnias in Tibbits Park. Rosie said that down on the Points they're calling Geronimo a hero."

CJ laughed and rubbed his shoulder. "Guess Geronimo spent a better night than that gangster Telano. Did Billy tell you he kept him locked in the trunk of his car for almost two hours? Damn near suffocated the bastard."

Julie nodded as she began aerating the soil in a flat of marigolds with a fork.

"Have you heard from Tyrone?" said CJ, engrossed in what Julie was doing.

"He called about an hour ago. Said he's fine except for having a bandage the size of a grapefruit on his ear. He also said to tell you thanks, that he's got your thousand, and that construction on the Stax of Wax music palace and the R&B museum will be on hold until he, Clothilde, Hampoli, and that guy from Chicago, Roland Jefferson, work out their differences over ownership of the Stax of Wax name and the tapes. Tyrone also said he talked to Jefferson first thing this morning. He'd been hiding because he knew he was a suspect in LeRoy Polk's murder. A few days of hiding were all he could take. Seems like Jefferson had wind of what LeRoy was up to and he came out here and hired a lawyer to take him on over the whole Stax of Wax ownership issue on the very day he was killed. Tyrone said LeRoy even made Jefferson a dupe of one of the stolen tapes and promised him he'd cut him in on the whole deal if he called the lawyer off."

CJ tried to picture a summit meeting between Clothilde, Tyrone, Roland Jefferson, and Hampoli. "Strange bedfellows," he said, shaking his head at the thought. "At least they're out of my hair."

"Not quite," said Julie, giving Mavis one of her *should I tell him now* looks.

CJ recognized the look. "Okay, what's up?"

"Clothilde called right after Tyrone. Seems like she's so thrilled about you finding her father's killer she wants to come by and deliver your expense and per diem money and a twenty-five-hundred-dollar bonus in person on her way to talk to Sergeant Fuller about how she was suckered in by Vanetta. My guess is she's looking for a little revenge."

CJ knew Clothilde Polk well enough to know that revenge against Vanetta probably wasn't the only thing she had on her mind. More than likely she was also looking for some way to involve him in trying to screw Tyrone, Roland Jefferson, and Hampoli. "I'm gonna let you handle Clothilde," said CJ with a wink. "I plan to be unavailable. Just make sure she leaves a check and give Tyrone's thousand to Billy for his truck."

Mavis smiled, pleased that Clothilde Polk was out of CJ's life for good. She reached over, borrowed Julie's fork, and began aerating her flats of plants. She finished the first flat and moved it out to the edge of the porch. "They have to be hardened off for a day or two," said Mavis, glancing up at CJ's puzzled look, knowing that he didn't appreciate the need for the plants to be gradually exposed to their new environment. CJ watched for another couple of minutes before his puzzlement turned back to disappointment at being left behind by his boys. Mavis knew the time had arrived for her to tweak a few of CJ's emotional strings.

"Don't pout, baby," she said getting up off her knees. She wrapped her arms around CJ's neck and pulled him toward her, careful to avoid his injured shoulder as she gave him a wet, tender kiss. Then she stepped back, smiled, and dusted the mud off her hands. "You've still got us girls."